BARRY EISLER 雨

A LONELY RESURRECTION

A JOHN RAIN NOVEL

THOMAS & MERCER

Published by Thomas & Mercer, Seattle in 2014.

www.apub.com

Amazon, the Amazon logo, and Thomas & Mercer are trademarks of Amazon. com, Inc., or its affiliates.

ISBN-13: 9781477820810

ISBN-10: 1477820817

Cover design by Jeroen ten Berge

Printed in the United States of America

A LONELY RESURRECTION

Previously published as *Hard Rain* and *Blood from Blood*

All John Rain wants is to get out of the killing business. But with his discretion, his reliability, and his unique talent for death by "natural causes," no one is willing to let him just retire. So when an old nemesis from the Japanese national police force comes to him with a new job—eliminate Murakami, a killer even more fearsome than Rain himself—Rain knows he can't refuse.

Aided by an achingly desirable half Brazilian, half Japanese exotic dancer he knows he shouldn't trust, Rain pursues his quarry through underground no-holds-barred fight clubs, mobbed-up hostess bars, and finally into the heart of a shadow war between the CIA and the yakuza. It's a war Rain can't win, but also one he can't afford to lose—a war where the distinctions between friend and foe and truth and deceit are as murky as the rain-slicked streets of Tokyo.

"… a superlative job… entertaining and suspenseful enough to keep you turning the pages as fast as your eyes can follow."

—*Chicago Sun-Times*

Includes a note from the author introducing the new edition.

For Emma
You make my heart sing.

INTRODUCTION TO THE NEW EDITION

Having just finished rereading and slightly revising *A Lonely Resurrection* exactly ten years after first writing it, I'm struck by two things. First, how well the book has held up. Part of the credit for this goes to Tokyo, where the story is largely set—a city whose face is constantly changing but whose essence never does. I lived there again in 2008 and 2009, fifteen years after my first sojourn in Rain's city, and I loved that despite the new surface contours, despite the loss of a few *A Lonely Resurrection* locales and changes to some others, the feeling of the place was exactly as I remembered. I expect it always will be.

The second thing that struck me was the prescience of the plot in light of the nuclear catastrophe that followed the earthquake and tsunami of March 11, 2011. I tend to get my plot ideas from real-world occurrences, and here are a few that appear in the book:

> *Universal Studios Japan, it turned out, had been serving food that was nine months past its due date and falsifying labels to hide it, while operating a drinking fountain pumping out untreated industrial water. Mister Donut was in the habit of fortifying its wares with meat dumplings containing banned additives. Snow Brand Food liked to save a few yen by recycling old milk and failing to clean factory pipes. Couldn't cover that one up—fifteen-thousand people were poisoned. Mitsubishi Motors and Bridgestone got nailed hard, concealing defects in cars and tires to avoid safety recalls. The worst, shocking even by Japanese standards, was the news that TEPCO, Tokyo Electric Power, had been caught submitting falsified nuclear safety reports going back twenty years. The reports failed to list serious*

problems at eight different reactors, including cracks in concrete containment shrouds...

I wrote that in 2002. I had access only to open-source materials. The potential for calamity was visible to anyone who wanted to see it. As, indeed, my character Tatsu did:

> *He pulled himself up and sat on the edge of the tub to take a break from the heat. "You know, Rain-san," he said, "societies are like organisms, and no organism is invulnerable to disease. What matters is whether an organism can mount an effective defense when it finds itself under attack. In Japan, the virus of corruption has attacked the immune system itself, like a societal form of AIDS. Consequently, the body has lost its ability to defend itself. This is what I mean when I say that all countries have problems, but only Japan has problems it has lost the ability to solve. The TEPCO managers resign, but the men charged with regulating their activities for all those years remain? Only in Japan..."*
>
> *He wiped his brow. "So. Consider this state of affairs from Yamaoto's perspective. He understands that, with the immune system suppressed, there must eventually be a catastrophic failure of the host. There have been so many near misses—financial, ecological, nuclear—it is only a matter of time before a true cataclysm occurs. Perhaps a nuclear accident that irradiates an entire city. Or a countrywide run on banks and loss of deposits. Whatever it is, it will finally be of sufficient magnitude to shake Japan's voters from their apathy..."*

It remains to be seen whether the corruption and collusion that led to Japan's nuclear nightmare will be enough to shake voters from their apathy. I might have been mistaken about that. And I obviously was mistaken in suggesting that Japanese apathy in the face of extraordinary corruption is somehow unique. The last decade in America has seen a war sold to the public on false pretenses, high officials confessing to ordering torture in violation of treaty and domestic law, and an economic meltdown even former Federal Reserve Chairman Alan Greenspan acknowledges involved massive fraud—and no one has been prosecuted, no one has gone to prison, and Americans continue to dutifully cast their votes for the Democratic/Republican duopoly responsible for these disasters.

A last thought: it's not just the politics in these books that subsequent events keep validating; it's also the technology. In *A Lonely Resurrection*, Tatsu tracks Rain to Osaka using a nationwide system of video cameras tied to advanced facial recognition software. Here's what's going on today, ten years later:

http://digitaljournal.com/article/321848

So despite the presence of the odd anachronistic pager or two, I think on balance *A Lonely Resurrection* has proven itself not only stalwart, but indeed not-so-surprisingly ahead of its time. See for yourself—and I hope you'll enjoy it.

A NOTE ON THE NEW TITLES

Why have I changed the titles of the Rain books? Simply because I've never thought the titles were right for the stories. The right title matters—if only because the wrong one has the same effect as an inappropriate frame around an otherwise beautiful painting. Not only does the painting not look good in the wrong frame; it will sell for less, as well. And if you're the artist behind the painting, having to see it in the wrong frame, and having to live with the suboptimal commercial results, is aggravating.

The sad story of the original Rain titles began with the moniker *Rain Fall* for the first in the series. It was a silly play on the protagonist's name, and led to an unfortunate and unimaginative sequence of similar such meaningless, interchangeable titles: *Hard Rain*, *Rain Storm*, *Killing Rain* (the British titles were better, but still not right: *Blood from Blood* for #2; *Choke Point* for #3; *One Last Kill* for #4). By the fifth book, I was desperate for something different, and persuaded my publisher to go with *The Last Assassin*, instead. In general, I think *The Last Assassin* is a good title, but in fairness it really has nothing to do with the story in the fifth book beyond the fact that there's an assassin in it. But it was better than more of *Rain This* and *Rain That*. The good news is, the fifth book did very well indeed; the bad news is, the book's success persuaded my publisher that assassin was a magic word and that what we needed now was to use the word assassin in every title. And so my publisher told me that although they didn't care for my proposed title for the sixth book—*The Killer Ascendant*—they were pleased to have come up with something far better. The sixth book, they told me proudly, would be known as *The Quiet Assassin*.

I tried to explain that while not quite as redundant as, say, *The Deadly Assassin* or *The Lethal Assassin*, a title suggesting an assassin might be notable for his quietness was at best uninteresting (as opposed to, say, Margret Atwood's *The Blind Assassin*, which immediately engages the mind because of the connection of two seemingly contradictory qualities). The publisher was adamant. I told them that if they really were hellbent on using assassin in a title that otherwise had nothing to do with the book, couldn't we at least call the book *The Da Vinci Assassin*, or *The Sudoku Assassin*? In the end, we compromised on *Requiem for an Assassin*, a title I think would be good for some other book but is unrelated to the one I wrote—beyond, again, the bare fact of the presence of an assassin in the story.

Now that I have my rights back and no longer have to make ridiculous compromises about these matters, I've given the books the titles I always wanted them to have—titles that actually have something to do with the stories, that capture some essential aspect of the stories, and that act as both vessel and amplifier for what's most meaningful in the stories. For me, it's like seeing these books for the first time in the frames they always deserved. It's exciting, satisfying, and even liberating. Have a look yourself and I hope you'll enjoy them.

A
LONELY
RESURRECTION

Evening cherry blossoms:
I slip the inkstone back into my kimono
this one last time.

—death poem of the poet Kaisho, 1914

PART I

Had I not known
that I was dead
already
I would have mourned
my loss of life.

—last words of Ota Dokan,
　　scholar of military arts and poet, 1486

PART 1

CHAPTER 1

Once you get past the overall irony of the situation, you realize that killing a guy in the middle of his own health club has a lot to recommend it.

The target was a yakuza, an iron freak named Ishihara who worked out every day in a gym he owned in Roppongi, one of Tokyo's entertainment districts. Tatsu had told me the hit had to look like natural causes, like they always do, so I was glad to be working in a venue where it was far from unthinkable that someone might keel over from a fatal aneurism induced by exertion, or suffer an unlucky fall onto a steel bar, or undergo some other tragic mishap while using one of the complicated exercise machines.

One of these eventualities might even be immortalized in the warnings corporate lawyers would insist on placing on the next generation of exercise equipment, to notify the public of yet another unnatural use for which the machine was not intended and of which the manufacturer would have to remain blameless. Over the years, my work has made me the anonymous recipient of at least two such legal encomia—one on a bridge traversing the polluted waters of the Sumida River, in which a certain politician drowned in 1982 ("Warning—Do Not Climb On These Bars"); another, a decade later, following the aquatic electrocution of an unusually diligent banker, on the packaging of hair dryers ("Warning—Do Not Use While Bathing").

The health club was also convenient because I wouldn't have to worry about fingerprints. In Japan, where costumes are a national pastime, a weightlifter wouldn't pump iron without wearing stylish padded gloves any more than a politician would take a bribe in his underwear. It was a warm early spring for Tokyo, portending, they said, a fine cherry blossom season, and where else but at a gym could a man in gloves have gone unnoticed?

In my business, going unnoticed is half the game. People put out signals—body language, gait, clothes, facial expression, posture, attitude, speech, mannerisms—that can tell you where they're from, what they do, who they are. Most importantly, *do they fit in.* Because if you don't fit in, the target will spot you, and after that you won't be able to get close enough to do it right. Or a cop will spot you, and you'll have some explaining to do. Or a countersurveillance team will spot you, and then—congratulations!—the target will be you.

But if you're attentive, you begin to understand that the identifying signals are a science, not an art. You watch, you imitate, you acquire. Eventually, you can shadow different targets through different societal ecosystems, remaining anonymous in all of them.

Anonymity wasn't easy for me in Japan when my parentage was a matter of public record and schoolyard taunts. But today, you wouldn't spot the Caucasian in my face unless someone tipped you off that it was there to be found. My American mother wouldn't have minded that. She had always wanted me to fit in in Japan, and was glad that my father's Japanese features had prevailed in that initial genetic struggle for dominance. And the plastic surgery I had undergone when I returned to Japan after my fling with U.S. Special Forces in Vietnam largely completed the job that chance and nature had begun.

The story my signals would tell the yakuza was simple. He'd only begun seeing me at his gym recently, but I was already obviously in shape. So I wasn't some middle-aged guy who'd decided to take up weightlifting to try and regain a lost college-era physique. The more likely explanation would be that I worked for a company that had transferred me to Tokyo, and, if they had sprung for digs near Roppongi, maybe in Minami-Aoyama or Azabu, I must be someone reasonably important and well compensated. That I was apparently into body building at all at this stage in my life probably meant affairs with young women, for whom a youthful physique might ameliorate the unavoidable emotional consequences of sleeping with an older man in what at root would be little more than an exchange of sex and the illusion of immortality for

Ferragamo handbags and the other implicit currencies of such arrangements. All of which the yakuza would understand, and even respect.

In fact, my recent appearance at the yakuza's gym had nothing to do with a company transfer—it was more like a business trip. After all, I was in Tokyo just to do a job. When the job was finished, I would leave. I'd done some things to generate animosity when I'd been living here, and the relevant parties might still be looking for me, even after I'd been away for a year, so a short stay was all I could sensibly afford.

Tatsu had given me a dossier on the yakuza a month earlier, when he'd found me and persuaded me to take the job. From the contents, I would have concluded the target was just mob muscle, but I knew he must be more than that if Tatsu wanted him eliminated. I hadn't asked. I only wanted the particulars that would help me get close. The rest was irrelevant.

The dossier had included the yakuza's mobile number. I had fed it to Harry, who, compulsive hacker that he was, had long since penetrated the cellular network control centers of Japan's three telco providers. Harry's computers were monitoring the movements of the yakuza's mobile phone within the network. Any time the phone got picked up by the tower covering the area around the yakuza's health club, Harry paged me.

Tonight, the page had come at just after eight o'clock, while I was reading in my room at the New Otani Hotel in Akasaka-Mitsuke. The club closed at eight, I knew, so if the yakuza was working out there after hours there was a good possibility he'd be alone. What I'd been waiting for.

My workout gear was already in a bag, and I was out the door within minutes. I caught a cab a slight distance from the hotel, not wanting a doorman to hear or remember where I might be going, and five minutes later I exited at the corner of Roppongi-dori and Gaienhigashi-dori in Roppongi. I hated to use such a direct route because doing so limited my opportunities to ensure I wasn't being followed, but I had only a little time to pull this off the way I'd planned and decided it was worth the risk.

I had been watching the yakuza for over a month now, and knew his routines. I'd learned that he liked to vary the times of his workouts, sometimes arriving at the gym early in the morning, sometimes at night.

Probably he assumed the resulting unpredictability would make him hard to get to.

He was half right. Unpredictability is the key to being a hard target, but the concept applies to both time and place. Half measures like this guy's will protect you from some of the people some of the time, but they won't save you for long from someone like me.

Strange, how people can take adequate, even strong security measures in some respects, while leaving themselves vulnerable in others. Like double-locking the front door and leaving the windows wide open.

Sometimes the phenomenon is caused by fear. Fear not so much of the requirements, but rather of the consequences of life as a hard target. Seriously protecting yourself calls for the annihilation of ties with society, ties that most people need the way they need oxygen. You give up friends, family, romance. You walk through the world like a ghost, detached from the living around you. If you were to die in, say, a bus accident, you'd wind up buried in an obscure municipal graveyard, just another John Doe, no flowers, no mourners, hell, no mourning. It's natural, probably even desirable, to be afraid of all this.

Other times there's a form of denial at work. Circuitous routes, extensive security checks, an ongoing internal dialogue consisting of *If I were trying to get to me, how would I do it?* all require a deep acceptance of the notion that there are people out there who have both the motive and the means to cut short your time on earth. This notion is innately uncomfortable for the human psyche, so much so that it produces enormous stress even for soldiers in battle. A lot of guys, the first time they come under close-range fire, they're shocked. "Why's he trying to kill *me?*" they're asking themselves. "What did I ever do to him?"

Think about it. Ever look in a closet or under the bed, when you're alone in the house, to ensure an intruder isn't hiding there? Now, if you really believed the Man in the Black Ski Mask was lurking in those places, would you behave the same way? Of course not. But it's more comfortable to believe the danger only in the abstract, and to act on it only halfheartedly. That's denial.

Finally, and most obviously, there is laziness. Who has the time or energy to inspect the family car for improvised explosive devices before every drive? Who can afford a two-hour, roundabout route to get to a place that could have been reached directly in ten minutes? Who wants to pass up a restaurant or bar because the only seats available face the wall, not the entrance?

Rhetorical questions, but I know how Crazy Jake would have answered. *The living,* he would have said. *And the ones who intend to go on that way.*

Which leads to an easy rationalization, one I'm sure is common to people who have taken lives the way I have. *If he'd really wanted to live,* the rationalization goes, *I wouldn't have been able to get to him. He wouldn't have permitted himself that weakness, the one that did him in.*

The yakuza's weakness was his addiction to weights. Who knows what fueled it—a history of childhood bullying that made him want to appear visibly strong afterward, an attempt to overcome a feeling of inadequacy born of being naturally slighter of build than Caucasians, some suppressed homoeroticism like the one that drove Mishima. Maybe some of the same impulses that had led him to become a gangster to begin with.

His obsession had nothing to do with health, of course. In fact, the guy was an obvious steroid abuser. His neck was so thick it looked as though he could slide a tie up over his head without loosening the knot, and he sported acne so severe that the club's stark incandescent lighting, designed to show off to maximum effect the rips and cuts club members had developed in their bodies, cast small shadows over the pocked landscape of his face. His testicles were probably the size of raisins, his blood pressure likely rampaging through an overworked heart.

I'd also seen him explode into the kind of abrupt, unprovoked violence that is another symptom of steroid abuse. One night, someone I hadn't seen before, no doubt one of the club's civilian members who liked the location and thought that rubbing elbows with reputed gangsters made them tougher by osmosis, started removing some of the numerous iron plates weighing down the bar the yakuza had been using to bench-press. The yakuza had walked away from the station, probably to take a break, and the new guy must have mistakenly assumed this meant he was through. The guy was pretty sizable himself, his colorful spandex sleeveless top showing off a weightlifter's chest and arms.

Someone probably should have warned him. But the club's membership consisted primarily of *chinpira*—low-level young yakuza and wannabe punks—not exactly good Samaritan types who were interested in helping their fellow man. Anyway, you have to be at least mildly stupid to start disassembling a bar like the one the yakuza had been using without looking around for permission first. There were a hundred and fifty kilos on it, maybe more.

Someone nudged the yakuza and pointed. The yakuza, who had been squatting, reared up and bellowed, *"Orya!"* loud enough to vibrate the plate glass in the front of the rectangular room. What the fuck!

Everyone looked up, as startled as if there had been an explosion—even the new guy who had been so clueless just an instant earlier. Still bellowing expletives, the yakuza strode directly to the bench-press station, doing a good job of using his voice, either by instinct or design, to disorient his victim.

Everything about the yakuza—his words, his tone, his movement and posture, screamed *Attack!* But the man was too frozen, either by fear or denial, to move off the line of assault. And though he was holding a ten-kilo iron plate with edges considerably harder than the yakuza's cranium, the man did nothing but drop his mouth open, perhaps in surprise, perhaps in inchoate and certainly futile apology.

The yakuza blasted into him like a rhino, his shoulder driving into the man's stomach. The man tried to brace for the impact, but again he failed to move off the line of attack and his attempt was largely useless. The yakuza drove him backward into the wall, then unleashed a flurry of crude punches to his head and neck. The man, in shock now and running on autopilot, dropped the plate and managed to raise his arms to ward off a few of the blows, but the yakuza, still bellowing, slapped the attempted blocks out of the way and kept on punching. One of the shots connected to the left side of the man's neck, the real estate over the carotid sinus, and the man began to crumble as his nervous system overcompensated from the shock of the blow by reducing blood pressure to the brain. The yakuza, feet planted widely as though he had an axe and was splitting logs, continued to hammer at the top of his victim's head and neck. The man fell to the floor, but retained enough consciousness to curl up and protect himself to some extent from the hail of kicks that followed.

Huffing and swearing, the yakuza bent and caught the prostrate man's right ankle between an enormous bicep and forearm. For a moment, I thought he was going to apply a leglock and try to break something.

Instead, he straightened and proceeded to drag the man's prone form to the club's entrance and out into the street.

He returned a moment later, alone, and, after taking a moment to catch his breath, resumed his rightful place on the bench without looking at anyone else in the room. Everyone returned to what they were doing: his affiliates, because they didn't care; the civilians, because they were unnerved. It was as though nothing had happened, though the pervading silence indicated that indeed something had.

A part of my mind that's always running in the background logged what I saw as the yakuza's assets: raw strength, experience with violence, familiarity with principles of continuous attack. Under weaknesses, I placed lack of self-control, shortness of breath after a brief and one-sided fight, and a lack of real skill, as evidenced by the relatively minimal damage he had caused despite the ferocity of his assault.

Unless he was a borderline sociopath, which was statistically unlikely, I knew the yakuza would now be feeling slightly uneasy about what people must have made of his outburst. I took the opportunity to stroll over to the bench-press station and ask him if he needed a spot.

"*Warui na,*" he thanked me, grateful, I knew, for the comfort this simple interaction afforded him.

"*Iya,*" I replied. It's nothing. I stood over him and helped him get the bar in the air. I noted that he was moving a hundred and fifty-five kilos. He managed two repetitions, with some assistance from me on the second. He would still be fully adrenalized from his recent altercation, and I made a mental note of the limits of his strength at this exercise.

I helped him guide the bar back onto the uprights, then whistled quietly through my teeth in slightly theatrical deference to his power. I moved to the foot of the bench as he sat up and told him if he needed another spot, he should just ask me. He nodded his head in gruff thanks and I began to turn away.

I paused as though considering whether to add something, then turned back to him. "That guy should have checked to see if you were done with this station," I said in Japanese. "Some people have no manners. You taught him a lesson."

He nodded again, pleased at my astute assessment of the important social service he had provided in pulverizing some harmless idiot, and I knew he would be comfortable calling on me, his new friend, from time to time when he needed a spot.

Like tonight, I hoped. I moved quickly down Gaienhigashi-dori, easing past pedestrians on the crowded sidewalk, ignoring the cacophony of traffic and sound trucks and touts, using the chrome and glass around me to gauge whether there was anyone to my rear trying to keep up. I turned right just before the Roi Roppongi building, then right again onto the club's street, where I paused behind a thicket of parked bicycles, my back to the incongruous pink exterior of a Starbucks, waiting to see who might be trailing in my wake. A few groups of young partygoers drifted by, caught up in the urgent business of entertaining themselves and failing to notice the man standing quietly in the shadows. No one set off my radar. After a few minutes, I made my way to the club.

The facility occupied the ground floor of a gray commercial building hemmed in by rusting fire escapes and choked with high-tension wires that clung to the structure's façade like rotting vegetation. Across from it was a parking lot crowded by Mercedes with darkened windows and high-performance tires, the status symbols of the country's elite and of its criminals, each aping the other, comfortably sharing the pleasures of the night in Roppongi's tawdry demimonde. The street itself was illuminated only by the indifferent glow of a single arched lamplight, its base festooned with flyers advertising the area's innumerable sexual services, in the shadows of its own luminescence looking like the elongated neck of some antediluvian bird shedding diseased and curling feathers.

The shades were drawn behind the club's plate-glass windows, but I spotted the yakuza's anodized aluminum Harley-Davidson V-Rod parked in front, surrounded by commuter bicycles like a shark amidst pilot fish. Just past the windows was the entrance to the building. I tried the door, but it was locked.

I backed up a few steps to the club windows and tapped on the glass. A moment later the lights went off inside. *Nice,* I thought. He had cut the lights so he could peek through the shades without being seen from outside. I waited, knowing he was watching me and checking the street.

The lights went back on, and a moment later the yakuza appeared in the entranceway to the building. He was wearing gray sweatpants and a black cutaway A-shirt, along with the obligatory weightlifting gloves. Obviously in the middle of a workout.

He opened the door, his eyes searching the street for danger, failing to spot it right there in front of him.

"*Shimatterun da yo,*" he told me. Club's closed.

"I know," I said in Japanese, my hands up, palms forward in a placating gesture. "I was hoping someone might be here. I was going to come by earlier but got held up. You think I could squeeze in a quick one? Just while you're here, no longer than that."

He hesitated, then shrugged and turned to go back inside. I followed him in.

"How much longer have you got to go?" I asked, dropping my gear bag and changing out of my unobtrusive khakis, blue oxford-cloth shirt, and navy blazer. I had already slipped on the gloves, as I always did before coming to the club, but the yakuza hadn't noticed this detail. "So I can time my workout."

He walked over to the squat station. "Forty-five minutes, maybe an hour," he said, getting into position under the weight.

Squats. What he usually did when he was finished bench-pressing. *Shit.*

I slipped into shorts and a sweatshirt, then warmed up with some pushups and other calisthenics while he did his sets of squats. The warm-up might actually be useful, I realized, depending on the extent of his struggles. A small advantage, but I don't give away anything for free.

When he was through, I asked, "Already done benching?"

"Yeah."

"How much you put up tonight?"

He shrugged, but I detected a slight puffing of his chest that told me his vanity had been kindled.

"Not so much. Hundred and forty kilos. Could have done more, but with that much weight, it's better to have someone spot you."

Perfect. "Hey, I'll spot you."

"Nah, I'm already done."

"Come on, do another set. It inspires me. What are you putting up, twice your body weight?" My underestimate was deliberate.

"More."

"Shit, *more* than twice your body weight? That's what I'm talking about, I'm not even close to that. Do me a favor, do one more set, it'll motivate me. I'll spot you, fair enough?"

He hesitated, then shrugged and started walking over to the bench-press station.

The bar was already set up with the hundred and forty kilos he'd been using earlier. "Think you can handle a hundred and sixty?" I asked, my tone doubtful.

He looked at me, and I could tell from his eyes that his ego had engaged. "I can handle it."

"Okay, this I've got to see," I said, pulling two ten-kilo plates off the weight tree and sliding them onto the ends of the bar. I stood behind the bench and gripped the bar about shoulder-width with both hands. "Let me know when you're ready."

He sat at the foot of the bench, his shoulders hunched forward, and rotated his neck from side to side. He swung his arms back and forth and grunted a series of short, forceful exhalations. Then he lay back and took hold of the bar.

"Give me a lift on three," he said.

I nodded.

There were several additional sharp exhalations. Then: "One... two... three!"

I helped him get the bar in the air and steady it over his chest. He was staring at the bar as though enraged by it, his chin sunk into his neck in preparation for the effort.

Then he let it drop, controlling its descent but allowing enough momentum to ensure a good bounce off his massive chest. Two thirds of the way up, the bar almost stopped, suspended between the drag of gravity and the power of his steroid-fueled muscles, but it continued its shaky ascent until his elbows were straightened. His arms were trembling from the effort. There was no way he had another one in him.

"One more, one more," I urged. "Come on, you can do it."

There was a pause, and I prepared to try some fresh exhortations. But he was only mentally preparing for the effort. He took three quick breaths, then dropped the bar to his chest. It rose a few centimeters from the impact, then a few more from the northward shove that followed, but a second later it stopped and began to move inexorably downward.

"Tetsudatte kure," he grunted. Help. But calmly, expecting my immediate assistance.

The bar continued downward and settled against his chest. *"Oi, tano-mu,"* he said again, more sharply this time.

I pushed downward instead.

His eyes popped open, searching for mine.

Between the weight of the bar and plates and the pressure I was delivering, he was now struggling with almost two hundred kilos.

I focused on the bar and his torso, but in my peripheral vision I saw his eyes bulging in confusion, then fear. He made no sound. I continued to concentrate on the clinical downward pressure.

With his teeth clenched shut, his chin almost buried in his neck, he threw everything he had into moving the bar. In extremis he was actually able to get the weight off his chest. I hooked a foot under the horizontal supports at the bottom of the bench and used the leverage to add additional pressure to the bar, and again it settled against his chest.

I felt a tremor in the weights as his arms began to shake with exertion. Again the bar moved slightly north.

Suddenly I was struck by the reek of feces. His sympathetic nervous system, in desperation, was shutting down nonessential bodily activities, including sphincter control, and diverting all available energy to his muscles.

The rally lasted only another moment. Then his arms began to shake more violently, and I felt the bar moving downward, more deeply into his chest. There was a slight hissing as his breath was driven out through his nostrils and pursed lips. I felt his eyes on my face but kept my attention on his torso and the bar. Still he made no sound.

Seconds went by, then more. His position didn't change. I waited. His skin began to blue. I waited longer.

Finally, I eased the pressure I'd been putting on the bar and released my grip.

His eyes were still on me, but they no longer perceived. I stepped back, out of their sightless ambit, and paused to observe the scene. It looked like what it almost was: a weightlifting addict, alone and late at night, tries to handle more than he can, gets caught under the bar, suffocates and dies there. A bizarre accident.

I changed into my street clothes. Picked up my bag, moved to the door. A series of cracks rang out behind me, like the snaps of dried tinder. I turned to look one last time, realizing as I did that the sound was of his ribs giving way. No question, he was done. Only his convulsive grip on the bar remained, as though the fingers refused to believe what the body had already accepted.

I stepped into the dark hallway and waited until the street was clear. Then I eased out onto the sidewalk and into the shadows around me.

CHAPTER 2

slipped away from the area on foot along a series of secondary streets in Roppongi and Akasaka, cutting across narrow alleyways in a manner which, to the uninitiated, would have looked like a series of simple short-cuts to wherever I was going, but which were in fact designed to force a follower or team of followers to reveal themselves in an effort to keep up. With a few deliberate exceptions, all my surveillance detection moves are accomplished under the guise of seemingly normal pedestrian behavior. If I'm being followed because some organization has taken an interest but hasn't yet managed to confirm who I am, I'm not going to give away the game by acting like anything other than John Q. Citizen.

After about a half hour, I was confident I wasn't being tailed, and my pace began to slow in accompaniment to my mood. I found myself moving in a long, counterclockwise semicircle that I only half acknowledged was taking me in the direction of Aoyama Bochi, the enormous cemetery laid out like a triangular green bandage at the center of the city's fashionable western districts.

On the north side of Roppongi-dori, I passed a small colony of cardboard shelters, the way stations of wandering homeless men whose lives were, in a sense, as detached and anonymous as my own. I set down the gym bag I was carrying, knowing the bag and its contents of workout clothes and weightlifting gloves would quickly be distributed and assimilated among the gaunt and trackless wraiths nearby. Within days, perhaps hours, the discarded remnants of this last job would have been bleached of any trace of their origins, each just another nameless, colorless item among nameless, colorless souls, the flotsam and jetsam of loneliness and despair that fall from time to time into Tokyo's collective blind spot, and from there into oblivion.

Freed of the burden I had been carrying, I moved on, this time circling east. Under an overpass at Nogizaka, north of Roppongi-dori, I saw a half-dozen *chinpira*, gaudy in sleek racing leathers, squatting in a tight semicircle, their low-slung metal motorcycles parked on the footpath alongside them. Fragments of their conversation skipped off the concrete wall to my right, the words unintelligible but the notes tuned as tight as the tricked-out exhaust pipes of their machines. They were probably jacked on *kakuseizai*, the methamphetamine that has been the Japanese drug of choice since the government distributed it to soldiers and workers during World War II, and of which these *chinpira* were doubtless both purveyors and consumers. They were waiting for the drug-induced hum in their muscles and brains to hit the right pitch, for the hour to grow suitably late and the night more seductively dark, before emerging from their concrete lair and answering the neon call of Roppongi.

I watched them take notice of me, a solitary figure approaching from the southern end of what was in effect a narrow tunnel. I considered crossing the street, but a metal divider made that maneuver unfeasible. I might simply have backed up and taken a different route. My failure to do so made it more difficult for me to deny that I was indeed heading toward the cemetery.

When I was three or four meters away, one of them stood. The others continued to squat, watching, alert for whatever distraction was promised.

I had already noted the absence of any of the security cameras that were growing more pervasive in the streets and subways with every passing year. Sometimes I have to fight the feeling that those cameras are looking specifically for me.

"Oi," the one who had stood called out. Hey.

I stole a quick glance behind me to ensure that we were alone. It wouldn't pay to have anyone see what I would do if these idiots got in my way.

Without altering my pace or direction, I looked into the *chinpira's* eyes, my expression obsidian flat. I let him know with this look that I was neither afraid nor looking for trouble, that I'd done this kind of thing many times before, that if he was in search of some excitement tonight the smart thing would be to find it elsewhere.

Most people, especially those even loosely acquainted with violence, understand these signals, and can be relied on to respond in ways that increase their survival prospects. But apparently this guy was too stupid, or too jacked on *kakuseizai*. Or he might have misinterpreted my initial backward glance as a sign of fear. Regardless, he ignored the warning I had given him and started edging into my path.

I recognized the procedure: I was being interviewed for my suitability as a victim. Would I allow myself to be forced out into the street and the oncoming traffic? Would I cringe and flinch in the process? If so, he would know I was a safe target, and he would then escalate, probably to real violence.

But I prefer my violence sudden. Keeping him to my right, I stepped past him with my left leg, shooting my right leg through on the same side immediately after and then sweeping it backward to reap his legs out from under him in *osoto-gari,* one of the most basic and powerful judo throws. Simultaneously I twisted counterclockwise and blasted my right arm into his neck, taking his upper body in the opposite direction of his legs. For a split instant he was suspended horizontally over the spot where he had been standing. Then I drilled him into the sidewalk, jerking his collar up at the last instant so the back of his head wouldn't take excessive impact. I didn't want a fatality. Too much attention.

The sequence had taken less than two seconds. I straightened and continued on my way as before, my eyes forward but my ears trained behind me for sounds of pursuit.

There were none, and as the distance widened I indulged a small smile. I don't like bullies—they formed too large a portion of my childhood on both sides of the Pacific—and I had a feeling it would be a long time before these *chinpira* worked up a fresh appetite to dispute someone's passage along that sidewalk.

I continued along, cutting left east of the cemetery, then right on Gaiennishi-dori, taking advantage of the turn as I always automatically do to monitor the area to my rear while ostensibly checking for traffic. The cemetery was now to my right, but there was no sidewalk on that side of the street, so I stayed on the left until I was opposite a long riser of stone steps, a byway between the green piazza of the dead and the living city without. I stood looking at those steps for a long time. Finally I decided the urge to which I had almost succumbed was ridiculous, as I had decided so many times in the past. I turned and moved slowly down the street, back the way I had come.

As always after finishing a job, I was aware of the urge to be among other people, to find some comfort in the illusion that I'm part of the society through which I move. A few meters down the street I ducked into the Monsoon Restaurant, where I could enjoy the Southeast Asian-derived cuisine and the anodyne sounds of other people's conversation.

I chose a seat set slightly back from the restaurant's open-air façade, facing the street and entrance, and ordered a simple meal of rice noodles with vegetables. Although it was late for dinner, the tables were mostly occupied. To my left were the remnants of a small office party: a few young men with loosened ties and identical navy suits, two women with them, pretty and more stylishly dressed than their companions, at ease with the traditional Japanese female role of serving food, pouring drinks, and fostering conversation. Behind them, a solitary couple, high school or college kids, leaning toward each other and holding hands across the table, the boy talking with his eyebrows raised as though suggesting something, the girl laughing and shaking her head no. To the other side, a group of older American men, dressed more casually than the other patrons, their voices appropriately low, their skin shining slightly in the light of the table lamps.

It was slightly surreal, finding myself back in a restaurant or bar after finishing a job, my mind starting to drift, relief settling in after the adrenaline rush had ended. The sensations weren't new, but the context rendered them strange, like the feel of a familiar business suit donned to attend a funeral.

I had thought I was out of all this after finishing things with Holtzer, the late chief of the CIA's Tokyo Station. My cover had been blown, and it was time to reinvent myself, not for the first time. I had thought about the States, maybe the West Coast, San Francisco, someplace with a large Asian population. But establishing a new identity in America, without the sort of groundwork that I had long since prepared in Japan, would have been difficult. Besides, if the CIA had been looking for payback for Holtzer, they might have had an easier time coming after me on their home turf. Staying in Japan left Tatsu to contend with, of course, but

Tatsu's interest in me had nothing to do with revenge, so I had judged him the lesser of the risks.

I had to smile at that. I had learned that the danger Tatsu posed to me, while certainly less acute than the straightforward possibility of getting put to sleep by some lucky CIA contractor, was far more insidious.

He had tracked me down in Osaka, Japan's second largest metropolis, where I had gone after disappearing from Tokyo. I had moved into a high-rise community called Belfa in Miyakojima, the northwest of the city. Belfa was inhabited by sufficient numbers of corporate transferees from other places so that a recent arrival wouldn't provoke undue attention. It was also home primarily to families with small children, the kind of people who stay aware of the composition of their neighborhood, whose presence makes it difficult to mount effective surveillance or a successful ambush.

At first I had missed Tokyo, where I had lived for two decades, and was disappointed to find myself in a city the average Tokyoite would reflexively dismiss as a backwater in every category save brute geographical sprawl. But Osaka had grown on me. Its atmosphere, though arguably less sophisticated and cosmopolitan than Tokyo's, is also lacking in pretense. Unlike Tokyo, whose financial, cultural, and political center of gravity is so strong that at times the city can feel self-satisfied, even solipsistic, Osaka compares itself ceaselessly to other places, its cousin to the northeast chief among them, emerging victorious, of course, in matters of cuisine, financial acumen, and general human goodness. I found something endearing in this scrappy, self-declared contest for supremacy. Maybe we don't have the refined—read effete—manners, or the most powerful—read corrupt—political establishment, Osaka seems to declare to a Tokyo that isn't even listening, but we've got a bigger heart. Over time, I began to wonder if the city didn't have a point.

I had spotted Tatsu behind me one night as I was making my way to Overseas, a jazz club in Honmachi that I had come to like. Although I gave no sign, I had recognized him immediately. Tatsu has a squat build and a way of rolling his shoulders from side to side when he walks that makes him hard to miss. If the tail had been someone else, I would have doubled back and questioned him, if possible. Eliminated him, if not.

But since Tatsu himself was the one behind me, I knew I was in no immediate danger. As a department head with the Keisatsucho, Japan's

FBI, he easily could have had me picked up already, if that's what he had wanted. *The hell with it,* I had decided. Akiko Grace, a young pianist who had electrified Japan's jazz world with her debut CD *From New York,* was appearing that night, and I wanted to see her play. If Tatsu was inclined to join me, he could.

He had arrived midway through the second set. Grace was doing "That Morning," a melancholy piece from *Manhattan Story,* her second CD. I watched him pause just inside the entrance, his eyes scanning the tables in back. I would have signaled him, but he knew where to look.

He made his way to my table and squeezed in next to me as though it was the most natural thing in the world that he should be meeting me here. As usual, he was wearing a dark suit that fit him like an after-thought. He nodded a greeting. I returned the gesture, then went back to watching Grace play.

She was facing away from us, wearing a shoulderless gold-sequined gown that shimmered under the cool blue spotlights like heat lightning in a night sky. Watching her made me think of Midori, though as much by contrast as by association. Grace's attitude was funkier, with more swaying, more sideways approaches to the piano, and her style was gen-erally softer, more contemplative. But when she got going, on numbers like "Pulse Fiction" and "Delancey Street Blues," she had that same air of having been possessed by the instrument, as though the piano was a demon and she its exhilarated amanuensis.

I remembered watching Midori play, standing in the shadows of New York's Village Vanguard, knowing it would be the last time. I'd seen other pianists perform since then. It was always a sad pleasure, like making love to a beautiful woman, but not to the woman you love.

The set ended and Grace and her trio left the stage. But the audience wouldn't stop applauding until they had returned, with an encore of Thelonious Monk's "Bemsha Swing." Tatsu was probably frustrated. He wasn't there to enjoy the jazz.

After the encore, Grace moved to the bar. People began to get up to thank her, perhaps to have her sign the CDs they had brought, then to move on to whatever else the night had in store.

When the people next to us had departed, Tatsu turned to me. "Retirement doesn't suit you, Rain-san," he said in his dry way. "It's making you soft. When you were active, I couldn't have tracked you down like this."

Tatsu rarely wastes time on formalities. He knows better, but can't help himself. It's one of the things I've always liked about him.

"I thought you wanted me to retire," I said.

"From your relationship with Yamaoto and his organization, yes. But I thought we might then have the opportunity to work together. You understand my work."

He was talking about his never-ending battle with Japanese corruption, behind much of which was his nemesis Yamaoto Toshi, politician and puppet master, the man who had suborned Holtzer, who for a time had been my unseen employer as well.

"I'm sorry, Tatsu. With Yamaoto and maybe the CIA after me, things were too hot. I wouldn't have been much good to you even if I'd wanted to be."

"You told me you would contact me."

"I thought better of it."

He nodded, then said, "Did you know that, just a few days after the last time we saw each other, William Holtzer died of a heart attack in the parking garage of a hotel in suburban Virginia?"

I remembered how Holtzer had mouthed the words, *I was the mole... I was the mole...* when he thought I was going to die. How he had set me against my blood brother, Crazy Jake, in Vietnam, and gloated about it afterward.

"Why do you ask?" I said, my tone casual.

"Apparently, his death came as a surprise to people who knew him in the intelligence community," he went on, ignoring my question, "because Holtzer was only in his early fifties and also kept physically fit."

Not physically fit enough for three hundred and sixty joules from a modified defibrillator, I thought.

"It just goes to show you, you can't be too careful," I said, taking a sip of the twelve-year-old Dalmore I was drinking. "I take a baby aspirin myself, once a day. There was an article about it in the *Asahi Shinbun* a few years ago. Supposed to dramatically reduce the chances of heart problems."

He was silent for a moment, then shrugged and said, "He was not a good man."

Was this his way of telling me he knew I did Holtzer but didn't care? If so, what was he going to ask in return?

"How did you hear about all this?" I asked.

He looked down at the table, then back at me. "Some of Mr. Holtzer's associates from the CIA's station in Tokyo contacted the Metropolitan Police Force. They were less concerned about the fact of his death than they were about the manner of it. They seem to believe you killed him."

I said nothing.

"They wanted the assistance of the Metropolitan Police Force in locating you," he went on. "My superiors informed me that I was to offer full cooperation."

"Why are they coming to you for help?"

"I suspect the Agency has been tasked with trying to eliminate some of the corruption that is paralyzing Japan's economy. The United States is concerned that if the situation worsens, Japan's finances could collapse. A ripple effect, and certainly a global recession, would follow."

I understood Uncle Sam's interest. Everyone knew the politicians were focused more on ensuring that they got their share of graft from rigged public works and yakuza payoffs than they were on resuscitating a dying economy. You could smell the rot from afar.

I took another sip of the Dalmore. "Why do you suppose they'd be interested in me?"

He shrugged. "Perhaps revenge. Perhaps as part of some anticorruption effort. Perhaps both. After all, we know Holtzer was issuing intelligence reports identifying you as the 'natural causes' assassin behind the deaths of so many Japanese whistleblowers and reformers."

Just like Holtzer, I thought. Getting credit for the intelligence reports while using the subject for his own ends. I remembered how he had looked when I left him slumped and lifeless in his rent-a-car in that suburban Virginia parking garage, and I smiled.

"You don't seem terribly concerned," Tatsu said.

I shrugged. "Of course I'm concerned. What did you tell them?"

"That, so far as I knew, you were dead."

Here it comes, then. "That was good of you."

He smiled slightly, and I saw a bit of the wily, subversive bastard I had liked so much in Vietnam, where we had met when he was seconded there by one of the precursors of the Keisatsucho.

"Not so good, really. We're old friends, after all. Friends should help each other from time to time, don't you agree?"

He knew I owed him. I owed him just for letting me go after I'd ambushed Holtzer outside the naval base at Yokosuka, despite all the years he'd spent trying to ferret me out previously. Now he was putting the Agency off my scent, and I owed him for that, too.

The debts were only part of it, of course. There was also an implicit threat. But Tatsu had a soft spot for me that kept him from being too direct. Otherwise, he would have dispensed with all the win-win, we're old pals bullshit and would have just told me that if I didn't cooperate he'd share my current name and address with my old friends at Christians In Action. Which he could very easily do.

"I thought you wanted me to retire," I said again, knowing I'd already lost.

He reached into his breast pocket and took out a manila envelope. Placed it on the table between us.

"This is a very important job, Rain-san," he said. "I wouldn't ask for this favor if it weren't."

I knew what I would find in the envelope. A name. A photograph. Locations of work and residence. Known vulnerabilities. The insistence on the appearance of "natural causes" would be implicit, or delivered orally.

I made no move to touch the envelope. "There's one thing I need from you before I can agree to any of this," I told him.

He nodded. "You want to know how I found you."

"Correct."

He sighed. "If I share that information with you, what would stop you from disappearing again, even more effectively this time?"

"Probably nothing. On the other hand, if you don't tell me, there's no possibility that I would be willing to work with you on whatever you've got in that envelope. It's up to you."

He took his time, as though pondering the pros and cons, but Tatsu always thinks several moves ahead and I knew he would have anticipated this. The hesitation was theater, designed to convince me afterward that I had won something valuable.

"Customs Authority records," he said finally.

I wasn't particularly surprised. I had known there was some risk that Tatsu would learn of Holtzer's death and assume I had been behind it, that if he did so he would be able to fix my movements between the time he last saw me in Tokyo and the day Holtzer died outside of D.C., less than a week apart. But killing Holtzer had been important to me, and I had been prepared to pay a price for the indulgence. Tatsu was simply presenting me with the bill.

I was silent, and after a moment he continued. "An individual traveling under the name and passport of Fujiwara Junichi left Tokyo for San Francisco last October thirtieth. There is no record of his having returned to Japan. The logical assumption is that he stayed in the United States."

In a sense, he did. Fujiwara Junichi is my Japanese birth name. When I learned Holtzer and the CIA had discovered where I was living in Tokyo, I knew the name was blown and no longer usable. I had traveled to the States to kill Holtzer under the Fujiwara passport and then retired it, returning to Japan under a different identity I had previously established for such a contingency. I had hoped anyone looking for me might be diverted by this false clue and conclude I had relocated to the States. Most people would have. But not Tatsu.

"Somehow, I could not see you living in the States," he went on. "You seemed… comfortable in Japan. I did not believe you were ready to leave."

"I suppose you might have been onto something there."

He shrugged. "I asked myself, if my old friend hadn't really left Japan, but only wanted me to believe he had, what would he have done? He would have reentered the country under a new name. He would have then relocated to a new city, because he had become too well known in Tokyo."

He paused, and I recognized the employment of a fortuneteller's trick, in which the party ostensibly charged with supplying information instead cleverly elicits it, probing under the guise of informing. So far, Tatsu had offered only suggestions and generalities, and I wasn't going to fill in the blanks for him by confirming or denying any of it.

"Perhaps he would have used the same new name to reenter the country, and then to relocate within it," he said, after a moment.

But I hadn't used the same new name when I had relocated. Doing so would have presented too obvious a nexus for a determined tracker to follow. Tatsu must not have been sure of that, and, as I suspected, was hoping to learn more by getting me to react. If I were to slip and confirm that I had used the same name, he would tell me that it was by this he had managed to find me, thereby avoiding the need to reveal how he had really done it, and leaving the vulnerability intact, perhaps to be exploited again later.

So I said nothing, effecting a slightly bored expression instead.

He looked at me, the corners of his mouth creeping up into the barest hint of a smile. It was his way of acknowledging that I knew what he was up to, meaning it was useless for him to keep at it, and that he would now get to the point.

"Fukuoka was too small," he said. "Sapporo, too remote. Nagoya was too close to Tokyo. Hiroshima was possible because the atmosphere is good, but I thought the Kansai region more likely because it's less distant from Tokyo, to which I guessed you might want to maintain some proximity. That meant Kyoto, possibly Kobe. But more likely Osaka."

"Because…"

"Because Osaka is bigger, more bustling, so there is more room to hide. And it has a larger transient population, so a new arrival draws less attention. Also I know how you love jazz, and Osaka is known for its clubs."

I might have known Tatsu would key on the clubs. During the Taisho Period, from 1912 to 1926, jazz migrated from Shanghai to Kansai, the western region of Honshu, Japan's main island, where Osaka is located. A host of dance halls and live houses were built in the Soemoncho and Dotonbori entertainment districts, and jazz took off in cafés everywhere. The legacy lives on today in establishments like Mr. Kelly's, Overseas, Royal Horse, and, of course, the Osaka Blue Note, and I couldn't deny that the presence of these places had been a factor in my thinking.

I had even recognized, for the very reasons Tatsu had just articulated, that Osaka might be a somewhat predictable choice. But I had also found that I was reluctant to forego the lifestyle advantages the city would afford me. When I was younger, I would have reflexively foregone any such comforts in favor of the imperative of personal security. But I found my priorities were changing with age, and this, as much as anything else, was a clear sign that it was time for me to get out of the game.

So sure, knowing me as he did, it wouldn't be too difficult for Tatsu to assume Osaka. But that wouldn't have been enough for him to pinpoint me the way he ultimately had.

"Impressive," I told him. "But you haven't explained how you were then able to pick me up in a city of almost nine million."

He raised his head slightly and looked at me directly. "Rain-san," he said, "I understand your desire to know. And I will tell you. But it's important that the information goes no further, or the crime-fighting effectiveness of the Metropolitan Police Force will be inhibited. Can I trust you with this information?"

The question, and the revelations that might follow it, were intended to show that I could trust him, as well. "You know you can," I told him.

He nodded. "Over the last decade or so, the major prefectural and ward governments have been independently installing security cameras in various public places, such as subway stations and major pedestrian thoroughfares. There is substantial evidence, much of it gathered from the experience of the United Kingdom, that such cameras deter crime."

"I've seen the cameras."

"You can see some of them. Not all. In any event, the cameras themselves are not really the issue. What is behind them is what matters. After the events of September eleventh in the United States, the Metropolitan Police Force undertook a major initiative to link up these informal networks of cameras with a central database that runs advanced facial recognition software. The software reads characteristics that are difficult or impossible to obscure—the distance between the eyes, for example, or the precise angles of the triangle formed by the corners of the eyes and the center of the mouth. Now, when a camera gets a match for a photograph from the database, an alert is automatically sent to the appropriate authorities. What had been primarily a psychological deterrent is now a potent anticrime and investigative tool."

I knew of the existence of the software Tatsu was describing, of course. It was being tested in certain airports and stadiums, particularly in the United States, as a way of spotting and preempting known terrorists. But from what I'd read, the early tests had been disappointing. Or perhaps that was just disinformation. In any event, I hadn't known Japan was so far ahead in deployment.

"The cameras are tied to Juki Net?" I asked.

"Possibly," he answered in his dry way.

Juki Net, a vast data snooping and centralization program, went live in August 2002, perhaps inspired by the U.S. Defense Department's similar Total Information Awareness initiative. Juki Net assigns every Japanese citizen an eleven-digit identification number, and links that number to the person's name, sex, address, and date of birth. The government maintains that no other information will be compiled. Few people believe that, and there have already been abuses.

I considered. As Tatsu noted, if word got out, the efficacy of the camera network would be compromised. But there was more.

"Weren't there protests about Juki Net's introduction?" I asked.

He nodded. "Yes. As you may know, the government introduced Juki Net without passing an accompanying privacy bill. Attempts to do so belatedly have been less than convincing. In Suginami-ku there is a boycott. Nonresidents are now seeking to establish an address in that ward to escape the system's dominion."

Now I understood why the government would take such care to maintain the secrecy of Juki Net's connection to the network of security cameras. After all, even if you know it's there, avoiding video surveillance is hell, so the danger of inadvertently tipping off criminals would be a marginal problem. The real issue, no doubt, was the government's fear of the protests that would surely result if the public were to learn the announced scope of the system was really only the tip of the iceberg. If the security cameras were tied together with Juki Net, people would rightly think they had a serious Big Brother situation on their hands.

"You can't blame people for not trusting the government on this," I said. "I read somewhere that, last spring, the defense ministry got caught creating a database on people who had requested materials under the new Freedom of Information Act, including information on their political views."

He smiled his sad smile. "When the news broke, someone tried to delete the evidence."

"I read about that. Didn't the LDP try to suppress a forty-page report on what had happened?"

This time his smile was wry. "The Liberal Democratic Party officials involved in the attempted cover-up were punished, of course. They had their pay docked."

"Now there's a deterrent to future abuses," I said, laughing. "Especially when you know they were greased with twice what got docked."

He shrugged. "As a cop, I welcome Juki Net and the camera networks as a crime-fighting tool. As a citizen, I find it all appalling."

"So why swear me to secrecy on this? Sounds like a few leaks would be just the thing."

He cocked his head to the side, as though marveling at how my thinking could be so crude. "If such leaks were timed incorrectly," he said, "they would be as useless as a powerful but misplaced explosive charge."

He was telling me he was up to something. He was also telling me not to ask.

"So you used this network to find me," I said.

"Yes. I kept the mug shots that were taken of you at Metropolitan Police Headquarters when you were detained after the incident outside of Yokosuka naval base. I had these photographs fed into the computer so the network could look for you. I instructed the technicians to focus their initial efforts on Osaka. Still, because the system turns up so many false positives, the problem took a long time and significant human resources to solve. I have been looking for you for almost a year, Rain-san."

I realized from what he was telling me that the relentless advance of technology was going to force me to return to the nomadic existence I had adopted before my return to Japan, when I had wandered the earth without an identity, drifting from one mercenary conflict to another. There was no pleasure in the thought. I had done my penance for Crazy Jake and didn't wish to repeat the experience.

"The system is not perfect," he went on. "There are numerous gaps in coverage, for example, and, as I mentioned, too many false positives. Still, over time, we were able to identify certain commonalities in your movements. A high incidence of sightings in Miyakojima, for example. From there, it was simple enough to check the records of the local ward office for new resident registrations, weed out false leads, and uncover your address. Eventually, we were able to track you sufficiently closely so that I could travel to Osaka and follow you here tonight."

"Why didn't you just come to my apartment?"

He smiled. "Where you live is always where you are most vulnerable because it represents a possible choke point for an ambush. And I would not wish to surprise a man like you where he felt most vulnerable. Safer, I judged, to approach you on neutral ground, where you might even see me coming, *ne?*"

I nodded, acknowledging his point. If you're a likely target for a kidnapping or assassination attempt, or for any other kind of ambush, the bad guys can only get to you where they know you're going to be. Meaning outside your home, most likely, or the place where you work. Or at some point in between where they can rely on you to show up— maybe the only bridge crossing between your home and office, something like that. These choke points are where you need to be the most sensitive to signs of danger.

"Well?" he asked, raising his eyebrows slightly. "Did you see me?"

I shrugged. "Yes."

He smiled again. "I knew you would."

"Or you could have called."

"In which case, you might have disappeared again after hearing my voice."

"That's true."

"All in all, I think this was the best approach."

"The way you went about this," I said, "a lot of people were involved. People in your organization, maybe people with the CIA."

He might have said something to intimate that any such lack of security was my fault, for having failed to contact him as I had suggested I would. But that wouldn't have been Tatsu's style. He had his interests in this matter, as I had mine, and he wouldn't have blamed me for disappearing any more than he expected me to blame him for tracking me down.

"There has been no mention of your name in any of this," he told me. "Only a photograph. And the technicians tasked with checking for the matches the system spits out have no knowledge regarding the basis of my interest. To them, you are simply one of many criminals the Metropolitan Police Force is tracking. And I have taken other steps to ensure security, such as coming alone tonight and informing no one of my movements."

This was a dangerous thing for Tatsu to admit. If it were true, I could solve pretty much all my problems just by taking out this one man. Again, he was showing me that he trusted me, that I could trust him in return.

"You're taking a lot of chances," I said, looking at him.

"Always," he said, returning my gaze.

There was a long silence. Then I said, "No women. No children. It has to be a man."

"It is."

"You can't have involved anyone else in this. You work with me, it's an exclusive."

"Yes."

"And the target has to be a principal. Taking him out can't just be to send a message to someone. It has to accomplish something concrete."

"It will."

Having established my three rules, it was now time to apprise him of the consequences for breaking them.

"You know, Tatsu, outside of professional reasons—meaning combat or a contract—there's only one thing that has ever moved me to kill."

"Betrayal," he said, to show me he clearly understood.

"Yes."

"Betrayal is not in my nature."

I laughed, because this was the first time I had ever heard Tatsu say something naïve. "It's in everyone's nature," I told him.

We had worked out a system by which we could communicate securely, including simple codes and access to a secure site I continued to maintain for sensitive communications. I had told him I would contact him afterward, but now I wondered whether that would be necessary. Tatsu would learn of the yakuza's accident from independent sources and know I had held up my end. Besides, the less contact with Tatsu, the better. Sure, we had a history. Respect. Even affection. But it was hard to believe the alignment of our interests would last, and, in the end, that alignment, or its lack, would be all that mattered. A sad thought, in certain respects. There aren't many people in my life, and, now that things had turned out all right, I realized I had on some level enjoyed this latest encounter with my old friend and nemesis.

Sad also because it forced me to admit something I had been avoiding: I was going to have to leave Japan. I'd been preparing for such a contingency, but it was sobering to acknowledge the time might be at hand. If Tatsu knew where to find me, and came to believe I'd gotten back in the game in a way that was inhibiting his life's work of fighting corruption in Japan, it would be too easy for him to have me picked up. Conversely, if I agreed to play by his rules, it would be too easy for him to drop in periodically and ask for a "favor." Either way, he'd be running me, and I've lived that life already. I didn't want to do it again.

My pager buzzed. I checked it and saw a five-digit sequence that told me it was Harry.

I finished eating and motioned to the waiter that I was ready for the check. I looked around the restaurant one last time. The office party had broken up. The Americans remained, the white noise of their conversation warm and enthusiastic. The couple was still there, the young man's posture steadfastly earnest, the girl continuing to parry with quiet laughter.

It felt good to be back in Tokyo. I didn't want to leave.

I walked out of the restaurant, pausing to enjoy the feel of Nishi-Azabu's cool evening air, my eyes reflexively sweeping the street. A few cars passed, but otherwise it was as quiet as Aoyama Cemetery, brooding and dark, silently beckoning, across from where I stood.

I looked again at the stone steps and imagined myself traversing them. Then I turned left and continued the clockwise circle I had started earlier that evening.

CHAPTER 3

I called Harry from a public phone on Aoyama-dori.

"Are you on a secure line?" he asked, recognizing my voice.

"Reasonably secure. Public phone. Out of the way location." The location mattered, because governments monitor certain public phones—the ones near embassies and police stations, for example, and those in the lobbies of higher-end hotels, to which the nearby lazy can be counted on to repair for their "private" conversations.

"You're still in Tokyo," he said. "Calling from a Minami-Aoyama payphone."

"How do you know?"

"I've got things rigged so that I can see the originating number and location of calls that come in to my apartment. It's what 911 uses in the States. You can't block it."

Harry, I thought, smiling. Despite his SuperNerd clothes and constant case of bedhead, despite being at heart an oversized kid for whom hacking was just a video game, only better, Harry could be dangerous. The random favor I'd done him so many years earlier, when I'd saved his ass from a bunch of drunken Marines who were looking for a suitable Japanese victim, had paid a hell of a dividend.

And yet, despite my efforts, he could also be astonishingly naïve. I would never tell anyone the kind of thing he had just told me. You don't give away an advantage like that.

"The NSA should never have let you go, Harry," I told him. "You're a privacy nut's worst nightmare."

He laughed, but a little uncertainly. Harry has a hard time knowing when I'm teasing. "Their loss," he said. "They had too many rules, anyway. It's more fun working for a big five consulting firm. They've got so many other problems, they don't even bother trying to monitor what I'm up to anymore."

That was smart of them. They couldn't have kept up with him, anyway. "What's going on?" I asked.

"Nothing really. Just wanted to catch up with you while I could. I had a feeling that, if your business here was done, you might leave soon."

"I guess you were right."

"Is it... done?"

Harry has long since figured out what I do, though he also understands it would be taboo to actually ask. And he must have known what it meant when he had contacted me earlier that evening, at my specific request, to tell me precisely where and when I could find the yakuza. Regardless, he'd be reading about it in the papers soon enough.

"It's done," I told him.

"Does that mean you won't be around much longer?"

I smiled, absurdly touched by his hangdog tone. "Not much longer, no. I was going to call you before I left."

"Yeah?"

"Yeah." I looked at my watch. "In fact, what are you doing right now?"

"Just getting up, actually."

"Christ, Harry, it's ten at night."

"I've been keeping some strange hours lately."

"I believe it. Tell you what. Why don't we meet for a drink. For you, it can be breakfast."

"What have you got in mind?"

"Hang on a minute." I grabbed a copy of the Tokyo Yellow Pages from under the phone, and flipped through the restaurant section until I found the place I was looking for. Then I counted ahead five listings, per our usual code, knowing Harry would count five backward from whatever I told him. Not that anyone was listening—hell, I couldn't imagine who could listen, if Harry didn't want them to—but you don't take chances. I'd taught him to always use a layered defense. To never assume.

"How about Tip-Top, in Takamatsu-cho," I said.

"Sure," he said, and I knew he understood. "Great place."

"I'll see you when you get there," I told him.

I hung up, then pulled a handkerchief out of a pants pocket and wiped down the receiver and the buttons. Old habits die hard.

The place I had in mind was called These Library Lounge, pronounced *tei-ze* by the locals, a small bar with the feel of a speakeasy nestled on the second floor of an unremarkable building in Nishi-Azabu. Although it inhabits the city's geographical and psychological center, Teize is suffused by a dreamy sense of detachment, as though the bar is an island secretly pleased to find itself lost in the vast ocean of Tokyo around it. Teize has the kind of atmosphere that quickly seduces talk into murmurs and weariness into languor, peeling away the transient concerns of the day until you might find yourself listening to a poignant Johnny Hodges number like "Just a Memory" the way you listened to it the first time, without filters or preconceptions or the notion that it was something you already knew; or taking a saltwater and iodine sip of one of the Islay malts and realizing that this, this exactly, is the taste for which the distiller must have mouthed a silent prayer as he committed the amber liquid to an oak cask thirty years before; or glancing over at a group of elegantly dressed women seated in one of the bar's quietly lit alcoves, their faces glowing, not yet lined, their faith that havens like this one exist as if by right reflected in the innocent timbre of their laughter and the carefree cadences of their conversation, and remembering without bitterness what it felt like to think that maybe you, too, could be part of such a world.

It took me less than ten minutes to walk the short distance to the bar. I paused before the exterior stairs leading to the second floor, imagining, as I always do before entering a building, where I might wait if I hoped to ambush someone coming out. The area around Teize offered two promising positions, one of which, the entryway of an adjacent building, I especially liked because it was set back from the bar's entrance in such a way that you wouldn't see someone lurking there until after you'd reached the bottom of the stairs, when it might be too late to do anything about it. Unless, of course, before descending, you took the trouble to lean over the bar's front balcony in appreciation of the quiet street scene below, as I had now reminded myself to do.

Satisfied with the security layout outside, I took the stairs to the second floor and walked in. I hadn't been there in a long time, but the proprietors hadn't seen fit to change anything, thank God. The lighting was still soft—mostly sconces, floor lamps, and candles. A wooden table that had begun its life as a door before being elevated to its current, considerably higher, purpose. Muted Persian rugs and dark, heavy drapes. The white marble bar, confident but not dominating at the center of the main room, shining quietly beneath an overhead set of track lights. Everywhere there were books: mostly works on design, architecture, and art, but also seemingly whimsical selections such as *The Adventures of Two Dutch Dolls* and *Uncle Santa*.

"Nanmeisama?" the bartender asked me. How many? I held up two fingers. He looked around the room, confirming what I had already noticed, that no tables were available.

"That's fine," I told him in Japanese. "I think we'll just sit at the bar." Which, in addition to its other advantages, offered a tactical view of the entranceway.

Harry arrived an hour later, as I was beginning my second single malt of the evening, a sixteen-year-old Lagavulin. He saw me as he came in and smiled.

"John-san, hisashiburi," he said. It's been a long time. Then he switched to English, which would afford us marginally better privacy in these surroundings. "It's good to see you."

I stood and we shook hands. Despite the lack of formality of the occasion, I also offered him a slight bow. I've always liked the respect of a bow and the warmth of a handshake, and Harry merited both.

"Have a seat," I said, motioning to the bar stool to my left. "I hope you'll forgive me for starting without you."

"If you'll forgive me for avoiding what you're having and ordering some food instead."

"Suit yourself," I said. "Anyway, Scotch is a grownup's drink."

He smiled, knowing I was ribbing him, and ordered an herb salad with tofu and mozzarella and a plain orange juice. Harry's never been a drinker.

"You do a good SDR?" I asked him while we waited for the food to arrive. An SDR, or surveillance detection run, is a route designed to flush a follower or team of followers out into the open. I'd taught the subject to Harry and he'd proven himself an able student.

"You ask me that every time," he replied in a slightly exasperated tone, like a teenager remonstrating with a parent. "And every time I give you the same answer."

"So you did one."

He rolled his eyes. "Of course."

"And you were clean?"

He looked at me. "I wouldn't be here if I weren't. You know that."

I patted him on the back. "Can't help asking. Thanks again for the nice work with that yakuza's mobile phone."

He smiled. "Hey, I've got something for you," he said.

"Yeah?"

He nodded and reached into a jacket pocket. He fished around for a second, then pulled out a metal object about the dimensions of a half-dozen stacked credit cards. "Check this out," he said.

I took it. It was heavy for something of its size. There must have been a lot of circuitry packed in it. "Just what I've always wanted," I said. "A faux silver paperweight."

He moved as though to take it back. "Well, if you're not going to appreciate it…"

"No, no, I do appreciate it. I just don't know what the hell it is." Actually I had a good idea, but I prefer to be underestimated. Besides, I didn't want to deny Harry the pleasure of educating me.

"It's a bug and video detector," he said, pronouncing the words slowly as though I might otherwise fail to comprehend them. "If you come within shooting distance of radio frequency or infrared, it'll let you know."

"In a sexy female voice, I hope?"

He laughed. "If someone's trying to record you, you might not want them to know you know. So no sexy voice. Just a vibration mode. Intermittent for video, continuous for audio. Alternating for both. And only in ten second bursts, to conserve battery power."

"How does it work?"

He beamed. "Wide range circuitry that detects transmitters operating on frequencies from fifty megahertz to three gigahertz. Plus it's got an internal antenna that picks up the horizontal oscillator frequency radiated by video cameras. I've optimized it for the PAL standard, which is what you're most likely to encounter, but I can change it to NTSC or

SECAM if you want. Reception isn't great because it's so small, so you won't be able to tell where the bug or camera is, only that one is there. And the big security closed-circuit TV units you sometimes see in train stations and parks will usually be out of the unit's range."

Too bad about the CCTV units. If I had a reliable, portable way to detect those, I'd have a shot at getting my privacy back from Tatsu and whomever else.

"Any chance you can make the reception a little better?" I asked.

He looked a little hurt, and I realized I should have praised him before asking that. "Not for something this small," he said. "You'd need something with a much bigger antenna."

Oh well. Even with its limitations, the unit would be useful. I hefted it in my hand. I was familiar with functionally similar commercial models, of course, but I hadn't seen one this small. It was an impressive piece of work.

"Rechargeable battery?" I asked.

"Of course. Lithium ion. Just like a mobile phone." He reached into a jacket pocket and pulled out what looked like an ordinary mobile phone charger. "I ran it down testing it, so you'll need to charge it when you get home. And don't forget to juice it up every day. There's no low battery indicator or anything else like that. I built this thing for speed, not looks."

I took the charger and put it on the table next to me. Then I pulled out my wallet and slid the unit into it. It was a nice, snug fit. I would examine it back at the hotel, of course, to confirm that it was a bug detector and not some sort of bug. Not that I don't trust Harry. I just like to satisfy myself about these things.

I put my wallet back in my pants and nodded appreciatively. "Nice work," I said. "Thank you."

He smiled. "I know you're a professional paranoid, so I figured it was either this or a lifetime supply of Valium."

I laughed. "Now tell me, what's with the vampire hours?"

"Oh, you know," he said looking away, "just lifestyle stuff."

Lifestyle stuff? As far as I knew, Harry had no lifestyle. In my imagination he was always huddled in his apartment, worming his way into remote networks, creating backdoors to exploit later, mediating the world through the safety of a computer screen.

He was blushing. Christ, the kid was so transparent. "Harry, are you going to tell me you've got a girlfriend?" I asked.

The blush deepened, and I laughed. "I'll be damned," I said. "Good for you."

He looked at me, checking to see whether I was going to tease him. "She's not exactly my girlfriend."

"Well, never mind the taxonomy. How did you meet her?"

"Work."

I picked up my glass. "You going to give me details, or do I have to force feed you two or three of these to loosen your tongue?"

He made a face of exaggerated disgust. "One of the firm's clients, one of the big trading houses, was happy with some security work I did for them."

"Guess they didn't know about the backdoors you left for yourself in the process."

He smiled. "They never do."

"So the client is happy…"

"And my boss took me out to celebrate, to a hostess club."

Most westerners have a hard time grasping the concept of the Japanese "hostess club," where the women are paid only for conversation. The West accepts the notion that sex can be commoditized, but rebels at the idea that other forms of human interaction might be subject to purchase, as well. For hostesses are not prostitutes, though, like the geisha from whom they're descended, they might strike up an after-hours relationship with the right customer, after a suitable courtship. Rather, patrons at such establishments pay for the simple pleasure of the girls' company, and for their ability to smooth out the rough edges of business meetings, as well as for the hope that, eventually, something more might develop. If it were simple sex the hostesses' clients were after, they could buy it for much less elsewhere.

"What club?" I asked him.

"A place called Damask Rose."

"Haven't heard of it."

"They don't advertise."

"Sounds upscale."

"It is. It's a pretty refined place, in fact. In Nogizaka, on Gaienhigashi-dori. They probably wouldn't let you in."

I laughed. I love when Harry shows some spirit. "Okay, so the boss takes you to Damask Rose…"

"Yeah, and he had a lot to drink and was telling everyone that I'm a computer genius. One of the hostesses asked me some questions about how to configure a firewall because she just bought a new computer."

"Pretty?"

The blush reappeared. "I guess. Her computer was a Macintosh, so I liked her right off the bat."

I raised my eyebrows. "I didn't know that kind of thing could form the basis for love at first sight."

"So I answered a few of her questions," he said, ignoring me. "At the end of the night, she asked if I would give her my phone number, in case she had any more questions."

I laughed. "Thank God she didn't just give you her number. She would have died of old age waiting for you to call."

He smiled, knowing this was probably true.

"So she called you…" I said.

"And I wound up going over to her apartment and configuring her whole system."

"Harry, you 'configured her whole system'?" I asked, my eyes mock-wide.

He looked down, but I saw the smile. "You know what I mean."

"You're not going to… penetrate her security, are you?" I asked, unable to resist.

"No, I wouldn't do that to her. She's nice."

Christ, he was so smitten he couldn't even spot the sophomoric double entendre. "I'll be damned," I said again. "I'm happy for you, Harry."

He looked at me, saw that my expression was genuine. "Thanks," he said.

I raised my glass to my nose, took a deep breath, held it for a moment, and let it go. "So she's got you keeping odd hours?" I asked.

"Well, the club is open until three in the morning and she works every day. So, by the time she gets home…"

"I get the picture," I said. Though in fact, it was a little hard to imagine Harry with an attachment that didn't have an Ethernet cable and a mouse. He was an introverted, socially stunted guy, with no contacts

I knew of outside of his day job, which he kept at arm's length in any event, and me. Conditions that had always made him useful.

I tried to picture him with a high-end hostess, and couldn't see it. It didn't feel right.

Don't be a prick, I thought. *Just because you can't have someone in your life, don't begrudge Harry.*

"What's her name?" I asked.

He smiled. "Yukiko."

Yukiko means "snow child." "Pretty name."

He nodded, his expression slightly dopey. "I like it."

"How much does she know about you?" I asked, taking a sip of the Lagavulin. My tone was innocent, but I was concerned that, in the delirium of what I assumed was first love, Harry would be unnecessarily open with this girl.

"Well, she knows about the consultant work, of course. But not about the... hobbies."

About his extreme proclivity for hacking, he meant. A hobby that could land him in prison if the authorities caught wind of it. In the ground, if someone else did.

"Hard to keep that sort of thing secret," I opined, testing.

"I don't see why it would have to come up," he said, looking at me.

A waitress appeared from behind a curtain and set Harry's order on the bar in front of him. He thanked her, showing a deep appreciation for this newly wonderful class of being, *women who work in restaurants and bars,* and I smiled.

I realized on some level that if Harry was going to start living more like a civilian, he would be less useful, and possibly even dangerous, to me. His increasing transparency to the wider world might offer an enemy a window into my otherwise hidden existence. Of course, if someone connected Harry to me, they might come after him, too. And despite what I'd tried to teach him over the years, I knew that, out in the open, Harry wouldn't have the means to protect himself.

"Is she your first girlfriend?" I asked, my tone gentle.

"I told you, she's not really my girlfriend," he said, ducking the question.

"If she's occupying enough of your attention to keep you in bed until the sun sets, I feel safe using the word as shorthand."

He looked at me, cornered.

"Is she?" I asked again.

He looked away. "I guess so."

I hadn't meant to embarrass him. "Harry, I only ask because, when you're young, you sometimes think you can have it both ways. If you're just having fun, you don't need to tell her anything. You shouldn't tell her anything. But if the attachment gets deeper, you'll need to do some hard thinking. About how close you want to get with her, about how important your hobbies are. Because you can't live with one foot in daylight and the other in shadows. Believe me on this. It can't be done. Not long-term."

"I'm not stupid, you know."

"Everybody in love is stupid. It's part of the condition."

He blushed again, at my use of the word and the assumption behind it. But I didn't care how he referred to these new feelings in his own mind. I know what it's like to live walled off, isolated, and then suddenly, unbelievably, to have that pretty girl you'd longed for returning the feeling. It changes your priorities. Hell, it changes your damn values.

I smiled bitterly, thinking of Midori.

Then, as if reading my mind, he said, "There's something I've been meaning to tell you. But I wanted to do it in person."

"Sounds serious."

"A few months ago I got a letter. From Midori."

I finished off the Lagavulin before answering. If the letter had arrived that long ago, a few moments more for me to figure out how I wanted to respond weren't going to make a difference.

"She knew where to reach you…" I started, though I had already figured it out.

He shrugged. "She knew because we brought her over to my apartment to handle the musical aspects of that lattice encryption."

I noticed that, even now, Harry felt compelled to carve out Midori's precise role in that operation to clarify that he had been fully capable of handling the encryption itself. He was sensitive about these things. "Right," I said.

"She didn't know my last name. The envelope was only addressed to Haruyoshi. Thank God, otherwise I would have had to move, and what a pain in the neck that would have been."

Harry, like anyone else who values privacy, takes extreme pains to ensure there's no connection anywhere—not on utility bills, not on cable TV subscriptions, not even on lease documents—between his name and the place where he lives. This kind of disassociation requires some labor, involving the establishment of revocable trusts, LLCs, and other blind legal entities, and it can all be blown in a heartbeat if your Aunt Keiko visits you at your home, notes your address, and decides to send you, say, flowers to thank you. The flower shop puts your name and address into its database, which it then sells to marketing outfits, which in turn sell the information to everyone else, and your true residence is now available to anyone with even rudimentary hacking or social engineering skills. The only way to regain your privacy is to move again and repeat the exercise.

If what was sent to you was just an ordinary letter, of course, the only person who might make the connection is the postman. It's up to the individual to decide whether that would be an acceptable risk. For me, it wouldn't be. Probably not for Harry, either. But if only his first name had appeared on the envelope, he would be all right.

"Where was the letter from?" I asked him.

"New York. She's living there, I guess."

New York. Where Tatsu had sent her, after telling her I was dead, to protect her from suspicion that she might still have the computer disk her father had stolen from Yamaoto, a disk containing enough evidence of Japan's vast network of corruption to bring down the government. The move made sense for her, I supposed. Her career in America was taking off. I knew because I was watching.

He reached into a back pants pocket and pulled out a folded piece of paper. "Here," he said, handing it to me.

I took it and paused for a moment before unfolding it, not caring what he would make of my hesitation. When I looked, I saw that it was written in confident, graceful longhand Japanese, an echo, perhaps, of girlhood calligraphy lessons, and a reflection of the personality behind the pen.

Haruyoshi-san,

It is still cold in New York, and I am counting the days to Spring. I imagine that soon enough, the cherry blossoms will be blooming in Tokyo and I am sure they will be beautiful.

I trust that you, too, have heard the sad news that our mutual friend Fujiwara-san has passed away. I have been given to understand that Fujiwara-san's body had been returned to the United States for burial. I have hoped to visit the gravesite to present an offering for his spirit, but, regrettably, I have been unable to discover where he has been laid to rest. If you have any information that would be helpful to me in this matter, I would sincerely appreciate your assistance. You can reach me at the above address.

I humbly pray for your health and well-being. Thank you for your solicitude.

Yours,
Kawamura Midori

I read it again, slowly, then a third time. Then I folded it back up and extended it to Harry.

"No, no," he said, his hands raised, palms forward. "You keep it."

I didn't want him to see that I wanted it. But I nodded and slipped it into an inside pocket of my blazer.

I signaled the bartender that it was time for another Lagavulin. "Did you answer this?" I asked.

"I did. I wrote back, and told her that I had heard exactly what she had, that I didn't have any other information."

"Did you hear from her after that?"

"Just a thank-you. She asked me to let her know if I heard anything, and told me she would do the same."

"That's all?"

"Yeah."

I wondered if she had bought the story. If she hadn't thanked Harry for his response, I would have known she hadn't bought it, because she was classy and it wouldn't have been like her not to respond. But the thank-you might have been automatic, sent even in the presence of continued suspicions. It could even have been duplicitous, intended to lull Harry into thinking she was satisfied when in fact the opposite was true.

That's bullshit, some part of me spoke up. *She's not like that.*

Then a bitter smile: *Not like you, you mean.*

There was nothing duplicitous about Midori, and knowing it opened up a little ache. The environment I've inhabited for so long has conditioned me to assume the worst. At least I still occasionally remember to resist the urge.

It didn't matter. There were too many oddities surrounding the disk's disposition and my disappearance, and she was too smart to miss them. I'd spent a lot of time thinking about it over the last year or so, and I knew the way she would see it.

After what had happened between us, the doubts would have started small. But there would have been nothing to check their growth. *After all,* she would think, *the contents of the disk were never published.* That was Tatsu's doing, not mine, but she would have no way of knowing that. All she would know was that her father's last wishes were never carried out, that his death was ultimately futile. She would wonder again how I had known where to find that disk in Shibuya, go over my previous explanations, find them wanting. That would have led her to start thinking about the timing of my appearance, so soon after her father's death.

And she knew I was part of something subterranean, though not exactly what. The CIA? One of the Japanese political factions? Regardless, an organization with the resources to fake a death and backstop it reasonably effectively.

Yeah, with all these loose threads, and without me there to reassure her that what happened between us had been real, I knew that, eventually, she would conclude she had been used. That's how I would see it, in her shoes. *Maybe the sex was just opportunistic for him,* she would think. *Sure, why not, might as well have a little fun while I'm using her to get the disk. And then I'll just disappear afterward, after I've tricked her into cooperating.* She wouldn't want to believe all this, but she wouldn't be able to shake the feeling. And she wouldn't want to believe I might actually have been involved in some way in her father's death, but she wouldn't be able to let that suspicion go, either.

"Did I handle it right?" Harry asked.

I shrugged. "You couldn't have handled it any better than you did. But she's still not buying it."

"You think she'll let it go?"

That was the question I was always left with. I hadn't managed to answer it. "I don't know," I told him.

And there was something else I didn't know, something I wouldn't share with Harry. I didn't know if I *wanted* her to let it go.

What had I just told him? *You can't live with one foot in daylight and the other in shadows.* I needed to take my own damn advice.

CHAPTER 4

I saw Harry off around one. The subways were already closed and he caught a cab. He told me he was going home to wait for Yukiko.

I tried to picture a beautiful young hostess, pulling down the yen equivalent of a thousand dollars a night in tips in one of Tokyo's exclusive establishments, with her pick of wealthy businessmen and politicians for paramours, hurrying home to Harry's apartment after work. I just couldn't see it.

Don't be so cynical, I thought.

But my gut wasn't buying it, and I've learned to trust my gut.

It's still early. Just take a look. It's practically on the way to the hotel.

If Harry had changed his mind about going home and had gone to Damask Rose instead, though, he'd know I was checking up on him. He might not be surprised, but he wouldn't like it, either.

But the chances that Harry would stop by there on his own dime, when Yukiko was due to come to his place in just a few hours anyway, were slim. The risk was worth taking.

And Nogizaka was only a few kilometers away. What the hell.

I tried directory assistance from a public phone, but there was no listing for a Damask Rose. Well, Harry had said they didn't advertise.

Still, I could just go and have a look.

I walked the short distance to Nogizaka, then strolled up and down Gaienhigashi-dori. It took awhile, but I finally spotted it. There was no sign, only a small red rose on a black awning.

The entrance was flanked by two black men, each of sufficient bulk to have been at home in the sumo pit. Their suits were well tailored and, given the size of the men wearing them, must have been custom-made. Nigerians, I assumed, whose size, managerial acumen, and relative facility with the language had made them a rare foreign success story, in this case as both middle management and muscle for many of the area's entertainment establishments. The *mizu shobai,* or "water trade" of entertainment and pleasure, is one of the few areas in which Japan can legitimately claim a degree of internationalization.

They bowed and opened the club's double glass doors for me, each issuing a baritone *irasshaimase* as they did so. Welcome. One of them murmured something into a microphone set discreetly into his lapel.

I walked down a short flight of stairs. A ruddy-faced, prosperous-looking Japanese man whom I put at about forty greeted me in a small foyer. Interchangeable J-Pop techno music was playing from the room beyond.

"Nanmeisama desho ka?" Mr. Ruddy asked. How many?

"Just one," I said in English, holding up a finger.

"Of course." He motioned that I should follow him.

The room was rectangular, flanked by dance stages on either end. The stages were simple, distinguished only by mirrored walls behind them and identical brass poles at their centers. One stage was occupied by a tall, long-haired blonde wearing high heels and a green g-string and nothing more. She was dancing somewhat desultorily, I thought, but seemed to have the attention of the majority of the club's clientele regardless. Russian, I guessed. Large-boned and large-breasted. A delicacy in Japan.

Harry hadn't mentioned floorshows. Probably he was embarrassed. My sense that something was amiss deepened.

On the other stage, there was a girl who looked like a mix of Japanese and something Mediterranean or Latin. A good mix. She had that silky, almost shimmering black hair so many modern Japanese women like to ruin with *chapatsu* dye, worn short and swept over from the side. The shape of the eyes was also Japanese, and she was on the petite side. But her skin, a smooth gold like melted caramel, spoke of something else, something tropical. Her breasts and hips, too, appealingly full and slightly incongruous on her Japanese-sized frame, suggested some foreign origin. She was using the pole skillfully, grabbing it high, posing with her body held rigid and parallel to the floor, then spiraling down in time to the music. There was real vitality in her moves and she didn't seem to mind that most of the patrons were focused on the blonde.

Mr. Ruddy held out a chair for me at an empty table in the center of the room. After a routine glance to ensure the seat afforded a proper view of the entrance, I sat. I wasn't displeased to see that I also had a good view of the stage where the dark-haired girl was dancing.

"Wow," I said in English, looking at her.

"Yes, she is beautiful," he replied, also in English. "Would you like to meet her?"

I watched her for another moment before answering. I didn't want to wind up with one of the Japanese girls here. I would have a better chance of creating rapport, and therefore of eliciting information, by chatting with a foreigner while playing the role of foreigner.

I nodded.

"I will let her know." He handed me a drinks menu, bowed, and slipped away from the table.

The menu was written on a single page of thick, cream-colored parchment in double columns of elegant Japanese, the club's signature red rose placed discreetly at the bottom. I was surprised to see that it included an imaginative selection of single malts. A twenty-five-year-old Springbank, which I'd been looking for. And a Talisker of the same age. I might have to stay for a while.

A waitress came by and I ordered the Springbank. Ten thousand yen the measure. But life is short.

There were a dozen girls working the floor. About half were Japanese; the others looked indeterminately European. All were attractive and tastefully dressed. Most were engaging customers, but a few were free. None approached my table. Mr. Ruddy must have passed the word that I'd requested someone. Efficient operation.

At the table next to me was a Japanese man surrounded by three fawning hostesses. He looked superficially youthful, with radiant, white teeth and black hair swept back from a tanned face free of fissures. But I looked more closely and saw the appearance was ersatz. The hair was dyed; the tan courtesy of a sun lamp; the unseamed face likely the product of botox and surgery; the teeth porcelain caps. The chemicals and the knife, even the retinue of attractive young women with paid-for adoring smiles, all flimsy tools to prop up a shaky wall of denial about the inevitable indignities of aging and death.

The techno beat faded out and the dark-haired girl gyrated slowly to the floor, her legs scissoring the pole, her back arched, her head tilted back toward the room. The blonde was also finishing, albeit in less spectacular fashion. The audience applauded.

The waitress brought my Springbank, shimmering amber in a crystal tumbler. I raised the glass to my nose, closed my eyes for a moment, and inhaled a breath of clean, sherried sea air. I took a sip. Salt and brine, yes, but somewhere a hint of fruit, as well. The finish was long and dry. I smiled. Not bad for a twenty-five-year-old.

I took another sip and looked around. I didn't pick up any danger vibes. *The place could be legit,* I thought. Doubtless it would be hooked up with organized crime, but that was par for the course in the *mizu shobai,* not just for Japan but for the world. Maybe Harry had simply gotten lucky.

Maybe.

A few minutes later, the dark-haired girl appeared from behind the stage. She moved down a short riser of steps and walked over to my table.

She had changed into a strapless black cocktail dress. A thin diamond bracelet encircled her left wrist. *A gift from an admirer,* I thought. I expected she would have many.

"May I join you?" she asked. Her English was lightly accented with something warm, maybe Spanish or Portuguese.

"Please," I said, standing and pulling back a chair for her. "Is English all right?"

"Of course," she said, looking at me closely. "You… you're American?"

I nodded. "My parents are Japanese, but I grew up in America. I'm more comfortable in English."

I eased the chair in behind her. The cocktail dress laced up the back. Smooth skin glowed in the interstices.

I sat next to her. "I enjoyed watching you dance," I said.

I knew she would have heard that a thousand times before, and her smile confirmed it. The smile said, *Of course you did.*

That was fine. I wanted her to feel in control, to let her guard down. We'd have a few drinks, relax, get to know each other before I began to probe for what really interested me.

"What brings you to Tokyo?" she asked.

"Business. I'm an accountant. Once a year I have to come to Japan for some of the firm's local clients." It was a good cover story. No one ever asks follow-up questions when you tell them you're an accountant. They're afraid you might answer.

"I'm John, by the way," I added.

She held out her hand. "Naomi."

Her fingers were small in my hand but her grip was firm. I tried to place her age. Late twenties, maybe thirty. She looked young, but her dress and mannerisms were sophisticated.

"Can I get you something to drink, Naomi?"

"What's that you're having?"

"Something special, if you like single malts."

"I love single malts. Especially the old Islay whiskies. They say age removes the fire but leaves the warmth. I like that."

You're good, I thought, looking at her. Her mouth was beautiful: full lips; pink gums that almost glowed; even, white teeth. Her eyes were green. A small network of freckles fanned out on and around her nose, barely perceptible amidst the background of caramel skin.

"What I'm drinking isn't from Islay," I said, "but it's got some island character. Smoke and peat. A Springbank."

She raised her eyebrows. "The twenty-five?"

"You know the menu," I said, nodding. "Would you like one?"

"After a night of watered-down Suntory? I'd love one."

Of course she'd love one. Her pay would include a cut of her customers' tabs. A few ten thousand yen shots and she could call it an evening.

I ordered another Springbank. She asked me questions: how I knew so much about single malt whisky, where I lived in the States, how many times I'd been to Tokyo. She was comfortable in her role and I let her play it.

When our glasses were empty I asked her if she'd like another drink.

She smiled. "You're thinking about the Talisker."

"You're a mind reader."

"I just know the menu. And good taste. I'd love another."

I ordered two Taliskers. They were excellent: huge and peppery, with a finish that lasted forever. We drank and chatted some more.

When the second round was nearly done, I began to change tack.

"Where are you from?" I asked her. "You're not Japanese." This last I said with some hesitation, as though inexperienced in such matters and therefore unsure.

"My mother was Japanese. I'm from Brazil."

I'll be damned, I thought. I was planning a trip to Brazil. A long trip.

"Brazil, where?"

"Bahia."

Bahia is one of the country's coastal states. "Salvador?" I asked, to determine the city.

"Yes!" she exclaimed, with the first genuine smile of the evening. "How do you know Brazil so well?"

"I've been there a few times. My firm has clients all over the world. *Um pai brasileiro e uma mãe japonesa—é uma combinacao bonita,*" I said in the Portuguese I had been studying with cassettes. A Brazilian father and a Japanese mother—it's a beautiful combination.

Her eyes lit up and her mouth parted in a perfect O. "*Obrigada!*" she exclaimed. Thank you! Then: "*Você fala português?*" You speak Portuguese?

It was as though the real person had suddenly decided to reinhabit the hostess's body. Her eyes, her expression, her posture had all come alive, and again I felt that vital energy that had animated her dancing.

"Only a little," I said, switching back to English. "I'm good with languages and I try to pick up a bit from wherever I travel."

She was shaking her head slowly and looking at me as though it was the first time she had seen me. She took a swallow of her drink, finishing it.

"One more?" I asked.

"*Sim!*" she answered immediately in Portuguese. Yes!

I ordered two more Taliskers, then turned to her. "Tell me about Brazil," I said.

"What do you want to hear?"

"About your family."

She leaned back and crossed her legs. "My father is a Brazilian blue-blood, from one of the old families. My mother was second-generation Japanese."

Brazil's melting pot population includes some two million ethnic Japanese, the result of immigration that began in 1908, when Brazil needed laborers and Imperial Japan was looking to establish her people in different parts of the world.

"So you learned Japanese from her?"

She nodded. "Japanese from my mother, Portuguese from my father. My mother died when I was a child, and my father hired an English nanny so I could learn English, too."

"How long have you been in Japan?"

"Three years."

"The whole time at this club?"

She shook her head. "Only a year at the club. Before that I was teaching English and Portuguese here in Tokyo through the JET program."

JET, or Japan Exchange and Teaching, is a government-sponsored program that brings foreigners to Japan primarily to teach their native languages. Judging from the average Japanese's facility with English, the program could use some work.

"You learned to dance like that teaching language classes?" I asked.

She laughed. "I learned to dance by dancing. When I got here a year ago I was so shy I could barely move on the stage."

I smiled. "That's hard to imagine."

"It's true. I was raised in a very proper house. I never could have conceived of this kind of thing growing up."

The waitress walked over and set down two crystal tumblers, each with a measure of Talisker, and two glasses of water. Naomi expertly tipped a drop of the water into the whisky, swirled it once, and raised the tumbler to her nose. Had she still been in hostess mode she would have waited, taking her cue to drink from the customer. We were making progress.

"Mmmm," she purred.

We touched glasses and drank.

She closed her eyes. "Oh," she said. "That's so good."

I smiled. "How did you wind up here at world-famous Damask Rose?"

She shrugged. "My first two years in Japan, my salary was about three million yen. I was tutoring in the evening to make a little extra. One of my students told me he knew some people who were opening a club where I could make a lot more than I was making then. I checked it out. And here I am."

Three million yen a year—maybe twenty-five thousand dollars. "This certainly looks like an improvement," I said, looking around.

"It's a good place. We make most of our money with private lap dances. If you'd like, I can do one for you. But no pressure."

Lap dancing would be her economic bread and butter. That she had treated it as an afterthought was another good sign.

I looked at her. She really was lovely. But I was here for something else.

"Maybe later," I said. "I'm enjoying talking with you."

She smiled, perhaps flattered. Given her looks, my demurral must have been refreshing. Good.

I smiled back. "Tell me more about your family."

She took another sip of the Talisker. "I have two older brothers. They're both married and work in the family business."

"Which is?"

"Agriculture. It's a family tradition that the men go into the business."

The reference to agriculture felt deliberately vague. From what I knew about Brazil, it could have meant coffee, tobacco, sugar, or some combination. It could also have meant real estate. I gathered that her family was wealthy but that she was discreet about it.

"What do the women do?" I asked.

She laughed. "The women study something trivial in college, so they have a proper education and can be good conversationalists at parties, then they get married into the right families."

"And you decided to do something different."

"I did the college part—art history. But my father and brothers expected me to get married after that and I just wasn't ready."

"Why Japan, then?"

She glanced upward and pursed her lips. "It's silly, but whenever I hear Japanese it sounds like my mother to me. And I was starting to lose the Japanese I had acquired from her as a child, which was like losing part of her."

For an instant I saw an image of my own mother's face. She had died at home while I was in Vietnam.

"That's not silly at all," I said.

We were each quiet. *Now,* I thought.

"So, how do you like working here?" I asked.

She shrugged. "It's okay. The hours are crazy, but the money is good."

"Management treats you well?"

She shrugged again. "They're okay. No one tries to make you do anything you don't want to."

"What do you mean?"

"You know. When you do lap dances, some customers want more. If the customers are happy, they come back and spend big money. So, in places like this, sometimes management can pressure the girls to make the customers happy. And to do other things."

My expression was appropriately concerned. "'Other things'?"

She waved a hand. "Nothing," she said.

Change tack. "What about the other girls?" I asked, looking around. "Where do they come from?"

"Oh, all over the world." She pointed to a tall, auburn beauty in a red-sequined dress who was charming Botox Boy. "That's Elsa. She's from Sweden. And that's Julie next to her, from Canada. The girl who was dancing opposite me is Valentina, from Russia."

"What about the girls from Japan?"

"That's Mariko and Taeka," she said, pointing to a petite pair at a corner table who had just said or done something to elicit gales of laughter from their two obviously inebriated, American-looking customers. She turned her head one way, then the other, then back to me. "I don't see Emi or Yukiko. They must be getting ready to dance."

"Seems like a good mix," I said. "Do you all get along?"

She shrugged. "It's like anywhere else. Some of your coworkers are your friends. Others you're not so crazy about."

I smiled as though preparing to enjoy a bit of gossip. "Who do you like, and who do you not like?"

"Oh, I get along all right with pretty much everyone." It was a safe answer to a slightly different question. I admired her poise.

The house music faded out and was replaced by another round of J-Pop techno. Simultaneously, two Japanese girls, topless and high-heeled, appeared on the dance stages.

"Ah, that's Emi," Naomi said, indicating the pretty, appealingly zaftig girl on the far stage. She turned and nodded her head at the stage closer to us. "And that's Yukiko."

Yukiko. At last we meet.

I watched her, a tall girl with long hair so black that under the stage lighting it coruscated like moonlit liquid. It cascaded in waves around the smooth contours of her shoulders, past the alluring shadows of her waist, around the upturned curve of her ass. She was tall and fine-boned, with delicate white skin, high cheekbones, and small, high breasts. Put the hair up, add a little couture, and you'd have the world's classiest courtesan.

This girl with Harry? I thought. *No way.*

"She's beautiful," I said, feeling that her striking looks demanded some commentary.

"A lot of people say so," Naomi replied.

There was something lurking in her deliberately noncommittal reply. "You don't think so?" I asked.

She shrugged. "Not my type."

"I get the feeling you don't care for her."

"Let's just say she's comfortable doing things I'm not."

With Harry? "I'd be lying if I told you I wasn't curious."

She shook her head, and I knew I'd hit another dead end, even after three whiskies.

Snow child, indeed. There was something cold, even calculating, about the girl's beauty. Something was wrong here, though how the hell could I tell Harry that? I imagined the conversation: *Harry, I went to Damask Rose to check up on you. Trust me, my friend, this girl is way out of your league. Plus, I had a bad feeling about her generally. Steer clear.*

I knew where his mind was right now: she would feel like the best thing that had ever happened to him, and anything or anyone that threatened that comfortable sense would be rationalized away or ignored. A heads-up from a friend would be useless. Or worse.

I wasn't going to get any more out of Naomi. I'd do a little more digging when I got back to Osaka. Harry was a friend and I owed him that much. But finding out what this girl was up to wasn't really the problem. Getting Harry to acknowledge it, I knew, would be.

"Do you want to watch her?" Naomi asked.

I shook my head. "Sorry. I was thinking of something else."

We talked more about Brazil. She spoke of the country's ethnic and cultural variety, a mélange of Europeans, Indians, Japanese, and West Africans; its atmosphere of exuberance, music, and sport; its extremes of wealth and poverty; most of all, its beauty, with thousands of miles of spectacular coast, the vast pampas of the south, the trackless green basin of the Amazon. Much of it I knew already, but I enjoyed listening to her, and looking at her while she spoke.

I thought of what she had said about Yukiko: *Let's just say she's comfortable doing things I'm not.*

But that only meant Yukiko had been in the game longer. Innocence is a fragile thing.

I might have asked for her number. I could have told her my visit had been extended, something like that. She was too young, but I liked the way she made me feel. She provoked a confusing mix of emotions: affinity based on the shared experiences of mixed blood and childhood bereavement; a paternalistic urge to protect her from the mistakes she was going to make; a sad sexual longing that was like an elegy for Midori.

It was getting late. "Will you forgive me if I forgo the lap dance?" I asked her.

She smiled. "That's fine."

I stood to go. She got up with me.

"Wait," she said. She took out a pen. "Give me your hand."

I held out my left hand. She held it and began to write on my palm. She wrote slowly. Her fingers were warm.

"This is my private email address," she said when she was done. "It's not something I give customers, so please don't share it. Next time you have a trip to Salvador, let me know. I'll tell you the best places to go." She smiled. "And I wouldn't mind hearing from you if you find yourself back in Tokyo, either."

I smiled into her green eyes. The smile felt strangely sad to me. Maybe she didn't notice.

"You never know," I said.

I settled the bill at the door, in cash as always. I took a card, then walked up the stairs without looking back.

The early morning air of Nogizaka was cool and slightly damp. Light from streetlamps lay in weak yellow pools. The pavement was slick with urban dew. Tokyo slumbered around me, dreamless and indifferent.

Goodbye to all that, I thought, and began walking toward the hotel.

CHAPTER 5

I went straight to bed, but I couldn't sleep. I kept thinking of Harry, of Harry with Yukiko. I knew something was wrong there. What would this girl, or whoever she worked for, want with a guy like Harry?

I supposed he might have made an enemy with one of his hacking stunts. Even if he had, though, tracing the problem back to him would be a bitch. And what would be the point of setting him up with the girl?

Harry had told me his boss had taken him to Damask Rose to "celebrate" the night Harry had met Yukiko. If the girl had been a setup, Harry's boss must have been complicit. I chewed on that.

I thought about going to the guy. I could find out his name, where he lived, brace him one morning on his way to the office.

Tempting, but even if I got the information I wanted, the incident would cause problems for Harry, possibly severe ones. No go.

Okay, try something else. Maybe someone was interested in Harry only as a conduit to me.

But nobody knows about Harry, I thought. *Not even Tatsu.*

There was Midori, of course. She knew where he lived. She'd sent him that letter.

Nah, I don't see it.

I got up and paced the room. Midori had connections in the entertainment world. Use those connections, have someone get close to Harry as a way of finding me?

I remembered that last night with her at the Imperial Hotel, how we'd been standing, my arms around her from behind, her fingers intertwined with mine, the way her hair smelled, the way she tasted. I pushed away the memory.

I realized that, for the moment, there was no way of knowing who was behind Harry's improbable romance. So I put aside Midori and concentrated on what, not who.

What makes me a hard target is that I have no fixed points in my life—no workplace, no address, no known associates—that someone can hook into and use to get to me. If someone had established a connection from Harry to me, he'd have that fixed point. He could be expected to exploit it.

That meant people would be watching Harry. Not just through Yukiko. They'd have to tail him, as often as possible.

But he'd been clean when I'd seen him at Teize. He'd told me as much, and I knew for sure that I'd been clean afterward.

I decided to conduct an experiment. It was a bit risky, but not as risky as leveling with Harry about his situation, given his current state of mind. I'd need another night in Tokyo to do it right. No problem with that. While closing in on the weightlifter, I'd been staying in appropriately anonymous city hotels for one week at a time—not wishing to attract attention with longer stays—and the New Otani reservation was good for another three nights anyway.

I looked at the digital clock on the bedstand. It was past four in the morning. Christ, I was keeping the same hours as my lovesick friend.

I'd call him in the evening, when we'd both be awake. More importantly, when Yukiko would be at Damask Rose, and Harry, presumably, would be alone. Then, based on the outcome of my little experiment, I'd decide how much to tell him.

I got back in bed. The last thing I thought of before drifting off to sleep was Midori, and how she had said in her letter that she wanted to present an offering for my spirit.

I woke up the next day feeling refreshed.

Later I would call Harry and arrange a meeting for that night. But first, I wanted to map out an SDR that I'd ask him to use beforehand.

Putting together the route took most of the afternoon. Every element had to be done right or the route itself would be a failure. It had to move through areas with which Harry was already familiar because he wasn't going to have an opportunity to practice. Also, at several junctures, timing would be important, and I had to walk the entirety of both Harry's route and mine to ensure that our paths would cross only as planned. I took detailed notes as I went along, using some typing paper I picked up at a stationery store.

When I was done, I stopped at a coffee shop and created a map with notations on a single sheet of paper. Then I made my way to Shin-Okubo, north of Shinjuku and a bastion of the Korean mob, where, among the unlicensed doctors and unadvertised shops hidden in crumbling apartment buildings, I was able to purchase a cloned mobile phone for cash, with no ID.

Next stop was Harry's neighborhood in Iikura, just south of Roppongi, where I found a suitable Lawson's convenience store not far from his apartment. I browsed in the reading section, folding the map into one of the magazines there.

I called him from a payphone at seven that evening. "Wake up, sleepyhead," I told him.

"Hey, what's going on?" he asked. "I didn't expect to hear from you for a while."

He didn't sound groggy. Maybe he'd gotten up to see Yukiko off to the office.

"I missed you," I said. "You alone?"

"Yeah."

"I need a favor."

"Name it."

"Are you free right now?"

"Yeah."

"Okay. I need you to go outside and call me from a payphone. There's one outside the Lawson's at Azabu Iikura Katamachi, to the left as you're facing the store. Use it. I'll give you my number."

"This line is okay, you know that."

"Just in case. This is sensitive." I used our usual code to give him my mobile number.

Ten minutes later the unit rang. "Okay, what's so sensitive?" he asked.

"I think someone might be following you."

There was short silence. "Are you serious?"

"Stop looking over your shoulder. If they're there right now I don't want you to tip them off. You wouldn't see them that way anyway."

Another silence. Then: "I don't get it. I'm awfully careful."

"I know you are."

"Why do you think this?"

"Not over the phone."

"You want to meet?"

"Yes. But I want you to pick something up first. I've inserted a note behind the back cover of the second-to-the-back issue of this week's *TV Taro* in the Lawson's you're next to. Go inside and retrieve the note. Make sure you make it look natural, in case somebody's close. Pick up a carton of milk, some prepared food, like you're just grabbing something quick and easy for dinner to take back to your apartment. Take it all home, wait a half hour, then go out and call me again from a different phone. Be ready for a two-hour walk."

"Will do."

A half hour passed. The mobile phone rang again.

"You retrieve it?" I asked.

"Yeah. I see what you're up to."

"Good. Just follow the route. Start at eight-thirty sharp. When you're done, wait for me at the place I've indicated on the note. You know how to interpret the place I've indicated."

My reference to "interpretation" was a reminder that he wasn't to take our meeting place literally, but was instead to use the Tokyo Yellow Pages per our usual code to divine my true intent. If people were following Harry and they moved on him right now, presumably they'd pick up the note, see the location of the meet, and go to the wrong place to ambush me.

"Understood," he said.

"Be cool. You've got nothing to worry about. I'll explain everything when I see you. And don't worry if I'm a little late."

"No worries. I'll see you later."

I hung up.

Harry had been clean when we'd gotten together at Teize, but that didn't mean he'd been clean beforehand. I'd taught him to start out his

SDRs unobtrusively, acting like any other civilian so that anyone who might be watching him would be lulled into believing he was no more than that. But the low-level stuff was only for the outset. As the route progresses, it becomes increasingly aggressive, less concerned with lulling potential followers and more concerned with forcing them into the open. You get off a subway car and wait until the platform is completely empty, then get back on a train going in the opposite direction. You turn corners, stop, and wait to see who rushes around just behind you. You use a lot of elevators, which forces followers to snuggle up with you shoulder to shoulder or let you go. Et cetera. The idea is that it's better to get caught acting like a spy than it is to lead the bad guys to the source you're trying to protect in the first place.

Harry would have observed the protocol on his way to Teize when we met there. And, as his countersurveillance moves became more aggressive, his followers would have had to choose between being spotted, on the one hand, or giving up the quarry so as not to alert him and trying again another day, on the other. If they'd chosen door number two, Harry would have shown up at the meeting clean, never knowing he'd been followed a little while earlier.

And, having seen him engage in blatant countersurveillance tactics, his followers would then assume that he had something to hide, perhaps the very thing they were looking for. They would intensify coverage as a result.

Tonight's exercise was intended to determine whether all this was indeed the case. The route I'd devised was designed to take whoever might be following Harry in a circle through the Ebisu Garden Place, a multistoried outdoor shopping arcade that would afford me several opportunities to unobtrusively watch him and whatever might be trailing in his wake. It was aggressive enough to enable me to spot a tail, but not so aggressive as to scare the tail off. Except at the end, when Harry would pull away in front and I would close in from behind.

At eight o'clock, I made my way to the Rue Favart restaurant on the corner of Ebisu 4-chome, across from the Sapporo Building. I wanted to get there early to be sure I would get one of the three window seats on the restaurant's third floor, which would give me a direct view of the sidewalk Harry would shortly be using. If the tables were taken, I would have time to wait. I was hungry, too, and the Rue, with its eclectic collection of pastas and sandwiches, would be a good spot to fuel up. I had enjoyed the place from time to time while living in Tokyo and was looking forward to being back.

I followed a waitress up the wooden stairs to the third floor, taking in the zany décor on the way—lime green walls with enormous flower murals, helter-skelter chairs and tables of wood and metal and molded plastic. The window seats were indeed all occupied when I arrived, but I told the waitress not to worry, I'd be happy to wait for the privilege of such a splendid view. I sat on a small sofa, enjoying an iced coffee and the hallucinogenic ceiling murals of beetles and moths and dragonflies. After a half hour, the two office ladies at one of the window seats departed, and I took their table.

I ordered the shitake mushroom risotto and a minestrone soup, asking if they could bring it in a hurry because I was hoping to catch a nine-thirty movie. I would need to leave immediately after Harry passed by, and had to time things right.

I thought about what I would do if my experiment were successful—that is, if I confirmed that Harry was indeed being followed. The answer, I supposed, depended largely on who they were, and why they were interested. My main concern was that nothing should interfere with my preparations for departure, which, now that I had finished the "favor" for Tatsu, I was going to have to accelerate. I had to protect my plans, even if it meant leaving Harry on his own.

The risotto was good, and I would have liked more time to enjoy it at my leisure. Instead, I ate quickly, watching the street below. When I was done, I checked my watch. Just enough time for one of the Rue's celebrated hot cocoas, dense concoctions crafted with pure cocoa and dollops of whipped cream, of which the Rue serves no more than twenty a day. I ordered one and savored it while I waited and watched.

I saw Harry at a little after nine, heading clockwise from Ebisu Station toward Kusunoki-dori. He was moving quickly, as I'd instructed him. At this time of the evening, Ebisu comprises mostly pleasure-seekers attracted to the swank restaurants and bars of the Garden Place complex. The pace of the area is accordingly relaxed. Anyone attempting to match Harry's speed would find himself out of sync with the area's rhythms, and therefore conspicuous.

I spotted the first likely candidate as Harry turned right onto Kusunoki-dori at the Ebisu 4-chome police box. A young Japanese in a navy suit, slight of build, with gelled hair and wire-rimmed glasses. He was following about ten meters behind Harry on the opposite side of the street—sound technique, as most people are aware, if at all, only of what is transpiring directly behind them. I couldn't yet be sure, of course, but from his position, his manner, and his pace, I had a feeling.

Harry continued to move away from my position. Two groups of Japanese now appeared farther back in his wake, but I dismissed them as unlikely. Their manner was too relaxed, and they struck me as too young.

Next was a Caucasian, a big guy, the sack drape of his dark suit and the confident cadences of his gait both American, moving quickly down the sidewalk. Could be a businessman, staying at the nearby Westin Hotel, in a hurry for an appointment. Or not. I filed him as a possible.

Harry disappeared, obscured by the branches of one of the *kusunoki* trees for which the street is named. So did the young Japanese guy. I turned my attention to the American. He stopped, as though he had developed a sudden interest in one of the Most Wanted posters on the side of the police box.

Gotcha.

A moment later Harry reappeared, retracing his steps, now on the south side of the street. He paused to examine the illuminated map on the corner in front of the Sapporo Building, diagonally across from the police box where the American, suddenly no longer in a hurry for his appointment, indulged his newfound interest in Japan's Most Wanted.

Harry's U-turn had been moderately aggressive, but not so provocative, I thought, as to cause his pursuers to let him go for the night. They wouldn't feel he had made them. Not yet.

But let's see.

Harry moved right onto Platanus Avenue. The American held his position. A moment later the Japanese appeared from beyond my field of vision. When he, too, had turned right onto Platanus, the American fell in behind him.

I waited another minute to see whether anyone else tickled my radar, but no one did.

I got up and took the stairs to the first floor, where I paid and thanked the proprietor for an excellent meal. Then I cut across the Garden Place complex and took the stairs to the second floor of the outdoor promenade. I leaned against the waist-high stone wall in front of the Garden Place Tower office building like a sentry on a castle keep, watching the foot traffic moving through the esplanade below.

I knew Harry had taken one of the underground passages to the esplanade and was pausing for a bit of window-shopping en route to give me time to get in position. After a few minutes, he emerged from below me and began walking diagonally across the esplanade, away from where I was standing. Had I wanted to, I could have set up at the other end of the promenade, where I would have been able to watch him and any followers as they approached me, but I was now ninety percent certain I'd spotted the tails and didn't need to risk giving them an opportunity to spot me.

There they were, fanned out behind him like two points at the base of a moving scalene triangle. The Japanese was looking around now at the windows of the esplanade's stores and restaurants and at the people looking down from the promenade above. His head started to swivel to check his rear and, although I was likely to remain anonymous among the other onlookers around me, I moved back a few steps to ensure I would remain unseen.

The Japanese was showing decent, but in this case futile, countersurveillance awareness. He had obviously noted that Harry was leading him in a circle, a classic countersurveillance tactic that gives a static team multiple opportunities to try to spot a tail. I had anticipated such a reaction, though, and from here on, the route would be comfortingly straightforward, right up until the moment Harry would exit the scene and I would make a surprise appearance.

I waited ten seconds, then eased forward again. Harry had just reached the top of the incline that would take him out of the esplanade and toward the skywalk of Ebisu Station. The Japanese and American kept their positions behind him. I watched until all three of them had moved out of my field of vision, then waited to ascertain whether there might be more of them. I was unsurprised to discover no one of interest. If their numbers had been greater, they would have switched positions to avoid potential countersurveillance when they sensed they were being moved in a circle. That they hadn't was a strong indication this was only a two-person team.

I checked my watch. Fifteen minutes to go.

I took the underground passage to the Westin, where I caught a cab to nearby Hiro. Harry and his two admirers were now walking to the same place; taking the cab ensured that I would be there early to greet them.

I had the cab let me off on Meiji-dori, where I ducked into a Starbucks.

"What can I get you?" the counter girl asked me in Japanese.

"Just a coffee," I said. "Grande. And can you make it extra hot?"

"Sorry, the coffee drips at precisely ninety-eight degrees centigrade and is served at eighty-five degrees. I can't change it."

Christ, they really train these people, I marveled. "I see. I've got this cold, though, I could use something really hot for the vapors. What about tea?"

"Oh, the tea is very hot. There's no dripping, so it's made and served at ninety-eight degrees."

"Wonderful. I'll have a grande Earl Grey."

She made the tea and set it on the counter next to the register. I paid for it and picked it up.

"Wait," she said. She handed me an extra cup. "This will keep it hot."

I smiled at her thoughtfulness. "Thank you," I said.

The detour had taken about four minutes. I moved a few hundred meters farther up the right side of the street to a small playground, where I sat on a corner bench. I set down the tea and used the cloned mobile phone to confirm that the taxi I had ordered was waiting. It was indeed, and I told the dispatcher the passenger would be there in just a few minutes.

Five minutes later, I saw Harry heading in my direction. He made a left on a nameless street that would take him into a rather dark and quiet residential area. Not the kind of place where you could catch a cab. Luckily, Harry knew there would be one waiting for him. His two friends, of course, were going to be shit out of luck.

There they were, one on each side of the street. The American was now in the lead, on my side. He cut across and followed Harry into the neighborhood. Ten seconds later the Japanese followed. I picked up the tea and moved in behind them.

Fifty meters left, fifty meters right, fifty meters left again. These streets were exceptionally narrow, flanked by white concrete walls. Almost a labyrinth. I walked slowly. I couldn't see them from this far back, but I knew where they were going.

Three minutes later, a cab pulled out in front of me and headed in my direction. I glanced at the back window and saw Harry. I was glad this part had gone smoothly. Had there been a problem, Harry would have turned around and just kept walking and I would have improvised. What I wanted, though, was that this sudden and somewhat theatrical loss of their quarry would cause his pursuers to come together for a consultation. I would have an easier time of it if I could surprise them simultaneously.

Neither Harry nor I gave any sign of acknowledgment as the cab passed my position. I continued ahead, making a right onto the street from which the cab had just emerged.

The street was about thirty meters long, turning ninety degrees to the right at the end. No sign of Tweedle Dee and Tweedle Dum. No problem. The place Harry had led them to was a dead end.

I reached the end of the street and turned right. There they were, about twelve meters away. The Japanese guy had his left side to me. He was talking to the American. The American was facing me, an unlit cigarette in his mouth. He was holding a lighter at waist level, flicking it, trying to get it going.

I forced myself to keep my pace casual, just another pedestrian. My heart began to beat harder. I could feel it pounding in my chest, behind my ears.

Ten meters. I popped the plastic lid off the paper cup with my thumb. I felt it tumble across the back of my hand.

Seven meters. Adrenaline was slowing down my perception of the scene. The Japanese guy glanced in my direction. He looked at my face. His eyes began to widen.

Five meters. The Japanese guy reached out for the American, the gesture urgent even through my adrenalized slow-motion vision. He grabbed the American's arm and started pulling on it.

Three meters. The American looked up and saw me. The cigarette dangled from his lips. There was no recognition in his eyes.

Two meters. I stepped in and flung the cup forward. Its contents of ninety-eight degrees centigrade Earl Gray tea exited and caught the American directly in the face and neck. His hands flew up and he shrieked.

I turned to the Japanese. His eyes were popped all the way open, his head rotating back and forth in the universal gesture of negation. He started to raise his hands as though to ward me off.

I grabbed his shoulders and shoved him into the wall. Using the same forward momentum, I stepped in and kneed him squarely in the balls. He grunted and doubled over.

I turned back to the American. He was bent forward, staggering, his hands clutching at his face. I grabbed the collar of his jacket and the back of his trousers and accelerated him headfirst into the wall like a matador with a bull. His body shuddered from the impact and he dropped to the ground.

The Japanese guy was lying on his side, clutching his crotch, gasping. I hauled him up by the lapels and shoved his back against the wall. I looked left, then right. It was just the three of us.

"Tell me who you are," I said in Japanese.

He made retching noises. I could see he was going to need a minute.

Keeping my left hand pressed against his throat, I patted him down to confirm he didn't have a weapon, then checked his ears and jacket to ensure he wasn't wired for sound. He was clean. I reached into the inside pocket of his suit jacket and pulled out a wallet. I flipped it open. The ID was right in front, in a slip-in laminated protector.

Tomohisa Kanezaki. Second Secretary, Consular Affairs, U.S. Embassy. The bald eagle logo of the U.S. Department of State showed blue and yellow in the background.

So these characters were CIA. I slipped the wallet into one of my pants pockets so I could examine its contents later.

"Pull yourself together, Kanezaki-san," I said, switching to English. "Or this time I'll hurt you for real."

"Chotto matte, chotto matte," he panted, holding up one of his hands for emphasis. Wait a minute, wait a minute. *"Setsumei suru to yakusoku shimasu kara..."* I promise I'll explain everything, but...

His Japanese was American-accented. "Use English," I told him. "I don't have time to give you a language lesson."

"Okay, all right," he said. The panting had slowed a little. "My name is Tomohisa Kanezaki. I'm with the U.S. Embassy here in Tokyo."

"I know who you are. I just looked at your wallet. What were you doing following that man?"

He took a deep breath and grimaced. His eyes were watering from the ball shot. "We were trying to find you. You're John Rain."

"You were trying to find me, why?"

"I don't know. The parameters I was given…"

I shoved hard against his throat and got in his face. "I'm not interested in your parameters. Ignorance is not going to be bliss for you. Not tonight. Understand?"

He tried to push me away. "Just let me fucking talk for a minute, okay? If you keep choking me, I'm not going to be able to tell you anything!"

I was taken aback by his gumption. He sounded more petulant than afraid. I realized this kid didn't understand the kind of trouble he was in. If he didn't tell me what I wanted to know I would have to adjust his attitude.

I shot a quick glance at his prone friend, then back to him. "Talk," I told him.

"I was only supposed to locate you. I was explicitly told not to make contact."

"What was supposed to happen after you located me?"

"My superiors would take it up from there."

"But you know who I am."

"I told you, yes."

I nodded. "Then you know what I'm going to do to you if I find any of your answers unsatisfactory."

He blanched. I seemed to be getting through to him.

"Who's he?" I asked, gesturing with my head to the prone American.

"Diplomatic security. The parameters… I was told that under no circumstances was I to take a chance on encountering you alone."

A bodyguard. Sounded possible. The guy hadn't recognized me, I'd seen that. He was probably here just for protection and surveillance tag team.

Or he could have been the triggerman. The Agency relies on contractor cutouts for its wetwork, people like me. He might have been one of them.

"You're not supposed to encounter me alone because…"

"Because you're dangerous. We have a dossier on you."

The one Holtzer would have put together. Right.

"The man you were following. Tell me about that."

He nodded. "His name is Haruyoshi Fukasawa. He's your only known associate. We were following him to get to you."

"That's not enough."

He gave me a cold stare, looking like he was prepared to tough things out. "That's all I know."

His partner groaned and started to pull himself up onto his knees. Kanezaki glanced at him, and I knew what he was thinking: If his partner recovered, I would have a hard time controlling the two of them.

"You're not telling me what you know, Kanezaki," I said. "Let me show you something."

I took a step over to his partner, who was now facing us on all fours, grunting something unintelligible. I braced a knee against his back, took hold of his chin with one hand and the side of his head with the other, and gave a sudden, decisive twist. His neck snapped with a loud crack and he flopped to the ground.

I let go of his head and stepped back to Kanezaki. His eyes were bulging, shifting from me to the corpse and back again. "Oh my fucking God!" he spluttered. "Oh my God!"

"First time you've seen something like that?" I asked, my tone deliberately casual. "It gets easier as you go along. Of course, in your case, the next time you see it, it's going to be happening to you."

His face was white and getting whiter, and I wondered for a moment if there was some danger he might faint. I needed to help him focus.

"Kanezaki. You were telling me about Haruyoshi Fukasawa. About how you knew he's an associate of mine. Keep going, please."

He took a deep breath and closed his eyes. "We knew... we knew he was connected to you because we intercepted a letter."

"A letter?"

His eyes opened. "From him to Midori Kawamura, in New York. Mentioning you."

Goddamn it, I thought, at the mention of her name. I just couldn't get clear of these people. They were like cancer. You think you've cut it out, it always comes back.

And spreads, to the people around you.

"Keep going," I said, scowling.

"Jesus Christ, I'm telling you that's all I know!"

If he panicked completely, I wouldn't get anything useful. The trick was to keep him scared, but not so scared that he began to make things up just to please me.

"All right," I told him. "That's all you know about how. But you still haven't told me about why. Why you were trying to find me."

"Look, you know I can't talk about..."

I seized his throat hard. His eyes bulged. He snaked one arm between mine and tried to lever my grip open. It looked like something he might have picked up in one of the Agency's weekend personal security courses. Kudos to him for remembering it under pressure. Too bad it didn't work.

"Kanezaki," I said, loosening the grip enough so he could breathe, "in one minute you will either go on living or someone will find you next to your friend there. Which it is depends entirely on what you say to me in that minute. Now start talking."

I felt him swallow beneath the pressure from my hand.

"All right, all right," he said. He was talking fast now. "For ten years the USG has been pressuring Japan to reform its banks and get its finances in order. For ten years things have only gotten worse. The economy is beginning to collapse now. If the collapse continues, Japan will be the first domino to fall. Southeast Asia, Europe, and America will be next. The country has to reform. But the vested interests are so deeply entrenched that reform is impossible."

I looked at him. "You've got about forty seconds left. You're not doing well."

"Okay, okay! Tokyo Station has been tasked with an action program of furthering reform and removing impediments to reform. The program is called Crepuscular. We know what you've been doing freelance. I think... I think what my superiors want to ask you for is your assistance."

"For what purpose?" I asked.

"For removing impediments."

"But you aren't sure of that?"

"Look, I've been with the Agency for three years. There's a lot they don't tell me. But anyone who knows your history and knows about Crepuscular can put two and two together."

I looked at him, considering my options. Kill him? His superiors wouldn't know what had happened. But they'd assume I'd been behind it, of course. And though they wouldn't be able to get to me, they had a good fix on Harry and Midori.

No, killing this kid wasn't going to get the Agency out of my life. Or out of Harry's or Midori's.

"I'll think about your proposal," I told him. "You can tell your superiors I said so."

"I didn't propose anything. I was only speculating. If I tell my superiors what we just talked about, I'll be sent back to Langley for a desk job."

"Tell them anything you want. If I'm interested, I'll get in touch with you. You personally. If I'm not interested, I'll expect you to understand that my silence means no. I'll also expect you to stop trying to find me, especially through other people. If I learn you aren't respecting these wishes, I'll hold you responsible. You, personally. Do you understand?"

He started to say something, then gagged. I saw what was coming and stepped out of the way. He leaned over and vomited.

I took it as a yes.

I walked back to Ebisu and caught a Yamanote train to Shibuya. I took the Miyamasuzaka exit to Shibuya 1-chome, then walked the short distance to the Hatou coffee shop. Windowless Hatou, with its dark wood floors and tables and long *hinoki* counter, its hundreds of exquisite porcelain cups and saucers, and its expertly prepared brews, had been one of my regular haunts while I lived in Tokyo, or at least as regular as I allowed any one place to become. I missed it.

I walked in the street-level door. The counterman issued a low *irasshaimase* but didn't look up. Instead, he continued pouring steaming water from a silver pot into a filter perched over a blue porcelain demitasse. He was leaning to the side so that he was eye level with the pot, his arm describing small circles in the air to ensure the water dripped uniformly through the grounds in the filter. He looked like he was painting, or conducting a miniature orchestra. It was a pleasure to behold such practiced devotion and I couldn't help pausing to watch.

When he was done he bowed and welcomed me again. I returned the gesture and made my way to the back. I turned left at the end of the L-shaped room and saw Harry sitting at one of the three back tables.

"Hey," he said, standing up and offering his hand.

I shook it. "Glad to see you found the place okay."

He nodded. "Your directions were good."

I looked at the table, empty but for a glass of ice water. "No coffee?"

"I didn't know when you were going to get here, so I ordered two old beans demitasses. Something called the Nire Blend. It takes a half hour to prepare. I figured you'd like it—the waitress says it's 'exceptionally intense.'"

I smiled again. "It is. I'm not sure it'll be to your taste."

He shrugged. "I like to try new things."

Yukiko, I thought.

We sat. "Well? How did it turn out?" he asked.

I took out Kanezaki's wallet and slid it across the table to him. "You were being followed," I said.

He opened it and looked at the ID inside. "Oh, shit," he said softly. "CIA?"

I nodded.

"But how? Why?"

I briefed him on my conversation with Kanezaki.

"So it looks like they were interested in me only because they're interested in you," he said, when I was done.

I nodded slowly. "It looks that way."

"I wonder if they know who I am, other than that I'm somehow connected to you."

"Impossible to say. They might have cross-checked with other agencies, in which case they would know you were once with the NSA. But they're not always so thorough."

"They did a nice job of tracking me from that letter, though. Stupid of me to send it."

"There's more than meets the eye there. The letter alone doesn't sound like enough. But I didn't have time to ask."

We were quiet for a minute. Then he said, "It might have been enough. I only signed it with my first name, but my parents chose three *kanji,* not the usual two." On his hand he traced the characters for "spring," "giving," and "ambition," an unusual spelling for a common name.

"They must have been watching Midori, too," I said.

He nodded. "Yeah. She was a known point of contact. They might have been doing spot surveillance and mail checks, hoping she'd hear from you. Instead they got me."

"I'll buy that," I said.

"And I mailed that letter near the main Chuo-ku post office, not so far from where I work. There would have been a postmark. They could have used it to work outward in concentric circles. That was dumb. I should have mailed it from somewhere out of the way."

"You can't be too careful," I said, looking at him.

He sighed. "I'm going to have to move again. Can't have them knowing where I live."

"Don't forget, they also know where you work."

"I don't care about that. A lot of what I do now, I do remotely. On the days where I have to go to and from the office, I'll run an extra-careful SDR."

"You haven't been doing that already?"

"Sorry. Not as much as I should be. But believe me, I'm careful when I go to see you."

This was an unavoidable problem. Inside computer networks, Harry was pure stealth. But in the real world, he was mostly a civilian. A weak spot in my armor.

I shrugged. "If you weren't, those guys would have gotten to me by now. Maybe at Teize, maybe another time. Your moves shook them off."

He brightened a little, then said, "You don't think I'm in any danger, do you?"

I thought about it. I hadn't mentioned that Kanezaki's partner hadn't survived our meeting. I told him now.

"Shit," he said. "That's what I'm talking about. What if they want payback?"

"I don't think they'd look to extract it from you. If this were a yakuza thing, it might be a different story—they might come after my friends just to hurt me. But here, if they've got a beef, it's with me. You're no threat to them. Besides, they don't have much in-house muscle. Congress wouldn't like it. That's why they need people like me."

"What about the police? A taxi picked me up at the same spot where someone is going to find a body."

"Kanezaki will make a few calls and that body will be gone before anyone stumbles across it. And even if the cops were to get involved, what do they have? Even if they found a way to contact the cab driver, all he's got is a fake name and an average looking guy he barely saw in the dark, right?"

"I guess that's true."

"But you still have to be cautious," I said. "This girl you're involved with, Yukiko, you trust her?"

He looked at me. After a moment, he nodded.

"Because, if you're spending the night with this girl, she knows where you live. That's a weakness in your defenses right there."

"Yeah, but she's not involved with these people…"

"You never know, Harry. You never really know."

There was a long pause. Then he said, "I can't live that way. The way you do."

A thought flashed in my mind: *Maybe you should have figured that out before you got involved in my world.*

But that wasn't fair. Or particularly useful.

The waitress brought two demitasses of the Nire Blend and set them down with exquisite care, as though they were priceless artifacts. She bowed and moved away.

We drank the coffee. Harry said positive things about his, but there was some obvious effort behind this. It used to be that he would delight in mocking my gustatory recommendations. I couldn't help noticing the contrast, and I didn't care for it.

We made small talk. When the coffee was done, we said goodnight, and I left him to make my circuitous way back to the hotel.

I wondered if I really believed the Agency posed little danger to Harry. I supposed that mostly I did. Whether they posed a danger to me was another story. They might have wanted me for help, as Kanezaki had said. Or they might have been looking for payback for Holtzer. I had no way to be sure. Regardless, eliminating Kanezaki's escort earlier wasn't exactly going to engender endearment.

And there was Yukiko. She still didn't feel right to me, and I had no way of knowing whether she was hooked up with the Agency or with someone else.

Back at the hotel, I lay in bed and stared at the ceiling, again unable to sleep.

So it wasn't Midori, after all, I thought.

The Agency instead of Midori. Talk about a fucking consolation prize.

Enough. Let it go.

I was suddenly less certain than I had been the night before that this would be my last in Tokyo. I stared at the ceiling for a long time before descending into sleep.

CHAPTER 6

The next morning, I took the bullet train back to Osaka. Arriving early in the afternoon at bustling Shin-Osaka Station, I was surprised to find it felt good to be back. Maybe I'd gotten tired of living in hotels. Or maybe it was something about knowing I was going to have to leave again, this time permanently.

I knew I'd been clean when I left Tokyo, but the two-and-a-half-hour train ride had afforded me no new opportunities to check my back. That's a long time for me, especially given my recent run-in with Kanezaki and company, and to ease my discomfort I took an appropriately circuitous route before catching a Tanimachi line train to Miyakojima, where I took the stairs of the A4 exit to the street.

For no particular reason, I made a left around the police box at the Miyakojima Hon-dori intersection, maneuvering around the hundreds of commuter bicycles jammed in all directions around the exit. I could as easily have made a right, past the local high school and toward the Okawa River. One of the things that had attracted me to the high-rise in Belfa is that the complex is approachable from all directions.

I took a left at Miyakojima Kita-dori, then a right against traffic down a one-way street, then another left. The move against traffic would impede anyone's attempts at vehicular surveillance. And each turn gave me an opportunity to unobtrusively glance behind me while putting me on a narrower, quieter road than the last. Anyone hoping to follow me on foot would have to stay close or lose me. There were dozens of high-rises in the area, too, and the fact that I might have been going to any one of them was another factor that would have rendered ineffective anything other than close-range surveillance.

In some ways, the neighborhood was the poster child for bad zoning. There were shiny glass-and-steel condominiums across from corrugated and I-beam parking garages. Single-family homes perched alongside recycling plants and foundries. A new multistory school turned its proud granite façade away from its neighbor, a dilapidated relic of a car repair shop, like an ungrateful child ashamed of an ailing parent.

On the other hand, the residents didn't seem to mind the shambles. On the contrary: everywhere were small signs of the pride the locals took in their dwellings. The monotonous macadam and corrugated metal were relieved by small riots of potted bamboo, lavender, and sunflowers. Here was a carefully arranged cairn of volcanic rocks, there, a display of dried coral. One house had concealed what would have been an ugly ferroconcrete wall with a lovingly tended garden of angel's trumpet, sage, and lavender.

I lived on the thirty-sixth floor of one of the twin high-rises in the Belfa complex, in a three-bedroom corner apartment. The place was larger than I needed and most of the rooms went unused, but I liked living on the top floor, with a view of the city, above it all. Also, at the time I'd rented it, I thought it would be to my advantage to take a place that didn't fit the profile of what a lone man, recently disappeared and with minimal needs, would take for an apartment. In the end, of course, it hadn't mattered.

I tell myself I like to live in places like Belfa because parents are inherently watchful of strangers, and once they decide you belong they can form an unconscious but effective obstacle to an ambush. But I know there's more to it than that. I don't have a family and never will, and I'm probably drawn to such environments not just for operational reasons but for some other, more vicarious form of security, as well. There was a time when I didn't seem to need such things, when I would have been amused and perhaps even vaguely disgusted at the notion of living like some sort of psychic vampire, a lingering revenant pressed up against one-way glass, looking with forlorn and futile eyes at the ordinary life fate had denied him.

It changes your priorities. Hell, it changes your damn values.

I used a payphone to access a voicemail account attached to a special phone in my apartment, a sound-activated unit with a sensitive speakerphone that functions like a transmitter. The unit silently dials a voicemail account if someone enters the apartment without knowing the code that disengages the phone, letting me know in advance and from a safe distance whether I've had any unexpected visitors. An identical setup had saved me in Tokyo from a Holtzer-inspired ambush, and I tend to stick with what works. I'd been checking the account daily from Tokyo without incident, and the mailbox was empty this time as well, so I knew my apartment had gone unmolested during my absence.

From the payphone, I walked the short distance to the Belfa complex. A softball game was underway on the field to my right. Some children were playing kickball by a granite sculpture garden in front of the building. An old man swerved past me on a bicycle, a laughing grandchild perched on the handles.

I used the front entrance, taking care as always to approach in such a way that the security camera facing the building would get a picture only of my back. Such precautions are part of my routine, but, as Tatsu had pointed out, the cameras are everywhere and you can't hope to spot them all.

I took the elevator to the thirty-sixth floor and walked down the corridor to my apartment. I checked the small piece of translucent tape I had left at the bottom of the door and found it intact, still attached to the jamb. As I'd told Harry so many times, a good defense has to be layered.

I unlocked the door and went inside. Everything was as I'd left it. Which wasn't saying much. Beyond the futon and nightstand in one of the bedrooms, there was an olive leather couch, new but not new-looking, set against the wall facing the west of the city, where I sometimes sat to watch the sun set. A sprawling Gabeh rug covering an expanse of polished wooden floor, its strata of greens and blues interspersed with a dozen whimsical splotches of cream that were probably intended to denote goats in a pastoral setting, its weave dense and soft enough to have once served as a mattress for the nomads who made it. A massive double-bank writing desk that had made its way to Japan from England, its surface dominated by a black leather insert appropriately worn by more than a century of pressure from the pen points that moved over its surface to transact business across the oceans, conveying news that might be weeks old by the time it reached relatives abroad, announcing births and deaths, offering congratulations, felicitations, condolences, regrets. One of those fantastically complicated but astonishingly comfortable Herman Miller Aeron desk chairs that I'd picked up on a whim from a recently demised technology startup in Shibuya's Bit Valley. Atop the desk, several high-end laptops, about which I'd said nothing to Harry because he was under the impression that I was a computer primitive and I saw no advantage in letting him know I have my own knack for getting behind the odd firewall when the need arises.

Opposite the couch was a Bang & Olufsen home theater with a six-CD changer. Next to it, a bookshelf containing an extensive collection of CDs, most of them jazz, and my modest library. The library includes a number of books on the *bugei,* or warrior arts, some of them quite old and obscure, containing information on combat techniques thought to be too dangerous for modern judo—spine locks, neck cranks, and the like—techniques that are, consequently, largely lost to the art. There are also some well-thumbed works of philosophy—Mishima, Musashi, Nietzsche. And there are a number of slim volumes that I order from time to time from some unusual publishers in the States, volumes that are illegal in Japan and in other countries lacking America's perhaps overly strong devotion to freedom of speech, but which I manage to acquire nonetheless through techniques garnered from some of the volumes themselves. There are works on the latest surveillance methods and technologies; police investigative techniques and forensic science; acquiring forged identity; setting up offshore accounts and mail drops; methods of disguise and evasion; lock-picking and breaking and entry; and related topics. Of course, over the years I have developed my own substantial expertise in all these areas, but I have no plan to write a how-to account of my experiences. Instead, I read these books to learn what the opposition knows, to understand how the people I might be up against think, to predict where they might come after me, to take the appropriate countermeasures.

The only conspicuous item in the apartment was a wooden wing-chun training dummy, about the dimensions of a large man, which I had placed in the center of the apartment's lone tatami room. Had the apartment been occupied by a family, this might have been the location of the *kotatsu,* a low table with a heavy quilted skirt draping to the floor and an electric brazier underneath, around which the family would nestle in the winter, their shoeless feet warmed by the brazier, their legs tucked comfortably under the quilted skirt, as they gossiped about the neighbors, examined the household bills, perhaps planned for the children's future.

But the wooden dummy represented a better use for me. I'd been training in judo for the almost quarter century I'd been in Japan, and loved the art's emphasis on throws and ground fighting. But once Holtzer and the Agency had connected me to the Kodokan judo center in Tokyo, I knew joining the Osaka branch would have been too obvious a move, like a recent entrant to the federal witness protection program resubscribing to the same obscure magazines he'd always enjoyed before moving underground. For now, I felt safer training alone. The dummy kept my reflexes sharp and the striking surfaces of my hands callused and hard, and allowed me to practice some of the strikes and blocks I'd neglected to some degree while training in judo. It would have made an interesting conversation piece, if anyone ever visited my apartment.

During the days that followed, I busied myself with my preparations for leaving Osaka. Moving hastily would be a mistake: the transitions are where you're most vulnerable, and someone who couldn't track me now might very well find himself able to do so if I dove suddenly into a less securely backstopped life. And Tatsu might be expecting me to move quickly; if so, he would be prepared to follow me. Conversely, if I stayed put, he might be lulled, giving me the opportunity to lose him entirely when the timing and preparations were right. He had no reason to come after me for the moment, so the lesser risk was to take the appropriate time to set things up correctly.

I had decided on Brazil, and it was for this I'd been studying the Portuguese that had been so useful with Naomi. Hong Kong, Singapore, or some other Asian destination, or perhaps somewhere in the States, might have been a more obvious choice, but that was of course one of the things Brazil had going for it. And even if someone thought to look for me there, they would have a hell of a time: Brazil's multitudes of ethnic Japanese have branched out into all areas of the country's life, and one more transplant wasn't going to arouse any attention.

Rio de Janeiro, which offered culture, climate, and a significant transient population consisting largely of tourists, would be ideal. The city is far from the world's intelligence, terrorism, and Interpol focal points, so

I would have relatively few worries about accidental sightings, security camera networks, and the other natural enemies of the fugitive. I would even be able to return to judo, or at least one of its cousins: the Brazilian Gracie family had taken one of judo's forebears, jiu-jitsu, carried into the country by arriving Japanese, and developed it into arguably the most sophisticated ground fighting system the world has ever seen. It's practiced fanatically in Brazil, and has become popular all over the world, including Japan.

Along with the right location, I had an ice-cold alternate identity, something I'd been nurturing for a long time in preparation for a day when I might have to drop off the map more completely than I ever had before. About a decade earlier, as I was surveilling and preparing to eliminate a certain bureaucrat, I was struck by the degree to which the man superficially resembled me—the age, height, build, even the face wasn't too far off. The subject also had a wonderful name: Taro Yamada, the Japanese equivalent of John Smith. I had done some digging, and learned that Yamada-san lacked a close family. There seemed to be no one who would miss him enough to go looking for him if he happened to disappear.

Now, a lot of books claim you can build a new identity using the name of someone deceased, but that's only true if no one filed a death certificate. If the authorities were involved in any way—say, the person died in a hospice or hospital, or gets buried or cremated, which, if you think about it, applies to pretty much everyone, or if someone files a missing person report—a certificate will be filed. Or if a relative wants to get his or her hands on any aspect of the decedent's estate—in which case you're talking about the transfer of title to real and personal property and probably probate—again, a certificate will be filed. And if you decide to proceed anyway, then even if you do manage to get some additional new identification based on the dead person's particulars, the new ID will always be fatally flawed, and, eventually, when you apply for a driver's license, or for credit, or when you try to get pretty much any job, or file a tax return, or when you try to cross a border—in short, when you try to do any one of the innumerable things for which you needed your new identity in the first place—a "what's wrong with this picture" alert will pop up on someone's screen, and you will be promptly and thoroughly screwed.

So what about the identity of someone who's still living? This works fine for short-term scams, known colloquially as "identity theft" though perhaps better understood as "identity borrowing," but is infeasible for anything long-term. After all, who's going to be responsible for those new credit cards? And where do the bills get sent? Okay, then what about using someone who's, say, disappeared for some reason, assuming you even know of such a person? Well, what about it? Did the person have debts? Was he a drug dealer? Because if he had anyone looking for him before, now they'll be looking for you. And anyway, what do you do if Mr. Missing Person suddenly resurfaces?

Of course, if you happen to know of someone who's dead because you're the one who killed him, that's a little different. True, you'd have to dispose of the body—in a manner that ensures it will never be found—a risky and often grisly chore that isn't for everyone. But if you've come this far, and if you know no one is going to report the person dead, or even missing, you've got something potentially valuable on your hands. If you also know he's got a good credit history, because you've gone on paying bills incurred in his name, you might just have landed yourself a winner.

So yes, I did carry out the contract on the unfortunate Mr. Yamada, but I didn't tell the client that. Instead, the subject seemed to have gone "underground," I reported, unable to resist the pun. Perhaps he had somehow gotten wind of the fact that a contract had been put out on his life? The client hired a PI, who confirmed the presence of all the indicia of sudden flight: a closed bank account and other personal matters efficiently tied up; mail forwarded to a foreign drop; missing clothes and other personal items from the apartment. I, of course, had been taking care of all of this. The client let me know that, for his purposes, disappearance was as good as death, and that I needn't trouble myself tracking Yamada down to complete the contract. I was paid for my efforts anyway—no one wants someone like me to feel he may have been treated unfairly—and that was that. The client himself has long since come to his own unfortunate end, and enough time has elapsed for me to have resurrected Yamada-san, opening up a small consulting operation in his unobtrusive name, paying taxes, securing an appropriate postal address, incurring debt and paying it off—all the little things that, taken together, add up to existence as a thoroughly unremarkable, thoroughly legitimate, member of society.

All I had to do now was slip into the Yamada identity and begin my new life. But first, Taro Yamada had to do some of the things any guy in his position would do after deciding to give up on his failed consulting business and move to Brazil to teach third-generation Japanese their now forgotten language. He needed a visa, a legitimate bank account—as opposed to the illegitimate, pseudonymous ones I maintain offshore—assistance with housing, an office. He would be nominally based in São Paulo, where almost half of Brazil's ethnic Japanese are concentrated, which would make him even more difficult to track to Rio. It would have been easier to take care of much of this with the assistance of the Japanese consulate in Brasilia, of course, but Mr. Yamada preferred less formal, less traceable means.

While I went about setting Yamada up in Brazil, I read about a string of corruption scandals and wondered how they figured in Tatsu's shadow war with Yamaoto. Universal Studios Japan, it turned out, had been serving food that was nine months past its due date and falsifying labels to hide it, while operating a drinking fountain that was pumping out untreated industrial water. Mister Donut was in the habit of fortifying its wares with meat dumplings containing banned additives. Snow Brand Food liked to save a few yen by recycling old milk and failing to clean factory pipes. Couldn't cover that one up—fifteen thousand people were poisoned. Mitsubishi Motors and Bridgestone got nailed hard, concealing defects in cars and tires to avoid safety recalls. The worst, shocking even by Japanese standards, was the news that TEPCO, Tokyo Electric Power, had been caught submitting falsified nuclear safety reports that went back twenty years. The reports failed to list serious problems at eight different reactors, including cracks in concrete containment shrouds.

The amazing thing wasn't the scandals, though. It was how little people seemed to care. It must have been frustrating for Tatsu, and I wondered what drove him. In other countries, revelations like these would have precipitated a revolution. But despite the scandals, despite the economy, the Japanese just went right on reelecting the same usual Liberal Democratic Party suspects. Christ, half the problem Tatsu was fighting comprised his nominal superiors, the people to whom, in a sense, he had to salute. How do you keep going, in the face of such determined ignorance and relentless hypocrisy? Why did he bother?

I read the news and tried to imagine how Tatsu would interpret it, how, indeed, he might even be trying to shape it. Not all of it was bad, I supposed. In fact, there were some developments in the provinces that must have encouraged him. Kitagawa Masayasu beat the bureaucrats in Mie by simply deciding against a proposed nuclear power plant. In Chiba, Domoto Akiko, a sixty-eight-year-old former television reporter, prevailed against candidates backed by business, trade unions, and the various political parties. In Nagano, Governor Tanaka Yasuo stopped all dam building despite pressure from the country's powerful construction interests. In Tottori, Governor Yoshihiro Katayama opened the prefecture's books to anyone who wanted to see them, setting a precedent that must have caused his counterparts in Tokyo nearly to soil themselves.

I also spent time checking computer records on Yukiko and Damask Rose. Compared to Harry I'm a hacking primitive, but I couldn't ask for his help on this one without revealing that I'd been checking up on him.

Getting into the club's tax information gave me Yukiko's last name: Nohara. From there, I was able to learn a reasonable amount. She was twenty-seven years old, born in Fukuoka, educated at Waseda University. She lived in an apartment building on Kotto-dori in Minami-Aoyama. No arrests. No debt. Nothing remarkable.

The club was more interesting, and more opaque. It was owned by a succession of offshore corporations. If there were any individual names tied to its ownership, they existed only on certificates of incorporation in someone's vault, not on computers, where I might have gotten to them. Whoever owned the club didn't want the world to know of the association. In itself, this wasn't damning. Cash businesses are always mobbed up.

Harry could almost certainly have found more on both subjects. It was too bad I couldn't ask him. I'd just have to give him a heads-up and recommend that he do a little checking himself. It was frustrating, but I didn't see what else I could do. He might take it badly, but I wouldn't be around for much longer, anyway. *And who knows?* I thought. *Maybe you're wrong. Maybe he'll find nothing.*

Naomi checked out, too. Naomi Nascimento, Brazilian national, arrived in Japan August 24, 2000, courtesy of the JET program. I used the email address she had given me to work backward to where she lived—the Lion's Gate Building, an apartment complex in Azabu Juban 3-chome. No other information.

As my preparations for departure approached completion, I made a point of visiting some of the places near Osaka I knew I would never see again. Some were as I remembered them from childhood trips. There was Asuka, birthplace of Yamato Japan, with its long-vacant burial mounds, surfaces carved with supernatural images of beasts and semi-humans, their makers and their meaning lost in the timeless swaying of the rice paddies around them; Koya-san, the holy mountain, reputedly the resting place of Kobo Daishi, Japan's great saint, who is said to linger near the mountain's vast necropolis not dead but meditating, his vigil marked by the mantras of monks that drone among the nearby markers of the dead as ancient and eternal as summer insects in primordial groves; and Nara, for a moment some thirteen centuries earlier the new nation's capital, where, if the morning is young enough and the tourist floodwaters have not yet risen in their quotidian banks, you might find yourself passing a lone octogenarian, his shoulders bent with the weight of age, his slippers shuffling along the cobblestones, his passage as timeless and resolute as the ancient city itself.

I supposed it was strange to feel the urge to say goodbye to any of this. After all, none of it had ever been mine. I had understood even as a child that to be half Japanese is to be half something else, and to be half something else is to be... *chigatteiru*. *Chigatteiru,* meaning "different," but equally meaning "wrong." The language, like the culture, makes no distinction.

I also went to Kyoto. I had found no occasion to visit the city in over twenty years, and was struck to find that the graceful, vital metropolis I remembered was nearly extinct, disappearing like an unloved garden given over to vapid, industrious weeds. Where was the fulgent peak of Higashi Honganji Temple, sweeping upward among the surrounding tiled roofs like the upturned chin of a princess among her retainers? That magnificent view, which had once greeted travelers to the city, was now blotted out by the new train station, an abomination that sprawled along a half-mile length of tracks like a massive turd that had plummeted from space and embedded itself there, too gargantuan to be carted away.

I walked for hours, marveling at the extent of the destruction. Cars drove through Daitokuji Temple. Mount Hiei, the birthplace of Japanese Buddhism, had been turned into a parking lot, with an entertainment emporium on its summit. Streets that had once been lined with ancient wooden houses accented with bamboo trellises were now tawdry with plastic and aluminum and neon, the wooden houses dismantled and gone. Everywhere were metastasizing telephone lines, riots of electric wires, laundry hanging from prefabricated apartment windows like tears from idiot eyes.

On my way back to Osaka, I entered the Grand Hotel, more or less the geographic center of the city. I took the elevator to the top floor, where, with the exception of the Toji Pagoda and a sliver of the Honganji Temple roof, I was confronted in all directions by nothing but inter-changeable urban blight. The city's living beauty had been beaten back into clusters of cowering refugees, like the results of some inexplicable experiment in cultural apartheid.

I thought of the poem by Basho, the wandering bard, which had moved me when my mother had first related it, on my earliest visit to the city. She had taken my hand as we stood upon the towering scaffold of Kiyomizu Temple, looking out upon the still city before us, and, surpris-ing me with her accented Japanese, had said:

Kyou nite mo kyou natsukashiya...
Though in Kyoto, I long for Kyoto...

But the meaning of the poem, once a paean to ineffable, unfulfillable longing, had changed. Like the city itself, it was now sadly ironic.

I smiled without mirth, thinking that, if any of this had been mine, I would have taken better care of it. *This is what you get if you put your trust in government,* I thought. *People ought to know better.*

I felt my pager buzz. I unclipped it and saw the code Tatsu and I had established to identify ourselves, along with a phone number. I'd been half expecting something like this, but not quite so soon. *Shit,* I thought. *Things are so close.*

I took the elevator down to the lobby, and walked out into the street. When I had found a payphone in a suitably innocuous location, I in-serted a phone card and punched in Tatsu's number. I could have just ignored him, but it was hard to predict what he might do in response to that. Better to know what he wanted, while maintaining the appearance of cooperation.

There was a single ring, then I heard his voice. *"Moshi moshi,"* he said, without identifying himself.

"Hello," I replied, in Japanese.

"Are you still in the same place?"

"Why would I want to leave?" I asked, letting him hear the sarcasm.

"I thought that, after our last meeting, you might choose to… travel again."

"I might. Haven't gotten around to it yet. I thought you'd know that."

"I am trying to respect your privacy."

Bastard. Even when he was busily ruining my life, he could always coax a smile out of me. "I appreciate that," I told him.

"I would like to see you again, if you wouldn't mind."

I hesitated. He already knew where I lived. He didn't have to arrange a meeting elsewhere, if he'd wanted to get to me. "Social visit?" I asked.

"That is up to you."

"Social visit."

"All right."

"When?"

"I'll be in town tonight. Same place as last time?"

I hesitated again, then said, "Don't know if we'll be able to get in. There's a hotel very near there, though, with a good bar. My kind of place. You know what I'm talking about?"

I was referring to the bar at the Osaka Ritz-Carlton.

"I imagine I can find it."

"I'll meet you at the bar at the same time we met last time."

"Yes. I will look forward to seeing you then." A pause. Then: "Thank you."

I hung up.

CHAPTER 7

I took the Hankyu train back to Osaka and went straight to the Ritz. I wanted to be sure I was in position at least a few hours early, in case there was anything I would want to see coming. I ordered a fruit and cheese plate and drank Darjeeling tea while I waited.

Tatsu was punctual, as always. He was courteous, too, moving slowly and letting me see him to show he didn't intend any surprises. He sat across from me in one of the upholstered chairs. He looked around, taking in the light wood paneling, the wall sconces and chandeliers.

"I need your assistance again," he said, after a moment.

Predictable. And right to the point, as always. But I'd make him wait before responding. "You want a whisky?" I asked. "They've got a nice twelve-year-old Cragganmore."

He shook his head. "I'd like to join you, but my doctor advises me to refrain from such indulgences."

"I didn't know you listened to your doctor."

He pursed his lips as though in preparation for a painful admission. "My wife, too, has become strict about such matters."

I looked at him and smiled, faintly surprised at the image of this tough, resourceful guy deferring sheepishly to a wife.

"What is it?" he asked.

I told him the truth. "It's always good to see you, you bastard."

He smiled back, a network of creases appearing around his eyes. *"Kochira koso."* The same here.

He gestured to the waitress and ordered chamomile tea. Because he wasn't drinking, I stayed away from the Cragganmore. A small pity.

Then he turned to me. "As I said, I need your assistance again."

I drummed my fingers along my glass. "I thought this was a social visit."

He nodded. "I was lying."

I had already known that, and he knew that I knew. Still: "I thought you said I could trust you."

"On the important things, certainly. Anyway, a social visit doesn't preclude a request for a favor."

"Is that what you're asking for? A favor?"

He shrugged. "You are no longer obligated to me."

"I used to get paid a lot of money when I did favors for people."

"I am pleased to hear you say 'used to.'"

"I was able to say it pretty accurately, until just recently."

"May I continue?"

"As long as we're clear from the outset that there's no obligation here."

"As I have said." He paused to withdraw a tin of mints from inside his coat pocket. He opened the tin and extended it toward me. I shook my head. He withdrew a mint and placed it in his mouth without dipping his head or stopping to look at what he was doing. It wasn't Tatsu's way to take his eyes off what was going on around him, and it showed in the little things as well as the more significant.

"The weightlifter was a front man," he said. "It is true that he looked like a Neanderthal, but in fact he was part of the new generation of organized crime in Japan. His specialty, in which he had proven himself unusually adept, was the establishment of legitimate, sustainable businesses, behind which his less progressive cohorts could then hide."

I nodded, knowing the phenomenon. The new generation, recognizing that tattoos, loud suits, and an aggressive manner offered them only limited upside in the society, was casting off its criminal persona and foraying into legitimate businesses like real estate and entertainment. The older generation, still wedded to drugs, prostitution, and control of the construction industry, was coming to rely on these upstarts for money laundering, tax avoidance, and other services. And, at the same time, the newcomers went to their forebears whenever the competitive pressures of business might be eased by the timely application of some of the traditional tools of the trade—bribery, extortion, murder—in which the older generation continued to specialize. It was a symbiotic division of labor that would have made a classical economist flush with pride.

"The weightlifter had established an efficient system," he continued. "All the traditional *gumi* were using his services. The legitimacy this system afforded the *gumi* was making them less vulnerable to prosecution, and more influential in politics and the boardroom. More influential in society generally, in fact. Our mutual acquaintance, Yamaoto Toshi, had grown particularly dependent on the weightlifter's operation."

Gumi means "group" or "gang." In the yakuza context, the word refers to organized crime families, the Japanese equivalent of the Gambinos or the fictional Corleones.

"I don't see how his absence is going to make a difference," I said. "Won't someone just take his place?"

"In the long run, yes. Where there is enough demand, eventually someone will offer a supply. But in the meantime, the supply is disrupted. The weightlifter was critical to the smooth maintenance of his organization. He groomed no successors, fearing, as strongmen do, that the presence of a successor would make a succession more likely. There will be a struggle in his organization now that he is gone. Deceit and betrayal will be part of that struggle. Assets and connections that are now hidden will be exposed. Criminal influence on legitimate enterprises will be lessened."

"For a time," I said.

"For a time."

I thought of what Kanezaki had told me about Crepuscular.

"I had a run-in with someone from the CIA recently," I said. "He mentioned something you might want to know about."

"Yes?"

"His name is Kanezaki Tomohisa. He's American, ethnic Japanese. He mentioned a CIA program for 'furthering reform and removing impediments to reform.' Something called Crepuscular. Sounds like your bailiwick."

He nodded slowly for a moment, then said, "Tell me about this program."

I started to tell him the little I'd heard. Then I realized. "You know this guy," I said.

He shrugged. "He was one of the people who came to the Metropolitan Police Force requesting assistance in locating you."

Marvelous. "Who was the other?"

"Holtzer's successor as the CIA's chief of Tokyo Station. James Biddle."

"Haven't heard of him."

"He's young for the position. About forty. Perhaps part of a new generation at the CIA."

I told him how I had met up with Kanezaki and his escort, fudging the details to conceal Harry's involvement.

"How did they manage to find you?" he asked. "It took me an entire year, even with local resources and access to Juki Net and the cameras."

"A flaw in my security," I told him. "It's been corrected."

"And Crepuscular?" he asked.

"Just what I told you. I didn't get details."

He drummed his fingers on the table. "It doesn't matter. I doubt Kanezaki-san could have told you more than I already know."

I looked at him, as always impressed with the breadth of his information. "What do you know?"

"The U.S. government is funneling money to various Japanese reformers. This is the same kind of program the CIA ran after the war, when it was supporting the Liberal Democratic Party as a bulwark against communism. Only the recipients have changed."

"What about the 'removing impediments' part?"

He shrugged. "I imagine that, as Kanezaki-san suggested, they might want you to help with that."

I laughed. "Sometimes these guys are so presumptuous a certain grandeur creeps into it."

He nodded. "Or they could be under the misapprehension that you had something to do with William Holtzer's demise. Either way, you should stay away from them. I think we know they are not to be trusted."

I smiled at his use, probably deliberate, of "we" and "they," as though Tatsu and I were partners.

"All right," I said. "Tell me about the favor you want."

He paused, then said, "Another key Yamaoto asset. And also a man whose primitive appearance masks a more sophisticated set of skills."

"Who is he?"

He looked at me. "Someone you should understand quite well. A killer."

"Really," I said, affecting nonchalance.

The waitress brought his tea and set it down before him. He extended the cup in my direction in a silent toast, then took a sip.

"He is a strange man," he said, watching me. "From his background, you might conclude he is only a brute. There was a history of child abuse. Fights in school, and early evidence of sadistic tendencies. He dropped out of high school to train in sumo, but couldn't develop the necessary bulk. Then he took up Thai boxing, where he had a short but unspectacular professional career. About five years ago he became involved in a so-called 'no holds barred' sport, something called 'Pride.' Do you know of it?"

"Sure," I said. The Pride Fighting Championship is a mixed martial arts sport, based in Japan, with televised bouts held every two months or so. The idea behind so-called mixed martial arts, or MMA, is to pit against each other a combination of traditional martial disciplines: boxing, jiu-jitsu, judo, karate, kempo, kung fu, Muay Thai, sambo, wrestling. Audiences for Pride competitions have been growing steadily since the sport was founded, along with interest in related events, like King of the Cage and the Ultimate Fighting Championship in the States. The sport has had some difficulty with regulators, who seem more comfortable with a boxer being beaten unconscious than with an MMA guy tapping out to a submission hold.

"What is your impression?" he asked.

I shrugged. "The competitors are strong. Good skills, good conditioning. A lot of heart, too. Some of what I've seen is as close to a real fight as you can get while still calling it a sport. But the 'no holds barred' stuff is just marketing. Until they decide to allow biting, eye-gouging, and ball shots, and until they start leaving weapons of convenience lying around the ring for the contestants to pick up, it'll have its shortcomings."

"It's interesting that you say that. Because the individual in question seemed to have the same concerns. He left the sport for the world of bare-knuckled underground fighting, where there really are no holds barred. Where as often as not the fight truly is to the finish."

I had heard about these fights. Had once even met someone who participated in them, an American named Tom, who was practicing judo, for a time, at the Kodokan. He was a tough-looking but surprisingly articulate guy who shared some interesting and valuable unarmed combat philosophy with me. I had defeated him in judo, but wasn't sure how things would have turned out in a less formal setting.

"Apparently this individual was highly successful in these underground contests," Tatsu said. "Not just against other men. Also in bouts against animals. Dogs."

"Dogs?" I asked, surprised.

He nodded, his expression grim. "These events are run by the yakuza. It was inevitable that our man's skills, and his cruel proclivities, would come to the attention of the organizers, that they would then recognize he had a higher calling than killing for prize money in the ring."

I nodded. "He could kill in the wider world."

"Indeed. And, for the last year, that is precisely what he has been doing."

"You said he had a more sophisticated set of skills."

"Yes. I believe he has developed capabilities I once thought were your provenance only."

I said nothing.

"In the last six months," he went on, "there have been two deaths, apparently by suicide. The victims were both high-level banking executives in soon-to-be merged institutions. Each seems to have leaped to his death from the roof of a building."

I shrugged. "From what I've been reading about the condition of the banks' balance sheets, I'm surprised only two have jumped. I would have expected more like fifty."

"Perhaps twenty years ago, or even ten, that would have been the case. But atonement by suicide now exists in Japan more as an ideal than as a practice." He took a sip of his tea. "An American-style apology is now preferred."

"'I regret that mistakes were made,'" I said, smiling.

"Sometimes not even 'I regret.' Rather, 'It is regrettable.'"

"At least they're not claiming taking bribes is a disease, that they just need treatment to be cured."

He grimaced. "No, not yet."

He took another sip of tea. "Neither of the jumpers left a note. And I have learned that each was concerned the actual size of the nonperforming loans of the other party was significantly higher than advertised."

"So? Everyone knows the problem loans are much bigger than the banks or the government admits."

"True. But these men threatened to reveal the problem data as a way of blocking a merger that had no sound business rationale, but which was nonetheless favored by certain elements of the government."

"Apparently not a very smart move."

"Let me ask you something," he said, looking at me. "Hypothetically. Would it be possible, realistically, to throw someone off a building and make it look like suicide?"

I happened to know with certainty that it was possible, but I decided to accept Tatsu's invitation to keep things on a "hypothetical" level.

"Depends on how thorough a pathological exam would be conducted afterward," I said.

"Assume very thorough."

"With very thorough, it would be tough. Still possible, though. Your biggest problem would be getting the victim up to the roof with no one seeing it. Unless you had some way of tricking him into meeting you on a rooftop or otherwise knowing in advance that he was going to be there, you'd have to transport him yourself. If he were conscious for that journey, he'd be making a hell of a racket. Also, if he were fighting you, there would be evidence of a struggle. Your skin under his nails. Maybe a clump of your hair in his stiff fingers. Other items incommensurate with a voluntary act. And he'd be fighting with no regard for his own safety, no regard to pain, so there would be evidence of a struggle all over you, as well. You have no idea the way a man will fight when he understands he's fighting for his life."

"Tie him up first?"

"You tie someone up, it leaves marks. Even if he doesn't struggle."

"And he would be struggling."

"Wouldn't you?"

"Kill him first?"

"Maybe. But that's risky. Changes to the body set in quickly after death. The blood pools. Temperature drops. And the results of impact to a dead body aren't the same as the results to a live one. The examiner could spot the discrepancies. Besides, you'd still have to worry about evidence of the actual cause of death."

"What if he were unconscious?"

"That's the way I would go. If he were unconscious, though, you'd have to carry him like a body. And maneuvering seventy or a hundred kilos of dead weight isn't easy. Plus, if you used a drug to knock him out, most likely it would still be in his bloodstream after death."

"What about alcohol?"

"If he'd drunk enough to pass out, you'd be in good shape. A lot of suicides drink before pulling the trigger, so nothing suspicious there. But how are you going to get the guy to drink himself under the table to begin with?"

He nodded. "The two jumpers in question had blood alcohol levels high enough to have induced unconsciousness."

"Could be what you think. Or not. That's the beauty of it."

"An injection?"

"Possibly. But to get enough alcohol in to do the job, you'd have to leave a detectable puncture mark at the spot where you injected it. Plus there's alcohol in his bloodstream, but no residue of, say, Asahi Super Dry in his stomach? Not good."

"Maybe a setup. A woman, someone strengthening his drinks, getting him to drink more than he can handle."

"That could work."

"How would you do it?"

"Hypothetically?"

He looked at me. "Of course."

"Hypothetically, I would try to get to the target late at night, when there would be the fewest people around. Maybe in his apartment, if I were sufficiently confident he'd be there alone and that I had a reliable means of undetectable access. I'd dress like a janitor, because no one ever notices janitors, knock him out with a carefully applied strangle, and put him in an industrial-sized laundry cart, or a large rolling refuse container, whatever would be in keeping with the surroundings. I'd line it with something soft to make sure he didn't suffer any contusions that would be incommensurate with his fall. You might have to choke him out again if he came to, but with no people around that wouldn't be too difficult.

Get him up to the roof, roll him over to the edge, and dump him. That's how I would do it. Hypothetically."

"What would you think if you found a small strip of plastic caught in the band of the victim's wristwatch?"

"What kind of plastic?"

"Sheet plastic. Thick. The kind that comes in rolls, for protecting furniture and other large valuables."

I was familiar with some of the uses for that kind of plastic, and I thought for a moment. "Your killer could have gotten the victim drunk. Let's leave aside how for the moment. Then he rolls him in the plastic to prevent contamination from handling. Take him to the edge of the roof, grip one end of the plastic, and give a hard shove. The victim rolls out of the plastic and into the air. Very neat."

"Unless, somehow, the victim's watch snagged on the plastic."

"Not impossible. But if that's all you've got to go on, you haven't got much."

"There was also an eyewitness. A bellhop, working late in the hotel where one of the victims died. At three in the morning, the same time the coroner fixed the time of death, he got a good look at a janitor with a large cart going up in one of the elevators. Exactly the scene you just depicted."

"He described your man?"

"To the details. A crushed left cheek, from his Muay Thai days. Unusual scarring on the opposite side of his face, under the eye. These are healed dog bites. 'A frightening face,' he said. Entirely accurately."

"No such janitor employed in that building?"

"Correct."

"What happened to the bellhop?"

"Disappeared."

"Dead?"

"Probably."

"That's all you've got?"

He shrugged. "And two similar deaths, outside of Tokyo. Each to a family member of a key player in Parliament." His jaw clenched, then released. "One to a child."

"A child?"

Clench, release. "Yes. One with no history of emotional or other problems in school. No evidence of precursors for suicide."

I had once heard that Tatsu had lost an infant son. I wanted to ask him, but didn't.

"If those deaths were intended to send messages to the principals," I said, "they were being pretty subtle. If the principal thinks it was suicide, there's no impact on his behavior."

He nodded. "I had the opportunity to interview each of the principals. Each denied there had been any contact from anyone claiming the deaths were other than suicide. Each was lying."

Tatsu had a nose for that sort of thing, and I trusted his judgment. "I'm surprised you didn't suspect I was involved in some of this," I said.

He paused for a moment before answering. "I might have. But, though I don't pretend to understand how you do what you do, I know you. You could not kill a child. Not that way."

"I've told you as much," I said.

"I am not talking about what you told me. I am talking about what I know."

I felt bizarrely appreciative of his confidence.

"In any event," he continued, "some of your movements, as recorded on the Osaka security camera network, provided you with an alibi."

I raised my eyebrows. "Your cameras are good enough to track me, but not good enough to spot someone wrapping people in plastic and dumping them off roofs?"

"As I have told you, the networks are far from perfect. I do not have control over their operation." He looked at me. "And I am not the only one with access."

I took a last sip of tea and asked a waitress for some more hot water. We sat in silence until it had arrived.

I picked up the delicate china cup and looked at him. "Tell me something, Tatsu."

"Yes."

"These questions. You already know the answers."

"Of course."

"Then why are you asking me?"

He shrugged. "I believe this man we are dealing with is a sociopath. That he is capable of killing under any set of circumstances. I am trying to understand how such a creature operates."

"Through me?"

He nodded his head once in acknowledgment.

"I thought you just said I'm not the right model." My tone was more forceful than I had intended.

"You are as close to such a creature as I have known. Which makes you ideally suited to hunt him."

"What do you mean, 'hunt him'?"

"He is careful in his movements. Not an easy man to track. I have leads, but they would need to be followed."

I took another sip of tea, considering. "I don't know, Tatsu."

"Yes?"

"The first guy, with the business fronts, okay, he was strategic. I understand. But this guy, the dog fighter, he's just muscle. Why aren't you going after Yamaoto and the other kingpins?"

"The 'kingpins,' as you put it, are difficult to get to. Too many bodyguards, too much security, too much visibility. Yamaoto in particular has hardened his defenses, I believe out of fear that you may be hunting him, and is now as inaccessible as the Prime Minister. And even if they could be gotten to, there are many like them in the various factions, waiting to take their places. They are like shark's teeth. Knock one out, and there are ten rows waiting to fill in the gap. After all, to be a kingpin is not so hard. What does it take? Some political acumen. A capacity for rationalization. And greed. Not a particularly rare profile."

He took a sip of his tea. "Besides, this man is no ordinary foot soldier. He is ruthless, he is capable, he is feared. An unusual individual, whose loss would not be a trivial blow to his masters."

"All right," I said. "What are you offering me? Given that I'm under no obligation."

"I have no money to offer you. Even if I did, I doubt I could match what Yamaoto and the Agency were paying you previously."

He might have been trying to get a rise out of me with that. I ignored it.

"I'm sorry to be so blunt, old friend, but you're asking me to take a hell of a risk. Just spending time in Tokyo entails risks for me. You know that."

He looked at me. When he spoke, his tone was measured, confident. "It would not be like you to assume your risk from Yamaoto and the CIA is confined only to Tokyo," he said.

I wasn't sure where he was going with that. "It's where the risk is most pronounced," I said.

"I've told you, Yamaoto has felt compelled to live a much more heavily defended existence since the last time you saw him. He has curtailed his political appearances, he no longer trains at the Kodokan, he travels only surrounded by bodyguards. My understanding is that he does not enjoy these new restrictions. My understanding, in fact, is that he resents them. Most of all, he resents the cause of them."

"You don't have to tell me Yamaoto has a motive," I said. "I know what he'd like to do to me. And it's not just business, either. He's the kind of man who would feel humiliated, enraged by how I helped steal that disk from him. He's not going to forget it."

"Yes? And none of this keeps you awake at night?"

"If I let that kind of shit keep me awake at night, I'd have bags under my eyes the size of Sado Island. Besides, he can have all the motive he wants. I'm not going to give him the opportunity."

He nodded. "I'm certain you wouldn't. At least not deliberately. But, as I have mentioned, I am not the only one with access to Juki Net."

I looked at him, wondering whether there was a threat hidden in there. Tatsu was always subtle.

"What are you saying, Tatsu?"

"Only that if I could find you, Yamaoto will be able to, also. And he is not alone in his efforts. The CIA, as you know, is also eager to make your reacquaintance."

He took a sip of his tea. "Putting myself in your shoes, I see two possible courses. One is that you stay in Japan, but not in Tokyo, and try to return to your old ways. This is perhaps the easier course, but the less safe one."

He sipped again. "Two is that you leave the country and start over somewhere. This is the harder course, but would perhaps afford you greater security. The problem, in either case, is that you will have left things unfinished with certain parties who wish you ill, parties with global reach and long memories, and that you will have no allies against them."

"I don't need allies," I said, but the rejoinder sounded weak even to me.

"If you plan to leave Japan, we can part as friends," he said. "But if I cannot count on your help today, it will be difficult for me to help you tomorrow, when you may need that help."

That was about as direct as Tatsu ever got. I thought about it, wondering what to do. Drop everything and disappear for Brazil, even though my preparations weren't complete? Maybe. But I hated the thought of leaving a loose end, something someone could grab onto and use to track me. Because, despite his obvious self-interest in emphasizing the dangers of Yamaoto and the CIA, Tatsu's assessment was not so far off from my own.

The other possibility would be to do this last job and keep him off my back, keep him off balance while I finished my preparations. What he was offering me in return wasn't trivial, either. Tatsu had access to people and places even Harry couldn't hack. No matter what I did next, he would be a damn useful contact.

I thought it through for another minute. Then I said, "Something tells me you're carrying an envelope."

He nodded.

"Give it to me," I said.

CHAPTER 8

I took the envelope to my apartment and perused it there. I sat at my desk and spread out the papers. I highlighted passages. I scribbled thoughts in the margins. Parts I read in order. Other times I skipped around. I tried to get the pattern, the gist.

The subject's name was Murakami Ryu. The dossier was impressive on background, on much of which Tatsu had already briefed me, but light on the sorts of current detail I need to get close to a subject. Where did he live? Where did he work? What were his habits, his haunts, his routines? With whom did he associate? All blanks, or too vague to be immediately useful.

He wasn't a ghost, but he was no civilian, either. Civilians have addresses, places of employment, tax records, registered cars, medical files. The lack of such details surrounding Murakami was itself a form of information. Which provided a frame, but I still didn't have a picture.

That's okay. Start with the frame.

No information meant a careful man. Serious. A realist. A man who didn't take chances, who was careful in his movements, who could be expected to make few mistakes.

I shuffled papers. Even his known organized crime associates were from multiple families. He didn't exclusively patronize any of the known yakuza *gumi.* He was a freelancer, a straddler, connected to many worlds but a part of none.

Like me.

He liked hostess bars, it seemed. He had been spotted in several, typically high-end, where he would spend the yen equivalent of twenty thousand dollars in a night.

Not like me.

High rollers get remembered. In my business, careful means *not* being remembered. Evidence of impulsiveness? Lack of discipline? Maybe. Still, there was no pattern to the behavior, only its existence. No trail for me to follow.

But there was something there, something in those periodic splurges. I tagged that thought for reexamination, then closed my eyes and tried to let the bigger picture cohere.

The fighting. That was a common theme. But Tatsu's information on where the underground bouts occurred, when, and under whose auspices, was sketchy.

The police had broken up several, always in different locations. That the police were breaking up the fights at all meant they weren't being paid not to. Meaning in turn that the organizers were willing to purchase overall secrecy at the price of a few random interruptions. Which showed good judgment, and perhaps some greed.

Too bad, from my perspective. If there had been payoffs, there would have been leaks, leaks Tatsu would have uncovered.

Stay with the fights, I thought, trying to get a visual. *The fights. Not work for this guy. He's a killer. For him, it's fun.*

What would the purses be? How much do you have to pay two men to step into the ring when each knows that only one might walk away afterward?

How many spectators? How much would they pay to see two men fight to the death? How much would they bet? How much would the house collect?

They'd have to keep the crowds small. Otherwise word gets out and the police intrude.

Enthusiasts. Devotees. Maybe fifty men. Charge them a hundred, two hundred thousand yen each for admission. Betting is free. A lot of money would change hands.

I leaned back in the Aeron chair, my fingers laced behind my head, my eyes closed. Pay the winner the yen equivalent of twenty thousand dollars. The loser gets a couple thousand for his efforts, if he lives. The couple thousand goes to the crew that disposes of the body if he doesn't. Minimal overhead. The house pockets close to eighty grand. Not bad for an evening.

Murakami liked to fight. Hell, Pride wasn't enough for him. He needed more. And it wasn't the money. Pride, with promotions and pay-per-view, would pay a lot more, to the winners and losers.

No. It wasn't the money for this guy. It was the excitement. The proximity to death. The high you can only get from killing a man who's simultaneously doing everything in his power to kill you.

I know the sensation. It both fascinates and repulses me. And, in a very few men, most of whom can live out their lives and be true to their natures only as the hardest of hard-core mercenaries, it becomes an addiction.

These men live to kill. Killing is the only thing for them that's real.

I had known one of them. My blood brother, Crazy Jake.

I remembered how Jake would cut loose after returning from a mission. He'd be flushed, not just his mood but his whole metabolism jacked up and humming. You could see heat shimmers coming off his body. Those were the only times he would be talkative. He'd relate how the mission had gone, his eyes bloodshot, his mouth working a maniac grin.

He would show trophies. Scalps and ears. The trophies said: *They're dead! I'm alive!*

In Saigon he'd buy everyone's beer. He'd buy whores. He threw parties. He needed a group to celebrate with him. *I'm alive! They're dead and I'm fucking alive!*

I sat forward in the seat and pressed my palms on the surface of the desk. I opened my eyes.

The bar tabs.

You've just killed and survived. You want to celebrate. They paid you in cash. Celebrate you can.

It felt right. The first glimmers of knowing this guy from afar, of beginning to grasp the threads of what I'd need to get close to him.

He loved the fights. He was addicted to the high. But a serious man. A professional.

Work backward. He would train. And not at some monthly-dues neighborhood *dojo* alongside the weekend warriors. Not even at one of the more serious places, like the Kodokan, where the police *judoka* kept their skills sharp. He'd need something, he'd find something, more intense.

Find that place, and you find him.

I took a walk along the Okawa River. Hulking garbage scows slumbered senseless and stagnant on the green water. Bats dive-bombed me, chasing insects. A couple of kids dangled fishing poles from a concrete retaining wall, hoping to pull God knows what from the murky liquid below.

I came to a payphone and used the number Tatsu had given me.

He picked up on the first ring. "Okay to talk?" I asked him.

"Yes."

"Our man trains for his fights. Not at a regular *dojo.*"

"I expect that is correct."

"Do you have information about where?"

"Nothing beyond what is in the envelope."

"Okay. Here's what we're looking for. A small place. A hundred square meters, something like that. Not in an upscale neighborhood, but not too far downscale, either. Discreet. No advertising. Tough clientele. Organized crime, biker types, enforcers. People with police records. Histories of violence. You ever hear of a place like that?"

"I haven't. But I know where to check."

"How long?"

"A day. Maybe less."

"Put whatever you find on the secure site. Page me when it's done."

"I will."

I hung up.

The page came the next morning. I went to an Internet café in Umeda to check the secure site. Tatsu's message consisted of three pieces of information. The first was an address: Asakusa 2-chome, number 14. The second was that a man matching Murakami's memorable description had been spotted there. The third was that the weightlifter had been one of the backers of whatever *dojo* was being run there. The first piece of information told me where to go. The second told me it would be worthwhile to do so. The third gave me an idea of how I could get inside.

I composed a message to Harry, asking whether he could check to see if my former weightlifting partner had ever made or received calls on his mobile phone that were handled by the tower closest to the Asakusa address. Based on Tatsu's information, I expected the answer would be yes. If so, it would confirm that the weightlifter had spent time at the *dojo* and would be known there, in which case I would use his name as an introduction. I also asked if Harry had heard from any U.S. government employees of late. I uploaded the message to our secure site, then paged him to let him know it was there.

An hour later he paged me back. I checked the secure site and got his message. No visits from the IRS, with a little smiley face next to the news. And a record of calls the weightlifter had made that were handled by the Asakusa 2-chome tower. We were in business.

I uploaded a message to Tatsu telling him I was going to check the place out and would let him know what I found. I told him I needed him to backstop Arai Katsuhiko, the identity I'd been using at the weight-lifter's club. Arai-san would have to be from the provinces, thus explaining his lack of local contacts. Some prison time in said provinces for, say, assault, would be a plus. Employment records with a local company— something menial, but not directly under mob control—would be ideal. Anyone who decided to check me out, and I was confident that, if things went as I hoped, someone would, would find the simple story of a man looking to leave behind a failed past, someone who had come to the big city to escape painful memories, perhaps to try for a fresh start.

I caught a late bullet train and arrived at Tokyo Station near midnight. This time, I stayed at the Imperial Hotel in Hibiya, another centrally lo-cated place that lacks the amenities and flair of, say, the Seiyu Ginza or the Chinzanso or Marunouchi Four Seasons, but that compensates with size, anonymity, and multiple entrances and exits. The Imperial was also the last place I had been with Midori, but I chose it for security, not for sentiment.

The next morning, I checked the secure site. Tatsu had given me the identity I wanted, along with the location of a bank of coin lockers in Tokyo Station, from under one of which I could retrieve the relevant ID. I memorized the message, then deleted it.

I did an SDR that encompassed Tokyo Station, where I retrieved the papers I might need, and that ended at Toranomon Station on the Ginza line, the oldest subway route in the city. From there I caught a train to Asakusa. Asakusa, in the northeast of the city, is part of what's left of *shitamachi,* the downtown, the low city of old Tokyo.

Asakusa 2-chome was northwest of the station, so I approached it through the Sensoji, the Asakusa Temple complex. I entered through Kaminarimon, the Thunder Gate, said to protect Kannon, the goddess of mercy, to whose worship the temple complex is dedicated. My parents had taken me there when I was five, and the sight of the gate's ten-foot red paper lantern is one of my earliest memories. My mother insisted on waiting in line to buy *kaminari okoshi,* Asakusa's signature snack, at the Tokiwado shop, whose crackers are reputed to be the best. My father complained at having to wait for such touristy nonsense but she ignored him. The crackers seemed wonderful to me—crunchy and sweet—and my mother laughed as we ate them, urging me, *"Oishii, ne? Oishii, ne?"* Aren't they yummy? Aren't they yummy?, until my father broke down and partook.

I paused before the Sensoji Temple and looked back at the compound. Around me whirled the general din of excited tourists, of hawkers exhorting potential customers *"Hai, irasshiae! Hai, dozo!,"* of squealing schoolchildren being mobbed by the legions of pigeons that make the complex their home. Someone was shaking an *omikuji* fortune-telling can, full of hundred-yen coins deposited in the hope of good tidings. Incense from the giant brass *okoro* wafted past me, simultaneously sweet and acrid on the cool air. Clusters of people stood around the censer, pulling the smoke onto those parts of their bodies they hoped to cure with its supposed magical properties. One old man in a fishing cap gathered great heaps of it onto his groin, laughing with gusto as he did so. A tour guide tried to arrange for a group photo, but waves of passersby continually obliterated the shot. The giant Hozomon gate herself stood silent through it all, brooding, dignified, inured by the decades to the clamor of tourists, the frantic photographers, the guano amassed on her eaves like wax from immolated candles.

I headed west. The din receded, to be replaced by an odd, depressing silence that hung over the area like smoke. Outside the tourist-fueled activity of Sensoji, it seemed, Asakusa had been hit hard by Japan's decade-long decline.

I walked, my head swiveling left and right, logging my surroundings. Hanayashiki amusement park sulked to my right, its empty Ferris wheel rotating senselessly against the ashen sky above. The esplanade beyond was given over mostly to a few pigeons that had wandered there from the nearby temple complex, the occasional flapping of their wings echoing in the surrounding silence. Here and there were small clusters of homeless men smoking secondhand cigarettes. A mailman removed a few envelopes from the back of a postal box and hurried on, as though vaguely afraid he might catch whatever disease had decimated the area's population. The owner of a coffee shop sat diminished in the back of his deserted establishment, waiting for patronage that had long since vanished. Even the pachinko parlors were empty, the artificially gay music piping out of their entranceways bizarre and ironic.

I turned the corner at the end of the street I was looking for. A heavily built Japanese kid with a shaved head, his eyes hidden behind sunglasses, was leaning against the wall. I made him as a sentry. Sure enough, at the other end of the street, there was his twin.

I walked past the first guy. After a few steps I turned my head casually to look back at him. He was watching me, speaking into a radio. This was a quiet street and I didn't look like one of the pensioners who lived in the neighborhood. The call felt routine: somebody's coming, I don't know who.

I walked on and found the address—an unremarkable two-story building with a concrete façade. The door was old and constructed of thick metal. Three rows of large bolts ran across it horizontally, probably attached to reinforcing bars on the other side. The bolts said *Visitors Not Welcome.*

I looked around. Across from me was a blue corrugated shed, ramshackle, its windows caved inward like the sunken eyes of a corpse. To the right was a tiny coin laundry, its three washers and three dryers arranged facing each other in neat rows as though set out to be taken away and discarded. The walls were yellowed, decorated with peeling posters. Spilled laundry powder and cigarette butts littered the floor. A vending machine hung tilted from the wall, advertising laundry soap at fifty yen a packet to customers who might as well have been ghosts.

There was a small black button recessed in the mud-colored brick to the right of the building's door. I pressed it and waited.

A slat opened up at head level. A pair of slightly bloodshot eyes regarded me through wire mesh from the other side.

"I'm here to train," I said in curt Japanese.

A moment passed. "No training here," was the reply.

"I'm judo fourth *dan*. Your place was recommended by a friend of mine." I said the dead weightlifter's name.

The eyes behind the slat narrowed. The slat closed. I waited. A minute went by, then another five. The slat opened again.

"When did Ishihara-san recommend this club?" the owner of a new pair of eyes asked.

"About a month ago."

"It took you a long time to arrive."

I shrugged. "I've been out of town."

The eyes watched me. "How is Ishihara-san?"

"Last I saw him, he was fine."

"Which was when?"

"About a month ago."

"And your name is?"

"Arai Katsuhiko."

The eyes didn't blink. "Ishihara-san never mentioned your name."

"Was he supposed to?"

Still no blink. "Our club has a custom. If a member mentions the club to a nonmember, he also mentions the nonmember to the club."

No blink from me, either. "I don't know your customs. Ishihara-san told me this would be the right kind of place for me. Can I train here or not?"

The eyes dropped down to the gym bag I was carrying. "You want to train now?"

"That's what I'm here for."

The slat closed again. A moment later, the door opened.

There was a small antechamber behind it. Cinderblock construction. Peeling gray paint. The owner of the eyes was giving me the once-over. He didn't seem impressed. They never do.

"You can train," he said. He was barefoot, wearing shorts and a tee shirt. I placed him at five-feet-nine and eighty kilos. Tending toward the burly side. Salt-and-pepper crew cut, age about sixty. Past what I sensed had been a formidable prime, but still a hard-looking guy with no bullshit, no posturing.

Behind the burly guy and to his right was a smaller, wiry specimen, dark complected for a Japanese, his head shaved to black stubble. I recognized the bloodshot eyes—the same pair that had initially regarded me through the mesh. Though slighter than the first guy, this one radiated something intense and unpredictable.

The smaller guys can be dangerous. Never having been able to rely on their size for intimidation, they have to learn to fight instead. I know because, before filling out in the army, I had been one of them.

The antechamber was adjacent to a rectangular room, about twenty feet by thirty. It smelled of old sweat. The room was dominated by a judo tatami mat. A half-dozen muscular specimens were using it for some kind of *randori,* or live training. They wore shorts and tee shirts, like the guy who had opened the door, no *judogi.* On a corner of the mat, someone was practicing elbow and knee drops on a prone, man-shaped dummy. The dummy's head, neck, and chest were practically mummified with duct tape reinforcements.

In another corner, two canvas heavy bags dangled on thick chains from exposed rafters. Large bags, seventy kilos or more. Man-sized. A couple of thick-necked guys with yakuza-style punch perms were working them, no gloves, no tape, their blows not quick but solid, the *whap! whap!* of knuckles on leather reverberating in the enclosed space.

The lack of wrist and finger tape interested me. Boxers wear tape to protect their hands. But you get dependent on the tape, and then you don't know how to hit someone without it. Even Mike Tyson once broke a hand when he hit another fighter barehanded in a late night brawl. In a real fight, if you break your hand, you probably just lost the fight. If you were fighting for your life, you probably just lost that, too.

And no *judogi.* That was also interesting, especially in tradition-loving Japan. Purists will tell you that training with the *judogi* is more realistic than without, because after all, people rarely fight naked. But modern attire—a tee shirt, for example—is often more like naked than it is like the reinforced, belted *gi.* Training exclusively in the *gi,* therefore, while traditional, is not necessarily the height of realism.

All signs that these were serious people.

"You can change in the locker room," the salt-and-pepper guy told me. "Warm up and you can do some *randori.* We'll see why Ishihara-san thought this would be a good place for you."

I nodded and headed to the locker room. It was a dank space with a floor of dirty gray carpet. Its half-dozen battered metal lockers were positioned on either side of a solid-looking exterior door, secured with a combination lock. I changed into cotton judo pants and a tee shirt, leaving the judo jacket in the bag. Best to blend.

I returned to the main room and stretched. No one seemed to take particular notice of me—except for the dark-complected guy, who watched while I warmed up.

After about fifteen minutes he walked over to me. *"Randori?"* he asked, in a tone that was more a challenge than an invitation.

I nodded, averting my eyes from his hard stare. In my mind, our contest was already underway, and I prefer my opponents to underestimate me.

I followed him to the center of the mat, slightly meek, slightly intimidated.

We circled around each other, each looking for an opening. In my peripheral vision I saw that the other men had paused in their workouts and were watching.

I snagged his right arm with my left and dropped under it for a duck-under, a simple and effective entry from my high school wrestling days in America. But he was quick: he dropped his arm, crouched, and cut clockwise, away from my entry. I immediately switched my attack to his left side, but he parried nicely there as well. No problem. I was feinting, feeling for his defenses, not yet showing him what I could do.

I withdrew from attack mode and started to straighten. As I did so, I saw his hips swivel in, caught a blur off the right side of my head. Left hook. *Whoa.* I shot my right hand into the gap and ducked my head forward. The blow snapped across the back of my head, then instantly retracted.

I took a quick step back. "Are we doing *randori,* or boxing?" I looked more concerned than I actually was. I've done some boxing. Not all of it with gloves.

"This is the way we do *randori* around here," he answered, sneering.

"With no rules?" I asked, mock-concerned. "I'm not sure I like that."

"You don't like it, don't train here, *judoyaro,*" he said, someone laughed.

I looked around as though unsure of myself, but it was really just a routine check of my surroundings. Adrenaline causes tunnel vision. Experience and a desire to survive ameliorate it. The faces around the tatami radiated amusement, not danger.

"I'm not really used to this kind of thing," I said.

"Then get off the fucking tatami," he spat.

I looked around again. It didn't feel like a setup. If it were, they wouldn't have been dancing with me one at a time.

"Okay," I said, scowling to look like a soft guy trying to look like a hard guy. Playing the victim of idiot pride. "We'll do it your way."

We squared off again. I logged his feints. He liked to lead with his right foot. His timing was regular—a weakness for which his quickness had probably always compensated.

He liked low kicks. Right foot forward plant, left roundhouse kick, return to defensive stance. I took two such shots to my right thigh. They stung. They didn't matter.

The right foot came forward again. When it was a few millimeters above the tatami and he was fully committed to planting it, I shot straight in, my right hand hooking his neck from behind, my left hand darting in just behind his right ankle. I used his neck to support my weight, dragging his head down and ruining his balance. I drove through him, my elbow leading the way at his chest. His ankle was blocked and his body had nowhere to go but backward to the tatami.

I kept the ankle as he fell, jerking it northward and spinning clockwise so that I landed facing the same direction he was in. I was straddling his leg and holding the ankle in front of me. In one smooth motion I caught it in my right bicep, wrapped the fingers of my left hand around his toes, and clamped down in opposing directions. His ankle broke with a snap like the sound of a mallet on hard wood. Freed of its moorings, the foot arced savagely to the right. Tendons and ligaments tore loose.

He let out a high scream and tried to use his other leg to kick me away. But the kicks were feeble. His nervous system was overloaded with pain.

I stood and watched him. His face was colored I'm-going-to-puke green and beaded in oily sweat. He was holding the knee of his ruined leg and looking bug-eyed at the dangling foot at the end of it. He hitched a breath in, then deeper, then let out a long wail.

Ankle injuries hurt, I know. I've seen feet lost to landmines.

He sucked in another breath and screamed again. If we'd been alone, I would have broken his neck just to shut him up. I looked around the room, wondering if I was going to have trouble from any of his comrades.

One of them, a tall, long-legged guy with an Adonis physique and peroxide-dyed, close-cropped hair, yelled out, *"Oi!"* and started to come toward me. Hey!

The salt-and-pepper guy cut in front of him. "That's enough," he said, pushing Adonis back. "That's enough."

Adonis backed off, but continued to fix me with a hostile stare.

Salt-and-Pepper turned and walked over to where I was standing. He bore an expression of mild amusement that was not quite a smile.

"Next time, use a little more control when you put in a joint lock," he said, his tone matter-of-fact.

The dark-complected guy writhed. Adonis and a couple of the others went to help him.

I shrugged. "I would have. But he told me 'no rules.'"

"True. He'll probably be the last guy who suggests that to you."

I looked at him. "I like this place. You guys seem serious."

"We are."

"It's all right for me to train here?"

"Between four and eight every evening. Most mornings, too, you can work out from eight to noon. There are dues, but we can talk about that another time."

"You manage the place?"

He smiled. "Something like that."

Someone brought a stretcher. The dark-complected guy was gritting his teeth and whimpering. Someone admonished him, *"Urusei na! Gaman shiro!"* Shut up! Take the pain!

"I'm Arai," I said, with a slight bow.

"Washio," he said, returning the bow. "And by the way, did you know Ishihara-san died recently?"

I looked at him. "No, I didn't."

He nodded. "An accident at his gym."

"I'm sorry to hear that. Is the gym still open?"

"Some of his associates are running it now."

"Good. Though I have a feeling that, from now on, I'll be spending more time here."

He grinned. *"Yoroshiku."* Looking forward to it.

"Yoroshiku."

I stuck around for another two hours. Adonis glared at me from time to time but otherwise kept his distance. Murakami never showed.

Washio's questions about Ishihara's death were neither surprising nor particularly unnerving. His death looked like an accident. Even if they wondered whether the truth might be otherwise, they had no more reason to suspect my involvement than they did anyone else who had worked out there.

Of course, if I received further inquiries on that subject, particularly any pointed ones, I might change my assessment.

I came the next day, and the day after that, but still no sign. That was fine with me. It felt good to be back in Tokyo and I thought I could afford a few more days if I continued to be careful. Besides, getting in a workout on the job is great. Not quite the wholesome life of an aerobics instructor, but it beats sitting in a van all night on surveillance, drinking cold coffee and pissing in a plastic jug.

On the fourth day, I dropped by in the evening. Three sequential occasions in the same place at the same time was as much as my paranoid nervous system will allow. I was surprised to see many of the same faces. Some of these characters worked out twice a day. I wondered what they did for a living. Crime, I supposed. Be your own boss. Flexible hours.

I exchanged greetings with Washio and some of the others whom I had gotten to know, then changed in the locker room. One of the heavy bags was open, and I started working it with knee and elbow combinations. Drills of one-minute attack, thirty seconds rest. I used a small clock on the wall to time myself.

My speed and strength were still good. Endurance likewise. Recovery times weren't what they once were, but a steady diet of liquid amino acids for the muscles, glucosamine for the joints, and Cognamine for the reflexes all seemed to help.

During one of the rest periods, I felt people pause in their workouts, felt their attention shift. The atmosphere in the room changed.

I looked over and saw someone in a poorly fitting double-breasted navy suit. It had wide lapels and overly padded shoulders. The kind of suit that's supposed to impart a swagger even when you're standing still. He was flanked by two burly specimens, more casually dressed, with yakuza punch perms. From their size and deportment I assumed they were bodyguards.

They must have just come in. The guy in the suit was talking to Washio, who was paying close and somehow uncomfortable attention.

I watched, and noticed other people doing the same. The newcomer couldn't have been more than five-feet-eight, but his neck was massive and I put him at about eighty-five, ninety kilos. His ears were deformed masses of protruding scar tissue that would stand out even in Japan, where such scarification is not uncommon among *judoka* and *kendoka*.

Washio was gesturing to various men who were training. The newcomer was nodding. It felt like a briefing.

The thirty-second rest was up. I returned my attention to the bag. Left elbow. Right uppercut. Left knee. Again.

When the one-minute sequence was done I looked over. Washio and the newcomer were walking toward me. The bodyguards remained by the door.

"*Oi*, Arai," Washio called out when they were a couple meters away. "Hold up for a minute."

I picked up a towel from the floor and wiped my face. They came closer and Washio gestured to the man next to him. "I want to introduce you to someone," he said. "One of the backers of this *dojo*."

I already knew who he was. Per Tatsu's briefing, the left cheek was flattened, with the opposite side exhibiting what looked like a golf ball-sized fissure pocked with jagged edges. I imagined a dog getting hold of him there and hanging on even as he shoved the animal away.

Something told me the dog had come out the worse.

I felt the hairs on the back of my neck pop up, a fresh surge of adrenaline dump into my veins. My fight or flight reaction is finely honed, and this guy's presence was making it sing.

"*Arai desu,*" I said, bowing slightly.

"*Murakami da,*" he said with a nod, his voice not much more than a growl. "Washio tells me you're good." He looked doubtful.

I shrugged.

"There's a fight tomorrow night," he went on. "We put them on from time to time. Most people pay a hundred thousand yen to attend, but members of the *dojo* get in free. You interested?"

A hundred thousand yen—I'd been in the right neighborhood about the economics of these things. And if this guy was comfortable issuing the invitation, someone must have checked me out. I was glad I'd asked Tatsu to backstop the Arai identity.

I shrugged again and said, "Sure."

He looked at me, his eyes flat, as though focused somewhere behind and through me. "The fight starts at ten o'clock sharp. People get there a little early for betting. We're doing this one in Higashi Shinagawa, five-chome. Just across the canal from Tennozu Island."

"The harbor district?" I asked. The area is part of Tokyo but wasn't a place I ever frequented while living in the city. It's in Tokyo's southeast, the home of meat processing plants and sewage disposal, of steam power facilities and wholesale warehouses, all of it fed and fattened by Tokyo's great port. I supposed the attraction was that it would be deserted at night.

"That's right. The address is eight-twenty-five. A warehouse with the character for 'transport' painted in a big circle on the door. Across from the Lady Crystal Yacht Club. On your right as you walk from the monorail. Should be easy to find."

"It's important that you not tell anyone about this," Washio added. "Only people who are invited get in anyway, and we don't want trouble from the police."

Murakami nodded once, acknowledging Washio's point as though it had been barely worth mentioning. I gathered Murakami didn't particularly care who showed up at these things, as long as there was a fight. Washio, on the other hand, was probably responsible for logistics and would be accountable if there were problems.

"Are you fighting?" I asked, looking at Murakami.

For the first time he smiled. The front teeth were overlarge and too even, and I realized he was wearing a cheap dental bridge.

"Sometimes I fight. But not tomorrow," he said.

I waited to see whether there would be more. There wasn't.

I briefly considered whether it could be a setup. If they were on to me, though, this was already a pretty perfect venue. They didn't have to convince me to go somewhere else.

"I'll be there," I told him.

Murakami looked at me for a moment longer, the smile lingering, the eyes still flat, then walked away. Washio followed.

I let out a long breath and looked at the clock. When the second hand was at the twelve, I attacked the bag again, working off the excess adrenaline Murakami's presence had provoked.

He was a scary one, no doubt about it. And not just the ruined face. Even without the scarring, I would have recognized him. He exuded the same deadly air I had known, and respected, in Crazy Jake. The external scars were the least of what marked him for what he was.

I wouldn't want to try to take this guy out with anything less than a scoped rifle. Which is something that's hard to confuse with expiration by natural causes.

The hell with it, I thought. *Risks are one thing. This looks like suicide.* If Tatsu wanted him dead that much, I'd recommend a six-man squad and firearms. Much as I would have liked to do something to buy Tatsu's continued goodwill, this one wasn't worth it.

I wondered if my old friend would threaten me. I didn't think so. And if he did, I'd just step up my Rio plans. The preparations weren't entirely complete, but moving hastily wasn't a bad option if I found myself caught between a likely suicide mission on the one hand and pressure from Tatsu's Keisatsucho on the other.

But I'd go to the fight tomorrow and collect whatever intelligence I could. I'd feed it to Tatsu as a consolation prize for my bowing out.

The clock's second hand swept past the twelve. I unloaded a final flurry of elbow strikes and stepped back. The adrenaline dump was largely depleted, but I still felt tense. Usually a workout helps with that. Not this time.

I found a partner and drilled leg attacks for another hour. After that I stretched and headed for the shower. I was glad this was going to be over soon.

PART II

Music reveals a personal past of which, until then, each of us was unaware, moving us to lament misfortunes we never suffered and wrongs we did not commit.

—Jorge Luis Borges

CHAPTER 9

That night I took a long, wandering walk through Tokyo. I was restless and felt the need to move, to let the city's currents carry me where they would.

I drifted north from Meguro, keeping to the backstreets, the alleys, the lonely paths through lightless parks.

Something about the damn city continued to draw me, to seduce me. I needed to leave. I wanted to be able to leave. Hell, I'd tried to leave. But here I was again.

Maybe it's fate.

But I don't believe in fate. Fate is bullshit.

Then what?

I came to Hikawa Jinja in Hiro, one of several score of Shinto shrines dotting the city. At perhaps thirty square meters, Hikawa is one of the smaller, but by no means the smallest, of these solemn green spaces. I walked through the old stone gate and was instantly enveloped in comforting darkness.

I closed my eyes, tilted my head forward, and inhaled through my nose. I raised my hands before me and extended my fingers like a blind man trying to determine where he has found himself.

It was there, just beyond the limits of ordinary perception. That feeling of the city being alive, coiled and layered and thrumming all around me. And the feeling that I was alive as part of it.

I opened my eyes and lifted my head. The shrine was built on a bluff, and through the trees at its periphery I could see the lights of Hiro, and of Meguro beyond it.

Tokyo is so vast, and can be so cruelly impersonal, that the succor provided by its occasional oasis is sweeter than that of any other place I've known. There is the quiet of shrines like Hikawa, inducing a somber sort of reflection that for me has always been the same pitch as the reverberation of a temple chime; the solace of tiny *nomiya,* neighborhood watering holes, with only two or perhaps four seats facing a bar less than half the length of a door, presided over by an ageless mama-san, who can be soothing or stern, depending on the needs of her customer, an arrangement that dispenses more comfort and understanding than any psychiatrist's couch; the strangely anonymous camaraderie of *yatai* and *tachinomi,* the outdoor eating stalls that serve beer in large mugs and grilled food on skewers, stalls that sprout like wild mushrooms on dark corners and in the shadows of elevated train tracks, the laughter of their patrons diffusing into the night air like little pockets of light against the darkness without.

I moved deeper into the gloom and sat with my back to the *honden,* the symmetrical, tile-roofed structure housing the god of this small shrine. I closed my eyes and exhaled, long and complete, then listened, for a while, to the stillness.

When I was a boy, I'd gotten caught stealing a chocolate bar from a neighborhood store. The elderly couple that owned the place knew me, of course, and informed my parents. I was terrified of my father's reaction, and denied everything when he questioned me. He didn't get angry. He nodded slowly instead, and told me that the most important thing for a man is to acknowledge what he has done, that if he fails to do so he can only be a coward. Did I understand that? he had asked.

At the time, I didn't really grasp what he meant. But his words induced a burning shame, and I confessed. He took me to the store, where I offered a tearful apology. In the presence of the owners, his visage had been stern, almost wrathful. But as we left, while I continued to weep in my disgrace, he had briefly and awkwardly pulled me to his side, then gently laid his hand on my neck while we walked.

I've never forgotten what he told me. I know what I've done, and I acknowledge all of it.

My first personal kill was of a Viet Cong near the Xe Kong River, the Laotian border. In Vietnam it was called a "personal kill" when you killed a specific individual with a direct-fire weapon and were certain of having done it yourself. I was seventeen at the time.

I was part of a three-man recon team. The teams were small, and depended for success and survival on their ability to operate undetected behind enemy lines. So only men with the ability to move with absolute stealth were selected for recon. The missions required ghosts more than they required killers.

It happened at daybreak. I remember the way I could just make out the mist rising off the wet ground as light crept into the sky. I always thought it was a beautiful country. A lot of soldiers hated it because they hated having to be there, but I didn't feel that way.

We'd been in the field for two nights with no contact and were heading to the extract point when we saw this guy, alone, standing in a clearing. We froze and watched him from just inside the tree line. He was carrying an AK, so we knew he was VC. He was pacing, looking left, then right. He seemed to be trying to orient himself. I remember wondering whether maybe he'd gotten separated from his unit. He looked a little scared.

Our guidelines were to avoid contact, but our mandate was to collect intelligence, and we saw that he was carrying a large book. Some kind of ledger. It might be a nice prize. We looked at each other. The team leader nodded at me.

I knelt and brought up my CAR-15, finding the VC in the sights, waiting for a pause in the pacing.

A few seconds passed. I knew I had time and wanted to be sure of the shot.

He knelt and set down his rifle and the book. Then he stood, opened his pants, and pissed. Steam rose from where the hot liquid hit the earth. I kept him in my sights, thinking the whole time that he had no idea what was coming and that this was a fucked-up way to die.

I let him finish and get himself back in his pants. Then, *ka-pop!* I dropped him. I saw him go down. I had this feeling of incredible elation—I'd succeeded! I'd won! I was good at this!

We went over to where he lay. When we got there, I was surprised to see he was still alive. I'd hit him in the sternum and he had a sucking chest wound. He'd fallen on his back and his legs were splayed out. The ground underneath him was already dark with his blood.

I remember being struck by how young he was. He looked my age. I remember that thought shooting through my mind—*God, same as me!*—as we stood in a circle around him, not knowing what to do.

He was blinking rapidly, his eyes jumping from one face to another and then back again. They stopped on mine, and I thought it was because he knew I was the one who shot him. Later, I realized the explanation was likely more prosaic. He was probably just trying to make sense of my Asian features.

Someone undid a canteen and extended it to him. But he made no move to take it. His breathing became faster and shallower. Tears spilled out of the corners of his eyes and he mumbled words in a high, strained voice none of us could understand. I learned later that battlefield wounded and dying often call out to their mothers. He might have been doing that.

We watched him. The chest wound stopped sucking. The blinking stopped, too. His head settled into the wet ground at an odd angle, as though he was listening to something.

We stood around him silently. The initial sense of elation was gone, replaced with a weirdly intimate tenderness, and a horrified sadness so sudden and heavy it actually made me groan.

Same as me, I thought again. He didn't look like a bad guy. I knew that in some other universe we wouldn't have been trying to kill each other. Maybe we would have been friends. He wouldn't be lying dead on a jungle floor saturated with his own blood.

One of the men I was with started to cry. The other began moaning, *Oh Jesus, oh Jesus,* over and over again. Both of them vomited.

I did not.

We took the ledger. It turned out to contain some fairly useful information about VC payments to local village heads and other attempts to buy influence. Though of course, in the end, none of that had mattered.

Someone on the Huey that picked us up afterward laughed and told me I'd popped my cherry. No one talked about how it really felt, or what had happened while we stood in a silent circle and watched the man die.

When the army was assessing my suitability for the joint Special Forces-CIA program known as SOG, the psychiatrist had displayed a keen interest in that initial killing experience. He seemed to think it was noteworthy that I hadn't vomited. And that what he described as my "associated negative emotions" had dissipated. No bad dreams afterward, that was also considered a plus.

Later, I learned that I was categorized as belonging to a magical two percent of military men who are capable of killing repeatedly, without hesitation, without special conditioning, without regret. I don't know if I really belonged there. It wasn't as easy for me as it was for Crazy Jake. But that's where they put me.

The average person is surprised at the extent to which a soldier has to deal with hesitation before the fact and regret afterward. Of course, the average person has never been required to kill a stranger at close range.

Men who have survived close-quarters killing know that humans are possessed of a deep-seated, innate reluctance to kill their own species. I believe there are evolutionary explanations for the existence of this reluctance, but that doesn't really matter. What matters is that the fundamental purpose of basic training for most soldiers is to employ classical and operant conditioning techniques to suppress the reluctance. I know modern training accomplishes this objective with ruthless effectiveness. I also know the training deals better with the reluctance than it does with the regret.

I sat for a long time, picking through memories. Eventually, I started to get cold. I went back to the hotel, watching my back as always along the way. I took an excruciatingly hot bath, then slipped into one of the cotton *yukata* the hotel had thoughtfully provided. I pulled a chair in front of the window and sat in the dark, watching the traffic moving along Hibiya-dori, twenty floors below. I thought of Midori. I wondered what she might be doing at that very instant on the other side of the world.

When the traffic began to thin, I got in bed. Sleep came slowly. I dreamed of Rio. It felt far away.

CHAPTER 10

The next night, I ran an SDR as usual on my way to the fight. When I was confident I was clean, I caught a cab to the Tennozu monorail station. From there I walked. There was no one else around.

It was cooler here by the water. A sidewalk was being repaired, and a cluster of temporary signs advising *anzen daiichi!*—Safety First!—swayed stiffly in the wind, squealing like lunatic chimes. I moved across the rust-colored bulk of the Higashi Shinagawa Bridge. Around me was a network of massive train and automobile overpasses, their concrete darkened by the accumulated years of diesel fumes, their bulk so densely woven against the dark sky that the earth beneath felt vaguely subterranean. A solitary vending machine sat slumped on a street corner, its fluorescent light guttering like a dying SOS.

I spotted the Lady Crystal Yacht Club, probably an advertising euphemism for a restaurant that happened to be located on the water, and turned left. To my right was another overpass with warehouses beneath; opposite, a small parking lot, mostly empty. Beyond that, another Stygian canal.

I found the warehouse door Murakami had described. It was flanked by a pair of concrete flowerpots choked with weeds. A metal sign to the left warned of fire danger. Rust ran down the wall from behind it like dried blood from a peeling bandage.

I looked around. Across the water were brightly lit high-rise office buildings, apartments, and hotels, the names of their owners proudly glowing in red and blue neon: JAL, JTB, the Dai-ichi Seafort. It was as though the ground around me was poisoned and incapable of supporting the growth of such structures here.

To my left was an indentation in the long line of warehouses. I stepped inside and spotted a door on the right, hidden from the street outside. There was a small peephole at eye level. I knocked and waited.

I heard a bolt moving, then the door opened. It was Washio. "You're early," he said.

I shrugged. I rarely make appointments. You don't want to give someone the opportunity to fix you in time and place. On those infrequent occasions where I have no choice, I like to show up early to scout around. If someone's going to throw me a party, I'll get there before the musicians set up.

I glanced inside. I was looking at a cavernous room dotted with concrete pillars. Incandescent lights dangled from a ceiling eight meters up, their bulbs encased in wire. Cardboard boxes were stacked five meters high on all sides. Two forklifts rested against a wall, looking like toys in relation to the space around them. A couple of *chinpira* in black tee shirts were moving chairs to the edges of the room. Other than that we were alone.

I looked at Washio. "Is it a problem?"

He shrugged. "Doesn't matter. People will be here soon enough."

I stepped inside. "You work the door?"

He nodded. "I don't know your face, you don't get in."

"Who's fighting?"

"Don't know. I just run the fights, I don't promote them."

I smiled at him. "You ever participate?"

He laughed. "No. I'm a little old for this shit. Maybe I would have when I was younger. But these fights have only been going on for a year, year and a half, which is long after my prime."

I thought of the way I'd seen him talking to Murakami, as though he'd been delivering a briefing. "The people at the club," I said, "you're training them for these fights?"

"Some of them."

"What about Murakami?" I asked.

"What about him?"

"What does he do?"

He shrugged. "A lot of things. Some of the guys he trains. Sometimes he fights. We get a good turnout when he's fighting."

"Why?"

"Murakami always finishes his fights. People like that."

"'Finishes' them?"

"You know what I mean. When Murakami fights, for sure one of the fighters is going to die. And Murakami has never lost."

I had no trouble believing that. "What makes him so good?" I asked.

He looked at me. "Let's hope you never have to find out."

"Is it true he fights dogs?"

He paused. "Where did you hear that?"

I shrugged. "Just talk."

Another pause. Then: "I don't know whether it's true. I know he goes to underground dog fights. He's a breeder. Tosas and American Pit Bulls. His dogs are dead game, too. He feeds them gunpowder, pumps them full of steroids. They get irritated at the world and aggressive as hell. One dog, Murakami shoved a jalapeño pepper up its ass. Fought like a demon after that."

There was a knock at the door. Washio stood. I offered him a slight bow to acknowledge we were done.

He reached out and took my arm. "Wait. I'll need your mobile phone first."

I looked at his hand. "I'm not carrying one," I said.

He eyeballed me, his expression baleful. I stared back. What I had told him was true, though if I'd been lying it would take more than a scowl to make me admit it.

His expression softened and he released my arm. "I'm not going to search you," he said. "But no one's allowed in here with a mobile phone. Too many people like to call a friend, tell 'em what they're seeing. It's unsecure."

I nodded. "That seems sensible."

"If one of the bouncers sees you with one, they'll work you over good. Just so you know."

I nodded to show I understood, then moved off to one of the corners and watched as people began to arrive. Some I recognized from the club. Adonis was wearing sweatpants. I wondered if he was fighting.

I stood in a corner and watched the place gradually fill. After about an hour, Murakami came in, flanked by two bodyguards, a different pair than I had seen in the *dojo*. He exchanged a few words with Washio, who looked around and then pointed at me.

I had the sudden sense that this was more attention from Murakami than I really wanted.

I watched him nudge his two men. The three of them started moving toward me.

Adrenaline dumped into my veins. I felt the surge. I looked around casually, searching for a weapon of convenience. There was nothing handy.

They walked up and stood in front of me, three abreast, Murakami slightly in front of the other two.

"I wasn't sure you were going to come," he said. "Glad to see you did."

"It's good to be here," I said, rubbing my palms in front of me as though in anticipation of the evening's entertainment. In fact it was an expedient defensive stance.

"We do three fights or thirty minutes, whichever comes first. That way everyone gets his money's worth. I'll explain the rules."

I didn't understand why he was telling me this. "Who's fighting?" I asked.

He smiled. The bridged teeth were white. Predatory.

"You are," he said.

Oh shit.

I looked at him and said, "I don't think so."

The smile disappeared and his eyes narrowed. "I'm not going to waste time fucking around with you. Washio says you're good. Says you broke a guy's ankle inside thirty seconds. Now that guy's friend wants payback. You're going to fight him."

Adonis. Should have known.

"Or…"

"Or you can fight three people I pick. You're so good, I'll make sure they have police batons. The crowd will like that, too. It's all the same to me."

I was in a box. I picked the easier way out.

"I'll fight," I told him.

His eyes crinkled with suppressed mirth. "Yes, you will."

"Anything else I need to know?"

He shrugged. "No shirts, no shoes, no weapons. Other than that, anything goes. There's no ring. If you get too close to the edge of the crowd, they'll shove you back to the center. If they think you're running from the other guy, you'll take a few punches, too. Good news is, the winner gets two million yen."

"What does the loser get?"

He smiled again. "We take care of the burial expenses."

I looked at him. "I'll take the money."

He laughed. "We'll see. Now pay attention. You're up first. That gives you fifteen minutes. These guys will stay with you to help you get ready." He turned and walked away.

I looked at the two goons. They kept a respectful distance, reducing my chances of making a sudden move and getting past them. Even if I could, though, there were men working the door. Several of them were watching. My chances would be better with Adonis.

I wondered about the number of fights. Multiple payouts would reduce, maybe even eliminate, the house's take.

I pushed the thought aside and slipped off the navy blazer I was wearing, then my shirt and shoes. I looked over and saw Adonis doing the same.

Some vicious thing inside me stirred. I felt it in my gut, the back of my neck, my hands.

I thought of Musashi, the master swordsman, who wrote, *You must think of neither victory nor of defeat, but only of cutting and killing your enemy.*

I stretched and shadowboxed. I let my focus narrow. It didn't matter where I was.

Murakami walked over. He said, "Let's go."

I moved to the center of the room. Adonis was waiting there.

His pupils were dilated and his hands were shaking. He looked juiced, maybe *kakuseizai*. Speed would give him a short-term energy boost, help him focus his attention.

I decided to give him something to focus it on.

I approached him, not slowing until I was in his face. "How's your buddy's ankle?" I asked. "Sounded like it hurt."

He stared at me. His respiration was rapid. Pupils, black basketballs. Definitely *kakuseizai*.

"Try that on me," he said, around clenched teeth.

"Oh, no," I said. "I'm not going to break your ankle. I'm going to break your knee." I took a half step back and pointed. "That one right there."

The idiot actually let his glance follow my outstretched finger. I tensed to launch an uppercut to his gut, but Washio, wise to such things, had seen it coming and jumped in between us.

"You don't start until I say start," he growled, looking at me.

I shrugged. Can't blame a guy for trying.

"They'll be taking you out of here in a bag, fucker," Adonis said. "That's a promise."

Washio shoved us apart. The crowd tightened like a noose.

"Are you ready?" Washio asked Adonis, who was bouncing on his toes like a hyperactive boxer.

Adonis nodded, glaring at me.

Washio turned to me. "Are you ready?"

I nodded, my eyes on Adonis.

"*Hajime!*" Washio cried, and a collective shout went up around us.

Adonis immediately feinted with a kick and took a sidestep back. Then again. We started to move in small, migrating circles.

I saw what he was up to. For him this was effectively a hometown crowd. He would have friends in the audience. The movement of our circles would gradually take us closer to them, and give them access to me.

But the presence of those friends would also engage his ego. "*Doko ni ikunda?*" I taunted him, moving to the center. "*Koko da.*" Where are you going? I'm right here.

He took a step forward, but not enough to close the distance. My earlier taunts had focused him on his knees. He was afraid I would shoot in on him the way I had on his friend, and thought keeping his distance would prevent me.

I dropped my arms a few centimeters and kept my head and torso slightly forward. He steadied himself on his feet and I could feel him thinking *Kick*. His kicks were good, too. I'd seen him practicing. If I were him, I'd try to wear me down from extended range, try to keep me away with those long legs.

He planted his left foot forward and whipped in a right roundhouse kick. His foot smacked into my left thigh, then snapped back to the ground. I felt a bolt of pain and there was a shout of approval from the crowd. Adonis bounced on his toes again.

He was quick. Didn't give me a chance to grab the leg.

I'd have to let him feel that the kicks were working for him, so he'd try to land them with a little more authority. The extra couple of milliseconds of contact would make the difference.

He snapped the kick out again. It hit my thigh like a baseball bat and shot back to the floor. The crowd shouted again. There was a roaring in my ears.

The impact hurt worse this time. A few more like that and I'd start to lose the full use of the leg. I knew he was thinking the same thing.

I shifted back a half step and crouched, giving him more of my right side as though to protect my forward leg. I watched him in adrenalized slow motion.

His nostrils were flaring in and out, his eyes drilling into me. He shuffled forward, his feet staying close to the floor.

In my peripheral vision I was aware of his right foot taking the ground a little more firmly. His weight began to shift to his forward left. His hips cocked for the kick.

I reined in my urge to act, forcing myself to wait the extra half-second I knew I needed.

The kick started to come off the ground and I shot forward, shortening the distance by half. He saw his error and tried to correct, but I was already too close. I jammed the kick with my left hip and swept my left arm out and around his extended right knee.

The crowd breathed, "Ahhh."

He improvised quickly, encircling my left tricep with his right hand and thrusting his free hand at my face, the fingers forward, going for my eyes. I tightened the grip on his knee and took a drop-step forward with my left leg, levering him down toward the floor. He hopped backward on his left leg to try to recover his balance and I popped a sharp right uppercut into his exposed balls.

He grunted and tried to pull away. I took a long step forward with my right leg, ducking under his left arm and simultaneously releasing his knee. I swept behind him, clasped my hands around his waist, dropped my hips, and arched sharply backward. A suplex—more a wrestling throw than one from judo. Adonis arced over me like the last car on a rollercoaster, his arms and legs splayed at demented angles. His neck and shoulders took the impact and his legs rocketed over his head to the floor from the momentum the throw had generated.

Had I elected to release my grip around his waist, he would have done a complete somersault. I maintained the grip instead, and his feet flopped back to the floor, putting him on his back. I grabbed his face with my left hand and used it to simultaneously shove his head back and scramble from behind him. I rose up on my right knee, tensed my hips, and smashed down on his exposed throat with my right forearm, getting my weight behind the blow. I felt the crunch of systemic breakage—the thyroid and cricoid cartilage, probably the spinous process, as well. His hands flew to his throat and his body convulsed.

I stood and stepped away from him. The crowd was now silent.

His neck began to swell from a hematoma induced by the fractures. His legs kicked and scrabbled and he rolled from side to side. His face blued and contorted above his frantic fingers. Nobody made any move to help him. Not that they could have. After a few seconds his body started to shudder in odd spasms, as though he was being shocked. A few seconds later, the shuddering stopped.

Someone cried out, *"Yatta!"* I won!, and the room reverberated with a chorus of cheers. The crowd converged on me. People slapped my back and grabbed my hands to shake them. I was uncomfortably aware that one of Adonis's friends might use the moment to try to put a knife in me, but there was nothing I could do.

I heard Washio's voice: *"Hora, sagatte, sagatte. Ikisasete yare!"* Come on now, come on now, let him breathe! He and a few of the bouncers moved close to me and started to push the crowd back.

Someone handed me a towel and I wiped my face. The crowd eased away. I looked around and saw stacks of ten-thousand-yen notes changing hands.

Murakami stepped into the circle. He was smiling.

"Yokuyatta zo," he said. Good job.

I dropped the towel. "Where's my money?"

He reached into his breast pocket and took out a thick envelope. He opened it so I could see that it was stuffed with ten-thousand-yen notes, then closed it and returned it to his pocket.

"It's yours," he said. "I'll give it to you later." He looked around. "Some of these people, they might try to rob you for it."

"Give it to me now," I said.

"Later."

Fuck the money, I thought. I was glad just to be alive.

I started moving toward where I had left my jacket, shirt, and shoes. The crowd parted respectfully before me. A few random hands slapped my shoulders.

Murakami followed. "The money is yours. I want one more thing before I give it to you."

"Fuck you." I pulled on my shirt and started buttoning it.

He laughed. "Okay, okay." He took out the envelope and tossed it to me.

I caught it two-handed and glanced inside. It looked about right. I shoved it in a pants pocket and continued buttoning my shirt.

"The extra thing I wanted," he said, "was to tell you how you can make ten, twenty times what's in that envelope."

I looked at him.

"You interested?"

"I'm listening."

He shook his head. "Not here. Let's go somewhere we can celebrate." He smiled. "My treat."

I stepped into my shoes and knelt to lace them. "What did you have in mind?"

"A little place I own. You'll enjoy it."

I considered. A "celebration" with Murakami would afford me the opportunity to collect additional intel for Tatsu. I didn't see any real downside.

"All right," I said.

Murakami smiled.

Two guys were zipping Adonis into a body bag. *Christ,* I thought, *they really come prepared.* They loaded him onto a gurney and wheeled him toward the door. On the underside of the gurney was a stack of metal plates. One of the guys was carrying a length of chain, and I realized they were going to weight the body and dump it in one of the surrounding canals.

The next fight went for a long time. The fighters were conservative and seemed to have implicitly agreed not to employ potentially lethal or disfiguring techniques. After about ten minutes, Murakami said to me, "This isn't worth watching. Let's go."

He motioned to his bodyguards, and the four of us walked outside. Washio saw us leaving and bowed.

A black Mercedes S-Class with darkened windows was parked at the curb. One of the guards opened the rear door for us. A dog was curled up on the back seat. A white pit bull, its ears clipped short, its body roped with thick muscle. It had been fitted with a heavy leather muzzle, beyond the edges of which were fissures and scars that told me I was looking at one of Murakami's fighting animals. The beast looked at me as though sighting down the barrel of its own muzzled snout, and I thought I saw the canine equivalent of insanity in its slightly bloodshot eyes. Well, they say dogs come to resemble their masters.

Murakami motioned for me to get in. "Don't worry," he said. "He's okay as long as he's muzzled."

"Why don't you go first, just the same," I said.

He laughed and slid in. The dog moved to make way for him. I got in and the guard closed the door. He and the other guy took the front. We rode north on Kaigan-dori, to Sakura-dori, and then to Gaienhigashi-dori in Roppongi. No one spoke. The dog eyeballed me ceaselessly during the ride.

When we crossed Roppongi-dori I started to wonder. As we neared Aoyama-dori I knew.

We were going to Damask Rose.

CHAPTER 11

Any lingering attempts to rationalize that Harry had just gotten lucky with a hostess disappeared. The air-conditioned interior of the Benz felt suddenly warm.

But I had a more immediate problem than Harry. The last time I'd been to Damask Rose, I'd been using English, posing as an American citizen who spoke secondhand Japanese. I'd also been using a different name. I needed to decide how to handle this.

As the Benz pulled up to the club, I said, "Ah, good place."

"You've been here?" Murakami asked.

"Just once. The girls are beautiful."

His lips parted in a smile and the overly white bridge appeared between them. "They should be. I select them."

The driver opened the passenger-side door and we got out. The dog stayed, watching me with its hungry, demon eyes until the driver had closed the door and the dark glass separated us.

The Nigerians were gauntleting the entranceway. They bowed obsequiously low for Murakami and breathed *"Irasshaimase"* in unison. The one on the right spoke into his lapel mike.

We walked down the steps. The ruddy-faced man I had seen there last time looked up. He saw Murakami and swallowed.

"Ah, Murakami-san, good evening," he said in Japanese with a low bow. "It is always a pleasure to have you here. Is there anyone special you would like to see tonight?"

A thin band of sweat had broken out on his brow. His full attention was on Murakami and he had taken no notice of me.

Murakami looked around the room. Several of the girls smiled at him. I gathered they were already acquainted. "Yukiko," he said.

Harry, I thought.

Mr. Ruddy nodded and turned to me. *"Okyakusama?"* he asked. And you? That he used Japanese indicated he hadn't remembered me from the last time, when our exchange had been in English.

"Is Naomi here tonight?" I asked, also in Japanese. If she were here, I wanted to see her right away, when I would have a marginally better chance of taking control of the conversation. If things went badly, at least it wouldn't look as though I'd been trying to avoid her.

Mr. Ruddy's eyes might have narrowed slightly in recollection of someone who had asked for Naomi some weeks earlier. I wasn't sure.

He bowed his head. "I will bring her to you."

I had already decided on a cover story, should Naomi comment on my name change or other inconsistencies: I was married, and didn't want to take any chances on this sort of nocturnal foray getting back to my wife. My use of cash rather than credit cards would be consistent with such a story. Not the world's best explanation, but I had to have something to say if she noticed the disparities.

Mr. Ruddy took two menus and escorted us into the main room, pausing first to whisper to a girl I recognized as Elsa from the last time I'd been there. Elsa touched another girl, Emi, on the arm.

He walked us to a corner table. Murakami and I took adjacent seats, both facing the entrance. I watched Emi walk over to another table, where Yukiko was entertaining another customer. Emi sat and spoke into Yukiko's ear. A moment later Yukiko stood and excused herself. Elsa was repeating the scene at the table Naomi was working. Very smooth.

Yukiko walked over, her mouth stretching into a feline grin at the sight of Murakami. Naomi followed a moment later. She was wearing another elegant black cocktail dress, this one silk, fitted at the waist but loose above it. The diamond bracelet glittered on her left wrist as before.

She saw me, and her expression started to break into a smile that aborted itself when her eyes shifted from my face to Murakami's. She must have known him, and, based on the story I had told her, obviously didn't expect to see us together. She was trying to process the incongruity, certainly. But the suddenness of her change of expression told me there was more. She was scared.

Yukiko sat next to Murakami and across from me. She looked at me for a long moment, then briefly at Murakami, then back at me. Her lips moved in the barest hint of a cool smile. Murakami stared at her as though waiting for more, but she ignored him. I felt a tension building and thought, *Don't play with this guy. He could go off.* Then she turned her eyes to him again and permitted him a smile that said, *I was only teasing you, darling. Don't be such a child.*

The tension dropped away. I thought that if anyone had a measure of control over the creature sitting next to me, it was probably this woman.

Naomi took the remaining seat. *"Hisashiburi desu ne,"* I said to her. It's been a while.

"Un, so desu ne," she replied, her expression now neutral. Yes, it has. She might have thought it odd that I was now using Japanese when the other night I had insisted on English. But perhaps I was only deferring to our other companions.

"You know each other," Murakami interjected in Japanese. "Good. Arai-san, this is Yukiko."

Naomi gave no indication of having noticed my new name.

"Hajimemashite," Yukiko said. She continued in Japanese, "I remember seeing you here a few weeks ago."

I bowed my head slightly and returned her salutation. "And I remember you. You're a wonderful dancer."

She cocked her head to the side. "You look different, somehow."

My American and Japanese personalities are distinct, and I carry myself differently depending on which language I'm using and which mode I'm in. Probably it was this, as much as his nervousness in Murakami's presence, that had caused Mr. Ruddy not to remember me. Yukiko was responding to the difference but unsure of what to make of it.

I ran my fingers through my hair as though to straighten it. "I just came from a workout," I said.

Murakami chuckled. "You sure did."

A waitress came over. She set down four *oshibori,* hot washcloths with which we would wipe our hands and perhaps our faces to refresh ourselves, and a variety of small snacks. The arrangement completed, she looked at Murakami and, apparently knowing his preferences, asked, "Bombay Sapphire?" He nodded curtly and indicated that Yukiko would have the same.

The waitress looked at me. *"Okyakusama?"* she asked.

I turned to Naomi. "The Springbank?" I asked. She nodded and I ordered two.

The vibrant half Latina that had emerged the other night had retracted like a turtle into its shell. What would she be thinking? *New name, new Japanese persona, new* yakuza *pal.* All fodder for conversation, but she was saying nothing.

Why? If I'd run into her in the street, the first thing she would have said would have been, "What are you doing back in Tokyo?" If I had used a different name, surely she would have commented on that. And if she heard me speaking in unaccented, native Japanese, of course she would have said, "I thought you said you were more comfortable with English?"

So her reticence was situation-specific. I thought of the fear I had detected when her eyes had first alighted on Murakami. It was him. She was afraid of saying or doing something that would draw his attention.

The last time I had seen her, I had the sense that she knew more than she was willing to say. Her reaction to Murakami confirmed my suspicion. And, if she were inclined to give me away, she already would have done it. That she had failed to do so created a shared secret. It made her complicit. Something I could exploit.

Yukiko picked up an *oshibori* and used it to wipe Murakami's hands, cool as an animal handler grooming a lion. Naomi handed me mine.

"Arai-san is a friend of mine," Murakami said, looking at me and then at the girls and smiling his bridged smile. "Please be good to him."

Yukiko smiled deeply into my eyes as if to say *If we were alone, I would take suuuch good care of you.* In my peripheral vision, I saw Murakami catch the look and frown.

I wouldn't want to be on the wrong end of this bastard's jealousy, I thought, imagining Harry.

The waitress came and put the drinks on the table. Murakami drained his in a single draught. Yukiko followed suit.

"Ii yo," Murakami growled. Good. Yukiko set her glass down with practiced delicacy. Murakami looked at her. She returned the look, something almost theatrically nonchalant in her expression. The look went on for a long moment. Then he grinned and grabbed her hand.

"Okawari," he called to the waitress. Two more drinks. He pulled Yukiko to her feet and away from the table. I watched him lead her to a room to the side of one of the dance stages.

"What was that?" I asked Naomi in Japanese.

She was looking at me. Warily, I thought.

"A lap dance," she said.

"They seem to know each other well."

"Yes."

I looked around. The adjacent tables were filled with parties of Japanese men in standard *sarariiman* attire. Even with the ambient noise, they were too close to permit a private conversation.

I leaned closer to Naomi. "I didn't expect to be back here," I said softly.

She winced. "I'm glad you came."

I didn't know what to make of the inconsistency between her reaction and her words. "You must have a lot of questions," I said.

She shook her head. "I just want to make sure you enjoy yourself tonight."

"I think I know why you're acting this way," I started to say.

She cut me off with a suddenly raised hand. "How about that lap dance?" she asked. Her tone was inviting, but her eyes were somewhere between serious and angry.

I looked at her, trying to gauge what she was up to, then said, "Sure."

We walked to the same room that Murakami and Yukiko had gone to a few minutes earlier. Another Nigerian was waiting just inside the entrance. He bowed and pulled aside a high-backed, semicircular sofa. A matching unit was positioned on the other side of it. We stepped inside and the Nigerian pushed the front half closed behind us. We were now enclosed in a circular, upholstered compartment.

Naomi gestured to the cushioned sofa seat. I lowered myself onto it, watching her face.

She stepped back, her eyes on mine. Her hands went to her back and I heard the sound of a zipper. Then her right hand moved to the left strap of her dress and began to ease it over the smooth skin of her shoulder.

There was a sudden buzz in my pocket.

Son of a bitch. Harry's bug detector.

Continuous, intermittent, continuous. Meaning both audio and video.

I was careful not to look around or do anything else that might have seemed suspicious. I opened my mouth to say something to her, something any other excited beneficiary of an incipient lap dance might utter. But she made a face—half scowl, half exasperation—that stopped me. She raised a subtle index finger from the strap of her dress to the ceiling. Then she cocked her head slightly and shifted her finger to her ear.

I got the message. People were listening, and watching.

Not just here. At the table, too. That's why her responses had been so odd. She couldn't warn me there.

And why she had looked angry tonight, I realized. Was I just the American accountant I had claimed to be, or at least a neutral party? If so, silence would be her safest course. Was I involved with Murakami, who frightened her? If so, silence, and certainly a warning like the one she had just given me, would be dangerous. I had inadvertently forced her to choose.

But the detector hadn't buzzed at the table. Then I realized: Murakami. If the tables were monitored, they knew to turn off the equipment when the boss was around. Those would be the rules, and I imagined no one would want a guy like Murakami finding out the rules weren't being followed. And the last time I'd been here, the device hadn't been charged yet. That's why it hadn't warned me then.

I reached into my pocket to switch off the unit, nodding to indicate I understood.

She finished moving the strap away and slipped her arm through it, then slowly performed the identical action on the opposite side. She crossed her arms. Her nostrils were flaring slightly with her breathing. She paused for a moment. Then, still scowling, her body rigid, she moved her arms to her sides. The dress slid down, past her breasts, past her belly, gathering in black ripples at her waist.

"You can touch with your hands," she said. "Only above the waist."

I stood, keeping my eyes on hers. I leaned forward and put my mouth to her ear. "Thanks for the warning," I whispered.

"Don't thank me," she whispered back. "It's not as though you left me any choice."

"I'm not with these people."

"No? You were fighting tonight, weren't you?"

"Why do you say that?"

"Your face is scratched. And I understood Murakami's joke about your 'workout.'"

Adonis must have dented me a little. I hadn't even noticed.

"You know about those fights?" I asked.

"Everyone knows about them. The fighters come in here afterward and brag. Sometimes they act like we're deaf."

"I wasn't there voluntarily. I work out at a *dojo,* some people invited me to a fight. I didn't know what it was all about. Turned out I wasn't there to eat. I was supposed to be the main course."

"Too bad for you," she whispered.

"If you think I'm with these people," I said, "why are you talking to me now? Why did you warn me about the listening devices?"

"Because I'm as stupid as you are." She took a step back and looked at me, her hands on her hips, her chin high. She raised her eyebrows and smiled. "Are you afraid to touch me?"

I watched her face. What I wanted was information, not a damn lap dance.

"You're afraid even to look?" she asked, her smile taunting.

I held her eyes for another moment, then let my gaze go south.

"You like what you see?" she asked.

"It's okay," I said after a moment, though in fact it was better than that. Much better.

She turned around and pushed back against me, leaning forward slightly as she did so, molding the back of her body to the front of mine.

I realized suddenly that this was a game I could only lose.

She put her hands on her knees and moved her hips from side to side. The friction from her ass assumed a prominent place in my consciousness.

"You like that?" she asked, looking over her shoulder.

"It's okay," I said again, my voice lower this time, and she laughed.

"It feels like you like it better than 'okay,' no?"

"I want to talk to you," I said. I noticed I had put my hands on her hips. I removed them.

"So talk," she said, pressing into me harder. "Say anything you like."

She was trying to divert me. She didn't want to talk and I didn't know how to make her.

She arched her back and pushed her ass higher. A shadow formed like a dark pool in the cleft of her lower spine.

"Anything you like," she said again.

The shadow waxed and waned in time to her movements.

"Cut it out, damn it," I whispered. My hands were on her hips again.

"But you like it," she cooed. "I like it, too."

Disengage, I thought. But my hands stayed put. They were moving now. I watched them as though from afar. The sound of fabric against flesh was loud in the enclosure.

She's playing you, I thought.

Then: *The hell with it. You're supposed to be acting like an ordinary customer, anyway.*

I dropped to one knee, sliding my hands down to the backs of her thighs as I did so, then stood again, my hands sweeping the dress upward en route. She was wearing a black thong. The dress dangled slightly above it, gathered at her lower back. I gripped the dress in one hand like a bridle and took hold of her ass with the other.

"Only above the waist," she said, smiling over her shoulder, her cool voice in counterpoint to the heat in my head and gut. "Or I have to call the doorman."

I felt a surge of anger. *Let it go,* I thought. *Just get out of here. Like you should have before this bullshit began.*

I removed my hand from her ass and took a step back, but my anger got the better of me. Still gripping the dress with one hand, I swiveled my hips in and delivered a hard spank to her exposed right cheek. There was a loud *slap!* and she yelped, jerking away from me as though from an electric shock.

She spun and faced me, one hand on her wounded posterior. Her eyes were wide, her nostrils flared with shock and anger. In my peripheral vision, I saw her weight shift to her back leg, and thought she was going to try for a ball shot with her forward foot.

Instead, she stepped back. Her arms slipped to her sides and she drew up her shoulders and chin, the picture of suppressed regal rage. She looked at me.

"Mo owari, okyakusama?" she asked, as contemptuously as she could. Are we finished, honorable customer?

"Was that against the rules?" I asked, smiling into her eyes.

She pulled up the dress and slipped her arms through the straps. Her face was still red with anger, and I couldn't help admiring her composure in controlling it. She managed the zipper without assistance, then said, "That was three songs, so thirty thousand yen. And you should tip the doorman ten percent. Ken?"

Ken must have been the Nigerian, because a second later the semicircular sofa was pulled aside and there he was. I took out my billfold and paid each of them.

"Thank you," I said to Naomi. I beamed like a well-satisfied customer. "That was... special."

She smiled back in a way that made me glad she didn't have a weapon. *"Kochira koso,"* she replied. The pleasure was mine.

She escorted me back to my seat. I switched on the unit en route. Murakami and Yukiko were waiting for us.

"Yokatta ka?" Murakami asked me, showing me the false teeth. Good?

"Maa na," I told him. Good enough.

He took Yukiko's hand and started moving away. "We'll discuss our business another time," he said.

"When?"

"Soon. I'll find you at the *dojo.*"

He didn't like to make appointments any more than I did. "Morning? Evening?" I asked.

"Morning. Soon." He turned to Naomi and said, "Take good care of him." Naomi bowed her head to show that she most certainly would.

Murakami and Yukiko left. A minute later the detector started buzzing—continuous, so audio only. I'd been right about the house rules.

Naomi and I made small talk for a few minutes for the benefit of the microphones. Her tone was cool and correct. I knew our little encounter hadn't turned out quite the way she had planned, but she had managed to distract me from my questions, which was what she had really been after. Probably she was telling herself the fight had been a draw, that she could settle for that.

She didn't know it had only been round one.

I told her I was bushed and had to go. "Come back anytime," she said with a sarcastic smile.

"For another one of those lap dances?" I asked, returning the smile. "Absolutely."

I walked up the stairs and out onto Gaienhigashi-dori. When I got to the street a horn tooted. It was Yukiko, driving by in a white BMW M3, Murakami in the passenger seat. She waved, then disappeared onto Aoyama-dori.

It was just past one in the morning. The club closed at three. Naomi would be heading home at some point thereafter.

I'd done the computer check. I knew where home was. The Lion's Gate Building, Azabu Juban 3-chome.

The trains had already stopped running. I doubted she'd have a car: keeping one in the city is too expensive and the trains go everywhere, anyway. Getting home would mean a taxi.

I took a cab to Azabu Juban subway station, then walked around 3-chome until I found her building. Standard upscale apartment *manshon*, tan ferroconcrete, new and spiffy looking. Straightforward front entrance with double glass doors, electronically controlled. Security camera mounted on the ceiling just inside the glass.

The building was on the corner of a one-way street. I moved to the back, where I found a secondary entrance—smaller, more discreet than the first, something only residents would use. This one had no camera.

The second access point complicated things. If I waited at the wrong entrance, I would miss her entirely.

I considered. All these streets were one-way—one of Azabu Juban's trademarks. If she were coming from Damask Rose, the cab would have to pass the second entrance first. Most likely she would get out there. Even if the cab continued around to the front, though, I'd have time to dash around behind it and get to her before she went inside.

Okay. I looked around for the right place. Ordinarily, when I'm setting someone up, I try for maximum concealment and surprise. But that's prior to a fatal encounter. Here, I was hoping just to talk. If I scared her too much, made her feel too vulnerable, she would just run inside and that would be the end of it.

There was a perpendicular side street that led to where I was standing, dead-ending just to the side of the second entrance to her building. I walked down it. There was an awning on the side of the building to my left, under the shadow of which were stacked several large plastic garbage bins. I could wait in those shadows quietly, and even someone walking right past me would be unlikely to notice.

I checked my watch. Almost two. I killed time walking around the neighborhood. I passed no more than a half-dozen people. By three the area would be almost completely deserted.

I thought about what I'd seen at the club earlier. I knew from Tatsu that Yamaoto relied in part on blackmail and extortion to run his network of compliant politicians. Tatsu had told me the disk Midori's father had taken from Yamaoto contained, among other things, video of politicians in compromising positions. Tatsu had also told me Yamaoto and Murakami were connected. So it seemed likely that Damask Rose was one of the places at which Yamaoto went about capturing politicians in the midst of embarrassing acts.

Meaning someone in Yamaoto's network now had my face on film. That would have been bad under any circumstances. But Murakami's new interest made things worse. I judged it probable that Murakami might show the video to someone as part of a further background check. He might even show it to Yamaoto, who knew my face. And I'd used the weightlifter's name as an introduction to Murakami's *dojo*. If they figured out whom they were actually dealing with, they'd also figure out that the weightlifter's "accident" had been anything but.

I tried to put together the rest of it. Yukiko, meaning someone higher up at Damask Rose, meaning perhaps Yamaoto, was trying to get hooks into Harry. If they were interested in Harry, it would only be because Harry might lead them to me.

What about the Agency? They'd been following Harry. According to Kanezaki, as a conduit to me. The question was, were Yamaoto and the CIA working together in some capacity, or was their interest merely convergent? If the former, what was the nature of the connection? If the latter, what was the nature of the interest?

Naomi might be able to help me answer these questions, if I played it right. I needed to resolve things quickly, too. Even if Harry's relevance to these people was only as a means of getting close to me, he could still be in danger. And if Murakami figured out that Arai Katsuhiko was really John Rain, both Harry and I were going to have a significant problem on our hands.

At just before three, it started raining. I walked quickly back to her apartment and took my position in the shadows near her building. I was out of the rain under the awning, but it was getting chilly. My leg ached from where Adonis had kicked me. I stretched to stay limber.

At 3:20, a cab turned onto the street. I watched it from the shadows until it passed me. There, in back, Naomi.

The cab turned left and stopped just beyond the secondary entrance to the building. The automatic passenger door opened a crack and the dome light went on. I saw Naomi hand some bills to the driver, who returned change. The door swung wide and she stepped out. She was wearing a black, thigh-length coat, and she pulled it close around her. The door shut and the cab sped away.

She opened the umbrella and started toward the entrance. I stepped from under the awning. "Naomi," I said quietly.

She spun around and I heard her inhale sharply. "What the hell?" she exclaimed in her Portuguese-accented English.

I raised my hands, palms forward. "I just want to talk to you." I used English because it was the language of the persona she'd initially met me in—the one she had initially trusted.

She looked over her shoulder for a moment, perhaps gauging the distance to her door, then turned back to me, apparently reassured. "I don't want to talk to you." She emphasized the first and last words of the sentence, her accent thickening somewhat in her agitation.

"You don't have to if you don't want to. I'm just asking, that's all."

She looked around again. She had good danger instincts. Most people, perceiving a threat, give it their full focus. That makes them easy prey if the threat was a feint and the real ambush comes from the flank.

"How do you know where I live?" she asked.

"I looked it up on the Internet."

"Really? You think with this kind of job I'd just list my address?"

I shrugged. "You gave me your email address. With a little information to start with, you'd be surprised what you can find out."

Her eyes narrowed. "Are you a stalker?"

I shook my head. "No."

It was starting to rain harder. I realized that, some physical discomfort aside, the weather hadn't been such bad luck. She was dry and poised under her umbrella; I was wet and almost shivering. The contrast would help her feel more in control.

"Am I in trouble?" she asked.

That surprised me. "What kind of trouble?"

"I didn't do anything wrong. I'm not involved with anything, I'm just a dancer, okay?"

I didn't know where she was going, but I didn't want to stop her. "You're not involved?" I parroted.

"I'm not involved! And I don't want to be. I mind my own business."

"You're not in trouble, at least not with me. I really just want to talk with you."

"Give me one good reason why."

"Because you trust me."

Her expression was caught between amused and incredulous. "I trust you?"

I nodded. "You warned me about the listening devices in the club."

She closed her eyes for a moment. "Jesus Christ, I knew I was going to regret that."

"But you knew you would regret it more if you had said nothing."

She was shaking her head slowly, deliberately. I knew what she was thinking: *I do this guy a favor, now I can't get rid of him. And he's trouble, trouble I don't want.*

I pushed dripping hair back from my forehead. "Can we go someplace?"

She looked left, then right. The street was empty.

"All right," she said. "Let's get a taxi. I know a place that's open late. We can talk there."

We found a cab. I got in first and she slid in behind me. She told the driver to take us to 3-3-5 Shibuya-ku, south side of Roppongi-dori. I smiled.

"Tantra?" I asked.

She looked at me, perhaps a little disappointed. "You know it?"

"It's been around for a long time. Good place."

"I didn't think you'd know it. You're a little... older."

I laughed. If she'd been trying to get a rise out of me, she had missed the mark. I'm never going to be sensitive about my age. Most of the people I knew when I was younger are already dead. That I'm still breathing is actually a point of pride.

"Tantra is like sex," I told her, smiling a little indulgently. "Every generation thinks it's the one that discovered it."

She looked away and we drove in silence. I would have preferred to have the cab take us someplace within walking distance rather than to the actual address, per my usual practice. Given the overall circumstances of the evening, though, I judged the likelihood of a problem stemming from Naomi's lack of security consciousness to be manageably low.

A few minutes later we pulled up in front of a nondescript office building. I paid the driver and we got out. The rain had stopped but the street was empty, almost forlorn. If I hadn't known where we were, I would have thought it an odd place to get out of a cab in the middle of the night.

Behind us, a dimly lit "T" glowed softly above a basement stairwell, the only external sign of Tantra's existence. We moved down the steps, through a pair of imposing metal doors, and into a candlelit foyer that led like a short tunnel to the seating area beyond.

A waiter appeared and in a hushed tone asked whether it would be just the two of us. Naomi told him it would, and he escorted us inside.

The walls were brown concrete, the ceiling black. There were a few spotlights, but most of the illumination came from candles on tables and in the corners of the lacquered concrete floor. In alcoves here and there were statues depicting scenes from the Kama Sutra. Around us were a half-dozen small groups of people, all sitting on floor cushions or low chairs. The room hummed with murmured conversation and quiet laughter. Some sort of light, Arabic-sounding techno music issued softly from invisible speakers.

There were two additional rooms at the back, I knew, both partially concealed by heavy purple curtains. I asked the waiter whether either was available and he gestured to the one on the right. I looked at Naomi and she nodded.

We moved past the curtains into a room that was more like a small cave or opium den. The ceiling was low and candles played flickering shadows on the walls. We sat on floor cushions in the corner, at ninety degrees to each other. The waiter handed us a menu and departed without a word.

"You hungry?" I asked.

"Yes."

"Me, too." I rubbed my wet shoulders. "And cold."

The waiter returned. We ordered hot tea, their signature Ayu chips, and spring rolls. Naomi chose an eighteen-year-old Highland Park and I followed suit.

"How do you know about this place really?" Naomi asked when the waiter had departed.

"I told you, it's been around forever. Ten years, maybe more."

"So you live in Tokyo."

I paused. Then: "I did. Until recently."

"What brings you back?"

"I have a friend. He's in some kind of trouble with people from your club and doesn't even know it."

"What kind of trouble?"

"That's what I'm trying to find out."

"Why did you tell me that bullshit about being an accountant?"

I shrugged. "I was looking for information. I didn't see the need to tell you very much."

We were quiet for a few minutes. The waiter came by with the food and drinks. I went for the tea first. It warmed me considerably. The Highland Park was even better.

"I needed that," I said, leaning back against the wall, heat radiating from my gut.

She picked up a spring roll. "Have you really been to Brazil?" she asked.

"Yes." It was a lie, but perhaps the moral equivalent of the truth. I couldn't very well tell her I was learning all I could about the country in preparation for a first and permanent trip there.

She took a bite of the spring roll and chewed it, her head cocked slightly to the side as though in consideration of something. "Tonight, when I saw who you were with, I was thinking that maybe you learned a few lines of Portuguese just to get me to open up. That I was in some kind of trouble."

"No."

"So you weren't trying to meet me in particular."

"You were dancing when I came in that night, so I asked about you. It was just a coincidence."

"If you're not an American accountant, who are you?"

"I'm someone who… performs services for people from time to time. Those services put me in touch with a lot of different players in the society. Cops and yakuza. Politicians. Sometimes people on the fringe."

"You have that on your business card?"

I smiled. "I tried it. The print was too small to read."

"You're what, a private detective?"

"In a way."

She looked at me. "Who are you working for now?"

"I told you, right now I'm just trying to help a friend."

"Forgive me, but that sounds like bullshit."

I nodded. "I can see where it would."

"You looked pretty comfortable with Murakami tonight."

"Did that bother you?"

"He scares me."

"He should."

She picked up her Highland Park and leaned back against the wall. "I've heard some bad stories about him."

"They're probably true."

"Everyone's afraid of him. Except for Yukiko."

"Why do you think that is?"

"I don't know. She has some kind of power over him. No one else does."

"You don't like her."

She glanced at me, then away. "She can be as scary as he is."

"You said she's comfortable doing things that you're not."

"Yes."

"Something to do with those listening devices?"

She upended her drink and finished it. Then she said, "I don't know for sure there are listening devices, but I think there are. We get a lot of prominent customers—politicians, bureaucrats, businessmen. The people who own the club encourage the girls to talk to them, to elicit information. All the girls think the conversations are taped. And there are rumors that certain customers even get videotaped in the lap dance rooms."

I was gaining her confidence. And the way she was talking now, I knew I could get more. A gambler will agonize for hours over whether to put his chips on, say, the red or the black, and then, when the croupier spins the wheel, he'll double or even triple the bet, as a way of bolstering his conviction that he must have been betting right. If he were betting wrong, why would he be putting all that extra money down?

I pointed to her glass. "Another?"

She hesitated for a moment, then nodded.

I finished mine and ordered two more. The walls flickered in the candlelight. The room felt close and warm, like an underground sanctuary.

The waiter brought the drinks. After he had moved silently away, I looked at her and said, "You're not involved in any of this?"

She looked into her glass. Several seconds went by.

"You want an honest answer, or a really honest answer?" she asked.

"Give me both."

"Okay," she said, nodding. "The honest answer is no."

She took a sip of the Highland Park. Closed her eyes.

"The really honest answer is, is…"

"Is, not yet," I said quietly.

Her eyes opened and she looked at me. "How do you know?"

I watched her for a moment, feeling her distress, seeing an opportunity.

"You're being suborned," I said. "It's a process, a series of techniques. If you even half realize it, you're smarter than most. You've also got a chance to do something about it, if you want to."

"What do you mean?"

I sipped from my glass, watching the amber liquid glowing in the candlelight, remembering. "You start slow. You find the subject's limits and get him to spend some time there. He gets used to it. Before long, the limits have moved. You never take him more than a centimeter beyond. You make it feel it's his choice."

I looked at her. "You told me when you first got to the club you were so shy you could hardly move on the stage."

"Yes, that's true."

"At that point you would never have done a lap dance."

"No."

"But now you can."

"Yes." Her voice was low, almost a whisper.

"When you did your first lap dance, you probably said you would never let a customer touch you."

"I did say that," she said. Her voice had gone lower.

"Of course you did. I could go on. I could tell you where you'll be three months from now, six months, a year. Twenty years, if you keep going where you're going. Naomi, you think this is all an accident? It's a science. There are people out there who are experts at getting others to do tomorrow what was unthinkable today."

But for her breath, moving rapidly in and out through her nostrils, she was silent, and I wondered if she was fighting tears.

I needed to push it just a little further before backing off. "You want to know what's next for you?" I asked.

She looked at me but said nothing.

"You know Damask Rose girls are being used to blackmail politicians, or something like that. The other girls whisper about it, but that's not all. You've been approached, right? It was an oblique approach, but it was there. Something like, 'There's a special customer we think would like you. We'd like you to go out with him and show him a really good time. If he's satisfied afterward, we'll pay you X.' Maybe they had a suite at a hotel where they wanted you to take him. They'd bug him there, videotape him. You refused, I guess. But there was no pressure. Why would there be? They know you'll get worn down just from the exposure."

"You're wrong!" she said suddenly, jabbing a finger in my face.

I looked at her. "If I were wrong, you wouldn't react that way."

She watched me, her eyes hurt and angry, her lips twisting together as though trying to find words.

That was enough. Time to see if my words had the desired effect.

"Hey," I said softly, but she didn't look up. "Hey." I put my hand over hers. "I'm sorry." I squeezed her fingers briefly, then withdrew my hand.

She raised her head and looked at me. "You think I'm a prostitute. Or that I'm going to become one."

"I don't think that," I said, shaking my head.

"How do you know all this?"

Time for an honest, but safely vague response. "A long time ago, and in a different context, I went through what you're in the middle of."

"What do you mean?"

For a moment I pictured Crazy Jake. I shook my head to show her it wasn't something I was willing to talk about.

We were quiet for a few moments. Then she said, "You were right. I wouldn't have reacted so sharply if what you were saying were untrue.

These are things I've been thinking about a lot, and I haven't been as honest with myself as you just were." She reached out and took my hand. She squeezed it hard. "Thank you."

I felt an odd confluence of emotions: satisfaction that my manipulation was working; sympathy because of what she was struggling with; self-reproach for taking advantage of her naiveté.

And beneath it all, I was still attracted to her. I was uncomfortably aware of the touch of her hand.

"Don't thank me," I said, not looking at her. I didn't squeeze back. After a moment she withdrew her hand.

"Are you really just trying to help a friend?" she asked.

"Yes."

"I would help you if I could. But I don't know any more than what I've already told you."

I nodded, thinking of the Agency and Yamaoto, wondering about the connection. "Let me ask you something," I said. "How many Caucasians do you see at the club?"

She shrugged. "A fair number. Maybe ten, twenty percent of the customers. Why?"

"Have you ever seen Murakami spending time with them?"

She shook her head. "No."

"How about Yukiko?"

"Not really. Her English is pretty bad."

Inconclusive. She didn't know anything. I was starting to doubt that she'd be of much help after all.

I looked at my watch. It was almost five. The sun would be coming up soon.

"We should get going," I said.

She nodded. I paid the bill and we left.

Outside it was damp but not raining. The lamplights on Roppongi-dori created glowing cones of slowly swirling mist. It was as late as it could get without getting early, and the street was momentarily silent.

"Walk me home?" she asked, looking at me.

I nodded. "Sure."

Halfway through the twenty-minute walk it started raining again.

Droga! she swore in Portuguese. "I left the umbrella at Tantra."

Shoganai, I said, turning up the collar of my blazer. What can you do.

We walked faster. It started to rain harder. I brushed my fingers through my hair and felt rivulets trickling down the back of my neck.

With about half a kilometer to go, a huge crack of thunder rang out and it really started pouring.

"Que merda!" she exclaimed with a laugh. "We're doomed!"

We ran for it, but to no real avail. We got to her apartment and ducked under the overhang in front of the rear entranceway. *"Meu Deus,"* she said, laughing, "I haven't gotten drenched like that in forever!" She unbuttoned her dripping coat, then looked at me and smiled. "Once you're already wet, it's actually kind of nice."

Wisps of vapor were rising off her damp dress. "You're steaming," I observed.

She glanced down, then back at me. She pushed a few strands of clinging hair back from her face. "That run made me warm," she said.

I wiped water from my face and thought, *Time to go.*

But I remained.

"Thanks for an interesting evening," she said, after a pause. "You're not a bad guy, for a stalker."

I gave her a half smile. "That's what people tell me."

There was an odd moment of quiet. Then she stepped in close and hugged me, her face against my shoulder.

I was surprised. My arms moved reflexively around her.

Just a little comfort, I thought. *You were rough on her before. Let her go feeling good.*

I was distantly aware that this sounded like a rationalization. It troubled me vaguely. Ordinarily, I get along well without.

I could feel her soft shape, the heat of her, conducted with electric clarity through the wet of our clothes.

I felt my body responding. I knew she felt it, too. *Ah, shit.*

She lifted her head from my shoulder. Her mouth was very close to my ear. "Come inside," she whispered.

The last person I'd gotten involved with when I should have treated her only as an asset was Midori. I was still paying the price on that one.

Don't be stupid again, I thought. *Don't get too close. Don't blur the line.*

But the thoughts were disconnected. No one seemed to be listening.

She's a bargirl. You don't know where her loyalties lie.

That one was unconvincing. No one had directed her against me—I was the one who had been pursuing her. She hadn't needed to warn me about the bugs. My gut told me she wasn't dissembling.

She put a hand on my chest. "You haven't... been with someone for a long time," she said.

I reminded myself this was part of the reason I've lived so long.

"Why do you say that?" I asked.

"I can tell. The way you look at me."

Her hand pressed closer. "I can feel your heart," she said.

Between her hand over my heart and her hips at my crotch, she might as well have been administering a polygraph.

I looked out at the street beyond the overhang. The rain was coming in at gray angled streaks. One of my hands moved to her cheek. I closed my eyes. Her skin was wet from the rain and I thought of tears.

She lifted her head and I felt the side of her face settle against mine. Her head moved up and down just slightly, as though in time to some music I could almost hear. I kept my eyes closed, thinking *Don't do it, don't be stupid.*

I could hear my own breath, flowing through my mouth, moving past my tongue and teeth.

I started to pull back, sliding my wet cheek past hers. She moved one of her hands to the back of my neck and stopped me.

I shifted my head slightly. The corners of our mouths brushed together. I felt her breath on my cheek.

Then we were kissing. Her mouth was warm and soft. Our tongues entwined and simultaneously I thought *Oh, you fucking idiot* and *Oh, that feels so good.*

My hands found their way inside her coat to her waist. She took my face between her palms and kissed me harder.

I squeezed her hips, then ran my hands up and over the curve of her ribs to her breasts. Her nipples were hard under the wet fabric of her dress. Her body radiated heat. I heard myself groan. It sounded like capitulation.

She stepped back and fumbled in her purse. She pulled out a key and looked at me, her eyes dark, her breathing heavy.

"Come inside," she said.

She turned and put her key in the lock. The door slid open and we went in.

We kept kissing in the elevator on the brief ride to the fifth floor. On the way down the corridor we were pulling at each other's clothes.

We moved inside her apartment, into a foyer at the end of a short hallway. There was a living area beyond. Everything was dimly illuminated by the reflected gray light of the street without.

She closed the door behind me and pushed me back against it. She started kissing me again, hungrily, her hands unbuttoning my shirt. Ordinarily I don't get comfortable in a place until I've had a chance to look around it, but the narrow hallway, with Naomi between me and any potential attackers, wouldn't have worked well for an ambush. I didn't pick up any danger vibes, at least not of those kind. And Harry's bug and video detector was blessedly quiescent.

I eased her coat off her shoulders and let it fall behind her. She kissed my neck, my chest, while her fingers worked on my belt and pants. I reached around and undid the zipper at the back of her dress. I moved the straps off her shoulders and the dress slipped soundlessly to the floor. I felt her kick off her shoes.

She pushed my blazer back, but the wet material clung to me. I shrugged out of it and pulled off my shirt. She put a warm hand against my belly for a moment as though to freeze me in that position. I felt the diamond bracelet, a small cold circle around her wrist. Then she reached lower and started to ease my pants down. I stopped her so I could get my shoes and socks off first. Pants-pooled-at-the-ankles is too helpless a posture for me.

I stepped out of my pants and undershorts and kicked them aside. She pushed me back against the door again, circled her arms around my lower back, and pulled us tightly together. Her breasts and belly pressed against me, warm and soft and insanely inviting, and at that instant I didn't care what this was all going to cost me. What it might cost her.

I took her face gently in both my hands and eased her head back slightly. I looked into her eyes. In the dim light of the hall they seemed to have their own quiet luminescence.

Her hands dropped to my hips and she lowered herself in front of me. I watched her, breathing faster now. The door was cold on my naked back and then her mouth engulfed me and for a moment I couldn't feel anything else.

One of her hands rose to my belly and I took it in mine, then let it go. My head dropped back against the door with a quiet thump. Some stray hair brushed against my thigh. I could feel every strand of it, as though I'd been stroked with hot filament.

One of my hands drifted down and traced the edge of her ear, the curve of her cheek, the line of her jaw. I exhaled hard, tightening my abdomen until there was nothing left in my lungs, then breathed in sharply through my nose.

I dipped my fingers under her chin and tried to draw her upward.

She tilted her head back and looked up at me. "I want to finish," she said.

I stooped, placed my hands on her upper ribs, and raised her to her feet. I slipped one arm behind her neck and the other under her ass, stepped forward, and scooped her up. She laughed in surprise and clasped her arms around my neck.

"There's something I want to finish," I told her.

The living room was attached to a small kitchen and an only slightly larger bedroom. I headed toward the latter. I was dimly aware of my hard-on swaying before me like some absurd blind man's cane as I walked.

There was a futon on the floor just inside the bedroom doorway. I stepped onto it and gently set her down on her back. She slipped her arms from around my neck, her palms brushing past my ears and face. I reached down with both hands and eased the thong over the flat of her pelvis. She raised her hips and the garment moved over the curve of her ass. I pulled it past her ankles and tossed it aside.

I put my hands on the futon on either side of her and kissed her throat, her breasts, her belly. I made my way to the creases of her thighs. She grabbed a fistful of hair at the back of my head and pulled hard enough to make it hurt, but I made her wait longer before I gave her what she wanted.

When I did, she exhaled sharply and tightened her grip on my hair. I drew my knees up and took her ass in both hands, raising it off the futon. I heard her say "*Isso, isso, continua,*" felt her other hand move to the back of my neck. I glanced up. Her stomach muscles were clenched tight, her breasts trembling slightly from the action of my head and hands.

I took my time with her. She tasted clean and salty and sweet. Her fingers ran through my hair, sometimes grabbing, sometimes pulling, in time to the way I was touching her. I didn't rush it, even when the pressure from her hands urged me faster.

I heard her say, *"Isso"* again, over and over. Her legs rose behind me and tightened across my ears, and her voice was suddenly far away, reaching me as though from underwater. Her legs tensed further, her knuckles dug into my scalp. Then her body slowly unwound and sound came back into the room.

I lowered her back to the futon and looked at her. The gray light of the room had grown a shade brighter. It picked up the green in her eyes, and without thinking I said, "You're beautiful."

She reached up and took my face in her hands. *"Agora, venha aqui,"* she said in Portuguese. Come here.

I went to her. She reached down for me but I found my own way in.

I slid my hands under her arms and around to her face. I dipped my head forward and closed my eyes, the way I had once been taught to pray. I felt her lips against my face, mouthing silent words.

A minute went by, maybe two. Our movement together, back and forth, gradually slowed, like waves advancing and receding on a beach. More than that and I knew I was done.

She arched her head up to mine and the kiss quickened. I felt a sensation, like purring or a low growl, across her lips and tongue.

"Agora, mete tudo," she said, her mouth moving against mine. Now, everything now.

She pushed against me, not holding anything back. I held her face in my hands and kissed her harder. She raised her knees and I felt her thighs and ankles sliding against my hips. We moved faster. She locked her legs around my back and moaned something in Portuguese. My back arched and my toes dug into the futon, and I let myself go with a long *kussouu* that sounded as much like pain as pleasure.

The strength flowed out of my body and I felt suddenly heavy. I lay down on the futon beside her, facing her, my hand resting lightly on her belly.

"Isso, foi otimo," she said, turning her head to me. That was delicious. I smiled. *"Otimo,"* I repeated. My limbs felt jellified.

She covered my hand with hers and squeezed my fingers. We were quiet for a moment. Then she said, "Can I ask you something?"

I looked at her. "Sure."

"Why were you so reluctant, at first? I could tell you wanted to. And you knew I wanted to."

I closed my eyes for a moment, flirting with sleep. "Maybe I was afraid."

"Afraid of what?"

"I'm not sure."

"I'm the one who should have been afraid. When you said you had something you wanted to finish, I half thought you were going to try to spank me again."

I smiled, my eyes still closed. "I would have, if you'd deserved it."

"I would have made you sorry."

"You didn't. You made me happy."

She laughed. "Good. You still haven't told me what you were afraid of."

I thought for a moment. Drowsiness was settling on me like a blanket.

"Of getting involved. Like you said, I haven't been with someone for a long time."

She laughed again. "How can we be involved? I don't even know who you are."

With an effort, I opened my eyes. I looked at her. "You know better than most," I said.

"Maybe that's what scares you," she replied.

If I stayed any longer I would fall asleep. I sat up and ran a hand over my face.

"It's okay," she said. "I know you have to go."

She was right, of course. "Yeah?" I asked.

"Yeah." She paused. Then: "I'd like to see you again. But not at the club."

"That makes sense," I said, my mind having defaulted to its usual security setting. She furrowed her brow at my response. I saw my mistake, smiled, and tried to correct. "After tonight, I don't think I could respect that 'no below the waist' rule, anyway." She laughed at that, but the laughter wasn't entirely comfortable.

I used the bathroom, then made my way back to the foyer, where I pulled on my still wet clothes. They were cold and clinging.

She came over as I was lacing my shoes. She had combed her hair back and was wearing a dark flannel robe. She looked at me for a long moment.

"I'll try to help you," she said.

I told her the truth. "I don't know how much you can really do."

"I don't either. But I want to try. I don't want… I don't want to wind up someplace where I can't find my way back."

I nodded. "That's a good reason."

She reached into a pocket of the robe and pulled out a piece of paper. She extended her arm to hand it to me, and I noticed the diamond bracelet again. I reached out and took her wrist, softly.

"A gift?" I asked, curious.

She shook her head slowly. "It was my mother's," she said.

I took the paper and saw she had written a phone number on it. I put it in my pocket.

I gave her my pager number. I wanted her to have a way to contact me if something came up at the club.

I didn't say, "I'll call you." I didn't hug her because of the wet clothes. Just a quick kiss. Then I turned and left.

I made my way quietly down the hallway to the stairwell. I could tell she thought she wasn't going to see me again. I had to admit she might be right. The knowledge was as damp and dispiriting as my sodden clothes.

I came to the first floor and looked out at the entranceway of the building. For a second I pictured the way she had hugged me here. It already seemed like a long time ago. I felt an unpleasant mixture of gratitude and longing, streaked with guilt and regret.

And in a flash of insight, cutting with cold clarity through the fog of my fatigue, I realized what I hadn't been able to articulate earlier, not even to myself, when she'd asked me what I was afraid of.

It had been this, the moment after, when I would come face to face with knowing that it would all end badly, if not this morning, then the next one. Or the one after that.

I used the rear entrance, where there was no camera. It was still raining when I got outside. The day's first light was gray and feeble. I walked in my wet shoes until I found a cab, then made my way back to the hotel.

CHAPTER 12

The next day I contacted Tatsu via pager and our secure site, and arranged to meet him at noon at the Ginza-yu *sento*, or public bath. The *sento* is a Japanese institution, albeit one that has been in decline since not long after the war, when new apartments began to feature their own tubs and the *sento* became less a hygienic necessity and more a periodic indulgence. But, like all indulgences that are valued not just for their product but for their process, the *sento* will never entirely disappear. For in the unhurried rituals of scrubbing and soaking, and in the perspective of profound relaxation that can only be derived from immersion in water the meek might describe as scalding, there are qualities of devotion, and celebration, and meditation, qualities that are necessary concomitants to a life worth living.

Ginza-yu exists at both geographical and psychological remove from the nearby shopping glitz for which its namesake is best known, hiding almost slyly in the shadow of the Takaracho expressway overpass, and making its presence known only with a faded, hand-painted sign. I waited in a doorway across the street until I saw Tatsu pull up in an unmarked car. He parked at the curb and got out. I watched him turn the corner into the bathhouse's side entrance, then followed him in.

He saw me as I came up behind him. He had already taken off his shoes, and was about to place them in one of the small lockers just inside the entrance.

"Tell me what you have," he said.

I retracted a bit as though hurt. He looked at me for a long moment, then sighed and asked, "How are you?"

I bent and took off my shoes. "Fine, thanks for asking. You?"

"Very well."

"Your wife? Your daughters?"

He couldn't help smiling at the mention of his family. He nodded and said, "Everyone is fine. Thank you."

I grinned. "I'll tell you more inside."

We put our shoes away. I had already purchased the necessary accouterments at the convenience store across the street—shampoo, soap, scrubbing cloth, and towels—and handed Tatsu what he needed as we went in. We paid the proprietor the government-mandated and subsidized four hundred yen apiece, walked up the wide wooden stairs to the changing area, undressed in the unadorned locker room, then went through the sliding glass door to the bath beyond. The bathing area was empty—peak time would be in the evening—and, like the locker room, spartan in its unpretentiousness: nothing more than a large square space, a high ceiling, white tile walls dripping with condensation, bright fluorescent lighting, and an exhaust fan on one wall that seemed to have given up on its long battle with the steam within. The only concession to an aesthetic not strictly utilitarian was a large, brightly colored mosaic of Ginza 4-chome on the wall above the bath itself.

We sat in front of the spigots to scrub. The trick is to use hot water, filling the *sento*-supplied low plastic pail with increasingly painful bucketfuls and pouring them over your head and body. If you bathe using only tepid water, the soaking tub will be unbearable when you first try to enter it.

Tatsu completed his cleaning cycle with characteristic brusqueness and got in the bath ahead of me. I took a bit longer. When I was ready, I eased in beside him. Immediately I felt my muscles trying to shrink back from the heat, and knew that in a moment they would give up their fruitless struggle and surrender to delirious relaxation.

"Yappari, kore ga saiko da na?" I said to him, feeling myself begin to unwind. This is great, isn't it?

He nodded. "An unusual place for a meeting. But a good one."

I settled deeper into the water. "You've been drinking all that tea, so I figured you'd appreciate a place that's good for your health."

"Ah, you were being considerate. I thought that perhaps this was your way of showing me you had nothing to hide."

I laughed. I briefed him on the *dojo* and the underground fights, and on Murakami's connection with both. I gave him my assessment of Murakami's strengths and weaknesses: deadly, on the one hand; unable to blend, on the other.

"You say the promoters of these fights are losing money," he said, when I was done.

I watched the mural, my eyes half closed. "Based on what Murakami told me, yes. At three fights a night with two-million-yen payouts to the winners, plus expenses, they've got to be in the red. Even on those nights where they have two or even one, they can't be doing more than breaking even."

"What does that tell you?"

I closed my eyes. "That they're not doing it for the money."

"Yes. The question, then, is why are they doing it? What is the benefit they derive?"

I pictured the bridged, predatory smile. "Some of these people, like Murakami, are pretty sick. I think they enjoy it."

"I'm sure they do. But I doubt entertainment alone would be sufficient motive to create and sustain this kind of enterprise."

"What do you think, then?"

"When you were with Special Forces," he asked, his tone musing and thoughtful, "how did you treat personnel who performed a vital function for the unit?"

I opened my eyes and glanced at him. "There had to be redundancy. A backup. Like an extra kidney."

"Yes. Now put yourself in Yamaoto's shoes. With you, he could quietly eliminate anyone who proved uninterested in his rewards, or invulnerable to his blackmail, or who otherwise presented a threat to the machine he has established. You served a vital function. Following your loss, Yamaoto would have learned not to allow such reliance on a single person. He would seek to build redundancy into the system."

"Even if Murakami had been a total replacement."

"Which you say he is not."

"So the *dojo* Murakami is running, the fights..."

"It seems they constitute a training course of sorts."

"A training course..." I said, shaking my head. He was looking at me, waiting, one step ahead as usual.

Then I saw it. "Assassins?" I asked.

He raised his eyebrows, as if to say, *You tell me.*

"The *dojo* is the course introduction," I said, nodding. "And with the kind of training they do there, they've already selected for individuals predisposed to violence. Exposure every day, sometimes twice a day, to that regimen desensitizes the individual further. Being a spectator at actual death matches is the next step."

"And the fights themselves…"

"The fights complete the process. Sure, the whole thing is just a form of basic training. Better, in fact, because only a relatively few soldiers who pass through basic training experience combat and killing afterward. Here, killing is part of the curriculum. And the cadre you create is composed only of the ones who survive, who are the most proficient at what they've learned."

It made sense. A resort to assassins wasn't even original. In past centuries, the *shogun* and *daimyo* employed ninja in their own internecine struggles. I remembered Yamaoto from our run-in a year earlier and knew he would be flattered by the comparison.

"Do you see how this development fits in with Yamaoto's longer-range plans?" he asked.

I shook my head. It was hard to think through the penetrating heat.

He looked at me the way you might look at a slow but still likeable child. "What are Japan's overall prospects for the future?" he asked.

"How do you mean?"

"As a nation. Where will we be in ten, twenty years?"

I considered. "Not so well off, I suppose. There are a lot of problems—deflation, energy, unemployment, the environment, the banking mess—and no one seems to be able to do anything about it."

"Yes. And you are correct in distinguishing Japan's problems, which all countries have, from our powerlessness to solve those problems, in which respect we are unique among industrialized nations."

He was looking at me, and I knew what he was thinking. Until recently, I had been one of the causes of that powerlessness.

"All that consensus building takes time," I said.

"Often it takes forever. But a cultural predisposition to consensus building is not the real problem." His lips moved in the trace of a smile. "Even you were not the real problem. The real problem is the nature of our corruption."

"Quite a few scandals lately," I said, nodding. "Cars, nuclear, the food industry… I mean, if you can't trust Mr. Donut, who can you trust?"

He grimaced. "What was happening at the TEPCO nuclear facilities was worse than a disgrace. The managers should be executed."

"Are you asking me for another 'favor'?"

He smiled. "I must take care in my phraseology when I'm talking to you."

"Anyway, didn't the responsible TEPCO managers resign?"

"Yes, they resigned. While the regulators remained—the same regulators who get a cut from the funds allocated to the building and maintenance of nuclear plants, who only just publicized dangers they had known about for years."

He pulled himself up and sat on the edge of the tub to take a break from the heat. "You know, Rain-san," he said, "societies are like organisms, and no organism is invulnerable to disease. What matters is whether an organism can mount an effective defense when it finds itself under attack. In Japan, the virus of corruption has attacked the immune system itself, like a societal form of AIDS. Consequently, the body has lost its ability to defend itself. This is what I mean when I say that all countries have problems, but only Japan has problems it has lost the ability to solve. The TEPCO managers resign, but the men charged with regulating their activities for all those years remain? Only in Japan."

He looked pretty depressed, and I wished for a moment he wouldn't take this shit so seriously. If he kept it up, he'd have an ulcer the size of an asteroid. I sat next to him.

"I know it's bad, Tatsu," I said, trying to give him a little perspective, "but Japan is hardly unique when it comes to corruption. Maybe it's a little worse here, but in America, you've got Enron, Tyco, WorldCom, analysts pumping their clients' stock to get their kids into the right preschools…"

"Yes, but look at the outrage those revelations have induced in America's regulatory system," he said. "Open hearings are conducted. New legislation is passed. Heads of corporations go to jail. But in Japan, outrage is considered outrageous. Our culture seems strongly disposed toward acquiescence."

I smiled and in response offered one of the most common phrases in the language. *"Shoganai,"* I said. Literally, There is no way of doing it.

"Yes," he said, nodding. "Elsewhere they have *Cest la vie,* or That's life. Where the focus is on circumstances. Only in Japan do we focus on our own inability to change those circumstances."

He wiped his brow. "So. Consider this state of affairs from Yamaoto's perspective. He understands that, with the immune system suppressed, there must eventually be a catastrophic failure of the host. There have been so many near misses—financial, ecological, nuclear—it is only a matter of time before a true cataclysm occurs. Perhaps a nuclear accident that irradiates an entire city. Or a countrywide run on banks and loss of deposits. Whatever it is, it will finally be of sufficient magnitude to shake Japan's voters from their apathy. Yamaoto knows that violent disgust with an existing regime historically tends to cause an extremist backlash. This was true in Weimar Germany and Czarist Russia, to list only two examples."

"People would finally vote for change."

"Yes. The question is, a change to what?"

"You think Yamaoto is trying to position himself to surf that coming wave of outrage?"

"Of course. Look at Murakami's training course for assassins. This will augment Yamaoto's ability to silence and intimidate. Such an ability is one of the historical prerequisites of all fascist movements. I've told you before, Yamaoto is at heart a rightist."

I thought of some of the good news from the provinces I'd been reading, how some of the politicians there were standing up to the bureaucrats and other corrupt interests, opening up the books, eschewing the public works projects that have all but buried the country under poured concrete.

"And you're working with untainted politicians to make sure Yamaoto isn't the outraged voters' only choice?" I asked.

"I do what I can," he said.

Translation: I've told you as much as you need to know.

But I knew the disk, practically a who's who of Yamaoto's network of corruption, would have provided by negative implication an invaluable roadmap to who was absent from that network. I imagined Tatsu working with the good guys, warning them, trying to protect them. Positioning them like stones on a *go* board.

I told him about Damask Rose and Murakami's apparent connection to the place.

"Those women are being used to set up and suborn Yamaoto's enemies," he said, when I was done.

"Not all of them," I said, thinking of Naomi.

"No, not all. Some of them might not even know what is happening, though I imagine they would at least suspect. Yamaoto prefers to run such establishments as legitimate enterprises. Doing so makes them difficult to ferret out and dislodge. Ishihara, the weightlifter, was instrumental in that capacity. It's good that he is gone."

He wiped his forehead again. "I find it interesting that Murakami seems to have an important function with regard to that end of Yamaoto's means of control, as well. He may be even more vital to Yamaoto's power than I had first suspected. No wonder Yamaoto is attempting to diversify. He needs to reduce his dependence on this man."

"Tatsu," I said.

He looked at me, and I sensed he knew what was coming.

"I'm not going to take him out."

There was a long pause. His face was expressionless.

"I see," he said, his voice quiet.

"It's too dangerous. It was dangerous before, and now they've got my picture on Damask Rose home video. If the wrong person sees that picture, they'll know who I am."

"Their interest is in politicians and bureaucrats and the like. The chance of that video making its way to Yamaoto, or to one of the very few other people in his organization who might recognize your face, seems remote."

"It doesn't seem remote to me. Anyway, this guy is a hard target, very hard. To take out someone like that and make it look natural, it's almost impossible."

He looked at me. "Make it look unnatural, then. The stakes are high enough to take that chance."

"I might do that. But I'm no good with a sniper rifle, and I'm not going to use a bomb because bystanders would get blown up, too. And short of those two options, putting this guy down and getting away clean is too much of a long shot."

I realized I'd allowed myself to start arguing with him on practical grounds. I should have just told him no and shut my mouth.

Another long pause. Then he said, "What does he make of you, do you think?"

I took a deep lungful of the moist air and let it out. "I don't know. On the one hand, he's seen what I can do. On the other hand, I don't send out danger vibes the way he does. He can't control that sort of thing, so it wouldn't occur to him that someone else could."

"He underestimates you, then."

"Maybe. But not by much. People like Murakami don't underestimate."

"You've proven you can get close to him. I could get you a gun."

"I told you, he's always with at least two bodyguards."

The second I said it I wished I hadn't. Now we were negotiating. This was stupid.

"Line them up right," he said. "Take out all three."

"Tatsu, you don't understand this guy's instincts. He doesn't let anyone line up anything. When we got out of the Benz in front of his club, I saw him scoping rooftops for snipers. He knew where to look, too. He'd feel me lining him up from a mile away. Just like I'd feel him. Forget it."

He frowned. "How can I convince you?"

"You can't. Look, this was a risky proposition to begin with, but I was willing to undertake the risk in return for what you can do for me. I've learned the risk is now greater than I had originally thought. The reward is the same. So the equation has changed. It's no more complicated than that."

Neither of us said anything for a long time. Finally, he sighed and said, "What will you do, retire?"

"Maybe."

"You can't retire."

I paused. When I spoke, my voice was quiet, not much more than a whisper. "I hope you're not saying you might interfere."

He didn't flinch. "There would be no need for me to interfere," he said. "You don't have retirement in you. I wish you could recognize that. What will you do, find an island somewhere, spend time on the beach catching up on all the books you've been missing? Join a *go* club? Anesthetize yourself with whisky when your restless memories refuse to permit sleep?"

But for the jellifying effects of the heat, I might have gotten upset at that.

"Maybe therapy," he went on. "Yes, therapy is popular these days. It could help you come to terms with all the lives you have taken. Perhaps even with the one you have decided to waste."

I looked at him. "You're trying to goad me, Tatsu," I said softly.

"You need goading."

"Not from you."

He frowned. "You say you might retire. I understand that. But what I'm doing is important and right. This is our country."

I snorted. "It's not 'our' country. I'm just a visitor."

"Who told you that?"

"Everyone who mattered."

"They would be glad to know you listened."

"Enough. I owed you. I paid. I'm done."

I got up and rinsed with cold water at one of the spigots. He did the same. We changed and walked down the stairs.

Just outside the entranceway, he turned to me. "Rain-san," he said. "Will I see you again?"

I looked at him. "Are you a threat to me?" I asked.

"Not if you are really going to retire, no."

"Then we might see each other. But not for a while."

"Then we needn't say *sayonara.*"

"We needn't say it."

He smiled his sad smile. "I have a request."

I smiled back. "With you, Tatsu, it would be a little dangerous to agree to anything up front."

He nodded, accepting the point. "Ask yourself what you hope to get out of retirement. And whether retirement will achieve it."

I said, "That I can do."

"Thank you."

He extended his hand and I shook it.

"*De wa,*" I said, by way of goodbye. Well then.

He nodded again. "*Ki o tsukete,*" he said, a farewell that can be intended as an innocuous *Take care* or as a more literal *Be careful.*

The ambiguity felt deliberate.

CHAPTER 13

I waited until after seven that evening, when I knew Yukiko would have left for the club, then called Harry. I was going to tell him what he needed to hear. I owed him that much. What he decided to do with the information would then be his problem, not mine.

We set up a meeting at a coffee shop in Nippori. I told him to take his time getting there. He understood the translation: With the Agency snooping around, do a damn thorough SDR.

I got there early per my usual practice and passed the time sipping an espresso and leafing through a magazine someone had left on the table. After about an hour Harry showed up.

"Hey, kid," I said when I saw him. I noticed he was wearing a stylish lambskin jacket, and wool trousers instead of the usual jeans. He'd gotten a haircut, too. He looked nearly presentable. I realized there was no way he was going to listen to me, and almost decided not to bother telling him.

But that wouldn't be right. I would give him the information, and it would be his responsibility to use it. Or not.

He sat and, before I could open my mouth, said, "Don't worry. There's no way I was followed."

"Doesn't that go without saying?"

His eyes started to widen, then he saw I was just giving him a hard time. He smiled.

"You look good," I told him, my expression slightly bemused.

He looked at me, trying to gauge, I knew, whether he was being set up for a ribbing of some sort. "You think so?" he asked, his tone tentative.

I nodded. "Looks like you got your hair cut at one of those expensive places in Omotesando."

He reddened. "I did."

"Don't blush. It was worth whatever you paid for it."

He blushed harder. "Don't tease me."

I laughed. "I'm only half teasing."

He smiled. "What's going on?"

"Why does something have to be going on? Maybe I just missed you."

He gave me an uncharacteristically streetwise look. I had a feeling I knew where he'd picked it up. "Yeah, I missed you, too."

I wasn't looking forward to the turn the conversation would take when I brought up Yukiko, and felt no hurry to get there.

A waitress came by. Harry ordered a coffee and some carrot cake.

"You hear from any of our new government friends lately?" I asked him.

"Not a peep. You must have scared them."

"I wouldn't count on that." I took a sip of espresso and looked at him. "You still in the same place?"

"Yeah. But I'm almost ready to move. You know how it is. The preparations take awhile if you want to do it right."

We were silent for a moment, and I thought, *Here we go.*

"Planning on spending time with Yukiko at the new place?"

He gave me a wary look. "Maybe."

"Then I wouldn't bother moving."

He flinched, his expression characteristically befuddled beneath the slick new haircut.

"Why?" he asked, his tone uncertain.

"She's mixed up with some bad people, Harry."

He frowned. "I know."

It was my turn to be surprised. "You know?"

He nodded, still frowning. "She told me."

"Told you what?"

"Told me the club is run by the yakuza. So what? They all are."

"She tell you she's involved with one of the owners?"

"What do you mean, 'involved'?"

"'Involved,' as in closely involved."

He was tapping his foot nervously under the table. I could feel the vibration.

"I don't know what she has to do at the club. It's probably better if I don't."

He was in denial. This was going to be a waste of time.

All right. I'd modify my approach and try one more time.

"Okay," I said. "I'm sorry for bringing it up."

He looked at me for a moment, off balanced. "How do you even know about any of this?" he asked. "Are you sneaking around behind my back?"

I didn't care for the question, though I supposed its substance wasn't too far off the mark. My answer wasn't exactly a lie. Just incomplete.

"I've developed a... relationship with the yakuza who I think owns Damask Rose. A stone killer named Murakami. He took me there. He and Yukiko were obviously well acquainted. I saw them leave together."

"That's what you wanted to tell me? It sounds like he's her boss. They left together, so what?"

Open your eyes, you idiot, I wanted to say. *This woman is a shark. She's from a different world, a different species. There's something way fucking wrong here.*

Instead: "Harry, my gut tends to be pretty good about these things."

"Well, I'm not going to trust your gut more than I trust mine."

The waitress came with his coffee and cake and moved off. Harry didn't seem to notice.

I wanted to tell him more, wanted to offer Naomi's thoughts as corroboration. But I could see it wouldn't do much good. Besides, Harry didn't need to know where I came across my information.

I tried one last time. "The club is wired for sound and video. The detector you gave me was going apeshit the whole time I was there. I think the place is being used to entrap politicians in embarrassing acts."

"Even if that's true, it doesn't mean Yukiko is involved in it."

"Haven't you even asked yourself whether it's a coincidence that you met this woman at about the same time we discovered you were being followed by the CIA?"

He looked at me as though I'd finally come unhinged. "Are you saying Yukiko is mixed up with the CIA? Come on."

"Think about it," I told him. "We know the Agency was tracking you to get to me. They got to you through Midori's letter. What did they learn about you from the letter? Just an unusually spelled name and a postmark."

"So?"

"So the Agency doesn't have the in-house expertise to do anything useful with information like that. They need local resources."

"So?" he said again, his tone petulant.

"So they know Yamaoto from his connections with Holtzer. They ask him for his help. He has his people check domiciles and employment records in concentric circles moving outward from the Chuo-ku postmark. Maybe they access tax records, find out where an unusually named Haruyoshi is employed. Now they've got your whole name, but they can't find out where you live, because you're careful to protect that. They try to follow you from work, maybe, but you show them you're too surveillance conscious and it doesn't work. So Yamaoto gets your boss to take you somewhere to 'celebrate,' somewhere where you'll meet a real heart-stopper, someone who can find out where you live so they can follow you more often, hoping you'll drop your guard and lead them to me."

"Then why is she still with me?"

I looked at him. It was a good question.

"I mean, if her job was just to get my home address, she would have been gone the first time I took her home. But she's not. She's still with me."

"Then maybe her role was to watch you, learn your routines, find some information that would help her people get closer to finding me. Maybe listen in on your calls, alert her people if or when one of us got in touch with the other. I don't know for sure."

"I'm sorry. It's too far-fetched."

I sighed. "Harry, you're not in a good position to be objective here. You have to acknowledge that."

"And you are?"

I looked at him. "What possible reason would I have to distort any of this?"

He shrugged. "Maybe you're afraid I won't help you anymore. You said it yourself: 'You can't live with one foot in daylight and the other in shadows.' Maybe you're afraid I'll move into the daylight and leave you behind."

I felt a wave of angry indignation and willed it back. "Let me tell you something, kid," I said. "In a very short while, I plan to be living in the daylight myself. I won't need your 'help' after that. So even if I were the selfish, manipulative piece of shit you seem to think I am, I wouldn't have any motive to try to keep you in the shadows."

He flushed. "I'm sorry," he said, after a moment.

I waved a hand. "Forget it."

He looked at me. "No, really. I'm sorry."

I nodded. "Okay."

We were quiet for a moment. Then I said, "Look, I've got an idea of what you feel for this woman, okay? I saw her. She's a head-turner."

"She's more than that," he said softly.

The dumb, sappy bastard. His only hope with that ice bitch would be that she'd recognize how helpless he was and have some scruples about whatever it was she was up to.

I wouldn't count on it, though.

"The point is," I said, "it doesn't give me any pleasure to give you reason to doubt. But I'm telling you, there's something wrong here, Harry. You need to be careful. And nothing makes you less careful than the kind of feelings that have taken hold of you right now."

After a while he said, "I'll think about what you've said. Okay?"

He didn't look like he'd think about it, though. He looked like he wanted to jam his hands over his ears. Stick his newly coiffed head in the sand. Hit the Delete key on everything I'd told him.

"Look, I'm going to see her tonight," he said. "I'll watch more closely. I'll keep in mind what you've said."

I realized I'd been wasting my time.

"I thought you were smarter than this," I said, shaking my head. "I really did."

I stood and dropped a few bills on the table. I left without even looking at him.

I walked to the train station, thinking about what I had told Tatsu earlier, about risk and reward.

Harry had a lot to offer. I supposed he always would. But he wasn't being careful anymore. Keeping him in my life now entailed more risk than it had previously.

I sighed. Two goodbyes in one night. It was depressing. And it wasn't as though I had a whole Rolodex full of friends.

But no sense being sentimental about it. Sentiment is stupid. On balance, Harry had become a liability. I had to leave him behind.

PART III

God. That bastard, he doesn't exist.

—Samuel Beckett

CHAPTER 14

I made my way back to the Imperial, entering the hotel through the Hibiya Park side. In my mind, any place I'm staying is a potential choke point for an ambush, and my radar bumped up a notch as I moved through the spacious lobby to the elevators. I automatically scanned the area around me, first keying on the seats offering the best view of the entranceway, the places where an ambush team would position a spotter, the person tasked with supplying a positive ID. I saw no likelies. My radar stayed on medium alert.

As I approached the elevators, I noticed a striking Japanese woman, midthirties, shoulder-length hair wavy and iridescent black, skin smooth and pale white in contrast. She was wearing faded blue jeans, black loafers, and a black V-neck sweater. She was standing in the middle of the bank of elevators and looking directly at me.

It was Midori.

No, I thought. *Look more closely.*

Since that last time, about a year earlier when I had watched her perform from the shadows at the Village Vanguard in New York, I've seen a number of women who resemble Midori at first glance. Each time it happens, a part of my mind fills in the details, perhaps wanting to believe it really is her, and the illusion lasts for a second or two before closer inspection convinces that hopeful part of my mind of its error.

The woman watched me. Her arms, which had been crossed, began to unfold.

Midori. There was no question.

My heart started thudding. A fusillade of questions erupted in my mind: *How can she be here? How can it be her? What is she doing back in Tokyo? How would she know where to find me? How would anyone know?*

I shoved the questions aside and started checking the secondary areas around me. Just because you've spotted one surprise doesn't mean there isn't another. In fact, the first one might have been a deliberate distraction, a setup for a fatal sucker punch.

No one seemed out of place. Nothing set off my now elevated radar. Okay.

I looked at her again, still half expecting the second examination would tell me I'd been hallucinating. I hadn't. It was her.

I glanced around the room again, then slowly walked over to where she stood. I stopped in front of her. I thought the *ba-boom, ba-boom* in my chest might be loud enough for her to hear.

Get it together, I thought. But I didn't know what to say.

"How did you find me?" is what came out.

Her expression was placid, almost empty. Her eyes were dark. They radiated their characteristic untouchable heat.

"I looked in a directory of people who are supposed to be dead," she said.

If she'd been trying to fluster me, she'd done a nice job of it. I glanced around the room again.

"Are you afraid of something?" she asked mildly.

"All the time," I said, settling my eyes on hers again.

"Afraid of me? Why would that be?"

A pause. I asked, "What are you doing here?"

"Looking for you."

"Why?"

"Don't play dumb. I know you're not."

My heart rate was starting to slow. If she thought I was going to start spilling my guts in response to her vague replies, she was mistaken. I don't play it that way, not even for her.

"You going to tell me how you found me?" I asked.

"I don't know."

Another pause. I looked at her. "You want to get a drink?"

"Did you kill my father?"

My heart rate reversed course.

I looked at her for a long time. Then I said, very quietly, "Yes."

I watched her. I didn't avert my eyes.

She was silent for a moment. When she spoke, her voice was low and husky.

"I didn't think you would admit it. Or at least not so easily."

"I'm sorry," I said, thinking how ridiculous it sounded.

She pressed her lips together and shook her head, as though to say, *You can't be serious.*

I looked around the lobby again. I didn't spot anyone who was positioned to do me harm, but there were a lot of people coming and going and I couldn't be sure. I wanted to move. If she had any accomplices, this would draw them out.

"Why don't we go to the bar," I said. "I'll tell you what you want to know."

She nodded without looking at me.

What I had in mind was not the lobby-level Rendezvous Bar, which is so heavily trafficked as to be useless from a security standpoint, but the mezzanine-level Old Imperial Bar. The latter is a relic from the original Frank Lloyd Wright-designed Imperial that was torn down in 1968, ostensibly in the name of earthquake safety, more likely in obeisance to misguided notions of "progress." A walk to the mezzanine level would mean moving back across the lobby, taking a flight of stairs, and making several turns around mostly deserted corridors with various points of egress. If Midori had anyone following her, either with her knowledge or without, they'd have a hard time remaining unexposed while we moved.

We took the stairs to the mezzanine level. With the exception of the dozen or so patrons seated in the restaurants we passed, there was no one about. I checked behind us while we waited at the bar entrance to be seated. No one approached. It seemed she was alone.

We sat next to each other in one of the high, semicircular booths, hidden from the entrance. Anyone hoping to confirm our presence now would have to come inside and reveal himself. I ordered us a couple of eighteen-year-old Bunnahabhains from the bar's excellent single malt menu.

The feeling was a bit odd under the circumstances, but I was glad to be back at the Old Imperial. Windowless and low-ceilinged, dark and subdued, intimate despite its spaciousness, the bar has an air of history, of gravitas, perhaps a consequence of being the sole surviving feature of the hotel's martyred progenitor. Like the hotel itself, the Old Imperial feels a bit past its prime, but retains a dignified beauty and mysterious allure, like a grande dame who has seen much of life, known many lovers, and kept many secrets, who doesn't bother dwelling on the glory of her more exuberant youth but who hasn't forgotten it, either.

We sat in silence until the drinks had arrived. Then she said, "Why?"

I picked up my Bunnahabhain. "You know why. I was hired."

"By whom?"

"By the people your father took that disk from. The same people who thought you had it, who were trying to kill you."

"Yamaoto?"

"Yes."

She looked at me. "You're an assassin, aren't you? When there are rumors the government has someone on the payroll, they're talking about you, right?"

I let out a long exhalation. "Something like that."

There was a pause. Then she asked, "How many people have you killed?"

My eyes moved to my glass. "I don't know."

"I'm not talking about Vietnam. Since then."

"I don't know," I said again.

"Don't you think that's too many?" The mildness of her voice made the question worse.

"I don't... I have rules. No women. No children. No acts against nonprincipals." The words echoed flatly in my ears like a moron's mantra, talismanic sounds suddenly stripped of their animating magic.

She laughed without mirth. "'I have rules.' You sound like a whore who wants credit for virtue because she won't kiss the clients she fucks."

It stung. But I took it.

"And then your friend from the Metropolitan Police Department told me you were dead. And you let me believe it. Do you know I grieved for you? Do you know what that's like?"

I grieved for you, too, I wanted to say.

"Why?" she asked. "Why would you put me through that? Even beyond what you did to my father, why would you put me through that?"

I looked away.

"Tell me, goddamn it," I heard her say.

I gripped my glass. "I wanted to spare you. From this... knowledge."

"I don't believe you. I half knew anyway. What did you think I would think when the evidence of corruption on that disk, which my father died trying to get, wasn't published? When I tried to find out what had been done with your remains so I could offer my respects, but couldn't?"

"I didn't know it wouldn't be published," I said, not looking at her. "In fact I thought it would be. But regardless, I expected you to forget about me. At times I had my doubts, but what could I do at that point? Just show up in your life and explain? What if I'd been wrong, what if you had forgotten, you didn't suspect, you'd gotten on with your life the way I'd hoped?" I looked at her. "I would have just caused you more pain."

She shook her head. "You couldn't have caused me more pain if you'd tried."

There was a long silence. I said, "Are you going to tell me how you found me?"

She shrugged. "Your friend from the Metropolitan Police Department."

I was taken aback. "Tatsu contacted you?"

She shook her head. "I contacted him. Several times, in fact. He kept blowing me off. Last week I came back to Tokyo and went to his office. I told a receptionist that if Ishikura-san didn't see me I would contact the press, I would do everything I could do to make a public scandal. And I would have, you know. I wasn't going to give up."

She'd been brave, even a little reckless. Tatsu wouldn't have harmed her, even in response to a threat, but she had no way of knowing that. Another indication of just how desperately angry she had been.

"He saw you?" I asked.

"Not right away. He called me this afternoon."

This afternoon. Right after I'd refused him, then.

"And he said you could find me here?"

She nodded.

How had he managed to track me down again? Probably those damn cameras. *You can see some of them. Not all,* I remembered him saying. Sure, use the cameras to get a general fix on my location, then send men to the likely hotels in the area, if necessary, with the same photo they had fed to the cameras and the facial recognition software, to narrow things down.

I'd been a fool to stay in Tokyo, though with the kind of warning I had to give Harry, an overseas phone call would have been less than optimal.

What was that wily bastard up to, though? "Any thoughts on why Tatsu would agree to see you after a year of stonewalling?" I asked.

She shrugged. "Probably my threat."

I doubted it. Tatsu didn't know her as well as I did. He would have mistakenly assumed she was bluffing.

"You really think that was all there was to it?" I asked.

"Maybe. Maybe he had some ulterior reason for wanting us to meet. But what was I going to do, spite him by refusing to see you?"

"I suppose not." And Tatsu would have supposed the same. I felt a momentary wave of annoyance, bordering on hostility, toward Tatsu and his ongoing machinations.

She sighed. "He said telling me you were dead was his doing, not yours."

This was supposed to get back to me. Did he think I was going to take out Murakami in gratitude, as a quid pro quo?

"What else did he tell you?"

"That you helped him get the disk expecting him to turn it over to the media for publication."

"Did he tell you why he didn't?"

She nodded. "Because its information was so explosive it might have brought down the Liberal Democrats and paved the way for Yamaoto's ascension."

"Sounds like you're pretty up to date, then."

"I'm a long way from up to date."

"What about Harry?" I asked after a moment. "Why didn't you go to him?"

She looked away and said, "I did. I wrote him a letter. He said he'd heard you were dead, and didn't know any more than that."

The way she had looked away... there was something she wasn't telling me.

"You believed him?"

"Should I not have?"

Good recovery. But there was something more there, I thought.

"Remember the last time I saw you?" she asked.

It had been here, at the Imperial Hotel. We'd spent the night together. The next morning I had left to intercept Holtzer's limousine. I had spent a few days in police custody after that. Meanwhile, Tatsu had told Midori I was dead and had deep-sixed the disk. Game over.

"I remember," I said.

"You said, 'I'll be back sometime in the evening. Will you wait for me?' Well, I waited for two days before I heard from your friend Ishikura-san. I had no one to contact, no way to know."

Her eyes moved to the ceiling for a moment, maybe looking away from memories she didn't want to see. Maybe willing back tears.

"I couldn't believe you were gone," she went on. "Then I started to wonder if you really were gone. And if you weren't gone, what would that mean? And then I doubted myself. I doubted myself. I thought, 'He can't still be alive, he wouldn't have done this to you.' But I couldn't get rid of the suspicions. I didn't know whether to grieve for you, or to want to kill you."

She turned and looked at me. "Do you understand what you put me through?" she asked, her voice dropping to a whisper. "You... you fucking tortured me!"

In my peripheral vision, I saw her quickly flick her thumb across one cheek, then the other. I looked down into my glass. The last thing she would want would be my witnessing her tears.

After a moment I turned to her. "Midori," I said. My voice was low and sounded strange to me. "I'm sorrier for all this than I can say. If I could change any of it, I would."

We were silent for a moment. I thought of Rio and said, "For what it's worth, I've been trying to get out."

She looked at me. "How hard are you trying? Most people get along pretty well without killing someone. They don't have to go out of their way to avoid it."

"It's a little more complicated than that with me."

"Why?"

I shrugged. "Right now the people who know me seem to be equally divided between wanting to kill me and wanting me to kill."

"Ishikura-san?"

I nodded. "Tatsu has devoted his life to fighting corruption in Japan. He's got assets, but the forces he's up against are stronger than he is. He's trying to even the odds."

"It's hard for me to picture him as one of the good guys."

"I'm sure it is. But the world he inhabits isn't as black and white as the one you do. Believe it or not, he was trying to help your father."

And suddenly I understood why he had sent her here. Not because he hoped I would assist him as a quid pro quo for a few exculpatory comments he'd made to Midori. Or at least not entirely that. No, his real hope was that, if Midori came to view Tatsu as in some way trying to continue the fight her father had begun, she might want me to help him. He hoped my seeing her would tap into my regrets about her father, make me malleable to a request that I do what he wanted.

"So now you're 'trying to get out,'" she said.

I nodded, thinking this would be what she wanted to hear.

But she laughed. "Is that your atonement after all you've done? I didn't know it was that easy to get into heaven."

Maybe I didn't have a right, but I was starting to get irritated. "Look, I made a mistake with your father. I told you I'm sorry for it, I told you I would change it if I could. What else can I do? You want me to pour gasoline on myself and light a match? Feed the hungry? What?"

She dropped her eyes. "I don't know."

"Well, I don't know, either. But I'm trying."

That fucking Tatsu, I thought. He'd seen all of this. He knew she would rattle me.

I finished my Bunnahabhain. I set the empty glass down on the table and looked at it.

"I want something from you," she said, after a moment.

"I know," I answered, not looking at her.

"I don't know what it is."

I closed my eyes. "I know you don't."

"I can't believe I'm even sitting here talking to you."

To that I only nodded.

There was another long silence while I ran through my mind all the things I wished I could say to her, things I wished could make a difference.

"We're not through," she said.

I looked at her, not knowing what she meant, and she went on.

"When I know what I want from you, I'm going to tell you."

"I appreciate it," I said dryly. "That way I'll at least see it coming."

She didn't laugh. "You're the killer, not me."

"Right."

She looked at me for a moment longer, then said, "I can find you here?"

I shook my head. "No."

"Where, then?"

"It's better if I find you."

"No!" she said with a sudden vehemence that surprised me. "No more of that bullshit. If you want to see me again, tell me where you'll be."

I picked up my empty glass and gripped it tightly.

Walk away, I told myself. *You don't even need to say anything. Just put a few bills on the table and go. You'll never see her again.*

Except I'd always be seeing her. I couldn't get away from it.

I've gotten used to hoping for so little that I seem to have lost any natural immunity to the emotion's infection. My hopes for Midori had gotten a foothold, and as ridiculous as they'd become, I couldn't seem to beat them back.

"Look," I said, already knowing it was futile. "I've lived this way for a long time. This is how I've managed to live for a long time."

"Forget it, then," she said. She stood.

"All right," I said. "You can find me here."

She looked at me and nodded. "Okay."

I paused. "Am I going to hear from you?" I asked.

"Do you care?"

"I'm afraid I do."

"Good," she said, nodding. "Let's see how you like the uncertainty."

She turned and walked away.

I paid the bill and waited for a minute, then left, using one of the basement exits.

I couldn't stay there any longer. I might be able to live with Midori knowing my whereabouts, but she had no security consciousness and I couldn't live with the possibility that she might inadvertently lead someone to me. I wanted to make things harder for Tatsu, too. It might not have mattered all that much at this point if he had a way to find me, but I didn't like the notion.

I would stay at the most anonymous business hotels, a different one every night. Doing so would protect me from anyone who might be following Midori and would keep Tatsu scrambling to try to keep up.

I'd keep the room at the Imperial, of course. That might help throw Tatsu off. Also, I'd be able to check the room voicemail remotely, in case Midori tried to reach me there. I could stop in from time to time, using extra care, just to maintain appearances.

I kept my head low and did everything I could to try to avoid presenting a pretty picture for the cameras, but there was no way to be sure. I felt boxed in, claustrophobic.

Maybe I would just bolt. First thing in the morning, Osaka, Rio, *finito.*

But I hated the thought that Midori might try to contact me again, only to find, again, that I was gone.

You're already lying to her, I thought. *Took you all of a half hour.*

Then maybe I would stay for another day, two at the most. Yeah, maybe. And after that, the next time Midori or Tatsu or anyone else heard from me it would be via postcard, *par avion.*

I made some aggressive moves to ensure I wasn't being followed. Then I slowed down and drifted through night Tokyo, not knowing where I was going, not caring.

I saw two young *furita*—"freeters"—slackers who had responded to Japan's decade-long recession by eschewing positions that were no longer available to them anyway, dropping instead into odd jobs like the late shift in convenience stores, where they would service the needs of other Tokyo night denizens: hollow-eyed parents in search of cleaning supplies for the household chores their long commutes and crying babies left no time to accomplish during daylight hours; lonely men still dressed in the interchangeable shirtsleeves of their day jobs, suffering in the midst of the vast city from solitude so acute that not even the narcotic of late-night television talk shows could distract them from occasional nocturnal forays in search of signs of other life; even other *furita,* on their way back to their parents' houses, which, to make their meager ends meet, they still inhabited, who might share a tired cigarette and an unfunny joke before sleeping off the morning, then rising to do it all over again later that day.

I passed sanitation workers, construction crews laboring under halogen lamps on the potholes of night-quiet streets, insomniac truck drivers silently unloading their wares onto deserted sidewalks and silent stoops.

I found myself near Nogizaka Station, and realized I had been unconsciously moving northwest. I stopped. Aoyama Bochi was just across from me, silent and brooding, drawing me like a gaping black hole whose gravity was even greater than that of surrounding Tokyo.

Without thinking, I cut across the road, hopping over the metal divider at its center. I paused at the stone steps before me, then surrendered and walked up to the graves within.

Immediately the sounds of the street below grew detached, distant, the meaningless echoes of urban voices whose urgent notes reached but held no sway over the park-like necropolis within. From where I stood, the cemetery seemed to have no end. It stretched out before me, a city in its own right, its myriad markers windowless tenements in miniature, laid out in still symmetry, long boulevards of the dead.

I moved deeper into the comforting gloom, along a stone walkway covered in cherry blossoms that lay like tenebrous snow in the glow of lamplights to either side. Just days earlier, these same blossoms had been celebrated by living Tokyoites, who came here in their drunken thousands to see reflected in the blossom's brief and vital beauty the inherent pathos of their own lives. But now the blossoms were fallen, the revelers departed, even the garbage disgorged by their parties efficiently removed and discarded, and the area was once again given over only to the dead.

I thought of how Midori had once articulated the idea of *mono no aware,* a sensibility that, though frequently obscured during cherry blossom viewing by the cacophony of drunken doggerel and generator-powered television sets, remains steadfast in one of the two cultures from which I come. She had called it "the sadness of being human." A wise, accepting sadness, she had said. I admired her for the depths of character such a description indicated. For me, sad has always been a synonym for bitter, and I suspect this will always be so.

I walked on, my footfalls melancholy, respectful of the thick silence around me. Unlike the surrounding city, Aoyama Bochi is changeless, and I had no difficulty finding what drew me despite the decades that had passed since I had last come here.

The marker was stark and simple, distinguished only by a brief declaration that Fujiwara Shuichi had lived from 1912 to 1960, and that all that remained of him was interred here. Fujiwara Shuichi, my father, killed in the street riots that rocked Tokyo one awful summer while I was a boy.

I stood before the grave and maintained a long bow, my palms pressed together before my face in the Buddhist attitude of respect for the dead. My mother would have wanted me to say a prayer, crossing myself at its conclusion, and had this been her grave, I would have done so. But such a western ritual would have been an insult to my father in his life, and why would I do something to offend him now?

I smiled. It was hard to avoid that kind of thinking. My father was dead.

Still, I offered no prayer.

I waited a moment, then lowered myself, cross-legged, to the earth. Some of the graves were adorned with flowers, in various stages of freshness and decay. As though the dead could smell the bouquets.

A breeze sighed among the markers. I put my forehead in my palms and stared at the ground before me.

People have rituals for communing with the dead, rituals that depend more on the idiosyncrasies of the individual than on the influence of culture. Some visit gravesites. Some talk to portraits, or mantelpiece urns. Some go to spots favored by the deceased during life, or mouth silent prayers in houses of worship, or have trees planted in memory in some far-off land.

The common denominator, of course, is a sense beyond logic that the dead are aware of all this, that they can hear the prayers and witness the deeds and feel the ongoing love and longing. People seem to find that sense comforting.

I don't believe any of it. I've never seen a soul depart from a body. I've never been haunted by a ghost, angry or loving. I've never been rewarded or punished or touched by some traveler from the undiscovered country. I know as well as I know anything the dead are simply dead.

I sat silently for several minutes, resisting the urge to speak, knowing it was stupid. There was nothing left of my father. Even if there were, it was ridiculous to believe it would be here, hovering around ashes and dust, jostling for position among the souls of the hundreds of thousands of others buried in this place.

People lay the flowers and say the prayers, they believe these things, because doing so avoids the discomfort of acknowledging that the person you loved is *gone*. It's easier to believe that maybe the person can still see and hear and care.

I looked at my father's marker. It was young by the standards of the cemetery, just over four decades, but already it was darkened by pollution. Moss grew thin and insensate up its left side. Without thinking, I reached out and ran my fingers over the raised lettering of my father's name.

"*Hisashiburi, papa,*" I whispered, addressing him like the young boy I was when he had died. It's been a long time, papa.

Forgive me father. It's been thirty years since my last confession.

Stop that shit.

"I'm sorry I don't come to visit you more often," I said in Japanese, my voice low. "Or even think of you. There are so many things I keep at a distance because they're painful. Your memory is one of those things. The first of them, in fact."

I paused for a moment and considered the silence around me. "But you're not listening, anyway."

I looked around. "This is stupid," I said. "You're dead. You're not here."

Then I dropped my head into my hands again. "I wish I could make her understand," I said. "I wish you could help me."

Damn, she'd been hard on me. Called me a whore.

Maybe it wasn't unfair. After all, killing is the ultimate expression of hatred and fear, as sex is the ultimate expression of romantic love and desire. And, as with sex, killing a stranger who has otherwise provoked no emotion is inherently unnatural. I suppose you could say that a man who kills a stranger is not unlike a woman who has sex under analogous circumstances. That a man who is paid to kill is like a woman who is paid to fuck. Certainly the man is subject to the same reluctance, the same numbing, the same regrets. The same damage to the soul.

"But goddamn it," I said aloud, "is it moral to kill someone you don't even know, a grunt probably just like yourself, just because the government says you can? Or you drop a bomb from thirty thousand feet to kill the bad guys, you bury women and children under the rubble of their own homes in the process, but you're not bothered because you didn't actually have to see the damage, that's moral? I don't hide behind mortar range, or behind the cartoon image in the thermal scope of a sniper's rifle, or behind the medals they give you afterward to reassure you the slaughter was just. All that shit is an illusion, a soporific fed to killers to anesthetize them after they've killed. What I do is no worse than what goes on all over the world, what has always gone on. The difference is, I'm honest about it."

I was quiet for a while, thinking.

"And how about a little slack?" I said. "Her old man was set to check out from lung cancer anyway, in a lot more pain than what I caused him. Whatever happened to 'no harm, no foul'? I mean, I practically did him a favor. Hell, in some cultures what I did wouldn't be looked at as much more than euthanasia. She almost ought to thank me for it."

Things had been okay for me in Osaka, reasonably okay. Looking back, I felt like it had all been falling apart since Tatsu had showed up.

I thought about taking him out. There were a dozen reasons why I didn't want to. The problem was, he was beginning to act like he knew I didn't want to, and that wasn't good.

I needed to get back to Osaka, finish my preparations as quickly as I could, and go. Tatsu could handle himself. Harry was hopeless. Midori knew what she'd come here to learn. Naomi was sweet, but she'd served her purpose.

I stood. My legs had stiffened on the cool ground and I massaged some blood back into them. I bowed to my father's grave, then stood looking at it for a long time.

"*Jaa,*" I said finally. Then: "*Arigatou.*"

I turned and walked out.

CHAPTER 15

The next morning, I went out to a payphone and called Harry. He'd done a lot for me over the years and I felt bad about the way we'd parted. I knew he'd be bothered by it, and that bothered me.

An unfamiliar male voice answered his phone. *"Moshi moshi?"*

"Moshi moshi," I said, my brow furrowing. *"Haruyoshi-san irass-haimasu ka?"* Is Haruyoshi there?

There was a pause. "Are you a friend of Haruyoshi's?" the voice asked in Japanese.

"I am. Is everything all right?"

"This is Haruyoshi's uncle. I regret to inform you that Haruyoshi passed away last night."

I gripped the phone tightly and closed my eyes. I thought of the last thing he'd said to me: *Look, I'm going to see her tonight. I'll watch more closely. I'll keep in mind what you've said.*

He'd gone to see her, all right. But he hadn't kept anything in mind.

"Forgive me for asking," I said, my eyes still closed, "but can you tell me how he passed away?"

There was another pause. "It seems Haruyoshi had drunk a bit too much, and had gone up to the roof of his building for a walk. Apparently he came too close to the edge and lost his balance."

I gripped the phone harder. I'd never known Harry to drink. Certainly not excessively. Though I knew he might try all sorts of new things if Yukiko were there to urge him on.

"Thank you for informing me," I said to the voice. "Please accept my deepest condolences on this sad occasion. Please convey these sentiments to Harry's parents. I will say a prayer for his spirit."

"Thank you," the voice said.

I put the phone back in its cradle.

My gut told me what I'd just heard had been legitimate. Still, I called the police box in his neighborhood to make sure. I told the cop who answered I was a friend of a Haruyoshi Fukasawa, I'd heard there had been bad news. The cop confirmed that Harry was dead. A fall. Apparently an accident. He told me he was sorry. I thanked him and hung up.

I stood there for a moment, feeling miserable and alone.

They'd gotten what they wanted from him. They were tying up loose ends.

Well, there was nothing I could do for him now. I'd tried to help him when it mattered. Now it was too late.

In some ways it was my fault. I'd known Yukiko was dangerous to him, but all I did was tell him about my suspicions. What I should have done was said nothing to him, and just made her have a little accident. Harry would have grieved, but he'd still be alive.

I realized I was grinding my teeth and made myself stop.

I thought of how happy he'd been when he'd first told me about her, how shy and sappy and obviously in love.

I remembered the way the ice-bitch had alternately teased, then soothed, Murakami. How Naomi had said, *She's comfortable doing things I'm not.*

I imagined her pumping him with drinks, his body unaccustomed to the alcohol. I imagined him doing it to please her. I imagined her suggesting a walk on the roof, Murakami waiting there.

Or maybe she did it herself. It wouldn't be hard. She'd spent time in the building, she knew its rhythms, its routines, the layout of its security cameras. And he trusted her. Even with what I'd told him, if he were drunk enough, he wouldn't have hesitated to walk to the edge. Maybe for a laugh. Maybe on a dare.

Without thinking, I snatched the receiver from its cradle and raised it overhead to smash down onto the phone. I stood there for a long moment, my arm cocked, my body tensed and trembling, willing myself not to make a scene, not to draw attention.

Finally, I set the receiver back in its cradle. I closed my eyes and breathed in, then let it all the way out. Once more. And again.

I went to a different phone and called Tatsu. I told him to check our secure site because I wanted to see him. Then I went to an Internet café to tell him when and where.

We met at Café Peshaworl, a coffeehouse and bar in the Nihonbashi business district, and another place I had liked during the years I was in Tokyo.

I got there early, as usual, and took the steps down from Sakura-dori to the subdued interior below. Peshaworl is shaped like an I-beam, and I took a seat in the corner of one of the short ends of the I. I was hidden from the entrance, but I could just see the bar, with its red steel scale for measuring precise quantities of beans; its battered pots for steeping coffee, their dents, like those in fine single malt stills, probably credited with producing the unique taste of Peshaworl's brews; and its curious implements, intimidating in their specificity, no doubt designed exclusively for the concoction of the most exalted blends, their correct use unknown except to craft initiates.

I ordered the house Roa blend and listened to Monica Borrfors singing "August Wishing" while I waited for Tatsu to show. At just after twelve, I heard the door open and close, followed by Tatsu's familiar shuffling gait. A moment later he poked his head around the corner and saw me. He came over and sat so that we were at ninety degrees to each other and could converse with maximum privacy. He grunted a greeting, then said, "Based on your recent meeting with Kawamura Midori, I can only assume that you asked me here either to thank me or to kill me."

I shook my head slowly. "Neither."

He looked at me for a moment, silent, perhaps sensing something in my face, my voice.

The waitress came over and asked him what he would like. He ordered a milk tea, more, I thought, as a concession to his surroundings than out of any real desire.

While we waited for his tea, he said, "I hope you understand why I did what I did."

"Sure. You're a manipulative, fanatical bastard who believes the end always justifies the means."

"Now you sound like my wife."

I didn't feel like laughing. "You shouldn't have dragged Midori back into this."

"I didn't. I had hoped she would want to believe you were dead. If she had wanted to believe, she would have. If she did not want to believe, she would investigate. She is quite tenacious."

"She told me she threatened you with a scandal."

"Probably a bluff."

"She doesn't bluff, Tatsu."

"Regardless. I told her where to find you because it was no longer useful to try to deceive her. In fact, she was not deceived. Also, I thought you might benefit from that encounter."

I shook my head. "Did you really think she could convince me to help you?"

"Of course."

"Why?"

"You know why."

"Don't lead me, Tatsu."

"All right. Consciously or unconsciously, you want to be worthy of her. I respect you for that sentiment because there is much about Kawamura-san to admire. But you may be going about it in the wrong way, and I wanted to give you the opportunity to see that."

"You're wrong," I said.

"Then why are you here?"

I looked at him. "I'm going to help you on this. It has nothing to do with Midori." I pictured Harry for a second, then said, "No, you're going to help me."

The waitress set down his tea and moved on.

"What happened?" he asked.

My reflex was to not tell him, to protect Harry, like I'd always tried to do before. But it didn't matter any more.

"Murakami killed a friend of mine," I said. "A kid named Haruyoshi. Yamaoto was using him, I think to find me. When they thought they'd gotten what they wanted, they got rid of him."

A long pause. Then: "I'm sorry."

I shrugged. "It works out well for you. If I didn't know you as well as I do, I might have been suspicious."

I regretted saying it as soon as it was out. Tatsu had too much dignity to respond.

"Anyway, I want you to look into something for me," I said.

"All right."

I told him about how Kanezaki had been following Harry, how Midori's letter had been the start of it, how Yukiko and Damask Rose were involved.

"I'll see what I can find out," he said.

"Thank you."

"Your friend was… young?" he asked.

I looked at him. "Young enough."

He nodded, his eyes sad.

I thought of how he had first briefed me on Murakami, how his jaw had clenched and unclenched when he told me he believed Murakami had been involved in the murder of a child. I had to ask. "Tatsu, was there… did you have a son?"

There was a long silence, during which he must have been digesting the realization that I knew something of his personal life, and deciding on how he wanted to respond.

"Yes," he said after a while, nodding. "He would have turned thirty-two this past February."

He seemed to be carefully weighing, even carefully pronouncing, the words. I wondered when he had last spoken of this.

"He was eight months old, just weaned," he went on. "My wife and I had not been out together in some time, and we hired a babysitter. When we came home, the sitter was distraught. She had dropped the little boy and he had a bruise on his head. He had cried, she told us, but now he seemed all right. He was sleeping.

"My wife wanted to take him to the doctor right away, but we checked on him and he seemed to be sleeping peacefully. 'Why trouble the little one's sleep unnecessarily?' I said. 'If there were a problem, we would know it by now.' My wife wanted to believe everything was all right, and so I was able to persuade her."

He took a sip of tea. "In the morning, the baby was dead. The doctor told us it was a subdural hematoma. He told us it would have made no difference if we had sought immediate medical attention. But of course I will always wonder. Because I had a choice, you see? It may be terrible for me to say it, but it would have been easier if my son had died instantly. Or if the sitter had been less decent, and had mentioned nothing to us. The same outcome, and yet completely different."

I looked at him. "How old were your girls, Tatsu?" I asked.

"Two and four."

"Christ," I muttered.

He nodded, not bothering to make a show of stoicism by arguing with me. "Losing a child is the worst thing," he said. "There is no greater grief. For a long time I wanted to take my own life. Partly on the chance that by doing so I might be reunited with my son, that I might be able to comfort him and protect him. Partly to atone for how I had wronged him. And partly simply to end my pain. But my duty to my wife and daughters was greater than these irrational and selfish impulses. And I came to view my pain as a just punishment, as my karma. But still, every day I think of my little son. Every day I wonder if I will have a chance to see him again."

We were silent for a moment. From behind the counter came the sound of beans being ground.

"We're going to take this guy out," I told him. "I can't do it alone, and neither can you, but maybe we can do it together."

"Tell me what you propose."

"Murakami shows up at the *dojo* from time to time, but you can't stake the place out. It's on a quiet street with minimal automobile or pedestrian traffic, so not much cover. Plus I spotted at least two sentries on my way in."

He nodded. "I know. I had a man make a casual pass."

"I figured you would. But we might not need a stakeout. If I show up, someone is likely to call Murakami. That's when we nail him."

He looked at me. "If Murakami killed your friend because they decided they didn't need him anymore to get to you, they probably know who you are."

"Exactly. That's why I know that, when I show up, someone will call him. And even if I'm wrong, and they don't know who I am, Murakami said he wanted to talk to me at the *dojo*. Sooner or later he'll show up there. And when he shows up, I'll call you. You come with picked men, arrest him, and take him into custody."

"He might attempt to resist arrest," he said dryly.

"Oh, yeah. A guy like that might resist fiercely. I'm sure lethal force would be justified in subduing him."

"Indeed."

"In fact, it's even possible that, after you have him handcuffed, someone who might be described afterward as 'one of his cohorts who got away' might appear and break his fucking neck."

He nodded. "I can see where something like that could occur."

"I'll go for two hours at a time," I said. "During those two-hour periods you have men mobile and nearby, ready to pounce on my signal."

He was quiet for a moment, then said, "I hesitate to suggest it, but it's possible Murakami will not show. He may simply subcontract the work to someone else. In which case you would be walking into extreme danger for nothing."

"He'll show," I said. "I know this guy. If he knows who I am, he's going to want a piece of me. And I'm going to give it to him."

CHAPTER 16

That night I stayed at a small business hotel in Nishi-Nippori. It was spare enough to make me miss the New Otani and the Imperial, but it was a quiet place in a lonely part of the city and I felt reasonably safe there for the night.

The next morning, I worked out at Murakami's *dojo* in Asakusa. When I arrived, the men who were already training paused and gave me a low collective bow—a sign of their respect for the way I had dispatched Adonis. After that, I was treated in a dozen subtle ways with deference that bordered on awe. Even Washio, older than I and with a much longer and deeper association with the *dojo*, was using different verb forms to indicate that he now considered me his superior. My sense was that, whatever Yamaoto and Murakami might have discovered about me, the knowledge had not been shared with the lower echelon.

Tatsu had given me a Glock 26, the shortest-barreled pistol in Glock's excellent 9-millimeter line. Definitely not standard Keisatsucho issue. I didn't know how Tatsu had acquired it in tightly gun-controlled Japan, and I didn't ask. Despite its relatively low profile, I couldn't keep it concealed on my person while I was working out. Instead I left it in my gym bag, which I kept close while I worked out.

Tatsu had also given me a mobile phone with which I would alert him when Murakami showed. I had created a speed dial entry so that all I had to do was hit one of the keys, let the call go through, and hang up. When Tatsu saw that a call had come from my number, he'd scramble his nearby men to the *dojo*.

But Murakami didn't show. Not that day, not the next.

I was getting antsy. Too much living out of hotels, a different one every night. Too much worrying about security cameras. Too much thinking about Harry, about the useless way he'd died, about how hard I'd been on him that very night.

And too much thinking about Midori, wondering whether she'd get in touch again, and what she would want if she did.

I went to the *dojo* for a third day. I was doing long workouts, trying to give Murakami the widest possible window in which to appear, but there was still no sign of him. I was starting to think he just wasn't going to show.

But he did. I was on the floor, stretching, when I heard the door buzzer. I looked up to see Murakami, wearing a black leather jacket and head-hugging shades, and his two bodyguards, similarly dressed, enter the room. As usual, the atmosphere in the *dojo* changed when he entered, his presence aggravating everyone's vestigial fight-or-flight radar like a mild electric current.

"*Oi, Arai-san, yo,*" he said, walking over. "Let's talk."

I stood. "Okay."

One of the bodyguards approached. I started toward my bag, but he got there ahead of me. He picked it up and slid it over his shoulder. "I'll take this," he said.

I gave no sign that this was a problem for me. The mobile phone, at least, was in my pocket. I shrugged and said, "Thanks."

Murakami motioned toward the door with a tilt of his head. "Outside."

My heart rate had doubled but my voice was cool. "Sure," I called to him. "Just going to take a leak first."

I walked to the back of the room and into the bathroom. I was already so juiced from adrenaline that I couldn't have pissed if I had to, but that wasn't what I had come to do.

I was looking for a weapon of convenience. Maybe some powdered soap that I could toss into someone's eyes, or a mop handle that I could break off into a nightstick. Anything that would improve the currently ugly odds.

My eyes swept the room but there was nothing. The soap was liquid. If there was a mop, they kept it elsewhere.

Damn it, you should have done this before it mattered. Stupid. Stupid.

One thing. There was a brass doorstop screwed into the wall just above the floor and behind the door. I knelt and tried to turn it. It was too close to the floor for me to get a hand around. And it was coated in probably ten layers of paint and looked as old as the building. It wouldn't budge.

"Fuck," I breathed. I could have tried stomping on it with my heel, but that might have broken off the point that was screwed into the wall.

Instead I tried pressing one way with my palm, then the other. Up, down. Left, right. I jiggled it but felt no new play. *Damn it, this is taking too long.*

I squeezed it between the thumbs and forefingers of both hands as hard as I could and rotated it counterclockwise. For a second I thought my fingers had slipped, but then I realized it had turned.

I unscrewed it the rest of the way and stood just as the bathroom door opened. It was one of the bodyguards.

He looked at me. "Everything okay?" he asked, holding the door open.

I palmed the doorstop. "Just washing my hands. Be right with you."

He nodded and left. The door closed behind him and I shoved the doorstop into my right front pocket, then immediately hit the speed dial key for Tatsu.

Of course, I didn't know for certain they were on to me. Murakami might have just been there to talk about whatever it was he had in mind at Damask Rose. But that didn't matter. The important thing is to accept the facts early. Most people don't want to believe the crime or the ambush or whatever the violence is going to be is really going to happen. At some level they know better, but they keep themselves in denial until the proof really comes in. At which point, of course, it's too late to do anything about it.

If I have to err, it's on the side of assuming the worst. This way, if I'm wrong, I can always apologize. Or send flowers. You err on the other side, the flowers will be coming to you.

The first thing I noticed as I exited the restroom was that the gym was empty. It was just Murakami and his two goons, standing between me and the door. They'd set my bag down near the front entrance. I didn't see the gun, so it seemed that they hadn't thought to open the bag during my brief absence.

"What's going on?" I asked, but casually, as though I was too stupid to realize anything was seriously amiss and was counting on Murakami for a straight answer.

"Everything's fine," he said, and they began to move toward me. "We just asked the others to wait outside so we could have some privacy."

"Oh, okay," I said with a shrug. I put my hands in my pockets, palming the doorstop with my right.

The bodyguards fanned out to his flanks. I would wait until they were in striking distance.

But they stopped just outside that range. I watched them with a quizzical, sheepish look, as if to say, "Hey, guys, what's all this about?"

Murakami eyeballed me for a long moment. When he spoke his voice was a low growl. "We've got a problem," he said.

"A problem?"

"Yeah. A problem as in, your name isn't Arai. It's Rain."

I let my eyes move fearfully from face to face, to the exit, then back again. I wanted them to think I might bolt. Which I sure as shit would if I could.

"Hold him," Murakami said.

The man to my left lunged. I was ready for it. My hands had already popped free of my pockets and I extended my left arm as though to block him. He took the bait, grabbing my forearm with both hands to immobilize it while his partner moved in from the right. I snaked the hand he was trying to hold over his left wrist, trapping it, and used the grip to yank myself toward him. He was braced for me to try to pull in the opposite direction and couldn't react in time to stop me from closing the distance. The doorstop was already out, palmed in my fist with the screw point jutting out between my middle and forefinger like the world's nastiest signet ring.

I popped a quick jab over his trapped left arm and up into his neck, aiming for just under the jawline. It wasn't a power shot but it didn't need to be; what it needed was accuracy, and that it had. The tip plunged in like a corkscrew hypodermic, and before he could pull away I twisted downward and ripped back. He yelped and leaped away, instinctively clapping his hand over the resultant tear. Blood jetted from between his fingers, and I knew I'd hit the carotid.

He made a horrified gurgling noise and clapped his other hand over the spot, but blood continued to pour out. I swung back to my right. His friend had pulled up short, unsure of what had just happened, shocked by all the blood. I slipped the doorstop between my thumb and forefinger as though it was a knife and brandished it at him Hollywood style, my arm extended and the weapon way too far from my body.

When he realized that I wasn't holding a machete, he tried to grab my juicy target of an arm. I let him get my wrist, then made as though I was trying to yank free. He braced against the pressure, straightening his forward knee, his eyes and all his focus on the weapon. Using our counterbalanced pulling to brace myself, I raised my right foot off the floor and shot it into his forward knee. At the last instant he saw it coming and tried to twist away, but he had too much weight on the leg. The kick blew through his knee and he crumbled to the floor with a shriek.

Murakami was still standing between me and the door. He looked calmly at the two fallen men, one screaming and writhing on his back, the other sitting and clutching his hands tightly to his spurting neck in a gesture of burlesque mortification. Then he looked back at me. He smiled, revealing the bridge.

"You're good," he said. "You don't look like much, but you're good."

"Your friend needs a doctor," I said, breathing hard. "If he doesn't get proper attention he's going to bleed out inside five minutes, maybe less."

He shrugged. "You think I want him as a bodyguard after this? If he wasn't going to die, I'd kill him myself."

The fallen man was drenched with blood and staring at Murakami blankly. His mouth opened and closed but no sound emerged. After a moment he slumped soundlessly to his side.

Murakami looked down at him, then back to me. He shrugged again. "Looks like you saved me the trouble," he said.

Come on, Tatsu, where the fuck are you?

He unzipped his jacket and took a respectful step backward before shrugging it off. If he'd stayed just a little closer I would have moved on him as soon as it was down around his elbows, and he knew it.

He looked at the doorstop, my hand bloody around it. "We're going to do this armed?" he asked, his tone dead-man flat. "Okay."

He reached into a back pocket and pulled out a folded knife. He flicked a thumb stud on the handle and the blade snapped into position.

From the instant, semiauto opening, I knew it was a Kershaw model, essentially a quality, street-legal switchblade, the blade about ten centimeters. *Shit.*

In my unpleasant experience, unarmed against a knife, you've basically got four options. Your best bet is to run like hell, if you can. Next best is to do something immediately that prevents the attack from getting started. Third is to create distance so you can deploy a longer-range weapon. Fourth is to go berserk and hope not to get fatally cut going through and over your attacker.

I don't care how much training you've had, these are your only realistic options, and none of them is particularly good except maybe the first. Unarmed techniques against the knife are a crapshoot, and against a determined attacker with a live blade, they offer piss-poor odds.

My macho years are at least two decades behind me, and I would have been thrilled to turn and run if I could have. But in the enclosed space of the *dojo*, with a younger, and probably faster, enemy standing between me and the exit, running wasn't really an option, and I realized that the ordinarily depressing odds of emerging unhurt against a knife looked downright desolate.

I glanced over at the bag. It was about ten meters away, and my chances of getting to it and accessing the gun before Murakami put that blade in me were not good.

He smiled, the bridge a predatory rictus. "Throw away yours, and I'll throw away mine," he said.

He really was deranged. I had no interest in fighting him, only in killing him now or running away to wait for a more opportune moment. But maybe I could play this out.

"You going to tell me what this is about?" I asked.

"Throw away yours, and I'll throw away mine," he said again.

So much for that. I knew there was a set of weights in back. I might be able to reach them before he got to me. If there were loose plates, I could use them like missiles, wear him down, create an opening that would give me time to deploy the gun. Not a happy prospect against a guy with the reflexes to fight dogs, but I was running out of ideas.

"You first," I said.

"All right, armed," he said, and started coming toward me. But slowly, taking his time.

I tensed to go for the weights.

A commanding series of knocks rang out from the front door, and I heard the words *"Keisatsu da!"* Police! bellowed through a bullhorn.

Murakami's head swiveled in that direction, but his eyes didn't leave me. The combination evinced surprise, but also discipline.

It came again, a fist banging on metal. Then *"Keisatsu da! Akero!"* Police! Open up!

We looked at each other for a long second, but I already knew what he was going to do. He might have been crazy, but he was a survivor. A survivor reassesses odds continually and doesn't disrespect them.

He gestured at me with the knife. "Another time," he said. Then he bolted for the back.

I dashed to the gym bag. But by the time I'd reached it, he'd already made it inside the locker room and had slammed the door behind him. Following him in alone would be dangerous. Better to have Tatsu as backup.

I sprinted to the entranceway. The door was secured with horizontal, spring-loaded bars, and it took me a few seconds to figure out how to work the mechanism. There was a gear in the center that wouldn't give. *There, that latch—press that first.* I pressed and turned, and the bars pulled in.

I pulled the door open. Tatsu and another man were on the other side of it, both with their guns drawn. "Inside," I said, gesturing with my head. "There's a back door he might use. He's got a knife."

"I've already sent a man around back," Tatsu said. He nodded to his partner and the two of them moved inside. I followed them in.

They noted the two men on the floor, but could see they weren't going to pose a problem. We made our way to the back of the *dojo*. Tatsu's man moved toward the bathroom. "Not there," I said. "There. The locker room. There's a back door inside, but he might still be in there."

They took up positions on either side of the door, crouching to reduce their profile. Each held his gun close in and at the high-ready, which demonstrated some tactical acumen. Tatsu nodded, and his man, who was on the knob side of the door, reached out and pushed the door inward while Tatsu sighted down the funnel. As the door swung in, Tatsu tracked it with his eyes and his weapon.

Another nod and they went in, Tatsu in the lead. The room was empty. The exterior door was closed, but its bolt was pulled back and the lock I had seen previously was gone.

"There," I said. "He went through there." I thought of Tatsu's other man, the one who had gone around back. He and Murakami would have been on a collision course.

They took up their positions again and went through. I followed. Behind the building was a tiny courtyard, choked with refuse containers, empty boxes, and abandoned construction materials. A rusting HVAC unit lay disconnected and inert to one side. Opposite, the carcass of a refrigerator leaned sideways against a corrugated wall, its door gone, two of its interior shelves hanging out like innards from a gutted animal.

The courtyard fed into an alley. In the alley we found Tatsu's man.

He was on his back, his eyes open, one hand still clutching the gun that had been useless to him. Murakami had opened him up and left him. The ground around him was soaked in blood.

"*Chikusho,*" Tatsu breathed. Fuck. He knelt to confirm the man was dead, then pulled out his mobile phone and spoke into it while his remaining man scanned the alley.

I noted the absence of defensive wounds on the corpse—no slash marks on the hands or wrists. He hadn't even gotten his arms up to protect himself, let alone managed to fire his weapon. The poor bastard. The gun might have made him feel overconfident. A common error. In some conditions, and a narrow alley can be one of them, a blade will beat a bullet.

Tatsu stood and looked at me. His tone was calm but I could see quiet rage in his eyes.

"Murakami?" he asked.

I nodded.

"Those men inside, they're his?"

I nodded again.

"There is a large Mercedes parked in front of the building. I am guessing he arrived in it, and was planning to leave in it. Now he will be forced to rely on taxis or public transportation. He could not have done that"—he gestured to the downed man—"without getting a substantial amount of blood on him. We'll have men here shortly to search the area. We may be able to track him."

"I don't think so," I said.

His nostrils flared. "One of the two men inside looked well enough to interrogate," he said. "That will also be useful."

"Was there anyone out front when you arrived?" I asked. "Murakami cleared the place out just before you got here."

"There were several men outside," he said. "They scattered when they saw us. They won't be of immediate use."

"I'm sorry about your man," I told him, not knowing what else to say.

He nodded slowly, and for a moment his features seemed to sag. "His name was Fujimori. He was a good man, capable and idealistic. Later today I will have to tell these things to his widow."

He straightened, as though collecting himself. "Brief me now on what happened, then go, before the other officers arrive."

I told him. He listened without a word. When I was done, he looked at me and said, "Meet me at Christie teashop in Harajuku tonight at seven o'clock. Don't disappear. Don't make me have to find you."

I knew Christie, having been there many times while living in Tokyo. "I'll be there," I said.

"Where is the gun?"

"Inside. In a gym bag, by the front entrance. I'd like to keep it."

He shook his head. "I was asked about it today. I need to account for it or there will be trouble. I may be able to get you another."

"Do that," I said, thinking of the confident way Murakami had drawn his Kershaw.

He nodded, then looked at his fallen comrade. His jaw clenched, then released. "When I catch him," he said, "that's what I'm going to do to him."

CHAPTER 17

I walked out to Kototoi-dori and found a cab. Although their functioning was temporarily disrupted by what had just gone down at the *dojo,* with Murakami's people aware I was in Asakusa, the subway station would have been too likely a spot for an ambush.

The meeting Tatsu had demanded was over six hours away, and the bizarre, floating feeling of having nowhere to go and nothing to do was getting to me. I felt a rush of what someone ought to name post-traumatic-extreme-horniness disorder, and thought about calling Naomi. She'd be home right now, maybe just waking up. But with Murakami onto me, I didn't want to go anywhere where there was even a small chance I might be anticipated.

My pager buzzed. I checked it, saw a number I didn't recognize.

I dialed the number from a payphone. The other party picked up on the first ring.

"Can you tell who this is?" a male voice asked in English.

I recognized the voice. Kanezaki, my latest friend from the CIA.

"Please, just listen to what I have to say," he went on. "Don't hang up."

"How did you get this number?" I asked.

"Phone records—calls made from payphones near your friend's apartment. But I had nothing to do with what happened to him. I just found out about it. That's why I'm calling you."

I thought about that. If Kanezaki had a way of accessing a record of calls made from those payphones, he might have managed to zero in on my pager number. Harry's practice had been to use various local payphones to page me, after which he would return to his apartment and wait for my call. With access to the records, you might spot a pattern—the same number being called from various payphones in the neighborhood. If there were several hits, and I imagined there would be, you just call them all and eliminate the false positives by trial and error. I supposed this was a possibility Harry and I should have considered, but it didn't really matter. Even if someone managed to intercept my number, as Kanezaki seemed to have done, they'd learn nothing more than a pager address.

"I'm listening," I said.

"I want to meet with you," he said. "I think we can help each other."

"Yeah?"

"Yes. Look, I'm taking a big chance doing this. I know you might think I had something to do with what happened to your friend, and that you might want payback."

"You might be right."

"Yeah, well, I know you can find me eventually anyway. I figure I'm better off explaining what I think happened, rather than having to worry for the rest of my life about you sneaking up behind me."

"What do you propose?" I asked.

"A meeting. Anyplace you want, as long as it's public. I know if you listen to me you'll believe me. But I'm afraid you might try to do something before you've listened. Like you did the last time we saw each other."

I considered. If it was a setup, there were two ways in which they might try to get at me. The first way would be to have people watching Kanezaki, people who would move in as soon as I appeared on the scene. The second would be to monitor him remotely, with some kind of a transmitter, the way they had once done when Holtzer had tried to nail me after proposing a similar "meeting."

The second way was more likely, because I would have a harder time spotting Kanezaki's team if they didn't have to keep him in visual contact. I could use Harry's bug detector to eliminate the second possibility. I'd have to take him someplace deserted to eliminate the first.

"Where are you right now?" I asked him.

"Toranomon. Near the embassy."

"You know Japan Sword? The antique sword shop in Toranomon three-chome, near the station?"

"I know it."

"Go there. I'll see you in thirty minutes."

"Okay."

I clicked off. Actually, I had no intention of going to the sword shop, much as I enjoy browsing there from time to time. But I wanted Kanezaki and anyone he was with to take the trouble to set up there, while I established myself in a more secure venue.

I took a series of cabs and trains to the Imperial Palace Wadakuramon Gate. With its swarms of tourists, batteries of security cameras, and phalanxes of cops protecting the important personages inside, the Wadakuramon Gate would be a highly inconvenient place to have to gun someone down, if that's what Kanezaki and company had in mind. Having him go there after I was already set up would force a potential surveillance team to move quickly, giving me a better chance to spot them.

I used Tatsu's mobile phone to call Kanezaki again when I had arrived. "Change of plans," I told him.

There was a pause. "Okay."

"Meet me at the Imperial Palace Wadakuramon Gate, across from Tokyo Station. Come right now. I'm waiting in front. Approach me from Tokyo Station so I can see that you're alone."

"I'll be there in ten minutes."

I clicked off.

I found a taxi on Hibiya-dori, which intersects the boulevard that leads from Tokyo Station to the Imperial Palace. I got in and asked the driver to wait, explaining that I would be meeting a friend here shortly. He clicked on the meter and we sat in silence.

Ten minutes later, I saw Kanezaki approaching as I had requested. He was looking around, but didn't spot me in the cab.

I cracked the window. "Kanezaki," I said. "Get in."

The driver activated the automatic door. Kanezaki hesitated—a cab obviously wasn't quite the "public" place he had been hoping for. But he got over it and slid in next to me. The door closed and we drove off.

I told the driver to take us in the direction of Akihabara, Tokyo's electronics mecca. I watched behind us but didn't see any unusual activity. No one was scrambling to keep up with him. It looked like he was alone.

I reached over and patted him down. Other than his mobile phone, keys, and a new wallet, he wasn't carrying anything. Harry's detector stayed quiet.

I had the driver use backstreets to lessen the chance that someone could be tailing us. We got out near Ochanomizu Station, and from there continued a series of swift moves in trains and on foot to ensure we were alone.

I finished the route in Otsuka, the extreme north of the Yamanote line. Otsuka is a neighborhood kind of place, albeit a somewhat seedy one, with a generous offering of massage parlors and love hotels. Beyond the locals who live and work there, it seems to cater primarily to older men in search of downmarket sexual commerce. Caucasians are rare. If there were a surveillance team and they were white CIA-issue, Otsuka would make for a difficult approach.

We took the stairs to the second-story Royal Host restaurant across from the station. We went in and I looked around. Mostly families enjoying a night out. A couple of tired-looking salarymen avoiding an evening at home. We sat in a corner that offered me a nice view of the street scene below.

I looked at him. "Go on," I said.

He rubbed his hands together and looked around. "Oh man, if I get caught doing this…"

"Cut the dramatics," I told him. "Just tell me what you want."

"I don't want you to think I had anything to do with your friend," he said. "And I want us to put our heads together."

I said nothing.

"Okay. To start with, I think… I think I'm being set up."

"What does this have to do with my friend?"

"Just let me start at the beginning, and you'll see, okay?"

I nodded. "Go ahead."

He licked his lips. "You remember the program I told you about? Crepuscular?"

A waitress came over and I realized I was starving. Without checking the menu I ordered a roast beef *sandoichi* and their soup of the day. Kanezaki asked for a coffee.

"I remember it," I told him.

"Well, Crepuscular was formally terminated six months ago."

"So?"

"So it's still going on anyway, and I'm still running it, even though the funding has been cut off. Why hasn't anyone said anything to me? And where is the money coming from?"

"Slow down," I said. "How did you find out about this?"

"A few days ago my boss, the Chief of Station, told me he wanted to see all the receipts I've collected from the program's assets."

"Biddle?"

He looked at me. "Yes. You know him?"

"I know of him. Tell me about the receipts."

"Agency policy. When we disburse funds, the asset has to sign a receipt. Without the receipt, it would be too easy for case officers to skim cash off the disbursements."

"You've been having these people... sign for their payouts?" I asked, incredulous.

"It's policy," he said again.

"They're willing to do that?"

He shrugged. "Not always, not at first. We're trained in how to get an asset comfortable with the notion. You don't even bring it up the first time. The second time, you tell him it's a new USG policy, designed to ensure all the recipients of our funding are getting their full allotments. If he still balks, you tell him all right, you're going out on a limb but you'll see what you can do on his behalf. By the fifth time he's addicted to the money and you tell him your superiors have reprimanded you for not getting the receipts, they've told you they're going to cut you off if you don't get the paperwork signed. You hand the guy the receipt and ask him to just scrawl something. The first one is illegible. Later, they get more readable."

Amazing, I thought. "All right. Biddle asks for the receipts."

"Right. So I gave them to him, but it felt weird to me."

"Why?"

He rubbed the back of his neck. "When the program got started, I was told that I would be responsible for maintaining all the receipts in my own safe. I was worried about why the Chief suddenly wanted them, even though he told me it was just routine. So I checked with some people I know at Langley—obliquely, of course. And I learned that, for a program with this level of classification, no one would ask to see documentation unless someone had first filed a formal complaint with the Agency's Inspector General with specific allegations of case officer dishonesty."

"How do you know that hasn't happened?"

He flushed. "First, because there's no reason for it. I haven't done anything wrong. Second, if there had been a formal complaint, protocol would have been for the Chief to sit me down with the lawyers present. Embezzling funds is a serious accusation."

"All right. So you give Biddle the receipts, but you feel weird about it."

"Yes. So I started going through the Crepuscular cable traffic. The traffic is numbered sequentially, and I noticed a missing cable. I wouldn't have spotted it except that it occurred to me to check the numerical sequence. Ordinarily you wouldn't notice something like that because no one ever searches the files by cable number, it's too much trouble, and anyway, ordinarily the number isn't even relevant. I called someone at East Asia Division at Langley and had her read the cable to me over the phone. The cable said Crepuscular was being terminated and should be discontinued immediately because the funding was being applied elsewhere."

"You think someone on this end pulled the cable so you wouldn't know the program had been terminated?"

"Yes."

The waitress brought our order. I started wolfing down the sandwich.

He was feeling talkative and I wanted to hear more. We would get to Harry soon enough.

"Tell me more about Crepuscular," I said, between bites.

"Like what?"

"Like when did it get started. And how you learned of it."

"I already told you. Eighteen months ago I was told Tokyo Station had been tasked with an action program of assisting reform and removing impediments. Code name Crepuscular."

Eighteen months ago, I thought. *Hmm.* "Who put you in charge of the program originally?" I asked, though, given the timeline, I already had a pretty good idea of the answer.

"The previous Station Chief. William Holtzer."

Holtzer, I thought. *His good works live on.*

"Tell me how he presented it to you," I said. "Be specific."

He glanced to his left, which for most people is a neurolinguistic sign of recall rather than of construction. Had he looked in the opposite direction, I would have read it as a lie. "He told me Crepuscular was compartmental classified, and that he wanted me to be in charge of it."

"What was your precise role?"

"Development of target assets, disbursement of funding, overall management of the program."

"Why you?"

He shrugged. "I didn't ask."

I suppressed a laugh. "Did you assume it was only natural that, despite your youth and inexperience, he was astute enough to recognize your inherent capabilities, and wanted to entrust you with something so important?"

He flushed. "Something like that, I suppose."

I closed my eyes briefly and shook my head. "Kanezaki, are you familiar with the terms 'front man' and 'fall guy'?"

His flush deepened. "I might not be as stupid as you think," he said.

"What else?"

"Holtzer told me support for reform would involve funneling cash to specified politicians with a reformist agenda, the kind of reforms favored by the USG. The theory was that, to compete in Japanese politics, you need access to large quantities of cash. You can't stay in office without it, so over time everyone either gets corrupted because they took the cash or weeded out because they refused to. We were going to change the equation with an alternate source of funds."

"Funds acknowledged with receipts."

"That's policy, yes. I've told you."

"I imagine that, when your assets are signing the receipts, they handle them?"

He shrugged. "Sure."

I wondered briefly why they hired these guys right out of college. "I'm curious," I said, "whether you can think of any uses to which someone might want to put signed, fingerprinted documents acknowledging receipt of CIA-dispersed funding."

He shook his head. "It's not what you're thinking. The CIA doesn't use blackmail."

I laughed.

"Look, I'm not saying we don't use it because we're nice people," he went on with almost comedic earnestness. "It's because it's been demonstrated not to work. Maybe you can use it to get short-term cooperation, but in the long-term it's just not an effective means of control."

I looked at him. "Does the CIA strike you as an organization that's particularly focused on the long-term?"

"We try to be, yes."

"Well, if you're not under investigation for embezzlement, and blackmail is an alien notion at the CIA, what do you think Biddle is doing with those receipts?"

He looked down. "I don't know."

"Then what do you want from me?"

"There's one more thing that's strange."

I raised my eyebrows.

"Protocol is, before every asset meeting, case officers have to fill out a form with particulars of the anticipated meeting: who, where, when. The purpose is to provide a record other case officers can use if anything goes wrong. After the Chief's request, I turned in the form saying I had an asset meeting tonight, though the truth is I don't, but I left the place of the meeting blank."

"And you got called on it."

"Right. Which is weird. No one should be taking an interest in these things before a meeting. They're for post-meeting contingencies. In fact, half the time, we don't even bother filling them out until afterward. It's too much of a pain. And you never hear anything about it."

"What are you thinking?"

"That someone is observing these meetings."

"For what?"

"I don't… I don't know."

"Then I don't see how I can help you."

"All right. It's possible someone is trying to gather some kind of evidence that I've been running Crepuscular by myself since it was terminated. Maybe in case it comes out, that way Biddle or whoever could just blame me." He looked at me. "As their fall guy."

Maybe the kid wasn't so naïve after all. "You still haven't told me what you want from me," I said.

"I want you to run countersurveillance tonight and tell me what you see."

"I'm flattered, but wouldn't you be better off going to the CIA Inspector General?"

"With what? Suspicions? Besides, for all I know, the IG and the Station Chief went to Yale together and they were buddies in Skull and Bones. Remember, as of six months ago, Crepuscular was shut down. At which point it effectively became illegal. And all this time I've been running it. Before I go through channels, I need to figure out just what is going on."

I was quiet for a moment. Then I said, "What are you offering me in return?"

"I'll tell you what I know about your friend."

"If what you tell me is convincing and valuable, I'll help you."

"You won't renege?"

"You're going to have to take that chance."

He pouted like a kid who thinks he's made a reasonable request and is hurt that he isn't being taken seriously.

"Okay," he said after a moment. "The last time we met, I told you we identified Haruyoshi Fukasawa as an acquaintance of yours by intercepting a letter from him to Kawamura Midori. All we had from the letter was his first name, which is spelled with an unusual combination of *kanji*, and a postmark for the main Chuo-ku post office."

That tracked pretty much with what Harry and I had come up with ourselves. "Keep going," I said.

"There was a lot of information to sift through if we were going to make effective use of those two small bits of information. Local ward domicile records, tax records, things like that. We'd have to work outward in concentric circles starting with the Chuo-ku postmark. That meant manpower and local expertise."

I nodded, knowing what was next. "So you outsourced it."

"We did. To a Station asset named Yamaoto."

Christ, they might as well have just put out a contract on Harry. I closed my eyes and thought. "Did you tell Yamaoto why you were interested in Fukasawa?"

He shook his head. "Of course not. We just told him we wanted to know where a person with that name lived and worked."

"What happened after that?"

"I don't know. Yamaoto got us the addresses we wanted. We tailed Fukasawa as closely as we could, but he was surveillance conscious and we never managed to stay with him long enough to follow him to you."

"You're not telling me much that I don't already know. What about Fukasawa's death?"

"I went to his apartment the other day with diplomatic security to try to surveil him as usual. I told Biddle I didn't think this was a good idea after our previous encounter, that it was personally dangerous for me, but he insisted. Anyway, I saw a lot of unusual activity. Police cars, and a... a cleanup crew for the sidewalk in front of his building. I looked into it and found out what had happened. When I told Biddle, he got totally pale."

"Meaning?"

"Meaning my impression was that he was both surprised and up-set. If he was surprised, it means someone else was responsible for this. I'm assuming it wasn't an accident. That leaves you and Yamaoto. Since you're here and seem to care, I'm also assuming you and Fukasawa didn't have some kind of falling out. That leaves Yamaoto."

"Let's assume you're right. Why?"

He swallowed. "I don't know. I mean, at a general level, I would guess it would be either because Fukasawa posed some sort of threat or because he was no longer useful, but I don't know more than that."

"You ever see Fukasawa with a woman?"

He nodded. "Yes, we saw him coming and going several times with a Yukiko Nohara. She works at a club in Nogizaka called Damask Rose."

I considered. My gut told me he was being straight. But I had no way of knowing for certain. Besides, for the little he'd given me, I wasn't going to take the kind of chances running countersurveillance for him could entail.

Tatsu might be interested, though. And he might be better able to use Kanezaki's meager information than I could.

"I've got a meeting in a few hours with someone who can help you with your problem," I said. "Someone who can do more than I can."

"Does that mean you believe me?"

I looked at him. "I haven't decided yet."

There was a pause, then he said, "My wallet."

I raised my eyebrows.

"Where is it?" he asked.

I chuckled. "It's gone."

"There were fifty thousand yen in it."

I nodded. "Just enough for a gustation menu and an '85 Rousseau Chambertin at a restaurant I like. Though I did have to go out of pocket on the '70 Vega Sicilia Unico I had with dessert, so next time you get it in your head to surveil me, bring along a few more yen, okay?"

He glowered. "You robbed me."

"You're lucky you didn't pay a much higher price than that for trying to follow me. Now let's see if the guy I'm going to see is willing to give you the assistance you want."

I took him to Christie Tea & Cake, the *kissaten* that Tatsu had proposed earlier. We walked the short distance from JR Harajuku Station. The proprietor, perhaps remembering me and my seating preferences from my Tokyo days, led us to one of the tables at the back of the long, L-shaped room, where we could sit hidden from the window in front.

Kanezaki ordered an Assam tea set. I asked for jasmine, both for myself and for our yet-to-arrive third party. After the day we'd just had, I figured Tatsu and I could use something low caffeine.

We made small talk while we waited for Tatsu. Kanezaki was surprisingly garrulous, perhaps out of nervousness at his circumstances. "How did you get into this business?" I asked him.

"I'm third-generation American Japanese," he told me. "*Sansei.* My parents speak Japanese, but they used English at home with me so I only learned what I picked up from my grandparents. In college I did a homestay program in Japan, in Nagano-ken, and I loved it. Kind of put me in touch with my heritage, you know? After that, I took all the Japanese courses I could and did another homestay. During my senior year, I met a CIA recruiter on campus. He told me the Agency was looking for people with hard language skills—Japanese, Chinese, Korean, Arabic. I figured what the hell. I took the tests, passed a background check, and here I am."

"Has the job met your expectations?" I asked, with a small smile.

"Not exactly. But I can roll with the punches. I might be tougher than you think, you know."

I thought of his surprising lack of fear during our initial encounter, the way he'd collected himself after watching me take out his partner, and wasn't inclined to disagree.

"Anyway," he went on, "the main thing is that the job puts me in a position to serve the interests of both countries. That's what really attracted me to it in the first place."

"How do you mean?"

"America wants Japan to reform. And Japan needs to reform, but lacks the internal resources to do it. So *gaiatsu* from the U.S. is in both countries' interests."

Gaiatsu means "foreign pressure." I wondered briefly whether there was a country outside Japan that had a dedicated word for the concept.

"Sounds idealistic," I said, probably failing to hide my dubiousness.

He shrugged. "Maybe. But we're one world now. If Japan's economy sinks, it'll drag America down with it. So U.S. ideals and U.S. pragmatism on the one hand, and Japanese needs on the other, are all aligned. I feel lucky to be in a position to work for the countries' mutual welfare."

I had a brief image of this kid ten years from now, running for office. "You given any thought to what you'll do if you ever have to choose?" I asked him.

He looked at me. "I'm American."

I nodded. "Then as long as America lives up to her ideals, you ought to be fine."

The waiter brought our tea. A moment later Tatsu appeared. If he was surprised to see me with Kanezaki, he didn't show it. Tatsu has a great poker face.

Kanezaki looked at me, then at Tatsu. "Ishikura-san," he said, half rising from his seat.

Tatsu bowed his head in greeting.

"You told us he was dead," Kanezaki said in English, inclining his head toward me.

Tatsu shrugged. "At the time, I believed he was."

"Why didn't you get in touch when you learned he wasn't?"

There was a trace of amusement in Tatsu's eyes at this kid's straightforwardness, and he said, "Something tells me it was fortunate I did not."

Kanezaki furrowed his brow, then nodded. "That may be true."

I looked at Kanezaki. "Tell him what you told me," I said.

He did. When he was done, Tatsu said, "It seems the most likely explanation for this unusual chain of events is that Station Chief Biddle or someone else in the CIA is preparing to turn you into a twenty-first century Oliver North."

"Oliver North?" Kanezaki asked.

"Yes," Tatsu went on, "from the Iran-Contra scandal. The Reagan administration had decided to circumvent a congressional ban on funds to the Nicaraguan Contras by selling arms to Iranian 'moderates' and channeling the resulting proceeds to the Contras without Congress's knowledge. Oliver North was a National Security Council staffer who ran the program day to day. When the program leaked, his betters in the NSC and the White House blamed him, as a way of escaping prosecution, for having instigated and run the program without their knowledge."

Kanezaki paled. "I hadn't thought about it that way," he said, looking from left to right as though trying to rediscover his bearings. "Oh, man, you're right, this really could be like Iran-Contra. I don't know who dreamed up Crepuscular in the first place, but someone terminated it, maybe Langley, or the NSC, or maybe even the Senate Select Committee on Intelligence. And now Tokyo Station is still running it, I'm still running it, with funds from some source outside of Congress's purview. Oh, man."

I had a feeling he was imagining himself getting sworn in before some special congressional committee established to investigate the latest scandal, sitting alone, his hand raised, the congressmen and their staffers prim and hypocritical behind their polished wooden dais, the video camera lights hot and blinding, while his superiors clucked their tongues and leaked to the press about the talented young CIA officer whose overly strong convictions had made him turn rogue.

Tatsu turned to me. "I have something for you."

I raised my eyebrows.

"Kawamura Midori. It seems that, in her zeal to locate you, she retained a Japanese private investigative firm. Many of these firms are staffed with ex-Keisatuscho and other law enforcement officials, and I have contacts among several. She knew where your friend lived and gave the firm his address. They attempted to follow him, but apparently were unable to do so because he was surveillance conscious. They did not learn your whereabouts. I believe this is why Kawamura-san came to my office recently with threats of a scandal. Her other means of locating you had not proven useful."

She must have been using an inheritance from her old man—the fruits of the corruption that had enriched him and disgusted her. There was some irony there.

I thought of the way she had seemed evasive at the Imperial. Now I knew why. She'd hired a PI to tail Harry and didn't want to tell me.

"These PI firms," I said. "Are any of them connected to Yamaoto?"

"Doubtless."

"That's why he put Yukiko on Harry," I said, finally seeing it. "It wasn't the Agency's request—they didn't tell him Harry was connected to me. It was Midori's PI people. She would have told them that they were following Harry to find me. When that information got back to Yamaoto, he wanted his own coverage—better coverage than the PI firm, or even the Agency, would be capable of. Her job was to stay close, really close, and learn as much as she could to help them get to me."

I pictured it. Yamaoto, probably through intermediaries, got Harry's boss to take Harry out to "celebrate" about that happy client. Harry's boss wouldn't know the purpose of all this, just where and when he was supposed to show up with Harry. Yukiko was waiting there, with a line about configuring her computer and bedroom eyes behind it. Harry swallowed the whole thing without a burp. He led Yukiko and her employers straight back to his apartment, and eventually to me.

"Why kill him, though?" Kanezaki asked.

I shrugged, thinking of the way Murakami had growled *Your name isn't Arai. It's Rain.* "They'd learned who I was and knew where to find me. They didn't need Harry after that. And Yukiko would have learned about some of his skills—he was former NSA, a top hacker. They would have viewed him as an asset of mine. Best to take him off the board."

I thought of how deeply Harry had been in denial, how hostile he'd been to any suggestion that Yukiko might be setting him up. I sighed. "That's probably how they found out who I was, too," I said. "Harry and I had an argument about the girl. He probably told her he had a friend who said this and that, a friend her boss had recently taken to Damask Rose. They might have put two and two together from that. Or they might have shown the video from the club to Yamaoto, who knows my face. It doesn't matter. Once they knew, they decided Harry had to go."

There was a long silence. Then Tatsu said, "Kanezaki-san, what do you propose to do?"

Kanezaki looked at him, his expression uncertain. "Well, originally I wanted someone non-Agency to run countersurveillance for me tonight. So I could know whether I'm being watched, or being set up, or whatever. But not you. You're…"

Tatsu smiled. "I am Keisatsucho."

"Right. It wouldn't do to have the Japanese FBI observing a CIA meeting with a sensitive national asset."

"I thought tonight's meeting was fictitious, designed to test your theory that someone wishes your assets ill."

"It is fictitious. But I've filled out paperwork saying it's real. If I get caught with you, the consequences will be the same."

Tatsu shrugged. "If someone sees us together, you can tell them you are developing me as an asset. Following up on the original contact you and Station Chief Biddle made when you were looking for our friend here."

Kanezaki looked at him. "Maybe I am developing you."

I thought, *Tatsu knew you were going to say that, kid.*

"You see?" Tatsu asked. "Not so far-fetched."

I thought of an old poker players' expression: *If you look around the table and can't spot the sucker, the sucker is you.*

No one said anything for a long time. Then Kanezaki let out a long breath and said, "I can't believe I'm doing this. I could go to jail."

"For a meeting with a potentially important asset?" Tatsu asked, and I knew the deal was closed.

"Right," Kanezaki said, more to himself than to anyone else. "That's right."

I thought of another saying I'd once heard: *It's easiest to sell to a salesman.*

All that training in how to suborn an asset into signing a receipt. Kanezaki had practically bragged about how adroitly a good case officer could do it. And yet he'd just stepped over a line without even looking down to see if it was there.

I thought of those pictorial representations of the food chain, a fish being swallowed by a bigger fish being swallowed by an even bigger one.

I glanced at Kanezaki and thought, *At least Tatsu won't betray you. Unless he absolutely has to.*

CHAPTER 18

We all departed so Kanezaki could go to his "meeting" and Tatsu could have men run countersurveillance for him. We agreed to meet back at Christie in two hours. I asked Tatsu before we left whether he'd managed to get another gun for me. He told me he hadn't.

I spent a short time browsing among the antiques in the basement of the nearby Hanae Mori Building. The shops were closed, but through the windows I admired the delicate Art Nouveau cameo glassware of artists like Daum Nancy and Emile Gallé. I lost myself in the little worlds depicted on the vases and tumblers: a green meadow inhabited by hovering dragonflies; windmills slumbering under a blanket of snow; a forest of trees so sensuous they seemed to sway in their glass etchings.

I returned to Christie well in advance of our follow-up meeting, but I didn't wait there. Instead, I checked the places a surveillance team would use if it were interested in someone in the shop, and then, confirming these spots were deserted, I perched like one of Tokyo's baleful ravens in the darkness atop the incline to the right of the shop, observing its entrance. Only after I had seen Kanezaki and then Tatsu return, and only after I had waited to ensure they weren't followed, did I descend and join them.

"We've been waiting," Tatsu said when I came in. "I didn't want to start without you."

"Sorry," I said. "I got held up."

He looked at me as though he understood exactly what had caused the delay, then turned to Kanezaki and said, "I took two men to observe the area around your ostensible meeting. We discovered someone who was there attempting to photograph the proceedings."

Kanezaki's eyes bulged. "Photograph?"

Tatsu nodded.

"What did you do?" he asked.

"We took the individual into custody."

"Oh, man," Kanezaki said, probably imagining the headlines in tomorrow's papers. "Official custody?"

Tatsu shook his head. "Unofficial."

"Who is he?" Kanezaki asked.

"His name is Edmund Gretz," Tatsu said. "He came to Tokyo three years ago, hoping to make a living as a freelance photographer, with visions of models on runways. Instead he found himself giving English lessons at various Japanese corporations. But eventually he did manage to find someone interested in his talents as a photographer."

"The Agency?" Kanezaki asked, his complexion pale.

"Yes. He is a contractor. Six months ago he was given training in surveillance and countersurveillance and various other clandestine arts. Since then, the Agency has contacted him three times. On each occasion, he was given a time and place where a meeting was to occur, and instructed to photograph the meeting as it progressed."

"How did he know who he was shooting?"

"He was given a photograph of an ethnic Japanese who would always be a participant."

"Me."

"Yes."

I shook my head in wonder and thought, *You ought to just have "fall guy" printed on your business cards.*

"And Gretz's handler..." Kanezaki said.

"The Station Chief," Tatsu answered. "James Biddle."

"The same guy who wanted the receipts," I said.

Tatsu nodded. "Yes."

"I imagine the contractor wasn't able to shed any light on why," I said.

Tatsu shook his head. "Gretz is only a flunky, with some skill behind the lens. He doesn't know anything. His biggest concern was that no one should find out we had picked him up, lest he lose his lucrative sidework or face deportation."

"You couldn't get anything more out of him?" Kanezaki asked.

Tatsu shrugged. "My men did not ask nicely. I don't believe there was anything more to be gotten."

"What does he do with the photos after he's taken them?" Kanezaki asked.

"He delivers the prints to Biddle," Tatsu said.

Kanezaki was drumming his fingers on the table. "What's he going to do with those photos? Why would he do this to me?"

"I may have a way of finding out," Tatsu said.

"What's that?"

Tatsu shook his head. "Not yet. Let me make some discreet inquiries. I will contact you soon."

Kanezaki's eyes narrowed slightly. "Why would you help me?" he asked.

Tatsu looked at him. "I have my own reasons for wishing to avoid a scandal," he said. "Among them, my desire that the reformers you have been trying to aid not be harmed by all this."

Kanezaki's expression loosened. He was scared. He wanted to believe he had a friend. "Okay," he said.

Kanezaki stood to go. He reached into his jacket pocket, took out a card, and handed it to Tatsu. "Please, contact me as soon as you know more," he said.

Tatsu stood, too. He gave him a card in return. "I will."

Kanezaki said, "Thank you."

Tatsu bowed low and said, *"Kochira koso."* The same here.

Kanezaki nodded to me and walked away.

I waited a minute to allow Kanezaki to get clear, then said, "Let's go."

Tatsu understood. When I was a teenager, I once won a fight at a party. The guy I'd beaten left, while I enjoyed the feeling of being a hero. Trouble was, the guy returned a half hour later, only this time with two friends. The three of them beat the crap out of me. The lesson was worth it. It taught me that when the meeting is done, you leave, unless you want to take a chance on someone backing up on you.

We walked toward Inokashira-dori, the still darkness of Yoyogi Park to our right.

"How did it go today?" I asked as we walked. "With your man's wife. His widow."

Several seconds went by before he answered. "Fujimori-san," he said, and I wasn't sure whether he was talking about his fallen comrade or the wife. "I am fortunate to have had only three such conversations in my time with the Keisatsucho."

We continued to walk in silence. Then I asked, "Any luck tracking Murakami today?"

He shook his head. "No."

"The guy you interrogated?"

"Nothing yet."

"Why did you want to see me tonight?"

"I wanted all my resources accessible, in case there was a hot lead on Murakami."

"It's personal now?" I asked.

"It's personal."

We walked in silence. "I'll tell you one thing," I said. "Just when I think I'm getting jaded, the CIA does something to really surprise me, like hiring a photographer to take pictures of its own case officers in case it needs to burn them. It's refreshing."

"There is no photographer," Tatsu said.

I stopped and looked at him. "What?"

He shrugged. "I made him up."

I shook my head and blinked. "There's no Gretz?"

"There is a Gretz, in case Kanezaki thinks to check. A small time dope dealer I once caught and let go. I had a feeling he might be useful later."

I didn't know what to say. "Tell me what I'm missing, Tatsu."

"Not that much, really. I simply offered Kanezaki corroboration that his fears are not mere paranoia, while positioning myself as a friend."

"Why?"

"I needed him to be thoroughly convinced he is indeed being set up. We don't yet have sufficient information to really know what action to take. I want him to be comfortable calling on me. Even eager."

"Is he being set up, do you think?"

He shrugged. "Who knows? Biddle's request for the receipts seems suspicious, as does that missing cable, but I don't pretend to understand all the CIA's bureaucratic procedures."

"Why would Biddle have been taking such an inordinate interest in Kanezaki's meetings?"

"I don't know. But it wasn't to photograph them. My men observed nothing out of place at the meeting site. Certainly no one with a camera."

He was being awfully open with me about his duplicity. Perhaps his way of telling me he trusted me. The in-group and the out-group. Us and them.

We started walking again. "It was lucky, then, that the kid came to me with his suspicions," I said.

"And that you came to me. Thank you for that."

We walked in silence for a moment. Then I asked, "What do you know about Crepuscular?"

"No more than what Kanezaki has told us."

"The politicians the program has been underwriting—are you working with any of them? Maybe the ones the disk didn't implicate?"

"Some of them."

"What happened? You learned from the disk they weren't in Yamaoto's network. Then what?"

"I warned them. Simply sharing my information on Yamaoto's methods, and on who among them was a Yamaoto stooge, turned them into considerably wiser, and harder, targets."

"And you knew they were taking money from the CIA?"

"I knew of some, not necessarily all. From my position, I can only help protect these people from Yamaoto's practices of extortion. But Kanezaki was correct in saying that, in Japan's system of money politics, honest politicians still need cash to compete against Yamaoto-funded candidates. And that I cannot provide."

We walked wordlessly for a minute. Then he said, "I admit I was surprised to learn these people would be foolish enough to sign receipts for CIA disbursements. I fault myself, for underestimating the depth of their gullibility. I should have known better. As a breed, politicians can be astonishingly stupid, even when they are not being venal. If it were otherwise, Yamaoto would have a much harder time controlling them."

I thought for a moment. "Forgive me for saying so, Tatsu, but isn't this whole thing just a waste of time?"

"Why do you say?"

"Because even if these guys have some ideals, even if you can protect them from Yamaoto, even if they have access to some cash, you know they can't make a difference. Politicians in Japan are just ornamentation. The bureaucrats run the show."

"Our system is strange, is it not," he said. "An uncomfortable combination of domestic history and foreign intervention. The bureaucrats are certainly powerful. Functionally, they are the descendents of the samurai, with everything that lineage entails."

I nodded. After the Meiji Restoration in 1868, the samurai became the servants of the emperor, who was himself believed to be descended from the gods. The association connoted tremendous status.

"Then the wartime system put them in charge of the industrial economy," he continued. "The American occupation maintained this system so America could rule through the bureaucracy rather than through elected politicians. All this led to an accrual of additional prestige, additional power."

"I've always said Japan's rule by bureaucracy is a kind of totalitarianism."

"It is. But it is distinguished in that there is no Big Brother figure. Rather, the structure itself functions as Big Brother."

"That's my point. What can you gain by protecting a handful of elected politicians?"

"For the moment, perhaps not much. Today, the politicians act mainly as mediators between the bureaucrats and the voters. Their job is to secure for their constituents the biggest slice possible from the pie the bureaucrats control."

"Like lobbyists in the U.S."

"Yes. But the politicians are elected. The bureaucrats are not. This means the voters do exercise theoretical control. If they elected politicians with a mandate to rein in the bureaucracy, the bureaucrats would bend, because their power is a function of their prestige, and to oppose a clear political consensus would be to risk that prestige."

I didn't say anything. I understood his point, though I suspected his planning was so long-term as to be ultimately futile.

We walked for a few moments in silence. Then he stopped and turned to me.

"I would like you to have a chat with Station Chief Biddle," he said.

"I'd love to. Kanezaki seems to think Biddle was surprised to hear about Harry's death, but I'd like to make sure. The problem is how to get to him."

"The CIA Chief of Station is declared to the Japanese government. Many of his movements are no mystery to the Keisatsucho." He reached into his jacket pocket and took out a photo. A mid-forties Caucasian with a narrow face and nose, and close-cropped, sandy-colored thinning hair, the eyes blue behind tortoiseshell glasses.

"Mr. Biddle takes afternoon tea weekdays at Jardin de Luseine, in Harajuku. Building Two," he said. "On Brahms-no-komichi."

"A man of habit?"

"Apparently, Mr. Biddle believes a faithful routine is good for the mind."

"It might be," I said, considering. "But it can be hell on the body."

He nodded. "Why don't you join him tomorrow?"

I looked at him. "I might do that," I said.

I walked for a long time after leaving Tatsu. I thought about Murakami. I tried to find the nexus points, the intersections between his fluid existence and the more concrete world around him. There wasn't much: the *dojo*, Damask Rose, maybe Yukiko. But I knew he'd be staying away from all of those for a while, possibly a long while, just as I would. I also knew he'd be running the same game against me. I was glad that, from his perspective, the good nexus points would seem to be in short supply.

Still, I wished I could have held onto Tatsu's Glock. Ordinarily, I don't like to carry an unambiguous weapon. Guns are noisy and ballistics tests can connect the bullet you left behind to the weapon that's still in your possession. Besides, getting caught with a firearm in Japan is a guaranteed ticket to jail. Knives aren't much better. A knife makes a mess that can get all over you. And any cop worth a damn in any country will treat someone caught with a concealed knife—even a small one—as dangerous and warranting additional scrutiny. With Murakami out there and onto me, of course, the risk and reward ratio of a concealed weapon had changed fairly dramatically.

I wondered whether Tatsu would get anything useful out of the guy whose knee I had broken. I doubted it. Murakami would know Tatsu was working that angle, and adjust his patterns to account for anything his captured man might reveal under pressure.

Yukiko might have some useful information. Murakami would have anticipated that route, too, but it was still worth exploring. Especially because, after what they had done to Harry, my interest in Yukiko had become independent of my interest in her boss.

I pictured her, the long hair, the aloof confidence. She might be taking precautions, after Harry. Murakami might even have warned her to be careful. But she was no hard target. I could get to her. And I thought I knew how.

I went to a spy paraphernalia shop in Shinjuku to buy a few things I would need. What the store offered to the public was almost scary: pinhole cameras and phone taps. Taser guns and tear gas. Diamond-bit drills and lock picks. All available "for academic purposes only," of course. I contented myself with a Secret Service-style ASP tactical baton, a nasty piece of black steel that collapsed to nine inches and telescoped to twenty-six with a snap of the wrist.

Next stop was a sporting goods store, where I bought a roll of thirty-pound-test high-impact monofilament fishing line, white sports tape, gloves, a wool hat, long underwear, and a canvas bag. Third stop, a drug store for some cheap cologne, a hand towel, and a pack of cigarettes and matches. Next, a local Gap for an unobtrusive change of clothes. Then a novelty shop for a fright wig and a set of rotted false teeth. Finally, a packaging supply house, for a twenty-five-meter roll of translucent packing tape. *Shinjuku,* I thought, like an advertising jingle. *For All Your Shopping Needs.*

I holed up in another business hotel, this time in Ueno. I set my watch alarm for midnight and went to sleep.

When the alarm woke me, I slipped the long underwear on under my clothes and secured the baton to my wrist with two lengths of the sports tape. I wet the towel and wrung it out, put it and other gear I had bought into the canvas bag, and walked out to the station, where I found a payphone. I still had the card I had taken on my first night at Damask Rose. I called the phone number on it.

A man answered the phone. It might have been Mr. Ruddy, but I wasn't sure.

"*Hai,* Damask Rose," the voice said. I heard J-Pop playing in the background and imagined dancers on the twin stages.

"Hello," I said, in Japanese, raising my voice slightly to disguise it. "Can you tell me who's there tonight?"

The voice intoned a half-dozen names. Naomi was among them. So was Yukiko.

"Great," I said. "Are they all there until three?"

"*Hai, sou desu.*" Yes, they are.

"Great," I said again. "I'll see you later."

I hung up.

I caught a cab to Shibuya, then did a foot SDR to Minami-Aoyama. I remembered Yukiko's address from the time I had checked her and Naomi's backgrounds from Osaka, and I had no trouble finding her apartment building. The main entrance was in front. An underground garage was off to one side, accessible only by a grated metal door controlled by a magnetic card reader in a center island. No other ways in or out.

I thought of her white M3. Assuming the night I had seen her in it wasn't an anomaly, it was her commuting vehicle. She wouldn't be driving it to Harry's tonight, and Murakami would either be unreachable for the moment or he would have told her to stay away. I judged there was an excellent possibility that she would be pulling in sometime after three.

I found a nearby building separated from its neighbor by a long, narrow alley. I moved into the shadows there and opened my bag of goodies. I took out the cologne and applied a heavy dose to my nostrils. Then I closed the bag and stashed it, and walked into nearby Roppongi.

It didn't take me long to find a homeless man who looked about the right size. He was sitting on a cinderblock in the shadows of one of the elevated expressways of Roppongi-dori, next to a cardboard and tarp shelter. He was wearing overlarge brown pants cinched tight with a worn belt, a filthy checked button-down shirt, and a fraying cardigan sweater that two generations earlier might have been red.

I walked over to him. *"Fuku o kokan shite kurenai ka?"* I asked, point-ing to my chest. You want to trade clothes?

He looked at me for a long moment as though I was unhinged. *"Nandatte?"* he asked. What the hell are you talking about?

"I'm serious," I said in Japanese. "This is a once-in-a-lifetime opportunity."

I shrugged off the nylon windbreaker I was wearing and handed it to him. He took it, his expression briefly incredulous, then wordlessly began to slip out of his rags.

Two minutes later I was wearing his clothes. Even through the heavy layer of cologne, the smell was horrific. I thanked him and headed back to Aoyama.

Back in the alley, I pulled on the fright wig and secured it with the wool hat, then popped in the false teeth. I lit a cigarette and let it burn down, then rubbed a mixture of ashes and spit onto my face. I lit a match and took a quick look at myself in a sawed-off dental mirror I keep on my keychain. I barely recognized what I saw, and I smiled a rotten-toothed smile.

I slipped on the gloves and walked out to the garage entrance of Yukiko's building. I took the fishing line and translucent tape, but left the bag and the rest of its contents in the alley. There was a security cam-era mounted just above the grated garage door. I cut a wide path around it, then reapproached from the side farther from the street. The corner of the building jutted out a few centimeters, apparently for aesthetic rea-sons. I slid down low, using the jutting design for partial concealment. The average person pulling in or out wouldn't notice me. Anyone who did would assume I was just some homeless man, probably drunk and passed out there. My getup was insurance against the very small chance that someone might call the cops. If anyone did show up to investigate, my appearance and smell would be strong incentive for them to just tell me to be on my way and leave it at that.

It was late, and not too many people were coming or going. After nearly an hour, I heard what I'd been waiting for: a car pulling into the driveway.

I heard it stop in front of the door, the engine idling. I pictured the driver rolling down the window, inserting a magnetic card into the reader. A moment later I heard the mechanical whine of the door rising. I counted ten seconds off before the sound stopped. I heard the car pull in.

The mechanical whine started again. I counted off five seconds, on the assumption that, with the assistance of gravity, the door would drop more quickly than it had risen. Then I darted out from my position, strode down to the door, dropped to my side, and rolled under it.

Lying on my back to keep my profile low, I raised my head and looked around. The structure was a large rectangle. There was a row of parked cars in front of each of the four walls, and two double rows lengthwise up the middle. The car that had just arrived pulled into a space in one of the middle rows. I rolled to a crouch and, keeping low, ducked behind a nearby car.

The elevators and a door marked "Stairs" were at the far end of the rectangle, opposite the grated doors I had just come through. A woman got out of the car that had come in, walked over to the elevators, and pressed a button. A second later, the doors opened. She went inside and the doors closed behind her.

I looked around. Concrete weight-bearing pillars were spaced every few meters throughout. There were no ramps, so I knew it was only one story. From its size and location, I gathered it was intended only to serve the residents of the building above.

Ideally, I would have gotten to Yukiko just as she left her car. But I had no way of knowing which parking space was hers, and she might easily see me coming if my guess left me too far away. The only choke point was the elevators. I decided to set up there.

I looked around for cameras. The only one I spotted was a large double CCTV installation mounted on the ceiling directly in front of the elevators, one unit facing the elevators, the other monitoring the garage. Except in high security installations, where CCTV is monitored in real time by guards, security cameras typically record to tape that gets recorded over every twenty-four hours unless there's an incident that makes earlier review worthwhile. In a residential setup like this one, it was a safe bet no one was watching the garage right now. But they'd sure as hell be reviewing the tapes the next day. I was glad I was disguised.

There was a U-shaped metal guardrail around the elevator entrance, with three breaks for access. It looked like something intended to force residents to use a separate freight elevator for bringing large items in and out of the building. For me it would serve a better purpose.

I took out the fishing line and tied one end to the top left of the U at knee level. Then I ran the line along the floor around the bottom points and the right top point of the U so that each break in access was covered. I secured it lightly to the floor with the translucent tape, then moved over to the nearest pillar, letting out the line as I walked.

Squatting low, I took out my keychain and used one of the keys to cut off the line. I put the spool back in one of the pants pockets along with the tape, then wrapped the excess line around one of my gloved hands. I stood and angled the dental mirror so I could see the garage door without having to expose myself from behind the pillar.

I waited like that for about an hour. Twice I heard the garage door and checked with the mirror. The first time was a blue Saab. The second was a black Nissan. The third one was white. A Bimmer. An M3.

My heart started kicking harder. I exhaled slowly and gripped the end of the fishing line.

I listened to the car as it got closer, closer. I heard it stop just a couple meters away. She had a good spot. Probably paid more for it.

I heard the door open and then close. Then the *chirp chirp* of an automatic door lock. I looked in the mirror to confirm it was Yukiko and that she was alone. Right on both counts.

She was wearing a black trench coat and high heels. A purse was slung across her neck and one arm. None of it was ideal attire for reaction or maneuver. But it looked good.

Her right hand was closed around a small canister. My guess was Mace or pepper spray. A woman, late at night, in a parking garage— maybe this was nothing out of the ordinary for her. But I had a feeling she was thinking about Harry, and about me. Good.

She was walking briskly. I watched as she approached the perimeter of the metal guardrail. My breath was moving in and out of my mouth in silent shallow drafts. One. Two. Three.

I jerked hard on the line. It popped up from its taped moorings to ankle level and I heard her cry of surprise as she tripped over it. She might have recovered her balance, but those stylish heels were on my side. I stepped out from behind the pillar just in time to see her spill to the ground.

I shoved my keys back in a pants pocket and darted up behind her. By the time I reached her, she had pulled herself up on all fours. She still had the canister in one hand. I stomped her wrist and she cried out. I reached down and yanked what she was holding from her fingers. I glanced at it quickly—oleoresin capsicum. Pepper spray. Five million SHU—the good stuff. I crammed it in a pocket and dragged her over to the nearest car, away from the cameras.

I shoved her up against the passenger-side door. She looked frightened, but I didn't see any recognition in her eyes. Given my disguise, she might have been thinking I was a mugger or rapist.

"You don't remember me, Yukiko?" I asked. "We met at Damask Rose. I'm Harry's friend. Was his friend."

Her brow furrowed for a moment as she tried to square the evidence of her eyes with that of her ears. Then she saw it. Her mouth dropped open but no sound came out.

"Where can I find Murakami?" I asked.

She closed her mouth. She was breathing rapidly through her nose, but other than that she had managed to suppress any outward sign of fear. I admired her poise.

"If you want to live, you'll tell me what I want to know," I said.

She looked at me but said nothing.

I popped an uppercut into her gut. It was hard enough to hurt, but not too hard. I needed her to be able to talk. She gasped and doubled over.

"The next one is to that beautiful face," I said. "I want to know who killed him. Was it you, or Murakami?"

I didn't really give a shit how she might answer. I certainly wouldn't trust anything she said. But I wanted to give her the opportunity to plead something exculpatory, so she might believe I'd let her live if she told me where I could find her boss.

"It was… it was him," she gasped.

"All right. Tell me where I can find him."

"I don't know."

"You better think of something."

"He's hard to find. I don't know how to reach him. He just shows up at the club sometimes."

She glanced behind me, toward the garage door. I shook my head. "I know what you're thinking," I said. "If you can just hold out long enough for another car to pull in, I'll have to run and let you go. Or maybe someone saw what happened on those cameras, maybe they're on their way now. But you've got it backward. If someone comes and you haven't told me what I want to hear, that's when I'll kill you. Now where is he?"

She shook her head.

"We're running out of time," I said. "I'm going to give you one more chance. Tell me and you live. Don't tell me and you die. Right here."

She clenched her jaw and looked at me.

Damn, she was tough. I might have known, after seeing the way she handled her nitroglycerin-volatile boss.

"All right," I said. "You win."

I popped another uppercut into her midsection, this one hard enough to cause damage. She doubled over with a sharp exhalation of breath. I stepped behind her, braced a knee against her back, took her head in one gloved hand and her chin in the other, and broke her neck. She was dead before she hit the floor.

I'd never done that to a woman before. I thought for a second of some of the things I had said to Naomi about subornment, about what Midori had said about atonement. But other than a detached observation about the relative ease of the maneuver because of the lighter muscle mass, I felt nothing.

"Say hello to Harry," I said. I picked up her purse to make it look like she'd been the victim of a random robbery, collected the fishing line and tape, and took the stairs to the first floor. I let myself out through the front entrance, keeping my head down to avoid the camera there. I ducked around the corner into the alley, where I pulled off the hat and wig, spat out the false teeth, and rubbed the ash off my face with the damp towel. I pulled off the homeless man's clothes and the long underwear and changed into the Gap outfit, then shoved everything back into the bag. I ran a mental list of the contents of the bag to ensure I wasn't leaving anything behind, then double-checked the ground to be sure. Everything was copacetic. I took a deep breath and strolled back out onto Aoyama-dori.

When I was a few blocks away, I stopped under a streetlight and quickly went through her purse. There was nothing in it of interest.

I walked down Roppongi-dori until I found an appropriate colony of homeless men. I left the bag and the purse close by them and walked on, peeling off and dropping the gloves as I did so. I would get rid of the teeth elsewhere. They had my DNA on them, and weren't the kind of item Tokyo's shifting populations of homeless men would assimilate and thereby sanitize.

Ducking into an alley, I discharged a shot from the canister of pepper spray to confirm it worked. I decided to keep it. When Murakami learned about Yukiko, I might want a little extra protection.

CHAPTER 19

The next afternoon, I did an SDR that ended at JR Harajuku Station. I exited and let the eternal river of hip-hop shoppers, attired in ways an extraterrestrial would probably find welcoming, carry me onto Takeshita-dori, Tokyo's teen shopping mecca. Only in Tokyo could the jam-packed bizarrerie of a byway like Takeshita-dori exist side by side with the elegant tea houses and antique shops of Brahms-no-komichi, and the stark contrast is one of the reasons Harajuku has always been one of my favorite parts of the city.

Tatsu had assured me that Biddle employed no bodyguards, but there's nothing like independent verification to lower the blood pressure. There were a number of points from which I might approach Jardin de Luseine, and I moved around each of them, probing, imagining where I might position watchers if I were protecting someone in the restaurant. I moved in tightening concentric circles until I was sure no one was positioned outside. Then I made my way back to Takeshita-dori, where I cut across an alley running alongside the restaurant itself.

I spotted him through the enormous plate glass on the alley side of the building. He was sitting alone, reading a newspaper, sipping something from a china cup. The same man I had seen in the photograph, elegantly dressed in a single-breasted blue pin-striped suit, a white shirt with a spread collar, and a burgundy rep tie. Overall the impression was fastidious, but not overly so; less American, more British; less spymaster, more CEO.

He was sitting in one of the window seats, with his profile to the alley, and that told me a lot: he was insensitive to his surroundings; he didn't understand that ordinary glass is no deterrent to a gunman; he thought like a civilian, not a spy. I watched him silently for a moment, imagining high native intelligence, in which he would take refuge when he found himself inadequate to the demands of the real world; Ivy League schools and possibly a graduate degree, from which he would have learned much about office corridors and nothing of the street; an adequate but passion-less marriage to a woman who had borne him the required two or three children while dutifully following him from post to career-building post, hiding her growing sense of loss and inchoate desperation behind cock-tail party smiles and repairing with increasing frequency to a refrigerated bottle of Chablis or Chardonnay, just a glass, and certainly no more than three, a semi-secret indulgence for beating back the long silences of list-less afternoons.

I went inside. The door opened and closed with an audible clack, but Biddle didn't look up to check on who had entered.

I moved across the dark wood floor, beneath the Art Deco chande-liers, around Victorian tables and chairs, alongside a grand piano. Only when I was actually standing in front of him did he raise his head from his reading. It took him a half second to recognize me. When he did, he recoiled. "What the hell!" he stammered.

I sat across from him. He started to get up. I restrained him with a firm hand on his shoulder.

"Stay seated," I said quietly. "Keep your hands where I can see them. I'm only here to talk. If I wanted to kill you, you'd be dead already."

His eyes bulged. "What the hell!" he said again.

"Calm down," I told him. "You've been looking for me. Here I am."

He exhaled sharply and swallowed. "Sorry," he said. "I just didn't expect to see you like this."

I waited.

"All right," he said, after a moment. "The first thing I should mention is that this has nothing to do with William Holtzer."

I kept waiting.

"I mean, he didn't have many supporters. He isn't missed."

I doubted Holtzer's own family would miss him. I waited some more.

"So what we want, the reason we've been looking for you," he went on, "is, we want you to, ah, interfere with someone's activities."

A new euphemism, I thought. *So exciting.*

"Who?" I asked, to let him know he was finally on the right track.

"Well, just a second. Before we talk about that, I need to know, are you interested?"

I looked at him. "Mr. Biddle, I'm sure you know I'm selective about whose activities I'll 'interfere' with. So without knowing who, I couldn't tell you whether I'd be interested or not."

"It's a man. A principal."

I nodded. "Good."

"'Good' meaning, you're interested?"

"Meaning you haven't made me uninterested, so far."

He nodded. "You know the person we're talking about. You met him recently, when he was following an acquaintance of yours."

Only long-practiced discretion prevented me from showing my surprise. "Tell me," I said.

"Kanezaki."

"Why?"

He frowned. "What do you mean, 'why'?"

"Let's just say my unhappy history with your organization necessitates higher than usual levels of disclosure."

"I'm sorry, I can't tell you more than I have already."

"I'm sorry, you'll have to."

"Or you won't take the job?"

"Or I will take your life."

He blanched, but other than that kept his composure. "I don't really think this conversation calls for threats," he said. "We're discussing a business proposition."

"'Threats,'" I said, my tone thoughtful. "I've survived for a long time by identifying and preemptively eliminating 'threats.' So here's my business proposition to you. Convince me you're not a 'threat,' and I won't eliminate you."

"I don't believe this," he said. "Do you know who I am?"

"Tell me, so we can get it right on the headstone."

He glowered at me. After a moment, he said, "All right, I'll tell you. But only because it makes sense for you to know, not because of your threats." He took a sip from the china cup. "Kanezaki is a rogue. He's been running a secret program that would cause a lot of embarrassment on both sides of the Pacific if it were to get out."

"Crepuscular?" I asked.

His mouth dropped open. "You know... how could you possibly know about that? From Kanezaki?"

You dumb bastard, I thought. *Whatever I knew, you just confirmed it.*

I looked at him. "Mr. Biddle, how do you think I've lasted as long as I have in this line of work? I make it my business to know what I'm stepping into and whether the reward is worth the risk. That's how I stay alive and my clients get their money's worth."

I waited while he digested this new worldview.

"What else do you know about this?" he asked after a moment, trying to be shrewd now.

"Plenty. Now tell me why you've decided that Kanezaki has become a liability. From what I understand, up until now he's been your golden boy."

He crinkled his nose as though at an offensive odor. "In his own mind he's golden. Forgive me, but simply having Japanese blood doesn't give someone special insights into this country."

I waved a hand to show that of course his comment didn't offend me.

"Insight into this country, any country, takes years of education, experience, sensitivity," he said. "But this kid, he thinks he knows enough to design and run his own damn foreign policy."

I nodded to show I was sympathetic to his point, and he continued.

"All right, you know there was a program. But it was shut down six months ago. I don't necessarily agree with the shutdown, but my private thoughts on the matter are irrelevant. What is relevant is that Kanezaki has been continuing it on his own."

"I can see where that would be a problem."

"Yes, well, it's a shame in some ways. He's got a lot of passion and he's not without talent. But this matter must be put to rest, before some real damage occurs."

"What do you want me to do?"

He looked at me. "I want you to... look, I understand that you can arrange these things so it looks as though the person did it himself."

"That's true," I said, noting that he had initially spoken of what "we" want and was now saying "I."

"Well, that's what needs to be done. Is there a usual fee?"

"For a CIA officer? The fee would be high."

"All right. What is it?"

He was eager enough so that I was half tempted to bilk him. Make him pay up front, then *Sayonara, asshole*.

And maybe I would. But I still had a few questions.

"Let me ask you," I said, furrowing my brow in my best Columbo imitation. "How do you know about me? About my services?"

"The Agency has a dossier on you," he said. "Most of it assembled through Holtzer's efforts."

"Oh," I said. "Of course. That makes sense. And when you first started looking for me, was it for the same job you're offering me today?"

He wouldn't know I was aware he was with Kanezaki when he had first approached Tatsu inquiring about my whereabouts. The question was designed to trip him up.

But it didn't. "No," he said. "The original thinking was that we could use you for Crepuscular. But the program is done now, as I said. There may still be some role in the future, but for now I just need you to tie up loose ends."

I nodded. "It's just that it's strange. I mean, you had Kanezaki looking for me, right?"

"Yes," he said. His tone was cautious, as though he was afraid of what I might ask next and was already trying to think of an answer.

"Well, isn't that odd? Given that you actually wanted me to 'interfere' with him."

He shook his head. "He was only supposed to locate you, not actually meet you. I was going to handle the meeting personally."

I smiled, seeing the truth.

"All right," he said. "I'd read your dossier. I thought it was possible that, if you learned someone was trying to find you, you might, as you put it, see that person as a threat and act accordingly."

I almost laughed. Biddle had been looking for a freebie.

"What about the guy who was with him at the time?" I asked. "Kanezaki said he was diplomatic security."

"He was. What of it?"

"Why would you offer a bodyguard to a guy you wanted taken out?"

He pursed his lips. "Solo surveillance against someone like you is impossible. Kanezaki needed a partner. I wanted someone from outside the Agency, someone who wouldn't know what was really going on."

"Someone expendable."

"If you want to put it that way."

"Mr. Biddle," I said, "I'm getting the feeling this is a personal matter."

There was a long pause, then he said, "What if it is?"

I shrugged. "It's all the same to me, as long as I get paid. But we're not off to a good start. You've been telling me the problem with Kanezaki is that he's a rogue, that his activities could cause embarrassment on both sides of the Pacific. It sounds as though the potential embarrassment is more localized than that."

He looked at me. "What I told you is not untrue. But yes, I have personal reasons, as well. What do you think is going to happen to me as Kanezaki's direct supervisor if his activities are discovered?"

"Likely a shit storm. But I don't see how Kanezaki's suicide would solve your problems. Won't there still be records of his activities? Receipts from disbursements, that kind of thing?"

His eyes narrowed. "I'm taking care of that," he said.

"Sure, you know better than I do. I'm just mentioning it. By the way, where do you suppose Kanezaki has been getting the money to run Crepuscular even after the higher-ups have shut off the spigot? I imagine we're talking about some significant sums."

He glanced to his right. The glance said, *Think of something.*

"I don't know," he said.

"If you keep lying to me," I said, my tone mild, "I'm going to start seeing you as a threat."

He looked at me for a long moment. Finally he said, "All right. Kanezaki has been getting the money from a man named Fumio Tanaka. Someone with inherited money and the right political sympathies. I don't see that as relevant to the job at hand."

I paused as though considering. "Well, even if Kanezaki goes away, Tanaka is still around, isn't he? Why don't I interfere with his activities, too?"

He shook his head violently. "No," he said. "That won't be necessary. I've asked for your assistance with a particular matter and would like an answer with regard to that matter only, please."

"I'll need a way to contact you," I said.

"Will you take the job?"

I looked at him. "I want to think about your story first. If I decide I can work with you safely, I'll do it."

He took out a Mont Blanc Meisterstück, unscrewed it, and scrawled a number on a napkin. "You can reach me here," he said.

"Oh, one more thing," I said, taking the napkin. "The guy you were using to try to get to me. Haruyoshi Fukasawa. He died recently."

He swallowed. "I know. Kanezaki told me."

"What do you think happened there?"

"From what Kanezaki told me, I gather it was an accident."

I nodded. "The thing is, Fukasawa was a friend of mine. He wasn't much of a drinker. But apparently he was loaded when he fell from that roof. Strange, isn't it?"

"If you think we had something to do with this…"

"Maybe you can just tell me who did."

He glanced to his right again. "I don't know."

"Your people were following Harry. And I know his death was no accident. If you can't do any better than what you've already told me, I'm going to start thinking it was you."

"I'm telling you, I don't know who did it. Even assuming it wasn't an accident."

"How did you find out where Harry lived in the first place?"

He repeated Kanezaki's story about Midori's letter.

"With only that to go on, you must have used local resources," I suggested.

He looked at me. "You seem to know a lot. But I'm not going to start confirming or denying the specifics of local resources for you. If you suspect local resources might have been involved in your friend's death, I can't help you. As I said, I don't know."

I wasn't going to get any more out of him in a place like this. I wished for a second we were alone.

I got up to go. "I'll be in touch," I said.

Tatsu and I had agreed to meet in Yoyogi Park after I'd braced Biddle. I went there, taking the usual precautions. He was already waiting, sitting on a bench beneath one of the park's thousands of maple trees, reading a newspaper, looking like some of the retirees in the area who were passing the day doing the same thing.

"How did it go?" he asked.

I briefed him on what Biddle had told me.

"I know of Tanaka," he said when I was done. "His father founded an electronics company in the twenties that survived the war and prospered afterward. Tanaka sold it when his father died and has been living off the considerable proceeds ever since. He is said to have an enormous libido, particularly for a man nearing seventy. He is also said to be addicted to codeine and other narcotics."

"What about his politics?"

"He has none, so far as I know."

"Then why would he want to fund an Agency program to aid reformers?"

"I'd like you to help me find out."

"Why?"

He looked at me. "I need a bad cop. And we may get a lead about Murakami."

"Nothing from the guy you took into custody?"

He shook his head. "The problem is that he is much more afraid of his boss than he is of me. But I've always been impressed by how much a man's attitudes will change at between forty-eight and seventy-two hours of sleep deprivation. We may learn something yet."

He took out his mobile phone and input a number. Asked a few questions. Listened. Issued instructions. Then he hung up and turned to me. "One of my men is on his way to pick us up now. He will take us to Tanaka's residence, which is in Shirokanedai."

Shirokanedai is arguably Tokyo's poshest neighborhood. Apart from the main artery of Meguro-dori, which runs through it, its narrow streets of elegant single-family homes and apartments are astonishingly hushed and peaceful, as though the neighborhood's money has managed to buy off the tumult of the surrounding city and send it somewhere else. There's a sort of relaxed class about the place. Its women, known locally as *shiroganeze*, look at home in their furs as they promenade their toy poodles and Pomeranians between visits to tea shops and boutiques and salons; its men, secure behind the wheels of the Bimmers and Benzes that carry them to their high-powered jobs; its children, relaxed, carefree, not yet even aware that their neighborhood is the exception to life in Tokyo and elsewhere, not the rule.

Tatsu's man picked us up as promised and drove us the ten minutes to Shirokanedai.

Tanaka lived in an oversized, two-story detached house in Shirokanedai 4-chome, across from the Sri Lankan Embassy. Its most distinguishing characteristic, aside from its size, were the cars parked in its driveway: a white Porsche 911 GT with a massive spoiler, and a bright red Ferrari Modena. Each was spotless and gleaming and I wondered whether Tanaka actually drove them or merely exhibited them as trophies.

The property was gated and sat on an elevated plot of land that gave it the feel of a castle looking down upon the lesser dwellings around it. Tatsu and I got out and went through the gate, which was unlocked. He pressed a button next to the double wooden doors and a long series of baritone chimes issued from within.

A moment later a young woman answered the door. She was pretty and looked Southeast Asian, maybe Filipina, and was dressed in a classic black-and-white maid uniform, complete with some sort of white lace cap atop her upturned coiffure. The getup was just this side of what a medium-class pervert might ask for in one of Tokyo's "image clubs," where customers can be serviced by girls dressed as students, nurses, or any other profession whose uniform might provoke a fetish, and I wondered what the full range of this woman's household duties might actually be.

"May I help you?" she asked in accented Japanese, looking first at Tatsu, then at me.

"I am Keisatsucho Department Head Ishikura Tatsuhiko," Tatsu said in English, producing his ID, "here to speak with Tanaka-san. Would you get him for me?"

"Is Tanaka expecting you?" she asked, switching to English.

"I don't believe so," Tatsu said, "but I am certain he will be happy to see me."

"Just a moment, please." She closed the door and we waited.

A minute later the door opened, this time by a man. I recognized him instantly: the guy I had noticed at Damask Rose, with the chemically and surgically maintained superficially youthful appearance.

"I am Tanaka," the man said in Japanese. "How may I be of assistance?"

Tatsu displayed his ID again. "I would like to ask you a few questions. For the moment, my interest in you is peripheral and unofficial. Your cooperation, or lack of it, will determine whether my interest changes."

Tanaka's expression was impassive, but the tension in his body and angle of his head told me Tatsu had his full attention. Despite all the lawyers I had no doubt were in his employ, despite likely entourages of sycophants and underlings, this was a man who was afraid of real trouble, the kind of real trouble he would have just seen when he looked in Tatsu's eyes.

"Yes, please, come in," he told us. We took off our shoes and followed him through a circular entranceway with a floor of checkerboard black-and-white marble tiles. At the rear was a winding stairwell; to the sides were reproductions of Greek statues. We entered a mahogany-paneled room with four sides of floor-to-ceiling bookcases. Like the cars out front, the books looked as though they were frequently dusted and never read.

Tatsu and I sat on a burgundy pincushion leather couch. Tanaka sat across from us in a matching armchair. He asked us if he could offer us something to eat or drink. We declined.

"I didn't get your associate's name," Tanaka said, looking at me.

"His presence here, like mine, is unofficial for now," Tatsu said. "I hope we can keep it that way."

"Of course," Tanaka said, in his nervous eagerness overlooking the fact that Tatsu had ignored his question. "Of course. Now, please tell me whatever it is you need."

"Someone is attempting to implicate you in a U.S. program that directs funds to certain Japanese politicians," Tatsu said. "Although I believe you are involved in this program, I don't believe you are responsible for it. But I need you to convince me I am correct in this belief."

The color drained from behind Tanaka's tan. "I think… it would be best for me to consult with my legal counsel."

I looked at him, imagining how I would kill him so he could see it in my eyes. "That would be uncooperative," I said.

Tanaka looked at me, then at Tatsu. "The money isn't even mine. It doesn't come from me."

Tatsu said, "Good. Tell me more."

Tanaka licked his lips. "This conversation will remain unofficial?" he asked. "If someone finds out, it would be very bad for me."

"As long as you cooperate," Tatsu said, "you have nothing to fear."

Tanaka looked at me for confirmation. I gave him a smile that said I was secretly hoping he would be uncooperative, so I could go to work on him.

Tanaka swallowed. "All right. Six months ago I was told to contact someone who works in the U.S. Embassy. A man named Biddle. I was told Biddle represented certain parties who hoped to secure a source of campaign funding for reformist politicians."

"Who told you to do this?" Tatsu asked.

Tanaka glanced at Tatsu, then down. "The same person who provides the money for this thing."

Tatsu looked at him. "Please be more specific."

Tanaka swallowed. "Yamaoto," he whispered. Then: "Please, I'm co-operating. This conversation must remain unofficial."

Tatsu nodded. "Keep going," he said.

"I met with Biddle and told him, as I was instructed, that I believed Japan needed radical political reform and that I wanted to help in any way I could. Since that time, I have provided Biddle with some one hundred million yen for distribution to politicians."

"These people are being set up," Tatsu said. "I want to know how."

Tanaka looked at him. "I was only following instructions," he said. "I'm not really involved."

"I understand," Tatsu said. "You're doing fine. Now tell me."

"For three months, I gave Biddle cash without asking for anything in return. Then I pretended to be concerned about whether I was being conned. 'Who is this money really going to?' I asked him. 'Tell me, or I'll cut you off!' At first he resisted. Then he told me I would know these people, in fact, that I could probably figure out who they were just from reading the paper. Then he gave me names. I pretended to be satisfied, and gave him more money.

"Then I acted paranoid again. I said, 'You're just making this up. Prove to me you really are giving my money to the people who need it and not keeping it for yourself!' Again, he argued at first. But eventually he agreed to tell me when and where a meeting would occur. And then another."

Jesus Christ, I thought.

"How many meetings did Biddle inform you of?" Tatsu asked.

"Four."

"And what did you do with that information?"

"I passed it along to... to the person who provides the funding, as I was instructed to do."

Tatsu nodded. "Give me the names of the participants in those four meetings, and the dates."

"I don't remember the exact dates," Tanaka said.

I smiled and started to stand. Tanaka flinched. Tatsu put a hand out to restrain me and said, "Be as accurate as you can."

Tanaka intoned four names. A ballpark date for each. I sat.

"Now give me every other name you got out of Biddle," Tatsu said.

Tanaka complied.

Tatsu didn't write anything down, and I realized he knew these people well. "Very good," he said, when Tanaka was done. "You have been most cooperative and I see no reason for anyone to learn that this conversation took place. Of course, should I need any further information, I may call on you again. With similar discretion."

Tanaka nodded. He looked sick.

The maid saw us to the door. The car was waiting outside. We got in back and drove off. I told them to drop me off at nearby JR Meguro Station. Tatsu's man drove the short distance to the station and waited in the car while Tatsu and I stood outside to wrap things up.

"What do you think?" I asked.

"He's telling the truth."

"Maybe. But who put him in touch with Biddle?"

He shrugged. "Probably one of the Agency's tainted assets, someone with connections to Yamaoto. If Biddle were canvassing these assets to try to find a supporter for Crepuscular, word would have gotten back to Yamaoto."

"And Yamaoto would have seen an opportunity to turn the program to his own ends."

He nodded, then said, "What do you think Yamaoto did on those four occasions in which he learned where and when Kanezaki would be meeting with his assets?"

I shrugged. "Observers. Using parabolic microphones, telephoto lenses, low-light video."

"Agreed. Now assume Yamaoto has audio and video recordings of these meetings in progress. What is the value of these materials to him?"

I thought for a moment. "Blackmail, mostly. 'Do as I tell you, or I release these photos to the media.'"

"Yes, that is Yamaoto's preferred method. And it is remarkably effective when the photos are of an extramarital affair in progress, or a liaison with a young boy, or some other socially unacceptable behavior. But here?"

I thought again. "You think video and audio of a meeting with Kanezaki wouldn't be damning enough?"

He shrugged. "The audio might be, if the recorded conversation were sufficiently incriminating. But the video would be of lesser consequence: a politician chatting with a man, apparently Japanese, in a public place."

"Because no one knows who Kanezaki is," I said, beginning to catch on.

He looked at me, waiting for me to put it together.

"They need a way to make Kanezaki a household name," I said. "To get his picture in the paper. That gives the photos punch."

He nodded. "And how to do that?" he asked.

"I'll be damned," I said, finally seeing it. "Biddle was playing right into Yamaoto's hands. He's been positioning Kanezaki as his fall guy, giving him full responsibility for Crepuscular so that, if it ever got out, he'd have a 'rogue' who could take all the heat. But now, if Kanezaki becomes publicly known as the poster child for CIA skullduggery, the politicians who have been photographed with him are going down, too."

"Correct. Biddle can no longer burn Kanezaki without burning the very reformers he presumably wants to protect."

"That's why he wants him dead," I said. "A nice, quiet suicide to preempt a scandal."

He nodded. "Biddle would meanwhile destroy the receipts and any other evidence of Crepuscular's existence."

I thought for a moment. "There's something off, though."

"Yes?"

"Biddle's a bureaucrat. In the ordinary course of things he wouldn't just resort to murder. He'd have to be feeling desperate."

"Just so. And what produces desperation?"

I looked at him, realizing he'd already put it together. "Personal reasons, as opposed to institutional ones."

"Yes. So the question is, what is Biddle's personal stake in all this?"

I considered. "Professional embarrassment? Problems with his career, if Kanezaki were burned and a scandal erupted about the CIA's Tokyo Station?"

"All that, yes, but something more specific."

I shook my head, not seeing it.

"What do you think precipitated Biddle's request for those receipts, and his request that you assist with Kanezaki's 'suicide'?"

I shook my head again. "I don't know."

He looked at me, perhaps mildly disappointed that I hadn't managed to keep up with him. "Yamaoto got to Biddle the same way he got to Holtzer," he said. "He created assets Holtzer and Biddle believed were real. They basked in the reflected glory of the intelligence the 'assets' produced. Then, when he judged the time was propitious, Yamaoto revealed to them, privately, that they had been duped."

I imagined Yamaoto's conversation with Biddle: *If word gets out that your "assets" are all run by the other side, your career is over. Work with me, though, and I'll keep things quiet. I'll even make sure that you get more assets and more intel, and your star will keep rising.*

"I understand," I said. "But somehow Yamaoto miscalculated this time, because Biddle thinks he's got a way out. Just get rid of Kanezaki and destroy all the evidence of Crepuscular's existence."

He nodded. "Yes. And what does that tell us?"

I considered. "That Crepuscular has an unusually small distribution list. That Langley doesn't know of it, because if they did, Biddle wouldn't be able to contain it just by eliminating Kanezaki and burning some paperwork."

"So it seems Mr. Biddle has been running Crepuscular on his own initiative. He told you the program was terminated six months ago, did he not?"

I nodded. "And Kanezaki told me he discovered cable traffic to that effect."

"Biddle's story is that Kanezaki has been running a rogue program since then. Given that Tanaka has only been dealing with Biddle, it seems likely the rogue is in fact Biddle, who was using Kanezaki as his unwitting front man."

"Yamaoto wouldn't know Crepuscular wasn't officially sanctioned," I said, nodding. "He would have assumed the program was within the knowledge of Biddle's superiors back at Langley. But it sounds like, outside of Biddle and Kanezaki, no one on the U.S. side is aware of it."

He bowed his head as though acknowledging the valiant efforts of a slow student who had shown a hint of progress. "Which is why Yamaoto missed the possibility that Biddle would see Kanezaki's elimination as a solution to Yamaoto's blackmail."

"You can't really fault Biddle's reasoning," I said, looking at him closely. "With Kanezaki gone, Yamaoto's blackmail evidence would lose most of its power. Meaning your network of reformers would be a lot safer if Kanezaki exited the scene."

He grunted, and I realized I was enjoying the sight of him struggling with what for him was a moral dilemma. "What about the reformers Kanezaki's been meeting with?" I asked. "If he gets exposed, they'll be at risk."

"Several of them may be."

"An acceptably small number?"

He looked at me, knowing where I was going. I said it anyway. "What would you do if there had been five? Or ten?"

He scowled. "These are decisions that can only be made case by case."

"Yamaoto doesn't make these decisions case by case," I said, still pushing. "He knows what needs to be done and he does it. That's what you're up against. You sure you're equal to the task?"

His eyes narrowed slightly. "Do you think I seek to be this man's 'equal'? Yamaoto would not account for the fact that these politicians are themselves to blame for their current predicament. Or for the fact that Kanezaki's motives are essentially good. Or for the fact that this young man presumably has a mother and father who would be ruined by his loss."

I bowed my head, acknowledging his point and the firsthand knowledge behind it. "Those men are finished, then?" I asked.

He nodded. "I have to assume Yamaoto owns them now, and warn the others."

"What about Kanezaki?"

"I'll brief him on our meetings with Biddle and Tanaka."

"Tell him his boss tried to put a contract out on him?"

He shrugged. "Why not? The young man already feels indebted to me. This sentiment might prove useful in the future. No harm in reinforcing it now."

"What about Murakami?"

"As I said, we will continue to question the man we took in. He may provide us with something useful."

"Contact me as soon as you have something. I want to be there when it happens."

"So do I," he said.

CHAPTER 20

I checked the Imperial voicemail account from a payphone. A mechanical female voice told me I had one message.

I tried not to hope, but the attempt felt pretty thin. The female voice instructed me to press the "one" key if I wanted to hear the message. I did.

"Jun, it's me," I heard Midori say. There was a pause, then, "I don't know if you're really still staying at the hotel, so I don't know if you'll even get this message." Another pause. "I'd like to see you tonight. I'll be at Body & Soul at eight o'clock. I hope you'll come. Bye."

The female voice told me the message had been left at 2:28 P.M., that I should press the "one" key if I wanted to repeat it. I pressed it. And again.

There was something so disarmingly natural about the way she called me Jun, short for Junichi. No one calls me Jun anymore. No one knows the name. I had been using Junichi, my real name, selectively even before leaving Tokyo, and had discarded it entirely afterward.

Hi, Jun, it's me. Such an ordinary message. Most people probably get ones like it all the time.

It felt as though the ground beneath me had borrowed some extra gravity from somewhere.

The part of my brain that's served me well for so long spoke up: *Place and time. Could be a setup.*

Not from her. I didn't buy that.

Who else might have heard that message, though?

I considered. To intercept the message, someone would have to know where I was staying and under what fictitious name, and they'd have to be able to hack the hotel voicemail system. Outside of Tatsu, who wasn't a current threat, there wasn't much chance of that.

A chance, though.

My response to that was, *The hell with it.*

I went to see her.

I took a long, meandering route, moving mostly on foot, watching as the city gradually grew dark around me. There's something so alive about Tokyo at night, something so imbued with possibilities. Certainly the daytime, with its zigzagging schools of pedestrians and thundering trains and hustle and noise and traffic, is the more upbeat of the city's melodies. But the city also seems burdened by the quotidian clamor, and almost relieved, every evening, to be able to ease into the twilight and set aside the weight of the day. Night strips away the superfluity and the distractions. You move through Tokyo at night and you feel you're on the verge of that thing you've always longed for. At night, you can hear the city breathe.

I stopped at an Internet café to check the Body & Soul website and see who was playing. It was Toku, a young vocalist and flugelhorn player who had already developed a reputation for a soulful sound that belied his twenty-nine years. I had two of his CDs but hadn't seen him perform.

It was possible Yamaoto had learned Midori was in Tokyo from the investigative firm she had retained. If so, there was a chance she was being watched, perhaps by Murakami himself. I did a thorough check of the likely spots around the club. They were all clear.

I went in at about eight-thirty. The place was full, but the doorman let me in when I told him I was a friend of Kawamura Midori, who was here for Toku's performance. Oh yes, he told me. Kawamura-san mentioned someone might come. Please.

She was sitting at the end of one of the two long tables that parallel Body & Soul's walls and overlook the floor, where the musicians were set up. I scanned the room but didn't spot any likely threats. In fact, the evening's demographic was young, female, and obviously there to see Toku, who, with his quintet, was now captivating them with his elegiac "Autumn Winds."

I smiled at what the band was wearing: tee shirts, jeans and sneakers. They all had long hair, died *chapatsu* brown. Their contemporaries would think it was cool. To me they looked young.

I made my way to where Midori was sitting. She watched my approach but made no move to greet me.

She was wearing a black, form fitting sleeveless turtleneck that looked like lightweight cashmere, her face and her arms luminous in contrast. She leaned back in her chair, and I saw a pair of leather pants, soft with age and use, and high-heeled boots. Other than a pair of diamond stud earrings, she'd left things unadorned. I'd always liked that she didn't overdo the jewelry or makeup. She didn't need it.

"I didn't really expect you," she said.

I leaned in so she could hear me over the music. "You didn't think I'd get your message?"

She cocked an eyebrow. "I didn't think you'd show up if I proposed the time and place."

She caught on fast. I shrugged. "Here I am."

There were no seats open, so she got up and we leaned against the wall, our shoulders not quite touching. She took her drink with her.

"What's that you're having?" I asked.

"Ardbeg. You introduced me to it, remember? It tastes like you now."

"I'm surprised you enjoy it, then."

She glanced at me, sidelong. "It's a bittersweet flavor," she said.

A waitress came by and I ordered an Ardbeg. We listened to Toku sing about sorrow and loneliness and regret. The crowd loved him.

When the set was over and the noise of the ensuing applause had died down, Midori turned to me. I was surprised to see concern on her face, even sympathy. Then I realized why.

"Did you... you must have heard about Harry," she said.

I nodded.

"I'm sorry."

I waited a second, then said, "He was killed, you know. Those PIs you put on him got word to the wrong people."

Her mouth dropped open. "They told me it was an accident."

"That's bullshit."

"How do you know?"

"Circumstances. At one point they thought they had me, so they figured they didn't need him. Besides, his stomach was full of alcohol. But Harry didn't drink."

"Oh, my God," she said, her hand over her mouth.

"Next time, hire a firm that takes its confidentiality obligations a little more seriously."

She shook her head, her hand still over her mouth.

"I'm sorry," I said, looking down. "That wasn't fair. This was nobody's fault but the people who did it. And Harry's, for not having known better." I told her a sanitized version of how they had set him up, and how he had refused to listen to me.

"I liked him," she said when I was done. "I wondered whether he was lying to me when he told me you were dead. That's why I hired those people to watch him. But he seemed like a good person. He was cute and shy and I could tell he looked up to you."

I smiled wanly. Harry's eulogy.

"If I were you," I said, "I'd be careful in Tokyo. They lost me, but they'll be looking for me again. If they know you're here, they might take an interest. Like they did with Harry."

There was a long pause. Then she said, "I'm going back to New York tomorrow anyway."

I nodded slowly, knowing what was coming.

"I won't see you after this," she said.

I went for a smile. Didn't quite make it. "I know."

"I figured out what I want from you," she said.

"Yeah?"

She nodded. "At first what I thought I wanted was revenge. I kept thinking of how to hurt you, how to cause you pain, like the pain you caused me."

I wasn't surprised.

"And I resented you for that," she went on, "because I've always believed hate is such an unworthy emotion. So weak and ultimately pointless."

I marveled briefly at how innocent a life someone would have to have led for such a philosophy to emerge credible and intact, and for a second I loved her for it.

She took a sip of her Ardbeg. "But seeing you the other day changed that. Part of it was realizing you really did try to get that disk back and finish what my father had started. Part of it was knowing you were trying to protect me from the other people who were trying to find the disk."

"But what was it really?"

She looked away, over to where the band had been playing, then back to me. "Understanding what you are. You're not part of the real world. Not my real world, at least. You're like a ghost, some creature forced to live in the shadows. And I realized someone like that isn't worthy of hatred."

Whether I was worthy of hatred and whether she hated me weren't the same thing. I wondered if she understood that. "Pity, instead?" I asked.

She nodded. "Maybe."

"I think I might have preferred hate," I said. I was trying for light, but she didn't laugh.

She looked at me. "So all we have left is tonight."

I almost said no. I almost told her it would hurt too much.

Then I decided I would deal with the hurt afterward. The way it's always been.

We went to the Park Hyatt in Shinjuku. She was staying at the Okura, but going back there together would have been too dangerous.

We took a cab to the hotel. We looked at each other on the way but neither of us spoke. I checked us in, and when we got to the room, we left the lights off. It seemed natural that we should walk over to the enormous windows, where we watched the urban mass of Shinjuku twinkling in the violet light around us.

I looked out at the city from my lofty perch and thought of all the events that had led to this precise instant, this moment I had imagined and ridiculously longed for so many times and that I was now trying to savor even as I felt it slipping irrevocably away.

At some point I felt her looking at me. I turned and reached out, tracing the outline of her face and neck with the back of my fingers, trying to burn all the details into my mind, wanting to have them with me later when she would be gone. I found myself saying her name, quietly, over and over, the way I say it when I'm alone and I'm thinking of her.

Then she stepped in close and put her arms around me and pulled us together with surprising strength.

She smelled the way I remembered, clean, with a trace of perfume that remains a mystery to me, and I thought of wine, the kind you wait and wait to decant and then hesitate to drink because afterward it'll be gone.

We kissed for a long time, gently, not hurrying, standing there in front of the window, and at some point I really did forget what had brought us here together and why we would have to depart alone.

We pulled off each other's clothes the way we had that first time, increasingly fast, almost angrily. I removed the baton from where it was taped to my forearm and set it down. She knew better than to ask about it. When we were naked, still kissing, she pressed against me so that I had to move backward toward the king-sized bed. My legs bumped against it and I sat on its edge. She leaned forward, one hand on the bed, the other on my chest, and pushed me down onto my back. She knelt astride me, one hand still on my chest, and reached down for me with the other. She squeezed for a second, hard enough to make it hurt. Then, looking at me with her dark eyes but still saying nothing, she guided me in.

We moved slowly at first, tentatively, like two people unsure of each other's motives. My hands roamed the landscape of her body, now moving on, now lingering somewhere in response to the pace of her breathing or the pitch of her voice. She put her hands on my shoulders, pinning me with her weight, and began to ride me harder. I watched her face, silhouetted by the reflected light of the windows, and felt some intangible thing like heat or current surging between our bodies. I brought my feet up to the bed and with the slightly altered angle of our bodies moved more deeply inside her. Her breathing shortened and quickened. I tried to hold back, not wanting to let go before she did, but she moved faster, more urgently, and I started to go over the edge. A sound, part growl, part whimper, came from her throat, and she leaned forward so her face was almost touching mine and she looked in my eyes and as I felt her coming and as I came, too, she whispered, "I hate you," and I saw that she was crying.

Afterward, she straightened, but kept her hands on my shoulders. She dipped her head forward so shadows obscured her face. She made no sound but her body shuddered and I felt her tears falling onto my chest and neck.

I didn't know what to say, or even whether to touch her, and we remained that way for a long time. Then she eased off me and walked silently to the bathroom. I sat up and waited. After a few minutes she came out, wearing one of the hotel's white terrycloth robes. She looked at me but didn't say anything.

"You want me to go?" I asked.

She closed her eyes and nodded.

"Okay." I got up and started pulling on my clothes. When I was done I faced her.

"I know you're doing well in New York," I said. *"Ganbatte."* Keep it up.

She looked at me. "What are you going to do?"

I shrugged. "You know how it is with us creatures of the night. Gotta find a rock to crawl under before the sun comes up."

She forced a smile. "After that."

I nodded, thinking. "I'm not sure."

There was a pause.

"You should work with your friend," she said. "It's the only thing for you."

"Funny, he's always saying that, too. Good thing I don't believe in conspiracies."

The smile reappeared, a little less forced this time. "His motives are probably selfish. Mine aren't."

I looked at her. "I'm not sure whether I can trust your motives, after what you just said to me."

She looked down. "I'm sorry."

"No, it's okay. You were being honest. Though I don't think anyone has ever been honest with me in quite that way. At least not at that moment."

Another smile. It was sad, but at least it looked genuine. "I'm being honest now."

I needed to get it over with. I moved in close, close enough to smell her hair and feel the warmth of her skin. I paused there for a moment, my eyes closed. Took a deep breath. Slowly let it out.

I used English to avoid the unambiguous finality of *sayonara.* "Goodbye, Midori," I said.

I walked to the door and, habitual as always, checked through the peephole. The corridor was empty. I moved into it without looking back.

The hallway was hard. The elevator was a little easier. By the time I got to the street I knew the worst was over.

A voice spoke up inside me, quiet but insistent. *So is the best,* it said.

CHAPTER 21

I made my way through the backstreets of Shinjuku, heading east, deciding where I wanted to stay for the night and what I would do when I awoke the following morning. I tried not to think about anything else.

It was late, but there were small clusters of people about, moving like dim constellations in the surrounding emptiness of space: vagrants and beggars; hustlers and pimps; the disheartened, the disenfranchised, the dispossessed.

I hurt, and couldn't think of a way to make the pain go away.

My pager buzzed.

Of course I thought, *Midori*.

But I knew it wasn't her. She didn't have the number. Even if she did, she wasn't going to use it.

I looked at the display, but didn't recognize the caller.

I found a payphone and dialed the number. It rang once, then a woman answered in English. She said, "Hey."

It was Naomi.

"Hey," I said. "I almost forgot I'd given you this number."

"You don't mind my using it, I hope."

"Not at all. Just a little surprised." I was surprised. My alertness had bumped up a notch.

There was a pause. "Well, things were slow tonight at the club and I got off a little early. I wondered if you might want to come by."

It was hard to imagine a slow night at Damask Rose, but maybe it was true. Even so, I would have expected her to want to go someplace

first—a late dinner, a drink. Not just a tryst at her apartment. My alertness edged up further.

"Sure," I said. "If you're not too tired."

"Not at all. Would love to see you."

That was odd. She'd pronounced "would" like something halfway to
"we'd." The blurring was contrary to her usual Portuguese accent. A message? A warning?

I looked at my watch. It was almost one-thirty. "I'll be there in about
an hour."

"I can't wait."

She clicked off.

Something didn't feel right. I couldn't put my finger on exactly what.

There was the oddity of her having contacted me. And the story
about having come home early, though I supposed the latter might ad-
equately explain the former. Her tone seemed pretty normal. But there
was that peculiarly pronounced word.

The question was, what would I do if I knew it was setup? Not what
I would do if I suspected, but if I *knew.*

I went to another payphone and called Tatsu. I got his voicemail. I
tried again. No dice. He must have been on a stakeout or something.

Well, he does have a day job, I thought. But shit.

The safe thing, the smart thing, would have been to stay away until I
could go in with backup. But there might be an opportunity here, and I
didn't want to let it slip. And Naomi might be in trouble.

I took a cab to the edge of Azabu Juban. I knew the security layout
outside Naomi's apartment well, of course, having reconnoitered and exploited it myself the night I had waited for her in the rain. The building
on that perpendicular side street, with the awning and the plastic garbage
bins, was a perfect spot. If someone were waiting for me, he'd wait there.
Just like I had waited for her.

I was making my way to the end of the street that led to the back of
the building when I heard the buzz of a two-cycle motorbike coming toward me. It was a pizza delivery scooter with a portable warmer strapped
to the back and a sign advertising the shop that had dispatched it. I
watched carefully to confirm it was nothing other than what it seemed.
Yeah, just a young guy trying to make a few extra yen with a late-night
job. I could smell pizza from inside the warmer.

I had an idea.

I flagged him down. He pulled up next to me.

"Can you do me a favor?" I asked him in Japanese. "For ten-thousand yen."

His eyes widened a bit. "Sure," he said. "What is it?"

"There's a building at the end of this street, on the right as you approach it from this direction. It's got an awning and a bunch of garbage containers stacked up along its side. I think a friend of mine might be waiting for me there, but I want to surprise him. Can you drive past it from the other direction, take a good look as you go by, and tell me if you see anyone there?"

His eyes widened more. "For ten-thousand yen? Yeah, I can do that."

I pulled out my wallet and took out a five-thousand-yen note. "Half now, half when you get back," I said.

He took the money and buzzed off. Three minutes later he was back.

"He's there," he said. "Right where you told me."

"Thanks," I said, nodding. "That was a lifesaver." I gave him the other five thousand yen. He looked at it, his expression momentarily unbelieving. Then he broke into an enormous, sunny grin.

"Thanks!" he said. "This is great! Anything else you need?"

I shook my head. "Not tonight."

He looked a little wistful, then smiled again as though he knew he'd been hoping for too much. "Okay, thanks again," he said. He gunned the engine and drove away.

I untaped the baton and palmed it in my right hand. I took out Yukiko's pepper spray and held it in my left. I moved with the furtiveness I had learned in long-range recon patrols in Vietnam, hugging the buildings I passed, checking each corner, each hot spot, confirming it was clear before advancing farther.

It took me almost a half hour to cover the hundred meters to the ambush site. When I was three meters away, the cover provided by the garbage bins had thinned too much for me to go any farther. I hunkered low, waiting.

Five minutes went by. I heard the strike of a match, then saw a cloud of blue smoke waft out from just beyond a stack of the containers. Whoever was waiting there wasn't Murakami. Murakami wouldn't have done something so stupid.

I eased the pepper spray back into a pocket and slowly extended the baton to its full length, tugging at the end to ensure the components were locked in position, gripping it in my right hand. I watched the smoke rising from in front of me and timed the inhalations and exhalations. I waited until I knew he was inhaling, when his attention would be somewhat distracted by the pleasure of sucking in all that tasty nicotine. In, out. In, out. In…

I leaped out from where I was crouching and shot forward, the baton arm curled past my neck as though I was trying to scratch my opposite shoulder, my free hand up, defending my face and head. I covered the distance in an instant and saw the man as soon as I cleared the edge of the garbage containers just behind him. It was one of Murakami's bodyguards, wearing a black waist-length leather jacket, with shades and a wool watch cap for light disguise. He'd heard the sudden sound of my approach and was in the midst of turning his head toward me when I burst into his position.

His mouth started to drop open, the cigarette dangling uselessly from his lips. His right hand went for one of the coat pockets. I saw everything slowly, clearly.

I stepped in with my right foot and whipped the baton into the side of his face. His head ricocheted left from the force of the blow. The shades flew off. The cigarette shot out of his mouth, tumbling like a spent rifle cartridge, followed by an explosion of teeth and blood. He staggered back into the building and started to slide down the wall. I stepped in close and brought the butt end of the baton up under his chin, arresting his descent.

"Where's Murakami?" I asked in Japanese.

He coughed up a mass of blood and dental matter.

I patted him down while he gagged and tried to collect himself. I found a Kershaw knife like Murakami's in his coat and a mobile phone in a belt clip. I pocketed both.

I pressed hard with the baton. "Where is he?" I asked again.

He coughed and spat. *"Naka da,"* he said, the words deformed by his injuries. Inside.

"Where's your other man?"

He groaned and tried to reach for his face. I shoved the baton up into his neck. He grimaced and lowered his arms.

"Where's your other man?" I asked again.

He sucked and wheezed. *"Omote da."* In front.

Made sense. That's the coverage I would have used.

I brought the baton down and jabbed its tip into his solar plexus. He doubled over with a grunt. I stepped behind him, brought the baton across his windpipe, and jammed a knee into his spine. I arched back, pulling him backward with the baton and pushing forward with my knee. His hands flew to the steel to relieve the pressure but it was already too late. His larynx was crushed. He struggled silently for another half minute, then sagged back into me.

I eased him down to the ground and looked around. All quiet. I pulled off his cap and coat and slipped them on. I hunted around on the ground for the shades—there they were. I pulled them on, too.

I dragged the body as deeply as I could into the shadows, then picked up his still-lit cigarette and stuck it in my mouth. I slammed the baton onto the pavement to close it, slipped it in one of the coat pockets, and palmed the pepper spray.

Unlike the back of the building, the front offered no perpendicular streets and thus fewer vantage points. There was really only one good spot there, I knew: the alley alongside the building directly across the street.

I walked around to the front of the building, the shades and hat on, the cigarette burning. I kept my head down and my eyes forward, the same posture these guys would have been using to avoid witnesses and cameras.

I saw him across the street as soon as I rounded the corner. He was dressed like his recently deceased partner. I made my way directly to his position, moving fast, confidently. The shades we were wearing were great for light disguise, but were hell on night-vision. He thought I was his partner. He stepped out of the shadows as though to greet me, perhaps unsure of why I had abandoned my post.

When I was three meters away, I saw him purse his lips in confusion. At two meters his jaw started to drop open as he realized something was definitely wrong. At one meter all his questions were answered with a mouthful of pepper spray.

His hands flew to his face and he staggered backward. I spat out the cigarette, dropped the canister into a jacket pocket, and withdrew the baton. I snapped it open, stepped behind him, and whipped it across his windpipe the way I had done to his buddy, this time with a stronger cross grip that crushed the carotids along with the larynx. His fingers clawed at the metal and his feet scrabbled for purchase for a few seconds as I dragged him back into the alley, but by the time we had reached the shadows he was dead. I patted him down and found another knife and another mobile phone. I left the knife. The mobile phone I took.

I collapsed the baton, pocketed it, and made my way to the end of the street, where I found a payphone. I didn't know if Naomi had caller ID, and didn't want to take a chance on trying her from one of the mobile phones I had just acquired.

I called her. She picked up on the third ring, her voice a little uncertain. "Hello?"

"Hey, it's me."

A pause. "Where are you?"

"I'm not going to be able to make it tonight. I'm sorry."

Another pause. "That's okay. It's fine." She sounded relieved.

"I just wanted to let you know. I'll be in touch soon, okay?"

"Okay."

I hung up and returned to the back of her building. I eased into the shadows next to the body I had left there.

One of the mobile phones I was carrying started to vibrate. I pulled it out and opened it.

"Hai," I said.

"He's not coming tonight," Murakami said in his signature growl. "I'll be down in a minute. Call Yagi-san and be ready to move."

I guessed Yagi was one of the guys I'd taken out. *"Hai,"* I said.

He clicked off.

I dropped the mobile back in the coat pocket. I took out the baton and kept it retracted in my right hand. I held the pepper spray in my left. My heart was thudding steadily in my chest. I took in a deep breath through my nose, held it, and let it out.

The back entrance was the less obvious, less trafficked choice. Also, it lacked a security camera. I knew he'd come out there, just like I had.

I stayed at the edge of the diffused light from a nearby streetlamp, where Murakami would see me but where my appearance would be obscured by shadows. I needed him to come as close as possible, to maximize the element of surprise. Surprise might be the only advantage I would have over him.

Two minutes later, he emerged from the rear door. I hung back just inside the shadows, the shades on, the hat pulled low.

There was a dog with him, straining on a leash. It took me a second to recognize it without the muzzle. The white pit bull, the one that had been in the car after my fight with Adonis.

Oh, fuck.

I almost turned and ran for it. But a dog's most atavistic instincts are triggered by flight, and there was too great a chance the thing would have caught me and brought me down from behind. I'd have to play this out.

At least Murakami's attention was partly engaged by the animal. He saw me and lifted his head in curt acknowledgment, then looked down at the dog, which had begun to growl.

Nice doggy, I thought. *Nice fucking doggy.*

They came closer. Murakami looked up at me again, then back to the dog. The damn thing was really growling now, staccato killing sounds that rumbled up from deep in its chest.

Murakami didn't seem unduly concerned. I guessed a dog that took gunpowder and steroids with its Alpo, and jalapeño pepper suppositories for dessert, might growl at the fucking wind, and that Murakami would be used to the behavior, might even welcome it.

They came closer. The dog was starting to get out of control, snarling and straining at the leash. Murakami looked down at it. *"Doushitanda?"* he said. What the hell is with you?

Then his head started to come up. He wasn't as close as I wanted, but I knew his next glance was going to put things together. I wasn't going to get a better opportunity.

I leaped out at them and closed the distance in two long strides. Murakami reacted instantly, releasing the leash and getting his hands up to protect his upper body and head.

It was a well-trained reaction and I'd been expecting it. Ignoring the dog, which I ranked as the lesser threat, I dropped to a crouch, cocked my right arm across my body, and whipped it forward like a tennis backhand. The baton started telescoping out. By the time it reached Murakami's lead ankle, it had achieved its proper twenty-six inches. The impact of that steel to his ankle was one of the best feelings I'd ever known. If I'd missed, I would have been dead a few seconds later.

But I didn't miss. I felt bone shatter under the steel and heard Murakami howl. An instant later all I could see was white dog, coming at me like a cruise missile.

I managed to get my left arm up in front of my throat. The dog shot forward and clamped onto it just above the wrist. There was an explosion of pain. The impact knocked me backward.

I knew if I fell to my back with that creature on top of me there wouldn't even be body parts for the clean-up crew afterward. Partly by instinct, partly by judo training, I let our paired momentum somersault us backward and rolled into a squat on the other end of it. The dog still had me just above the wrist, snarling and shaking its head, holding on in a dead-game grip the way it had been trained. I couldn't feel anything in my arm anymore.

I tried to bring the baton up and crack the thing over the head, but I couldn't get any leverage. The dog's claws scraped against the pavement, seeking purchase, leverage from which it could force me over onto my back.

I dropped the baton and reached around with my good hand, scrabbling for its testicles. The beast dodged left, then right, knowing what I was going for. I found it anyway. I grabbed that canine package and yanked downward as hard as I've ever yanked anything in my life. The jaws loosened and I jerked my arm free.

I lurched to my feet. The dog writhed for a moment, then got its legs under it. It snarled and stared up at me with bloodshot eyes.

I glanced at my left hand. It was clamped around the pepper spray canister with rigor mortis determination. The tendons must have locked up from the pressure of the animal's jaws.

The dog's muscles coiled together. I pried the canister loose with my good hand. The dog leaped. I turned the canister forward and depressed the trigger.

There was a satisfying sound of gas escaping under pressure, and a red cloud hit the beast directly in the face. Its momentum carried it into me and knocked me backward, but it was jerking and slobbering now, no longer attacking. I kicked out from under its twitching body and rolled to a crouch.

The dog started writhing on the ground, rubbing its snout frantically into the tarmac as though trying to wipe off the substance that was causing its agony. I held the canister closer. When the animal turned its wheezing face toward me, I aimed directly into its nose and mouth and depressed the trigger. A thick cloud jetted out, and then, just as suddenly, died, the canister's contents exhausted.

But it was enough. The dog's body launched into spasms that made its previous writhing look like playful stretching by comparison. Oleoresin capsicum irritant is ordinarily nonfatal, but I thought a concentrated double dose like the one the dog had just received might prove the exception.

I looked over at Murakami. He was on his feet, but was keeping his weight entirely off his wounded ankle. He had the Kershaw in his right hand, held close to his body.

I looked down and saw the baton. I swept it up in my good hand and approached him, my left arm hanging uselessly.

He was growling from deep in his chest, sounding not unlike his dog.

I moved around him in a wary circle, forcing him to adjust, trying to gauge the extent of his mobility. I knew the ankle shot had been potent. I also knew he might try to exaggerate the extent of the damage, to get me to overcommit and attempt to finish him too quickly. If he could grab the baton or otherwise get inside my guard, his knife and two good arms would prove decisive.

So I took my time. I feinted with the baton. Left, then right. I circled toward the knife hand, making it more difficult for him to snatch something with his free fingers, keeping him moving, stressing the ankle.

I let him get used to the left/right feints. Then I ran one straight up the middle, jabbing the steel directly at his face and neck. He parried with his free hand, trying to grab the baton, but I'd been expecting it and snapped the unit out of the way in time. Then, just as suddenly, I backhanded it in, cracking him along the side of his skull.

He dropped to one knee but I didn't rush in. My gut told me he was faking, again trying to lure me inside, where he could neutralize the greater distance afforded by the baton.

Blood ran down from the side of his head. He looked at me and for a split instant I saw fear sweep across his face like a sheet of driving rain. His feints hadn't worked and he knew it. He knew I was going to wear him down, carefully, methodically, that I wasn't going to do anything stupid he could exploit.

His only chance would be something desperate. I circled again and waited for it.

I let him get a little bit closer, close enough to give him hope.

I feinted and dodged, forcing him to move on the ankle. He was panting now.

With a loud *kiai* he lunged at me, reaching with his free hand, hoping to snag a jacket sleeve and reel me into the knife.

But his ankle slowed him down.

I took a long step back and to the side and snapped the baton down on his forearm. I traded force for accuracy and speed, but it was still a solid shot. He grunted in pain, and I took two more steps back to assess the damage. He held his injured arm against his body and looked at me. He smiled.

"Come on," he said. "I'm right here. Finish me off. Don't be afraid."

I circled again. His taunts meant nothing to me.

"Your friend screamed on the way down," he said. "He—"

I closed the distance with a single step and speared the baton into his throat. He raised his injured arm to try to grab it, but I had already retracted it across my body. In the same motion, I changed levels, dropping into a squat, and whipped the baton into his ankle again. He screamed and crumbled to his knees.

I stepped behind him, away from any possibility of a lunge.

"Did he sound like that?" I snarled, and brought the baton down on his head like a hatchet.

He sank to his side, then fought to regain his balance. I brought the baton down again. And again. Gouts of blood flew from his scalp. I realized I was yelling. I didn't know what.

I rained blows on him until my arm and shoulder ached. Then I took a long step backward and collapsed to my knees, sucking wind. I looked over at the dog. It was still.

I waited a few seconds to catch my breath. I tried to jam the baton closed, but couldn't. I looked and saw why. The straight steel rod had deformed into a bow shape from what I had done to Murakami.

Jesus. I stood and dragged his body into the shadows under the awning, next to what was left of his buddy. Dragging him one-armed was a bitch, but I managed it. The dog was easier.

I took out the mobile phones, wiped them down, and dropped them. Ditto for the shades. Last was the baton. I didn't want to be found walking around with a twenty-six-inch murder weapon bent into the shape of one of the victims' skulls. I shrugged off the leather jacket I had taken and dropped it on top of the mess.

Some of the buckets near the awning had collected rainwater. I used them to wash down the area and make the blood less obvious. I wiped them for prints when I was done.

Last stop was the front of the building, where I found the cigarette I had spat out before taking out the second guy. I stubbed it out and pocketed the butt.

I walked over to Naomi's building and pressed a knuckle to her apartment buzzer. A moment later I heard her voice. Her tone was fearful. "Who is it?" she asked.

For a second I couldn't even remember what I'd told her to call me when I'd first met her at the club. Then I remembered: my real name.

"It's me," I said. "John."

I heard her breathing. "Are you alone?" she asked.

"Yes."

"All right. Just come up. Hurry."

The door buzzed and I opened it. I kept my head low so whoever would surely be reviewing the building security tapes later that morning wouldn't get a good look at my face. I took the stairs to the fifth floor, headed to her door, and knocked.

For a moment, the light was blotted out behind the peephole. Then the door opened. Her mouth opened wide when she saw me.

"*Oh meu Deus, meu Deus,* what happened?"

"I ran into them on their way out."

She shook her head and blinked. "Come in." I walked into the *genkan* and she closed the door behind me.

"I can't stay," I said. "Someone is going to find them out there soon, and when that happens there are going to be cops swarming all over your neighborhood."

"Find them…" she said, then recognition hardened onto her features. "You… you killed them?" She shook her head as though she couldn't believe it. *"Oh, merda."*

"Tell me what happened."

She looked at me. "They came for me at the club tonight. They told me I had to leave with them but wouldn't say why. I was really scared. They made me take them here, up to my apartment. Murakami had a dog with him. He told me he would turn it on me if I didn't do exactly what he wanted."

She looked at me, afraid, I thought, of what I might be thinking.

"It's okay," I said. "Keep going."

"He told me he knew I'd been seeing you outside the club, that he knew I had a way to contact you. He told me to call you and ask you to come over."

"He was probably bluffing," I said. "Maybe the bugs picked it up when you gave me your email address that first night, and he played on that. Or maybe Yukiko sensed something and told him. It doesn't matter."

She nodded. "He asked me what language we used when we were together. I told him mostly English. His English isn't so good, but he told me if he heard anything wrong, anything that sounded like a warning, he would feed me to the dog. He was listening right next to me. I was afraid if I tried to warn you, you might say something back and he would know what I had done. But I tried to tell you, in a way you wouldn't notice or comment on right away. Did you notice?"

I nodded. "'Would love to,'" I said, pronouncing it the way she had.

"Sim. I'm sorry I couldn't do more. I was too scared. He would have known."

I smiled. "That was perfect," I said. "It was good thinking. *Obrigado.* "

I was cradling my wrist in front of me and she looked at it. "What happened to your arm?" she asked.

"Murakami's dog."

"Jesus! Are you all right?"

I looked at my forearm. The leather jacket had kept the animal's teeth from breaking the skin, but the area was purple and badly swollen and I thought something might be broken.

"I'll be okay," I said. "It's you I'm worried about. There was a triple murder outside your building just now. As soon as someone finds one of the bodies, which isn't going to be hard to do, the police are going to subpoena the security tapes from every building in the area. They'll see you getting escorted by a guy with a white dog, the same white dog that's getting cold now with its master a few meters from your building. You're going to have a lot of questions to answer."

She looked at me. "What should I do?"

"If you get picked up, tell the truth. You won't want to mention that you opened the door just now—it'll make you look complicit. But don't deny that someone came up here and tried to get in. They're going to see me on the security tapes, although I was careful to hide my face."

She nodded. "Okay."

"But the police aren't your real problem. Your real problem is going to be the associates of the men who came here tonight. They're going to come after you, either for revenge, or as a way to get to me, or as both."

The color drained from her caramel skin. "He would have killed me tonight, wouldn't he," she said.

I nodded. "If I had shown up as he hoped, they would have killed me and then eliminated you as a potential witness and loose end. My not showing up made you less of a liability. In their minds, killing you became not worth the trouble. It's that simple."

"Meu Deus," she said, swallowing. She was pale.

"Pack a bag," I said. "Do it quickly. Take a cab to Shinjuku or Shibuya, someplace where there are still people around. Get another cab there. Stay at a love hotel, someplace with automated check-in. Use cash, no credit cards. First thing in the morning, take a train to Nagoya or Osaka, someplace with a major airport. Get the first flight out. It doesn't matter where it's going. Once you're out of the country, you'll be safe. You can find your way home from there."

"Home?"

I nodded. "Brazil."

She was silent for a long moment. Then she took my good hand in both of hers. She looked at me. "Come with me," she said.

Looking into those green eyes, I almost could have said yes. But I didn't.

"Come with me," she said again. "You're in danger, too."

And then, in that instant, I realized I'd created a new nexus, another Harry or Midori, that a determined pursuer like the Agency or Yamaoto might follow as a way of getting to me. And this one was heading straight to Brazil. Where Yamada-san, my alter ego, had planned to establish himself.

I think I smiled a little bit at the irony, the jokes fate likes to play, because she said, "What?"

I shook my head. "I can't travel now. Even if I could, it would be too dangerous for you to try to travel with me. Just go. I'll find a way to contact you in Salvador after you're back there."

"Will you really?"

I nodded. "Yes."

There was a long pause. Then she looked at me. "I don't think you'll really come. That's okay. But contact me and tell me that. Don't make me wait, not knowing. Don't do that to me."

I nodded, thinking of Midori, the way she had said, *Let's see how you like the uncertainty.*

"I'll contact you," I said.

"I don't know where I'll be exactly, but you can contact me through my father. David Leonardo Nascimento. He'll know how to find me."

"Go," I said. "You don't have much time."

I turned to leave, but she caught me and stepped in close. She put her hands on my face and kissed me hard. "I'll be waiting," she said.

CHAPTER 22

I made my way out of the area on foot. I didn't want to be seen, not even by an anonymous taxi driver.

I cleaned myself up in an all-night sauna, then stopped at a twenty-four-hour drugstore and bought a bottle of ibuprofen. I ate a half-dozen dry. My arm was throbbing.

Finally, I found a business hotel in Shibuya and collapsed into coma-like sleep.

The sound of my pager awoke me. I heard it in my dreams as an automated garage door, then as a vibrating mobile phone, then finally in the wakeful world for what it was.

I checked the readout. Tatsu. About fucking time. I went out, found a payphone, and called him. It was already midday.

"Are you all right?" he asked me.

He must have heard about the carnage. "Never a cop around when you need one," I told him.

"Forgive me for that."

"If I'd gotten killed, I wouldn't have. Under the circumstances, though, I feel magnanimous. I could use a doctor for an injured arm."

"I'll find someone. Can you meet me right now?"

"Yeah."

"Where we parted last time."

"Okay."

I hung up.

I did an SDR that took me to Meguro Station. Tatsu and Kanezaki were standing by the wickets.

Oh good, I thought. *I needed a surprise.*

I walked over. Tatsu pulled me aside.

"The theory is that there is a gang war under way," he said to me. "An internal yakuza conflict. It will blow over."

I looked at him. "You've heard, then."

He nodded.

"Well?" I said. "Didn't your parents teach you to say thank you?"

His face broke into a surprised grin and he actually patted me on the back. "Thank you," he said. He looked at my arm, which I was cradling unnaturally close to my body. "I know someone who can take a look at that. But I think you'll want to hear Kanezaki first."

The three of us walked across the street to a coffee shop. As soon as we were seated and had ordered, Kanezaki said, "I learned something about your friend's death. It's not much, but you helped me out the way you promised, so I'll tell you."

I waited.

Kanezaki glanced at Tatsu. "Uh, Ishikura-san here briefed me on your meetings with Biddle and Tanaka. He told me Biddle asked you to kill me." He paused for a second. "Thanks for not taking him up on that."

"*Doitashimashite,*" I said, shaking my head slowly. Don't mention it.

"After the last time we met," he went on, "I wanted more information. For leverage over Biddle, to make sure he knew I had something on him in case he decided to try anything again."

Fast learner, I thought. "What did you do?"

"I bugged his office."

I looked at him, half-surprised, half-impressed by his apparent audacity. "You bugged the Chief of Station's office?"

He smiled in a young, self-satisfied way that reminded me for a moment of Harry. "I did. His office is only swept for bugs every twenty-four hours, at regular intervals. Back at Headquarters I took the locks and picks course, so getting into his office to place the bug was no problem."

"Impressive security."

He shrugged. "Security is generally effective against outside threats. But it wasn't designed with inside threats in mind. Anyway, I can get in and out pretty much as I need to, putting the bug down to listen in, then removing it to avoid the sweeps."

"You overheard something about Harry," I said.

He nodded. "Yesterday, the Chief was on the phone with someone. I could only hear his half of the conversation, but I know he was talking to someone big, because it was 'Yes, sir' this and 'No, sir' that."

"What did he say?"

"He said, 'Don't worry. The thread we were following to try to contact Rain has been cut.'"

"That's not much."

He shrugged. "To me it sounded like an acknowledgment that your friend's death wasn't an accident, that he was killed."

I looked at him, and what he saw in my eyes made him blink. "Kanezaki," I said, "if you feed me even the smallest bit of bullshit as a way of manipulating me into acting against your boss, it'll be the worst mistake you ever made."

He lost a bit of color, but other than that kept his cool. "I understand that. I'm not bullshitting you or trying to manipulate you. I told you before I'd tell you what I knew about your friend if you helped me, and you helped me. I'm just following through."

I kept my eyes on him. "Nothing more about who 'cut the thread'?"

He shook his head. "Nothing explicit. But the thrust of the conversation was about Yamaoto, so I think we can infer."

"All right, infer."

Tatsu broke in. "It seems Biddle's relationship with Yamaoto is not what I believed it to be. In certain critical ways they appear to be collaborators, not antagonists."

"What does this have to do with Harry?" I asked.

"One of the things I overheard," Kanezaki said, "is that Biddle plans to give the receipts to Yamaoto."

The waiter brought our coffee and departed.

"I don't get it," I said. "I thought we all agreed the USG wants to help Japan reform, while to Yamaoto reform is a mortal threat."

"That's true," Kanezaki said.

"But now you think they're working together."

"From what I overheard, yes."

"If that's true, then Biddle might have been involved in Harry's death. But why?"

"I'm not sure."

I looked at Tatsu. "If the Agency is working with Yamaoto, it can only be to fuck your reformers. And now Biddle has all those receipts."

Tatsu nodded. "We need to get them back. Before he turns them over to Yamaoto."

"But it's not just the receipts," I said. "From what Tanaka told us, you've got to assume several of Kanezaki's meetings have been caught on videotape, with audio intercepted by parabolic mics. What are you going to do about all that?"

"Nothing can be done," Tatsu said. "As we discussed, any politician thus caught meeting with a CIA case officer is compromised. But the ones implicated only by virtue of the receipts can still be saved."

"How?"

"A small percentage of politicians will be compromised both by the receipts and the photos. Doubtless Yamaoto plans to burn these unfortunates first. Then, during the ensuing media frenzy, he will release the balance of the receipts. The fact that there is no 'hard' video or audio evidence backing this second wave of revelations will be lost on the public."

"So even though Yamaoto might still be able to burn the group he's got on tape..."

"His efforts will be limited to that group. By reacquiring the receipts, we can contain the damage."

"Okay. How are you going to get the receipts?"

"They're in Biddle's safe," Kanezaki said. "I heard him say so on the phone."

"It sounds like you can pick a lock, kid," I said, "but cracking a safe is another story."

"He won't need to crack it," Tatsu said. "Biddle will give him the combination."

"What, are you going to just ask him nicely?"

Tatsu shook his head. "I thought it might be better if you would."

I considered for a moment. I wanted another chance to question Biddle about Harry, in more private surroundings than were available last time. Especially if it was true that he and Yamaoto were somehow aligned, which increased the probability that he might have been involved in Harry's death. Murakami and Yukiko were taken care of, but now it looked like there was still a little something I needed to wrap up.

"All right," I said. "I'll do it."

"I can help you set it up…" Kanezaki started to say.

"No," I said, shaking my head, already picturing how I would handle it. "I can take care of that myself. You just make sure you have access to Biddle's office when I tell you to."

"Okay," he said.

I looked at him. "Why are you doing all this? If the CIA finds out, they'll call you a traitor."

He laughed. "It's hard to be scared of something like that immediately after finding out that your boss has been trying to hire someone to have you killed. Besides, Crepuscular was officially shut down, remember? As far as I'm concerned, Biddle is the traitor. I'm just trying to straighten things out."

Tatsu took me to a doctor he knew, a guy named Eto. Tatsu told me he had done this guy a favor many years earlier, and as a result he was in Tatsu's debt and could be counted on for his discretion.

Eto didn't ask any questions. He examined my arm and told me I had a fractured ulna. He set it, put a cast on it, and gave me a prescription for a codeine-based painkiller. The prescription was written on generic Jikei Hospital stationery. The signature was illegible. No one would be able to trace it back to him.

I called Biddle afterward. Told him I was ready to take him up on his offer about Kanezaki. Arranged a meeting for ten o'clock that night to discuss details.

I went to another spy shop in Shinjuku. This time I bought a pair of high-resolution night-vision goggles with a binocular magnification function. I also picked up another ASP baton. I'd developed a certain fondness for the things.

Next I stopped at a sporting goods store and bought a pair of sweatpants and a matching sweatshirt, both in a flat black heavy cotton, and a pair of jogging shoes. It was hard to find the right footwear—almost everything the store had was multicolored and gaudy—but eventually I came upon a pair that was suitably dark. After I left the store I cut off the reflective strips the manufacturer had thoughtfully placed across the heels to make joggers more visible at night. Getting hit by a car that might fail to see me wasn't my primary concern.

I had told Biddle he should enter the Aoyama Bochi cemetery complex on Kayanoki-dori, from the Omotesando-dori entrance. That he should walk down the path about fifty meters, at which point he would see a tall obelisk on the left, the tallest structure in the cemetery. That he should wait there.

At eight o'clock, when it was sufficiently dark, I slipped into the cemetery from the Gaiennishi-dori side, avoiding the regular entrances just in case anyone was prepositioned and waiting for me. An odd place for a jog, but not unheard of. As soon as I was inside, I pulled on the goggles. I could make out every marker and bush in bright green. I saw bats sailing among the trees, a cat slinking from behind a stone.

I set up near the obelisk, inside a memorial shaped like a triple pagoda. The pagoda offered me excellent concealment and a three-hundred-sixty-degree vantage point.

Biddle showed up at ten sharp. He was as punctual about spycraft as he was about his tea.

I watched him make his way to the obelisk. He was wearing an open trench coat, a suit and tie beneath. Very cloak and dagger. For ten minutes I scanned the perimeter of the cemetery, using the goggles as night-vision binoculars, until I was satisfied he was alone. Then I eased out and made my way to where he was standing.

He didn't hear me until I spoke from a meter away. "Biddle," I said.

"Jesus!" he said, jumping and spinning to face me.

I could see him squinting in the darkness. In the white-green of the goggles, I logged every detail of his expression.

Harry's detector was motionless in my pocket. With my good arm, I slipped the baton out from one of the sweatpants pockets. Biddle missed the movement in the dark.

"There's a small problem," I said.

"What?"

"I need you to do a better job convincing me you had nothing to do with Haruyoshi Fukasawa's death."

I saw his brow furrow in the green glow. "Look, I already told you…" he started to say.

I snapped the baton out and backhanded it into his forward shin, holding back a little at the end because it was too soon to break anything. He shrieked and fell to the ground, clutching his wounded leg. I gave him a minute to roll around while I scanned the area. Except for Biddle, all was silent.

"No more noise," I told him. "Stay quiet, or I'll make you quiet."

He gritted his teeth and looked to where my voice had come from. "Goddamn it, I've told you everything I know," he said, gasping.

"You didn't tell me you're working with Yamaoto. That the one who's been keeping Crepuscular alive is you, not Kanezaki."

His eyes were wide, searching for me in the darkness. "Kanezaki is paying you, isn't he?" he groaned.

I considered for a moment. "No. No one's paying me. For once, I'm doing something just because I want to. Although I wouldn't call that good news, from your perspective."

"Well, I can pay you. The Agency can. It's a new world we're in, and I told you we want you to be a part of it."

I chuckled. "You sound like a recruiting billboard. Now tell me about Yamaoto."

"I'm serious. Post Nine-Eleven, the Agency needs people like you. This is why we've been looking for you."

"I'm going to ask my question again. For free. If I have to repeat myself after this, though, the shot that just put you on the ground is going to seem like a caress."

There was a long pause, then he said, "All right." He got slowly to his feet, keeping his weight off his injured leg. "Look, Yamaoto has his interests, and we have ours. There's just an alignment right now, that's all. An alliance of convenience."

"To what end? I thought Crepuscular was supposed to help reformers here."

He nodded. "Reform would be good for the U.S. in the long-term, but it would also create problems. Look, Japan is the world's largest creditor. It has over three-hundred-billion dollars invested in U.S. treasury bills alone. In the short term, real reform would mean Japanese bank closings, bank closings would mean bank runs, and bank runs would force banks to repatriate their overseas capital to cover fleeing depositors. If reforms eventually work, though, and the economy improves, yen-based holdings will become more attractive, and Japanese banks will move their dollar- and Euro-based holdings home, where they might earn a better return."

He had pulled himself together pretty nicely. Maybe I hadn't been giving him enough credit.

"So whoever's calling the shots in the USG right now prefers the status quo," I said.

"We like to refer to it as 'stability,'" he said, putting some weight on his injured leg and wincing.

I scanned the area around us. All quiet. "Because the status quo keeps all those trillions of yen safely parked in the U.S., where they prop up the American economy."

"That's right. To put it crudely, America is addicted to a continuing influx of foreign capital to support its deficit spending, and it gets the balance of its fix from Japan. There are elements in the USG that don't want that to change."

I shook my head. "That's not crude, it's nicely put. America is addicted to cheap oil, and props up brutal regimes in the Middle East to feed its habit. If the USG is supporting corrupt elements in Japan because those elements guarantee continued access to Japanese capital, Uncle Sam is just being consistent."

"I suppose that's not unfair. But I don't make policy. I just carry it out."

"So this is why Crepuscular was shut down six months ago," I said. "Some newly ascendant faction in the USG decided it wasn't in Uncle Sam's interest to further reform in Japan after all."

"The opposite," he said. He started to put his hands in his trench coat pockets.

"Keep your hands where I can see them," I said sharply.

He jumped. "Sorry, I'm just a little cold. How can you see anything, anyway? It's pitch dark in here."

"What do you mean, 'the opposite'?"

"Crepuscular was never intended to further reform. It was conceived as a way of suborning reformers from the beginning. Whoever ordered its termination was a supporter of reform. But certainly not a realist."

"You would be one of the realists, then."

He straightened slightly. "That's right. Along with some of the institutions that make U.S. foreign policy. The ones without blinders or the pressure of political constituencies. Look, the politicians press Japan to reform because they don't understand what's really going on. And what's really going on is that Japan is past reform. Maybe ten, even five years ago, it could have been done. But not anymore. Things have gone too far here. The politicians in America are always talking about 'biting the bullet' and 'strong medicine,' but they don't understand that if you try to bite this bullet, it'll go through your head. That the patient is so weak, an operation would kill him. We're past hope of a cure, it's time to move into more of a pain-management approach."

"It's a moving story, Dr. Kevorkian. But I'm ready to hear the end."

"The end?"

"Yes. The part that goes, 'Here's the combination to my safe.'"

"The combination… oh, no. No, no, no." Alarm was creeping into his voice. "How did he talk you into this? What did he tell you, those reformers are heroes? For God's sake, they're just like all the other politicians in this damn country, they're just as selfish and venal. Kanezaki doesn't know what he's doing."

I shot the baton into his wounded leg again. He screamed and went down.

"Quiet," I said. "Or I'll do the same to your arms."

He clenched his teeth and rocked on his back, one arm holding his leg, the other arm jerking left to right in front of his head in a vain attempt to ward off the next attack.

"I warned you about making me ask you something twice," I said. "Now spit it out. Or they won't even be able to use dental records to ID you."

He groaned and clutched his leg. Finally he said, "Thirty-two twice left, four once right, twelve left."

I took out the mobile phone and speed-dialed Kanezaki. He picked up instantly and I repeated the number.

"Hold on." A few seconds passed. "I'm in," he said.

"You find what you were looking for?"

I heard papers rustling. "Big time."

I clicked off.

"There's a marker about a meter to your right," I told him. "You can use it to stand."

He pulled himself in the right direction and got slowly to his feet, using the marker to support himself. He slumped against it, panting, his face slicked with sweat.

"You knew they were going to do Harry," I said.

He shook his head. "No."

"But you suspected."

"I suspect everything. I'm paid to suspect. That's not the same as knowing."

"Why did you ask me to kill Kanezaki?"

"I think you know," he said, his breathing getting a little more even. "If those receipts were used, someone would have to be blamed for it. It would be best if that person weren't in a position to tell his side of the story."

"Is he still in any danger?"

He chuckled ruefully. "Not if those receipts are no longer in play, no."

"You don't seem too upset."

He shrugged. "I'm a professional. None of this is personal for me. I hope the same goes for you."

"What happens to Crepuscular?"

He sighed and looked a little wistful. "Crepuscular? It's gone. It was shut down six months ago."

He was already reciting the official story. No wonder he'd recovered his serenity so quickly. He knew he wasn't going to face any personal—meaning career—repercussions.

I looked at him for a long time. I thought of Harry, of Tatsu, most of all of Midori. Finally I said, "I'm going to let you leave here, Biddle. The smart thing would be to kill you, but I won't. That means you owe me. If you repay that debt by trying to get back into my life, I'll find you."

"I believe you," he said.

"When we walk out of here tonight, we walk away—agreed?"

"We still need you," he said. "There's still a place for you."

I waited for a moment in the darkness. He realized he hadn't answered my question. He flinched.

"Agreed," he said, his voice low.

I turned and left. He could find his own way out.

I met Tatsu the next day, on a sunny boulevard beneath a maple tree in Yoyogi Park. I briefed him on what I'd learned from Biddle.

"Kanezaki recovered the receipts," he told me. "And promptly destroyed them. It's as though they never existed. After all, Crepuscular was discontinued six months ago."

"That kid is naïve, but he's got balls," I said.

Tatsu nodded, his eyes momentarily melancholy. "He has a good heart."

I smiled. It wouldn't be like Tatsu to admit that someone might have a good head.

"I have a feeling you haven't seen the last of him," I said.

He shrugged. "I would hope not. Getting those receipts back was lucky. But I have much more to do."

"You can only do so much, Tatsu. Remember that."

"But still we must do something, *ne?* Don't forget, modern Japan was born of samurai from the southern provinces seizing the imperial palace in Kyoto and declaring the restoration of the Meiji emperor. Perhaps something like that could happen again. Perhaps a rebirth of democracy."

"Perhaps," I said.

He turned to me. "What will you do, Rain-san?"

I looked out at the trees. "I'm thinking about that."

"Work with me."

"You're a broken record, Tatsu."

"You sound like my wife again."

I laughed.

"How does it feel, to have been part of something larger than yourself?" he asked.

I held up my taped and plastered arm. "Like this."

He smiled his sad smile. "That only means you are alive."

I shrugged. "I admit it beats the alternatives."

"If you need anything, ever, call me."

I stood. He followed suit.

We bowed and shook hands. I walked away.

I walked for a long time. East, toward Tokyo Station, toward the bullet train that would take me back to Osaka. Tatsu knew where to find me, but I could live with that for the time being.

I wondered what I would do when I got there. Yamada, my alter ego, was nearly ready to move. But I no longer knew where to send him.

I needed to contact Naomi. I wanted to contact her. I just didn't know what I was going to say.

Yamaoto was still out there. Tatsu had dealt him a few solid blows, but he was still standing. Probably still looking for me. And maybe the Agency with him.

As I walked, the sky grew darker. A wind shook the branches of the city's pollution-inured trees.

Tatsu had been upbeat. I wondered what deep wellspring fed his optimism. I wished I could share it. But I was too aware of Harry in the ground, of Midori gone for good, of Naomi waiting for an uncertain answer.

Fat droplets of rain started spattering against the city's concrete skin, against the glass windows of its eyes. A few people with umbrellas opened them. The rest ran for cover.

I walked on, through it all. I tried to think of it as a baptism, a new beginning.

Maybe it was. But what a lonely resurrection.

雨

AUTHOR'S NOTE

Readers familiar with Roppongi and Akasaka-Mitsuke in Tokyo will note that, while several hostess bars and "gentlemen's clubs" resemble Damask Rose, none is an exact match. Otherwise, the Tokyo and Osaka locales that appear in this book are described as I have found them.

DEEPEST THANKS

To a remarkable transpacific team: my agents, Nat Sobel and Judith Weber of Sobel Weber Associates in New York and Ken Mori of Tuttle Mori in Tokyo; and my editors, David Highfill of Putnam in New York and Masaru Suzuki of Sony's Village Books in Tokyo, for all their continued enthusiasm, insight, and support.

To my dear friend and *sensei* Koichiro Fukasawa of Wasabi Communications, for continuing to shine a clear light on so much of Japan and the Japanese—and for a great website, too.

To Evan Rosen, M.D. Ph.D., and Peter Zimetbaum, M.D., both of the Harvard medical system, for consistently overcoming their queasiness at my questions about the medical implications of killing techniques, for accepting that the Hippocratic Oath might not apply to fiction, and for assisting John Rain in all his endeavors with their considerable knowledge and imaginative faculties.

To Lori Kupfer, for her insights into what sophisticated, sexy women like Midori and Naomi wear and how they think, and for helpful comments on the manuscript.

To Ernie Tibaldi, a thirty-one-year veteran agent of the FBI, for generously sharing his extensive surveillance and investigative experiences, for recommending many good books and other sources of information, and for helpful comments on the manuscript.

To Carla Mendes, for furthering my understanding of Brazil and Brazilians and for refining Rain's attempts at Portuguese.

To Marc "Animal" MacYoung and Peyton Quinn, warrior philosophers both, for their many excellent books and videos on violence and street etiquette. In particular, John Rain owes to MacYoung his philosophy regarding unarmed defenses against the knife, and to Quinn the notion of being "interviewed" as a potential victim.

To Masao Miyamoto, for his horrifyingly humorous book *Straightjacket Society,* some of whose ideas on the nature of Big Brother in Japan Tatsu has borrowed.

To Lt. Colonel Dave Grossman, for his disturbing, original book, *On Killing: The Psychological Cost of Learning to Kill in War and Society,* which provided so many insights into the origins and psychology of John Rain.

To Alex Kerr, for his book *Dogs and Demons,* a meticulously researched and argued account of Japanese corruption and an insensate bureaucracy gone mad, which provided some of the backstory for the novel.

To Brian Koppelman, from whose movie *Rounders* Rain borrowed the excellent observation, "If you look around the table and can't spot the sucker, the sucker is you."

To Alan Eisler, Judy Eisler, Dan and Naomi Levin, Matthew Powers, Owen Rennert, David and Shari Rosenblatt, Ted Schlein, Hank Shiffman, and Pete Wenzel, for helpful comments on the manuscript and many valuable suggestions and insights along the way.

To Rick Kennedy and the staff of Tokyo Q, for introducing John Rain to several of the Tokyo bars and restaurants that appear in this book.

To the proprietors of the following establishments, all wonderful places to call one's office: Bar Satoh in Miyakojima-ku, Osaka; Café Borrone in Menlo Park, California; Las Chicas in Aoyama, Tokyo; the public library in Mountain View, California; These Library Lounge in Nishi Azabu, Tokyo.

Most of all, to a great editor, my fiercest supporter, and my best friend—my wife, Laura.

ABOUT THE AUTHOR

Barry Eisler spent three years in a covert position with the CIA's Directorate of Operations, then worked as a technology lawyer and startup executive in Silicon Valley and Japan, earning his black belt at the Kodokan International Judo Center along the way. Eisler's bestselling thrillers have won the Barry Award and the Gumshoe Award for Best Thriller of the Year, have been included in numerous "Best Of" lists, and have been translated into nearly twenty languages. Eisler lives in the San Francisco Bay Area and, when not writing novels, he blogs about torture, civil liberties, and the rule of law at www.BarryEisler.com.

ALSO BY BARRY EISLER

Novels

John Rain series

Graveyard of Memories

The Killer Ascendant (Originally published as Requiem for an Assassin)

Extremis (Originally published as The Last Assassin)

Redemption Games (Originally published as Killing Rain)

Winner Take All (Originally published as Rain Storm)

A Lonely Resurrection (Originally published as Hard Rain)

A Clean Kill in Tokyo (Originally published as Rain Fall)

Ben Treven series

Inside Out

Fault Line

Rain/Treven combined

The Detachment (an Amazon exclusive)

Novella

London Twist

Short Stories

The Khmer Kill (an Amazon exclusive)

Paris is a Bitch

The Lost Coast

Non-fiction

The Ass is a Poor Receptacle for the Head: Why Democrats Suck at Communication, and How They Could Improve

Be the Monkey: A Conversation About The New World of Publishing (with J.A. Konrath)

CONTACT BARRY

For updates, free copies, contests, and more, sign up for Barry's newsletter. It's a private list and your email address will never be shared with anyone else. The newsletter is also a great way to be the first to learn about movie news, appearances, and Barry's other books and stories. You can also find Barry on his website, his blog Heart of the Matter, Facebook, and Twitter.